THE
TELEPORTATION
ACCIDENT

Also by Ned Beauman

Boxer, Beetle

THE
TELEPORTATION
ACCIDENT

A Novel

NED
BEAUMAN

BLOOMSBURY

NEW YORK • LONDON • NEW DELHI • SYDNEY

Published by Bloomsbury USA, New York

All papers used by Bloomsbury USA are natural, recyclable products made from wood grown in well-managed forests. The manufacturing processes conform to the environmental regulations of the country of origin.

LIBRARY OF CONGRESS CATALOGING-IN-PUBLICATION DATA HAS BEEN APPLIED FOR.

ISBN: 978-1-62040-022-7

First published in Great Britain in 2012 by Sceptre, an imprint of Hodder & Stoughton, a Hachette UK company

First U.S. edition 2013

1 3 5 7 9 10 8 6 4 2

Typeset by Hewer Text UK Ltd, Edinburgh
Printed in the U.S.A.

I hate politics and belief in politics, because it makes men arrogant, doctrinaire, obstinate, and inhuman.

Thomas Mann, *Reflections of a Nonpolitical Man*

. . . all I had to do was go down into the subway. It was like fishing down there. Go down into the subway and come up with a girl.

Philip Roth, *The Human Stain*

Part I

Literary realism

1

BERLIN, 1931

When you knock a bowl of sugar on to your host's carpet, it is a parody of the avalanche that killed his mother and father, just as the duck's beak that your new girlfriend's lips form when she attempts a seductive pout is a quotation of the quacking noise your last girlfriend made during sex. When the telephone rings in the night because a stranger has given a wrong extension to the operator, it is a homage to the inadvertent substitution of telegrams that terminated your adulterous cousin's marriage, just as the resonant alcove between the counterpoised struts of your new girlfriend's clavicle is a rebuttal to the apparent beauty of your last girlfriend's fleshier décolletage. Or this is how it seemed to Egon Loeser, anyway, because the two subjects most hostile to his sense of a man's life as an essentially steady, comprehensible and Newtonian-mechanical undertaking were accidents and women. And it sometimes seemed as if the only way to prevent that dread pair from toppling him all the way over into derangement was to treat them not as prodigies but rather as texts to be studied. Hence the principle: accidents, like women, allude. These allusions are no less witty or astute for being unconscious; indeed, they are more so, which is one reason why it's probably a mistake to construct them deliberately. The other reason is that everyone might conclude you're a total prick.

And that was the final worry to flutter through Egon Loeser's mind before he pulled the lever on his Teleportation Device one morning in April 1931. If it went wrong, they would all say: for what possible reason did you name your experimental stagecraft prototype after the most calamitous experimental stagecraft prototype in the history of theatre? Why make that allusion? Why hitch those two horses together? Paint the devil on the wall and the devil will come, as every child knows. Or, to sieve the German idiom down to an English one, don't tempt fate. But Loeser was so unsuperstitious he was superstitious about it. He'd once got up on the stage of the Allien Theatre half an hour before a performance to shout 'Macbeth!' until he was hoarse. And one of his father's long-standing psychiatric patients had been an American financier who named his yacht *Titanic*, his daughters Goneril and Regan, and his company Roman Empire Holdings in the same spirit. So he couldn't credit the English idiom's characterisation of fate as something like a hack playwright who never missed a chance to work in an ironic pratfall, any more than he could credit the German idiom's characterisation of the devil as something like a preening actor who checked every gossip column in every newspaper every morning for a mention of himself (although perhaps God was like that). Accidents allude, but they don't ape. Naming one thing after another cannot, logically, increase the chances of the new thing turning out like the old thing. But if the test today went straight to ruin, people would still say he shouldn't have called it the Teleportation Device.

What choice did he have, though? This machine was primarily intended for use in a play about the life of Adriano Lavicini, the greatest stage designer of the seventeenth century. And the climax of the play portrayed the ghastly failure of Lavicini's Extraordinary Mechanism for the Almost Instantaneous Transport of Persons from Place to Place, better known in modern discourse as the Teleportation Device. Since Egon Loeser was, in his own opinion, Lavicini's closest modern counterpart, and since this new Teleportation Device was his finest innovation just as the old Teleportation Device had been Lavicini's, then to stifle the parallel between the two would have been even more perverse than to let it breathe.

Anyway, Lavicini himself had painted the devil on the wall with far bolder strokes than Loeser possibly could. Back in 1679, the Teleportation Device wasn't allowed a test run. Like a siege weapon, it had been constructed in total secrecy. No stagehand had seen more than a single jigsaw piece of the plans. Even Auguste de Gorge, the dictatorial owner of the Théâtre des Encornets, had not been permitted a peek, and even at the final dress rehearsal of Montand's new ballet *The Lizard Prince* the machine had not yet been in operation, so neither the dancers nor their choreographer had any idea what to expect on opening night. But Lavicini insisted that the operations of the Teleportation Device were so precise that it didn't matter, and the essential thing was that no rumours about the nature of the machine should escape.

The comparison to a siege weapon was especially apt here, Loeser always thought, because in the seventeenth century the struggle for supremacy between the great theatres and opera houses of Christendom resembled nothing so much as an arms race. For the ruling family of any major Italian city it would have been a political catastrophe to fall behind, and even within Paris the competition was fierce, which was why a set designer like Lavicini, who had in fact once held a job at the Venetian Arsenal, could expect to be bound as tightly by his contract of employment as the average twentieth-century germ-warfare scientist. (His salary, naturally, was large enough to make up for it.) This was an age in which the audience expected sphinxes pulling chariots, gods dancing in the air, lions transforming into girls, comets destroying city walls – all the really good stuff, of course, towards the middle of the play, because during the first act you would still be on the way to the theatre and by the fifth act you would already be doffing your hat to a platter of oysters. A typical published libretto might proudly list all nineteen contraptions that were to be set into motion during a performance, but neglect to mention the composer. Impresarios were bankrupted in their dozens, and enlightened critics complained that genuine dramatic values had been surrendered to this obsession with 'the marvellous', continuing a debate about the overuse of special effects that had begun with the Reformation and would presumably last until Hollywood fell into the San Andreas fault.

So Lavicini's employer could forgive him for wanting to keep the Teleportation Device a total secret. Still, even de Gorge, who had once strangled a man while dictating a love letter, must have felt a little nervous as the entire bejewelled elite of Paris, including, last of all, Louis XIV and his queen, arrived at the Théâtre des Encornets for the première of *The Lizard Prince*, greeting each other with hand-kissings so formalised and ostentatious they were like miniature ballets in themselves. For the thousandth time he must have reminded himself of what his mentor Lunaire had once taught him: as an impresario, you shouldn't flatter yourself that you were really anything to do with the show. You couldn't conjure a hit. Your job was just to sell tickets. And if you had done that to the best of your ability, said Lunaire, then the only thing left to pray for was that nobody in the audience arrived with a dog bigger than a child or a pistol bigger than an upholstery hammer. But all this without even rehearsing the new machine – that was painting the devil on the wall.

Loeser's Teleportation Device, by contrast, was about to be demonstrated at the little Allien Theatre in Berlin in front of only two other people: Adolf Klugweil, the putative star of *Lavicini*, and Immanuel Blumstein, the putative writer-director. The latter, at forty, was old enough to have been a founding member of the famous November Group, which seemed really pretty old to his two younger collaborators. Behind his back, they mocked him for his baldness, they mocked him for his nostalgia, and they mocked him for his habit, whenever he thought he might have misplaced his wallet or pipe (which was always), of patting himself down with such impatience, such savagery and such complete disregard for the actual location of his pockets that it began to resemble some sort of eroto-religious self-flagellation ritual – and yet they also had enormous respect for their mentor's refusal to let the convictions of his youth fall out along with his hair. The belief all three men shared was that Expressionism had not been pushed nearly far enough. 'Expressionism is no more a form of theatre than revolution is a form of state,' Fritz Kortner had written. Perhaps, but in that case the revolution had been botched. The New Objectivity that had replaced Expressionism in the middle of the 1920s was nothing but the old state with a new cabinet. In reply, the New Expressionism would be the old revolution with new bombs.

Klugweil, meanwhile, was a twenty-four-year-old so languid as to be almost liquid, except when he went on stage and broke open some inner asylum of shrieks and contortions, wild eyes and bared teeth – which made him perfectly suited to Expressionist acting and almost useless for any other type. He'd been at university with Loeser, who had always wondered what he was like during sex but had never quite had the cheek to make an enquiry with his dull girlfriend.

'Is everyone ready?' said Loeser, who stood in the wings with his hand on the lever. The Allien Theatre had been an old-fashioned music hall before Blumstein took it over, and renovations were still only half complete, so after a few hours backstage your clothes and hair were so thick with paint flakes, dust clumps, loose threads, cushion stuffing, cobwebs, and splinters that you felt like a veal cutlet rolled in breadcrumbs.

'Yes, get on with it,' said Blumstein, who sat in seat 3F of the empty auditorium.

'This pinches under the armpits,' said Klugweil, who stood on stage, strapped into a harness like a test pilot missing a plane.

Lavicini's Extraordinary Mechanism for the Almost Instantaneous Transport of Persons from Place to Place was, as it turned out, genuinely extraordinary. Once, as many as sixteen stagehands communicating with whistles had been required to change a scene. Giacomo Torelli's invention of a single rotating axle had since made possible the simultaneous movement of multiple flats, reducing that number from sixteen to one. But that leap forward was rendered instantly trivial by the magnificence of Lavicini's Teleportation Device. At the end of the first scene, the audience gave a gasp so great you could have marked it on a barometer as the stage suddenly took flight like a flock of birds. A vast hidden assembly of ropes, cranes, cranks, wheels, springs, runners, gantries, pulleys, weights, and counterweights was lifting every part of the set into the air – was rearranging it in a flurry of swoops and swaps and spins – and was setting it down again with barely an audible bump. The Third Temple of the Lizards was replaced by a Dagonite slave-cove before anyone in the room even thought of breathing out. All the violinists missed their cues and one ballerina fainted, but the cheering afterwards was so loud that it didn't matter. At the back of the theatre, Auguste de Gorge decided that, having gone to bed with eight whores after the last première and five whores after the première before that, he would go to bed tonight with thirteen. (Not long ago someone had told him about the Fibonacci sequence and he had construed it as a challenge.) In the wings, Adriano Lavicini stepped back from the controls with a temperate smile. A stagecraft machine so ambitious that it was indistinguishable from magic: that was painting the devil on the wall.

Loeser's Teleportation Device, by contrast, was not supposed to be spectacular. It was just a means to an end. The first half of *Lavicini*, before the protagonist's emigration to Paris, would take place during the Venetian Carnival, when the entire city strapped on masks – when lawyers would wear masks to plead in court, maids would wear masks to go to market, and mothers would put masks on their newborns – and not

8

just masks, in most cases, but also a long domino-cloak, so that it was impossible to tell a man from a woman until they spoke. Anyone could go anywhere, and anyone could mix with anyone: 'prince with subject', as Casanova wrote, 'the ordinary with the remarkable man, lovely and hideous together. There were no longer valid laws, nor law-makers.' The inquisition, omniscient and omnipotent for the rest of the year, gave up completely. To Loeser and Blumstein, the glamour and intrigue of the old Carnival were nothing compared to its unacknowledged political radicalism. At what other time in history had there been a social experiment on such a scale? No Bolshevik would have had the guts. The plays on which Loeser and Blumstein collaborated always stressed a notion they called Equivalence: the communist was shown to be no different from the Nazi, the priest from the gangster, the wife in furs from the prostitute in army boots. So the Carnival was perfectly suited to their themes. And so was the Teleportation Device. Like Lavicini's machine, Loeser's machine used springs and pulleys and counterweights, but whereas Lavicini's machine moved the scenery around the cast, Loeser's machine just moved the cast around the scenery, which was a lot easier. The idea was that a harnessed actor could make a speech as a stockbroker in the little bank at the top right of the stage, step back out of view, and be whipped across to the little casino at the bottom left, from which he would step back into view almost instantly as a compulsive gambler. This would be an effective if unsubtle way of driving home the point about how the two were just the same. And if in this new play there was some business with masks and cloaks coming on and off, the effect could be even more striking.

At the Théâtre des Encornets, by the time the second act drew to a close, the Teleportation Device was a novelty more than twelve minutes old, and yet the Paris upper crust weren't quite bored to death with it yet. Montand's lovely Dance of the Half-Fish came to an end, the dancers fluttered off stage to make way for an orchestral interlude, and the scenery began once again to lift into the air. And then there was a rumbling sound like thunder ground up with a pestle.

No two accounts quite agreed on what happened next. The confusion was understandable. Loeser knew only that the Théâtre des Encornets began to crumble – not the entire building, fortunately, but only its south-east corner, which meant one side of the stage and several of the nearby private audience boxes. There was a stampede, and even after all those centuries it was perhaps with a moistness in the eye that one recalled the tragic and senseless sacrifice of some of the most deliriously beautiful couture in the early history of the medium. Most of the inhabitants of that couture, as it happened, were unharmed – as were the musicians, who were shielded from tumbling marble by the position of the orchestra pit, and the dancers, who by great good luck had just exited stage right rather than stage left. The dead, in the end, numbered about twenty-five audience members from the private boxes nearest the collapse, who were recovered from the rubble after the fires had been put out but were in every case too badly mashed to be identified; the swooned ballerina, who had not been in the wings with her sisters but rather languishing on a couch backstage; Monsieur Merde, the Théâtre des Encornets' cat; and Adriano Lavicini himself.

The Teleportation Device, meanwhile, had deleted itself along with the building. No part of it could be salvaged for an investigation into what might have gone wrong, and no plans or even sketches could be found in Lavicini's workshop. Auguste de Gorge was, of course, ruined. And Louis XIV never went to the theatre again.

Two hundred and fifty years later, at the Allien Theatre, a spring sprang. A counterweight dropped. An actor shot across the stage. And a scream was heard.

The original Teleportation Accident was not notorious solely because it was the only time that a set designer was known to have inadvertently and suicidally wrecked a theatre and flattened sections of his audience. It was notorious also because of claims that appeared in certain reports of the cataclysm. Several reliable witnesses recalled that just before the end of the second act they had detected a stench somewhere between rotten metal and rusty meat. Others had felt an icy draught lunge through the theatre. And one (not very reliable) marquis insisted to friends that, as he fled, he had seen grey tentacles as thick as Doric columns slithering moistly out from behind the proscenium arch. Rumours began that – well, that an aforementioned German idiom was more literally applicable here than any post-Enlightenment historian would be willing to credit. Before his death, Lavicini had, after all, been nicknamed 'the Sorceror'.

Whatever the truth, that was Lavicini's Teleportation Accident. As for Loeser's Teleportation Accident, that wasn't nearly so bad. Nobody died. The Allien Theatre was not rended apart. Klugweil just dislocated a couple of arms.

They didn't confirm that until later, though. All Loeser and Blumstein could see as they rushed over was that Klugweil was dangling half out of the harness, limbs twisted, face white, eyes abulge. The overall effect reminded Loeser of nothing so much as a set of large pallid male genitalia painfully mispositioned in an athlete's thong.

'Why in God's name did you have to call it the Teleportation Device, you total prick?' hissed Blumstein to Loeser as they struggled to untangle the actor. 'I knew this would happen.'

'Don't be irrational,' said Loeser. 'It would have gone wrong whatever I called it.' Which, judging by the head-butt he then received from the pendulant Klugweil, was not felt to be a very satisfactory reply.

Two hours later Loeser arrived at the Wild West Bar inside the Haus Vaterland on Potsdamer Platz to find his best friend already waiting for him.

'What happened to your nose?' said Achleitner.

'To answer your question,' said Loeser indistinctly, 'I don't think we're going to be able to get all that coke from Klugweil tonight as we planned.' He lit a cigarette and looked around in disgust. The Haus Vaterland, which had been opened the year before last by a shady entrepreneur called Kempinski, was an amusement complex, a kitsch Babel, full of bars, cinemas, stages, arcades, restaurants, and ballrooms, with each nationally themed room (Italian, Spanish, Austrian, Hungarian, and so on, but no British or French, because of Versailles) given its own decor, music, costumes, and food. Up in the Wild West Bar where Loeser and Achleitner now sat, a sullen Negro jazz band wore cowboy hats to perform, which gave a sense of the Haus Vaterland's dogged commitment to cultural verisimilitude, while downstairs you could take a 'Cruise along the Rhine' with artificial lightning, thunder, and rain like in one of Lavicini's operas. It was as if, in some unfashionable district of hell, the new arrivals had established a random topography of small territorial ghettoes, each decorated to resemble a motherland that after a thousand years in purgatory they only half remembered. The whole place was full of tourists from the provinces, always strolling and stopping and turning and strolling and stopping again for no apparent reason as if practising some decayed military drill, and it was as loud as a hundred children's playgrounds. But Achleitner insisted on coming here, maintaining that it was good practice for living in the future. Loeser, he said, might think the whole twentieth century was going to look like a George Grosz painting, all fat soldiers with monocles and tarts with no teeth and gloomy cobbled streets, but that vision of darkness and corruption, that Gothic Berlin, was just as artificial and sentimentalised, in its own way, as the work of any amateur countryside watercolourist. When Loeser disputed Kempinski's prophetism, Achleitner just alluded to Loeser's ex-girlfriend Marlene.

Loeser had broken up with Marlene Schibelsky three weeks previously after a relationship of seven or eight months. She was a shallow girl, and Loeser knew that he ought not to settle for shallow girls, but she was good in bed, and until the day that either Brain or Penis could win a viable majority in Loeser's inner Reichstag there had seemed to be no hope of change. What finally broke the deadlock was something that happened at a small cast party in a café in Strandow.

Quite late in the night, Loeser had overheard part of a conversation in a nearby booth about dilettantism in Berlin cultural life, and one of the five or six occupants of that booth was the composer Jascha Drabsfarben. This was surprising for two reasons. Firstly, it was surprising to see Drabsfarben at a party at all, because Drabsfarben didn't go to parties. And secondly, it was surprising to hear that particular topic arise while Drabsfarben was sitting right there, because in any discussion about dilettantism in Berlin cultural life, Drabsfarben himself was the obvious and unavoidable counter-example, so either at some point someone would have to invoke Drabsfarben's reputation in the presence of Drabsfarben himself, which would be uncomfortable for everyone because it would sound like flattery and you didn't flatter a man like Drabsfarben, or else no one would, which would be uncomfortable for everyone too because that elision would throb more and more conspicuously the longer the discussion went on.

Loeser, like most of his friends, was mildly enthusiastic about his own artistic endeavours in the usual sort of way, but Drabsfarben was known to have a devotion so formidable that if he were ever shipwrecked on a rocky coast he would probably build a piano from dried kelp and seagull bones rather than let his work be interrupted even for an afternoon. Sex was nothing to him; politics were nothing to him; fame was nothing to him; and society was nothing to him, except when he thought a particular director or promoter or critic could help him get his work heard, in which case he would appear at precisely as many dinners and receptions as it took to get that individual on his side. His most recent work was an atonal piano concerto derived from an actuary's table of hot-air balloon accident statistics, and indeed most of his music seemed to demand that the intellectual tenacity of its listeners almost outmatch that of its creator. Drabsfarben, in other words, made Loeser feel like a bit of a fraud. But normally Loeser didn't resent this. In fact, Loeser sometimes felt that Drabsfarben might be the only man in Berlin he really respected. Which was why it was so upsetting when Hecht said, 'So many people only seem to have gone into the theatre in the first place because they have some narcissistic social agenda – you know, like . . . like . . .' And then Drabsfarben, who had been almost silent until this point, said, 'Like Loeser?'

While sober, Loeser could have brushed this off, but two bottles of bad red wine had transformed him into the emotional equivalent of one of those strange Peruvian frogs with transparent skin exposing their jumpy little hearts. He rushed from the party, and Marlene followed him out into the chilly street, where she found him sitting on the kerb, heels in the gutter, weeping, almost whimpering. 'Is that what they all think of me? Is that really what they all think of me?' Although he would probably have forgotten all about this small crisis by the following morning, or even by the end of the party, she did her best to comfort him.

And that was when she said it. 'Don't slip into the dark, my darling. Don't slip into the dark.'

Even while drunk, Loeser immediately recognised these words. They were from an atrocious American melodrama called *Scars of Desire* that they had seen at the cinema on Ranekstrasse. Loeser had mocked the film all through dinner and all the way back to his flat, finding himself so funny that he thought he might write a satirical piece for some magazine or other, and confident of Marlene's agreement, until finally he noticed her quietly sobbing, and she confessed that she had loved the film and felt it was 'meant just for [her]'. He dropped the subject. Marlene went to *Scars of Desire* four more times, twice with female friends, twice alone. To summarise: late in the film, the male romantic lead has a moral convulsion about marrying the female romantic lead, who was previously engaged to his brother, who was killed in the war. He starts crying and knocking over furniture, and we realise that he is not really angry at his new fiancée, but at the pointless death of his brother. The female romantic lead coaxes him back to his senses by whispering, 'Don't slip into the dark, my darling. Don't slip into the dark.'

The problem wasn't that Marlene was quoting from the film, although that would have been bad enough. The problem was that she said the line as if it had come not from any film but from deep in her own heart. She had internalised some lazy screenwriter's lazy offering to the point where she was no longer even vaguely conscious of its commercial origins. *Scars of Desire* had been screwed into her personality like a plastic prosthesis.

Naturally, he split up with her the next day.

'So you're trying to tell me that Marlene is herself a sort of avatar of the twentieth century,' said Loeser, sipping his schnapps.

'Yes,' said Achleitner. 'Because she nurses sentiments that have been sold to her as closely as she nurses sentiments of her own. Or perhaps even more closely. Like a magpie with discount cuckoo's eggs. Did you ever bring her here?'

'Once, remember. You were with us.'

'Did she like it? I would have thought she'd be quite at home.'

The jazz band concluded 'Georgia on My Mind' and trooped off stage, presumably ready to return to some sort of art deco hog ranch. 'That is cruel,' said Loeser. 'You know she'll probably be at the party tonight? Which is why I'm absolutely not going if we don't get some coke.'

15

'Egon, why is it that every single time you're obliged to be in the same room with one of your ex-girlfriends you have to make it into a huge emergency? It's incredibly boring.'

'Come on. You know how it is. You catch sight of an old flame and you get this breathless animal prickle like a fox in a room with a hound. And then all night you have to seem carefree and successful and elated, which is a pretence that for some reason you feel no choice but to maintain even though you know they're better qualified than anyone else in the world to detect immediately that you're really still the same hapless cunt as ever.'

'That's adolescent. The fact that you are so neurotic about your past lovers makes it both fortunate and predictable that you have so few of them. It's one of those elegant self-regulating systems that one so often finds in nature.'

'I can't lose this break-up. We've all seen what happens to the defeated.'

'You didn't even like her.'

'I know. But at least she had sex with me. And it was really good. When am I ever going to have sex with anyone again? I mean, without paying. Honestly – when? Sometimes I wish I was queer like you. I've never seen you worry about all this. Upon how many lucky pilgrims have you bestowed your blessing this year?'

'No idea. I gave up keeping count while I was still at school. Remind me what you're on now?'

'Five. Still. In my whole life. Not counting hookers. Sometimes when I walk down the street I look around at them all and I feel as if I'm being crucified on a cross made of beautiful women. Sometimes when I get out of the bath I catch sight of myself in the mirror and I feel as if even my own penis is bitterly disappointed in me.'

Throughout the 1920s, Germany had been full of teachers, doctors, psychoanalysts, sociologists, poets, and novelists who were eager to talk to you about sex. They were eager to inform you that sex was natural, that sex ought to be pleasurable, and that everyone had the right to a fulfilling sex life. Loeser broadly agreed with the first two claims, and he even agreed, in principle, with the third, but, given his present situation, the establishment of a global Marxist workers' paradise seemed a modest and plausible aim in comparison to this ludicrously optimistic vision of a world in which he, Egon Loeser, actually got close to a non-mercenary vulva once in a while. These well-meaning experts honestly seemed to believe that as soon as people were told that they ought to be having sex, they would just start having sex, as if there could not possibly be any obstacle to twenty-four-hour erotic festivities other than moral reluctance. 'Oh, thank you so much,' Loeser wanted to say to them. 'That's so helpful. I should be enjoying fantastic sex all the time, should I? That had really never occurred to me until you mentioned it. Now that I have been liberated by your inspiring words, I shall go off and enjoy some fantastic sex right away.'

Then again, it was sometimes possible to use this nonsense to one's advantage. Apparently there had been a short halcyon period in the early 20s when all you had to do to make a girl go to bed with you was to convince her that she was inhibited and politically regressive if she didn't, rather in the same way that you might nag someone into contributing to a strike fund. You could cite all manner of progressive thinkers, sometimes by chapter and paragraph. But that trick had expired long before Loeser had been old enough to use it.

Loeser felt particularly unlucky because, as a young man rising through Berlin's experimental theatre scene, he moved in perhaps the most promiscuous social circles of perhaps the most promiscuous city in Europe. If he had lived in, say, a village outside Delft, the contrast probably wouldn't have been quite so agonising. He half envied Lavicini, who got squashed twenty years before Venice entered its century of utter carnal mayhem. Loeser hated politics, but he knew there

17

were plenty of politicians who wanted to reverse Germany's descent into libertinism, and he wished them the best. A bit of good old-fashioned sexual repression could only improve his comparative standing. Back in the 1890s, for instance, he wouldn't have felt nearly so depressed that he never got laid, because no one else would have been getting laid either – the same principle they now used in Russia with potatoes and electricity and so on. Before the Great War, women knew that their dear daddies had spent years saving up to pay for them to be married, so they wanted their wedding night to mean something. But ever since all those dowries had been turned to dead leaves by the Inflation, women had realised that they might as well just have fun. That was Loeser's theory, anyway.

'So how long has it been now?' said Achleitner.

'Since the day I broke up with Marlene.'

'Before or after you told her?'

'Shortly before.' This final strategic indulgence had been especially enjoyable for Loeser because for once he didn't feel as if he had to bother about giving Marlene an orgasm. Normally, there was only one damnable way this could be done: Loeser would sit up in the bed with his back against the wall like an invalid receiving his breakfast, Marlene would straddle him, they would begin to rock back and forth, and then Loeser would simultaneously stick his tongue deep in her ear and reach down between their jostling bellies to – well, he sometimes had dreams afterwards where he was a vet in handcuffs who had to deliver a tiny, tiny calf from a tiny, tiny cow. The procedure with Marlene was incredibly awkward, it took so long that his fingertips wrinkled, and by the end his wrist and forearm were so embattled with cramp that he scarcely had the patience to attend to the needs of any other appendage. But for most of their time together he had been quite content to perform this little duty because she was such an exceptional lover in every other category. 'So that's three weeks,' he told Achleitner.

'Three weeks? You've gone longer than three weeks before.'

'Of course I've gone longer than three weeks. I seem to remember I once went nineteen years.'

'So why are you complaining?'

'If my platoon is stranded in the mountains and our rations have just run out, I'm not allowed to start worrying until we actually begin to starve?'

'Won't be long before you resort to cannibalism, I imagine.'

'Anton, I resorted to cannibalism one afternoon in 1921 and I have hardly stopped since. The point is, it could be another six months before even the most rudimentary lines of supply can be re-established. It could be a year. Or, who knows? I may never have sex again without paying. Never. It could happen.'

'You'll meet someone.'

'That is a groundless probabilistic calculation, and therefore of no value. I thought you knew better than to try to reassure me. There is nothing more sickening than reassurance.'

'If you are going to be like this all evening then I really am going to need some coke too. I wish you hadn't pissed off Klugweil.'

And Littau was in Munich, and they both owed money to Tetzner, and the toilet attendant at Borchardt would sell them crushed aspirin. 'Or the one at the Mauve Door?' said Achleitner finally. 'The one with no ears.'

'Even worse – I don't know what he sold us last time but it nearly made me soil myself in the street on the way back to Brogmann's house. I'm fed up with buying it from strangers. Come on, you must be able to think of someone. You lot' – by which Loeser meant homosexuals – 'always seem to know twice as many people for this sort of thing.'

'Thank you for your confidence, but I don't think I can help in this case. Oh, although that Englishman from last night had excellent stuff with him.'

'Which Englishman?'

'Some blond aspiring writer from London. I met him at the Eden Bar. Hung like one of those Norse giants from the *Ring Cycle*.'

'Can we find him again?'

'I think I've got a number for his boarding house.'

Loeser sighed. 'Listen, Anton, as fondly as I remember the many, many evenings of our youth that we've squandered running round Berlin searching in vain for adequate drugs, I just don't think I'm in the mood tonight. And anyway, my septum is still convalescing.'

'But we have to go to this party. I heard Brecht is going to be there.'

'Oh, ha ha.' There was nobody in Berlin that Loeser loathed more than Bertolt Brecht, and there was nothing about Berlin theatre parties that he loathed more than the ubiquitous cry of 'I heard Brecht is going to be there'.

'And Adele Hitler.'

'What?'

'She's back from Switzerland, apparently.'

Adele Hitler was a giggly teenage girl from a rich family whom Loeser had tutored in poetry for two lucrative years before she went off to finishing school. 'So? I'd stop to chat if I saw her in the street but I'm not going to the party just to catch up with the latest on her doll collection.'

'She's eighteen now,' said Achleitner, raising an eyebrow.

'What are you implying? I'm hardly likely to try to get her into bed.'

'Pedagogical ethics?'

'None whatsoever, but she was a grotesquely fat little thing.'

'They say she looks very different. Ugly duckling and all that.'

Loeser considered this. 'I did always think she had a bit of a crush on me.' He finished his drink. 'Well, all right, it's not as if I have any dignity left to lose. Let's find this Wagnerian gallant of yours.'

An hour later they met the Englishman in the street outside his boarding house on Konigslandstrasse. The evening was blustery, and nearby a hunchbacked balloon seller with two dozen red balloons stood shifting his weight against the tug of the wind like a Zeppelin breeder out promenading a whole litter of excitable pups.

'I'd love to introduce the two of you,' said Achleitner, nodding at the Englishman, 'but I'm afraid on this napkin next to your telephone number I seem just to have written "London, blond, incomparable dong".'

'Rupert Rackenham. And for accuracy's sake I'm originally from Devon. Have you been in a fight?' he asked Loeser.

'Of a kind.'

'We were wondering if you had any more of that coke,' said Achleitner.

'Quite a cache of it, yes,' said Rackenham. His German was good.

'Can we buy some?' said Loeser. 'We're going to a party later and it's the only way we know how to endure the company of our friends.'

'What sort of party?'

'It's in an old corset factory up in Puppenberg,' said Achleitner. There had been a craze recently for parties like this: in disused ballrooms, bankrupt coffin warehouses, condemned gymnasia. Loeser's attitude was that if a place was abandoned it was probably abandoned for a reason and reviving it voluntarily was perverse.

'Well, as we're all intimates now, why don't I give you each a few lines as a gift? And then perhaps you'd be kind enough to bring me along to this party and introduce me to a few more of these unendurable friends that you mentioned.'

'How many lines between the two of us?'

'Let's call it a sonnet.'

Achleitner shrugged at Loeser and Loeser shrugged back at Achleitner. So Achleitner said, 'Fine. I should think once

21

you're there you'll sell out the rest of your stock in about thirty seconds.'

'Splendid. I'll just go upstairs and get my camera.' He had an educated, ironic, very English manner, at once sharply penetrating and affably detached, like someone who would always win the bets he made with strangers at weddings on how long the marriage would last but would never bother to collect the money.

'We'll find a cab.'

When he came back down, Rackenham had a Leica on a strap around his neck. He took a photo of Loeser and Achleitner and then the cab set off for Puppenberg. At the corner, a coachman was feeding his nag out of a wide-mouthed coal scuttle, pigeons pecking grudgingly at the spilled oats as if what they really craved was a few scraps of fresh horse brisket.

'I assume you're an artist of some kind, Herr Loeser,' said Rackenham.

'Why do you assume?'

'Because since coming to Berlin I never seem to meet anyone who isn't an artist. At least by their own description.'

Loeser thought of what he'd overheard at that cast party. 'Yes, it's a state of affairs I find pretty sickening, but as you correctly surmise I'm guilty of contributing to it myself. I'm a set designer. I work mostly at the Allien Theatre.'

'What have you got on at the moment?'

'Nothing quite yet. We're just starting a new project.' Loeser gave Rackenham a brief sketch of *Lavicini* as it was currently conceived. He always felt a bit self-conscious talking about his work in the earshot of taxi drivers.

'So it's a historical drama? I hope you won't take offence, Herr Loeser, but I've never seen the point of historical drama. Or historical fiction for that matter. I once thought about writing a novel of that kind, but then I began to wonder, what possible patience could the public have for a young man arrogant enough to believe he has anything new to say about an epoch with which his only acquaintance is flipping list-lessly through history books on train journeys? So I stick to the present day. I really think it's the present day that needs our attention.'

'By accident, Herr Rackenham, you've led me to one of the great themes of the New Expressionist theatre,' said Loeser. And he explained Equivalence. Yes, whenever one began a play or a novel, there was a choice to be made: whether to plot your Zeppelin's course for present-day Berlin, or seventeenth-century Paris, or a future London, or some other destination entirely. But the choice meant nothing. Consider Germany under the Weimar Republic in 1931. Thirteen years since its inception, five years since its acknowledged zenith, two years since there was last any good coke: a culture old enough, in other words, that journalists were already beginning to judge it in retrospect, as history. And they were calling it a Golden Age, an unprecedented flourishing. But if you were part of it – and even if you were only part of its decline, like Loeser – you couldn't help but say to yourself: all these thousands of young people, all in a few nearby neighbourhoods, all call-ing themselves artists, as Rackenham had said. And all this spare time. And all these openings and all these premières and all these parties. And all this talk and talk and talk and drink and talk. For nearly fifteen years. All of this. And what had it produced for which anyone would really swap a bad bottle of Riesling in eight decades' time? A few plays, a few paintings, a few piano concertos – most of which, anyway, went quite unnoticed by the boys and girls who made such a fuss about being at the heart of it all. If that was a Golden Age then an astute investor might consider selling off his bullion before the rate fell any further. There had been so many Golden Ages now, and Loeser was confident that they had all been the same, and always would be. Compare the Venice of the late Renaissance, where Lavicini came of age, to the Berlin of Weimar, or compare the Berlin of Weimar to whatever city would turn out to be most fashionable in 2012, and you would find the same empty people going to the same empty parties and making the same empty comments about the same empty efforts, with just a few spasms of worthwhile art going on at the naked extremities. Nothing ever changed. That was Equivalence. Plot a course for another country, another age, and the best you could hope for was that you would circumnavigate the globe by accident, and arrive at the opposite coast of your own homeland, mooring your Zeppelin trepidatiously in this rich mud to find a tribe you did not recognise speaking a language you could not understand. If Loeser could ever get his Teleportation Device working, then in future productions it might sling actors not just through space but through time.

'Equivalence is all very well,' said Rackenham. 'But political conditions, at least, must change. And for a revolutionary dramatist that must mean something.'

'Good grief, don't talk to me about politics,' said Loeser. 'In the thirteen years since the war there have been how many governments, Anton?'

'Fifteen?' guessed Achleitner. 'Seventeen?'

'Exactly. And we're supposed to keep biting our nails as we wait for the next arbitrary plot development? Politics is pigshit. Hindenburg and MacDonald and Louis XIV, they're just men. I will bet you anything you like that . . . Anton, you still read the newspapers: name somebody who's making a lot of noise at the moment.'

'Hitler.'

'I will bet you anything you like – sorry, Hitler? Do you mean Adele's father?'

'No relation.'

'Right. As I was saying, I will bet you anything you like that this other Hitler, whoever he is, will never make one bit of difference to my life.'

'Careful, Egon,' said Achleitner. 'That's the sort of remark that people quote in their memoirs later on as a delicious example of historical irony.'

'What about the Inflation?' said Rackenham. 'That was politics' fault. And you can hardly say it didn't affect you.'

'Actually, he can,' said Achleitner. 'He's a special case. His parents were psychiatrists and most of their clients paid in Swiss francs or American dollars. The Inflation worked out very well for the Loeser family. That's why he's such a cosseted little darling. He wasn't eating cakes made of fungus like the rest of us.'

'Anton is partly correct,' said Loeser, 'but he neglects to mention that both my parents then died in a car accident. Thus cancelling out any egalitarian guilt I might otherwise have felt.'

'I'm sorry to hear that,' said Rackenham.

'Yes, I think of them often.'

'No, I mean, I'm sorry to hear that people here have to feel guilty about growing up in comfort. In England even my socialist friends wouldn't be so tiresome.'

'And this so-called Depression makes no difference to us either,' said Achleitner. 'Six million jobless doesn't seem like so many when none of us ever had any wish for a real job in the first place.'

'Still, what is one supposed to do with six million surplus people?' said Rackenham.

'Perhaps they can all become full-time set designers,' said Achleitner.

'We'd better stop and get some wine,' said Loeser. 'There won't be anywhere open near the party.'

When Loeser came back with four cheap bottles they got the driver to carry on waiting so they could do some of Rackenham's coke. Rackenham obligingly opened the back of his camera and took out a little paper parcel like a mouse's packed lunch.

'Is that where you always keep your coke?' said Loeser.

'Yes.'

'Isn't that where the film is supposed to go?'

'Yes.'

'So how does it take pictures?'

'Don't be so literal. Photography, as a ceremonial gesture, is a convenient way to make people feel like they're having a good time, but the technical details are a bore. I picked this machine up for a song because it wouldn't work even if there were film in it. Meanwhile, I may as well point out that the meter is running.' There was no flat surface near by so they just sniffed the coke off the sides of their hands and then licked up the residue. One of the great skills of Berlin social life was to make this awkward self-nuzzling into an elegant gesture; Loeser knew that he resembled a schoolboy trying to teach himself cunnilingus. Then, afterwards, always that furtive, startled look, as if somehow you'd only just realised that you weren't alone in the room.

The cab drove on. Now that they were further up into Puppenberg, most of the buildings they passed had sooty bricks and squinty windows. 'Whatever I may just have said about drugs these days, this stuff is not bad,' said Loeser. And then they pulled up outside the corset factory.

No one could remember whose party it was. Inside, long black rows of sewing machines still stood ready like cows for milking, but the electricity was disconnected so the whole factory had been lit up with candles, and at the far end a jazz band (Caucasian, hatless) played on a stage made out of upturned wooden crates – all of which Loeser would have found very imaginative and refreshing four or five years ago.

The first familiar faces they saw were Dieter Ziesel and Hans Heijenhoort, which was not an auspicious start. Both were research physicists who had hung on to the scrubby cliff edge of Loeser's social circle with the help of some old university friendships that had withered but not quite died. They were both olympically dull, but Loeser had nonetheless felt a special warmth for Dieter Ziesel ever since one drunken evening in the third year of his degree.

He had been in the college bar and something had just happened – he couldn't now remember what, but it was most likely some rejection by a girl – to melt him into the same sort of doldrums that would one day prove indirectly fatal to his relationship with Marlene Schibelsky. 'I know perfectly well that I'm better than everyone else around here, except maybe Drabsfarben,' he had said to Achleitner. 'But what if that makes no difference? I mean, girls don't seem to care, so why should the rest of the world? If I achieve anything really important, I won't mind about being unhappy, and if I did end up really happy, I suppose I could just about tolerate not achieving anything important. But what if I get neither? My whole life I've been so scornful of anyone who could make peace with failure, but what if I have to? Not everyone can get to the top. Someone's got to be at the bottom. It could happen. Except I think I'd gnaw out my own spleen first.'

'You're never going to be at the bottom,' Achleitner had said.

'How can you know?'

'Because of Dieter Ziesel.'

'Who's that?'

Achleitner had pointed, and Loeser had looked over to see a fellow student with all the classical good looks and muscle definition of a shop-window dummy dipped in birthday-cake icing, who sat alone with a glass of beer. Ziesel was in their year at university, Achleitner explained, but almost nobody knew him. He was still a virgin because he had been too nervous ever to undress in front of a prostitute, and in fact he had never even kissed a girl. He vomited down his shirt whenever he had more than two drinks. He was miserably conscious of his flab jiggling up and down whenever he ran for the tram, which he often did because he was always late. Every weekend he took the train back to his parents' house in Lemberg and all afternoon would cry into his mother's lap while she cooed to him like a baby. He spent his evenings drawing maps of imaginary planets. 'And he even plays the tuba! Isn't that too perfect? So you'd think he'd be a mathematical genius, wouldn't you? Specimens like him usually are. But he's not. He does all right in his exams because he spends so many hours in the library without bothering to wash, but all his Professors say he lacks any real feeling for his subject.'

'How do you know all this?'

'He left his diary somewhere and somebody found it. The point is, however bad you may think your life is, you can be sure that Dieter Ziesel's is worse. You're never going to be at the bottom, because Dieter Ziesel is always going to be at the bottom. In mathematical terms, he is the n minus one.'

'That may be the most gladdening thing I have ever heard,' Loeser had said.

'Yes. Dieter Ziesel is a gift to us all. I often feel that in some respects he is our Jesus.'

In the years that followed, Loeser took strength thousands of times from the thought of Dieter Ziesel. At one point he considered commissioning a miniature portrait of Ziesel and keeping it in his wallet. When his great redeemer won a prestigious research fellowship it was a bit of a blow, but apparently a particular Professor had championed Ziesel's cause to the selection committee, and that Professor was no doubt taking pity on the fellow, knowing that he would have no prospects in any other walk of life.

What Loeser found especially hilarious was that Ziesel still refused to accept his role. When he heard about a party thrown by people he knew, he always turned up, even though it must have been clear that nobody wanted him there. He had recently bought a suit in the gross American style that was now fashionable among the middlebrow public – huge shoulders, slim legs, leather belt – as if everyone would suddenly change their opinion about him as soon as they had a chance to admire this up-to-date garb. And, most absurd of all, he maintained his abusive relationship with Heijenhoort. The two had been good friends at university, but at some point Ziesel must have realised that his skinny classmate was the one person he could bully who was certain not to bully him back. This was because Heijenhoort – also a bit like Jesus, but in a less useful way – was basically the nicest man in the entire world. He wasn't all that charming or funny, he was just nice. He had incomprehensible reserves of friendliness, optimism, self-effacement, generosity, and tact. A gang of dockers could kick him to mush in the street and even his death rattle would be polite. Ziesel was safe with Heijenhoort. So he made constant little jokes at Heijenhoort's expense whenever he was in the presence of anyone who he thought might be impressed, hoping that it might at least infinitesimally elevate his social status, like a provincial civil servant writing to a minister about the incompetence of a colleague and expecting a promotion in return. But in fact it only had the effect of making Ziesel look like even more of a failure, since no sane person could possibly dislike Heijenhoort.

No sane person, that is, except Egon Loeser. To be that nice all the time, thought Loeser, just didn't make sense. It was inhuman, illogical, saccharine, and cowardly. You couldn't truly love anything if you didn't hate at least something. Indeed, perhaps you couldn't truly love anything if you didn't hate almost everything. What, he wondered, would it actually mean to be 'friends' with Heijenhoort, knowing that Heijenhoort, the skimmed milk to Ziesel's rancid butter, would bestow his insipid affection so indiscriminately? But even Achleitner said he didn't mind Heijenhoort, so Loeser kept his contempt to himself.

Loeser introduced Rackenham to the two mismatched messiahs and then asked them how the party was. 'Not very good,' Ziesel replied. 'There's no corkscrew.'

'What do you mean?' said Achleitner.

'No corkscrew,' said Ziesel. 'No one can open their wine. And there are no shops for miles.'

'There must be two hundred people here. How can there not be one corkscrew?'

'Hildkraut does have a penknife with a corkscrew attachment but he's hiring it out and no one wants to pay,' said Heijenhoort.

'There have already been some casualties.' Brogmann, apparently, had smashed his bottle on the wall to break off the neck and then tried to drink from what was left and cut his lip, while Tetzner had told Hannah Czenowitz that, given her curriculum vitae, she should have no trouble sucking out a cork, and she'd punched him in the eye.

'This is ridiculous,' said Achleitner.

'Yes, it's a disappointment, but at least Brecht is supposed to be coming later,' said Ziesel.

'If there's not even any wine, thank God we found some coke,' said Loeser. Then he felt a tap on his shoulder, and turned.

Achleitner had been right. Adele Hitler had changed.

The first thing Loeser noticed was her hair. It was hopelessly unfashionable. Where every single one of his female friends had a bob that looked like a geometric diagram of itself, often snipped so close at the back that in the morning there would be stubble at the nape, pale Adele wore a flock of black starlings, a drop of ink bursting in a glass of water, an avalanche of curls that could hardly be called a cut because if it were ever to come across a pair of scissors it would surely just swallow them up.

And where most 1931 frocks, like the medieval Greek merchant and geodesist Cosmas Indicopleustes, argued for flatness in the face of all available evidence, Adele had on a blue dress that wrote limericks about her bust and hips, no matter that her figure was actually pretty girlish – with a printed pattern of clouds, skyscrapers and biplanes that seemed to be the garment's lone, almost touchingly clumsy, concession to the zeitgeist.

And then, above all, her eyes. She didn't wear goggles of eyeshadow like the other girls did, just a little eyeliner and a little mascara, but both were quite redundant, since no artificial pigment could possibly augment what were not only the biggest and brightest and most tender eyes that Loeser had ever seen but also the most astonishingly baroque, with each iris showing a spray of gold around the pupil like the corona around an eclipse, within a dappled band of blue and green, within an outline of grey as distinct as a pencil mark, and then beyond that an expanse of moist white that did not betray even the faintest red vein but sheltered at its inner corner a perfect tear duct like a tiny pink sapphire. They were eyes that should have belonged to the frightened young of some rare Javanese loris.

Loeser could hardly believe that a beauty this intense had ever existed under all those layers of puppy fat – or not so much puppy fat, he recalled, as pony fat. He could hardly believe that lesson after lesson had seemed so tedious, that he had once felt positively unlucky to have been hired to teach this particular schoolgirl and not one of those schoolgirls one sometimes saw on the tram who had so much more . . . well, one shouldn't dwell on that. He could hardly believe that he had been so ungrateful when right in front of him, hanging tightly on his every word, had been this revelation, his pupil in pupa. And he could hardly believe that his blinkered pursuit of modish girls like Marlene Schibelsky who knew how to dress and paint their face and cut their hair had just been rendered so utterly absurd.

He had never wanted to fuck anything so much in his life.

'Herr Loeser,' she said. 'Do you remember me?'

He composed himself. 'Adele Hitler! I certainly do. You're looking . . . very well.'

'Thank you. And I see you've smartened up. Do you know a lot of people here?'

'Too many.'

'Is it true Brecht is going to come?'

'I'm afraid so.'

'I'd love to meet him.'

'You'd be disappointed. You'd see right through the man.'

'How can you be so sure?'

'Because of that exquisite critical eye that I remember so well from all our hours of Schiller.' He remembered no such thing. 'Unless those jealous Swiss matrons have quite gouged it out.'

Adele smiled. 'Do you still teach, Herr Loeser?'

'You can call me Egon now. And, no, I don't teach any more. I'm in the theatre.'

'Oh, I'm thrilled, I always thought you might become a playwright! I've been so desperate to meet some writers. You're my first. Are you even bolder than Brecht?'

There was almost no component of his self-respect that Loeser wasn't occasionally willing to leave at the pawnbrokers, but he did have one rule: he wouldn't falsify himself to please. No one was worth that. The world could take him as he was. So although it would have been very easy to skate along with Adele's assumption, he had no choice but to correct her. 'I'm not a writer, actually. I'm a set designer.'

'You mean a sort of carpenter?'

Loeser was about to explain that his work was fundamental to the conception of *Lavicini*, but then he heard something click behind his head. He looked round. There was Rackenham with his Leica. Another interruption, but this was all right: it would be good if Adele thought he was ringed with cosmopolitan associates.

'Oh, you didn't give me a chance to pose,' said Adele, fussing belatedly at her fringe.

'I don't think it would be possible to take an unflattering photo of you, my dear,' said Rackenham.

'Certainly not with that particular camera,' said Loeser evenly.

'Why don't you introduce me, Egon?'

'Fraulein Hitler, this is Herr Rackenham. He's a very distinguished young novelist.'

'A real writer! What's your book called?'

'My latest is *Steep Air*,' said Rackenham.

'Oh, I haven't heard of that. I'm sorry to say I don't read much English fiction.'

'Don't be sorry. You're very wise. English fiction is dead. It's disloyal of me to say, because I went to university with so many of its brightest hopes, but it is dead.'

'Then who am I to read?'

'The Americans. A critic friend of mine says that deciding between English fiction and American fiction is like deciding between dinner with a corpse and cocktails with a baby; but at least the baby has a life ahead of it.'

'I love American books,' said Adele.

Loeser, at present, was reading *Berlin Alexanderplatz* by Alfred Döblin. Unfortunately, after seventeen months, he was still only on page 189. Achleitner, who had bought it the same day, was about three quarters of the way through page 12. 'I cannot tolerate this infatuation with the Yanks,' he said. 'Rackenham, you're as bad as Ziesel over there in his new suit.'

'I think he might have heard you,' said Rackenham.

'I hope he did. If you want to understand what American culture really is you should go and look at the new escalators in the Kaufhaus des Westens on Tauentzienstrasse. They're American-made. Never in your life will you have seen so many apparently healthy adults queueing up for the privilege of standing still.'

'What about jazz?' said Adele.

'Jazz is castration music for factory workers. This band are playing in the right place but they got here too late.'

'There must be something American you like.'

'Nothing.'

'Nothing?'

'Nothing.'

This was a lie, but it didn't feel like a lie, because it had only one very specific exception. About a year earlier, he had taken a slow train to Cologne to visit his great aunt, and on the journey he had deliberately brought nothing to read but *Berlin Alexanderplatz*, on the basis that after six hours either he would have finished the book or the book would have finished him. He lasted one stop before turning to the other man in the carriage and saying, 'I will give you fifty-seven marks, which is everything I have in my wallet, for that novel you're reading.'

'I'm sorry, I don't speak German,' said the man in a thick American accent.

Loeser repeated the offer in English. (He had grown up speaking both languages to his parents.)

'Don't you care what it is?'

'Is it by any chance *Berlin Alexanderplatz*?' said Loeser.

'No.'

'Then I don't care what it is.'

The book turned out to be *Stifled Cry* by Stent Mutton. It was set in Los Angeles and it was about a petty criminal who meets a housemaid on a tram, becomes her lover, and then makes a plan to steal a baby so that the housemaid can sell it to her infertile mistress for enough money to elope. Loeser finished it in less than two hours, which might have represented bad value for money if he hadn't been delighted to have the chance to read it a second and third time before they arrived in Cologne, and then a fourth time by candle-light in his great aunt's guest room. The narrator had no name, no history, no morals, and no sense of humour. He had a vocabulary about the size of a budgerigar's, and yet he had a strangely poetic way with the grease-stained American vernacular. He seemed to find everyone and everything in the world pretty tiresome, and although he rarely bothered to dodge the women who threw themselves at him, the only true passion to which he was ever aroused was his ferocious loathing for the rich and those deferential to the rich. Loeser found all this captivating, but what he found most captivating of all was that Mutton's protagonist always, always, always knew what to do. No dithering, no procrastination, no self-consciousness: just action. Loeser yearned to be that man. He had soon afterwards sent off to Knopf in New York for all five of Mutton's remaining books, which were now hidden under his bed beside an expensive photo album of Parisian origin called *Midnight at the Nursing Academy*.

But he didn't tell Adele and Rackenham any of this. Instead, he started trying to nudge the conversation back to his impressive work in the theatre. Before he had done so, though, Achleitner appeared. Loeser introduced Achleitner to Adele. 'I shall enjoy watching you make a fool of yourself with this girl,' is what Achleitner said with the smile he gave Loeser. 'Apparently Brecht has just got here,' is what he said out loud.

Back at the entrance to the factory there was indeed a small crowd of what might have been Brecht's parasites. But Loeser didn't see Brecht. He did, however, see Marlene, who had evidently also just arrived. He felt dispirited by how chic she looked. She was even wearing a vogueish monocle. Adele, meanwhile, was standing on tiptoes to try and catch sight of the playwright.

A monstrous thought sank its fangs into Loeser's brain.

He blurted something to Achleitner about how he ought to tell Adele the story of Brogmann and the lifeguards while he had a word with Rackenham. Then he took Rackenham aside.

'I know we've only just met,' he said, 'but I'm going to ask a favour. Brecht will leave after twenty minutes. He always does. Could you just sort of distract Adele until then? Dance with her or something. Take some more "photos".'

'Why?'

'I'm sure even a man of your proclivities can tell that Adele is the most beautiful female at this party. And not only that but she's new blood. If he sees her, Brecht will go after her like Ziesel after a coffin full of ice cream sundae. And she's hardly going to say no to him. Even though he doesn't wash or brush his teeth.'

'Why don't you distract her yourself?'

'My ex-girlfriend's here.' He looked around. 'I'm not sure where she's gone now, but she is. And if she sees me trying to seduce a naive eighteen-year-old ex-pupil then she may get the impression that my new life without her is not quite the model of mature sexual prosperity that you and I know it absolutely is. I can't have that.'

'Loeser, the child seems very lovely, but if I don't sell the rest of this coke I shall have to hide from my landlady all weekend.'

'Please, Rackenham. If Brecht doesn't fuck her then I really think I might be able to. And I know it's silly but I can't help feeling that if I did fuck her . . .'

'What?'

'I can't helping feeling that if I did fuck her, just once, then everything would be all right,' said Loeser hesitantly. 'For me. Even if I didn't fuck anyone else this year. I know it sounds pathetic, but look at her. Look at her eyes. And I'd probably be her first. Imagine that! You and Achleitner wouldn't understand because you two can just fuck whomever you want whenever you want. But it doesn't work like that if you prefer women. Unless you're Brecht.' Or a Stent Mutton hero.

'Well, I can hardly say no after you've been so frank, can I?' There was a sardonic edge to Rackenham's tone but there was also a genuine sympathy, and for just a moment, as Loeser looked into the Englishman's handsome blue eyes, he felt a befuddling combination of tearful gratitude, unaccustomed optimism, and perhaps even a small homoerotic tremor. Probably something in the coke. Regardless, he thanked Rackenham warmly and they rejoined Adele and Achleitner, then Rackenham went off with the girl. He was about to explain the situation to Achleitner when he saw Tetzner standing near by, and he didn't want a conversation about his drug debts, so he rushed off in the other direction, and that was when he collided with Klugweil.

The actor had his arms in a double sling that bore a regrettable resemblance to the harness that had injured him the first place. And he was in mid-conversation with, of all people, Marlene, which was unfortunate but wasn't a total surprise, since he had always been the first man she flirted with at parties, even when she was going out with Loeser. Thankfully, Klugweil was devoted to his boring girlfriend Gretel, and in Loeser's experience it was always boring girlfriends who lasted the longest – like some Siberian brain parasite, they seemed to shut down their host's capacity to imagine a more exciting life.

'Hello, Adolf,' said Loeser. 'Hello, Marlene.'

Klugweil just glared at him, and Marlene said, 'The doctor says that his arms will never quite go back to how they were before. That's what you accomplished today, and here you are at a party as if nothing had happened.'

'I did almost get my nose broken.'

'And worst of all, Adolf says you made some comment afterwards about how the machine was actually designed to injure him, and that's why you gave it that name.'

'No, I didn't say that, I was only making a theoretical point about how the name of the thing couldn't logically make any difference to whether or not—'

'Oh God, you're always making some point, aren't you? Always some useless fucking point. Well, what about his arms?'

Loeser shrugged. 'At least they didn't get ripped off completely.'

Marlene gasped in disgust and led Klugweil away, presumably to counsel him not to slip into the darkness. 'Hey, calm down,' Loeser called after them. 'I was joking. Adolf! You know I'm sorry about it really. I am!'

'Oh, just fuck off!' Klugweil shouted back at him, not very languidly.

Loeser thought this might be a good time to do some more coke. So he found Achleitner and they went off into a corner and started drafting lines on top of a sewing machine.

'That wasn't actually Brecht, by the way,' said Achleitner. 'It was Vanel, but he happened to be wearing one of those long red overcoats like Brecht always wears.'

'So why was there all that commotion by the door?'

'It turned out he had a corkscrew on him.'

'Oh, I might as well get Adele back from Rackenham, then.'

'What do you mean?'

'I left her with him so that Brecht wouldn't notice her. He was very helpful about it.'

'That was brave,' said Achleitner.

'Brave?' said Loeser. Near by he heard one of those startling explosions of communal laughter that are distributed at random intervals through parties like moisture pockets in a fireplace log.

'He's very charming.'

'Yes, but he's hardly going to make a move himself, is he? He's queer. Ideal chaperone.'

Achleitner cocked his head. 'Not exactly.'

Another monstrous thought sank its teeth into Loeser's brain, which made the previous monstrous thought look like an adorable snuffly pet. 'What do you mean?'

'As everyone knows, all those English public-school boys are Gillette blades. They cut both ways.'

'But you said he was queer.'

'I didn't, Egon. I just said I fucked him. Not the same thing.'

'You're playing games with me.'

'No.'

'You must be.'

'No.'

'You must be because otherwise I will kill you and then kill myself.'

'I'm afraid I'm not.'

Loeser made a run for the dance floor, but Adele and Rackenham were nowhere to be seen. He collared Hildkraut, who looked as if he were mourning the loss of his corkscrew monopoly. 'Have you seen that girl with the long black hair and the big eyes?' he shouted over the music. 'She's with an Englishman in a waistcoat.'

'The short bony girl? Looks about twelve?' said Hildkraut.

'I suppose so,' said Loeser. That others might not find Adele as attractive as he did had not even occurred to him.

'They were here, but they left.'

'Where did they go?'

'Well, they were doing some coke, not very discreetly—'

'He gave her coke?'

'Yes. And then I think they went out by the back entrance.'

'Fuck!'

Outside, there was nobody but Klein vomiting methodically into an upturned copper corset mould. Loeser dashed past him and out into the street beyond, but it was deserted, so he hurried back to the party, wondering if Hildkraut might have got it wrong about the other two leaving.

Like a faithful old butler who quietly begins preparations to auction the antique furniture and dismiss the French chef several weeks before his master has even begun to wonder if all that fuss about the stock market might have cut a little bit into his income, there was an inferior part of Loeser's brain which had long since accepted that it was going to be Rackenham, not him, who fucked Adele tonight, and which was already getting ready for the moment when the superior part had no choice but to accept the same thing. Until then, however, Loeser would just go on running back and forth, looking in cupboards, tripping over dancers, asking incoherent questions of possible witnesses, inventing optimistic excuses (she might have become suddenly and disruptively menstrual!), and generally behaving as if what was now obviously true might still, somehow, be false. In the end, though, after a frantic, undignified and predictable twelve-minute crescendo of desperation, the last hope finally departed Loeser like a last line of credit finally withdrawn. 'That worthless cunt!' he howled, stamping on the ground. He realised he didn't have a drink, and just at that moment he saw Gobulev put down his bottle of black-market vodka to light a cigarette, so he grabbed it and sloshed as much of its contents into him as he could before it started to dribble down his chin. Then he slipped unsteadily back into the crowd, away from the dance floor.

What now? The main thing was not to dwell on it. There were alternatives. He could just go back to his flat, where whatever hour happened to show on the clock it was always, mercifully, *Midnight at the Nursing Academy*. But for once the book might not quite be enough to satisfy him. He could try and fuck someone else at this party. But he didn't have the spiritual stamina to fix upon a new target and begin a whole seduction from nothing when he was almost certain to fail as usual. What about Marlene? Could he persuade Marlene to go to bed with him for old times' sake? That was the sort of thing people did, wasn't it? But she hated him too much. Which only left the Zinnowitz Tearooms. He wasn't often drunk enough to want to go to the Zinnowitz Tearooms. But if he forced down the rest of Gobulev's vodka, he would definitely be drunk enough before long.

If some confidant had learned that the sole reason Loeser didn't like going to prostitutes was that they made him feel so uncomfortable, he might have deduced that Loeser had no moral sentiments at stake in the matter – or otherwise he might have deduced that this very feeling of awkwardness was itself a sort of moral sentiment – a sickly, selfish, and impotent sort of moral sentiment, but a moral sentiment nonetheless. Whatever the case, Loeser hadn't gone to a prostitute sober since he was nineteen, and he hadn't even gone to a prostitute drunk since late last year. That last occasion had been particularly bad. About a minute into the act he had stopped thrusting and cleared his throat nervously.

The girl, who called herself Sabine, turned her head to look back at him. 'What's wrong?' she said. Loeser's forehead felt riverine with sweat but hers, as usual, was somehow still talcum dry.

'Look, if it's all the same to you . . .'

'What do you want me to do, darling?'

'It's not that I don't appreciate the effort you put in, with all the moans and the lofty commendation of my dick and so forth, but the truth is . . .' He'd never had the courage to say this before. 'I don't like it when a waiter or a clerk pretends to be a bosom friend, and I don't like it when you pretend to be enjoying all this, either. No offence meant. I know it's part of the job. But we both know you're not really enjoying it. The suspension of disbelief isn't quite there. And on the whole it just puts me off.'

He'd expected her to get a bit sulky but in fact she just said, 'Whatever you say.' Relieved, he went back to work, but straight away she started squirming away from him and gasping, 'No, no, please, let me go, please, it's too big!'

He stopped in horror. 'I'm so sorry.'

She looked back at him again. 'Why did you stop? Did I get it wrong?'

He hadn't realised she'd been acting. 'What were you doing?'

'You told me to pretend I wasn't enjoying it.'

'No, I just told you to stop pretending that you *were* enjoy-ing it.'

'So am I supposed to be enjoying it or not?' she said.

'No,' he said.

'Well, then.'

'But not in that way.'

'If I'm not enjoying it, then I'm going to want you to stop, aren't I?'

'But you weren't enjoying it previously, and you didn't want me to stop. Well, I mean, I'm sure on some level you did want me to stop, actually, that's part of my point, but the difference is you didn't say anything.'

'You didn't ask me to say anything.'

The exasperation in her voice was murdering Loeser's erec-tion. 'I know, but . . . Look, can we just agree that I'm not giving you hundreds of orgasms, but I'm also not raping you, I'm just a polite stranger offering you a fair wage in exchange for the efficient completion of a specific service within a capi-talist system of alienated labour, all right? That's my shame-ful fantasy.'

From then on she was as silent and still as a coma patient. Which was by far the worst of the three scenarios. After another few minutes he had to pretend he'd ejaculated just so that he could leave, which was not something he'd ever anticipated he'd have to do with a paid consort, but he knew it was his own fault.

So it was with a rucksack of apprehension that he stepped out of the taxi outside the Zinnowitz Tearooms on Lieblingstrasse. At two in the morning the streets of Strandow were crowded with screeching drunks from the beer halls near by, many now queuing up like a congealed riot to buy boiled meatballs with caper sauce from stalls to eat on the way home. He nodded to the brothel's bouncer and went inside, where he was greeted straight away by Frau Diski, the dwarfish proprietor. 'Herr Loeser! What a pleasure. It's been

42

a long time, hasn't it? Sit down, sit down. What would you like to drink?'

'I suppose I've probably had enough tonight.' He couldn't remember what he'd done with the bottle of vodka.

'Some tea, then.'

'Fine.' Around the room sat six or seven other men, alone or in pairs, some of them with girls on their laps. Mercifully there was no one among them he knew. With its floral wallpaper, bentwood chairs, and Blandine Ebinger records playing softly on the gramophone in the corner, the Zinnowitz Tearooms, even after midnight, really did retain the stolid atmosphere of the sort of place your aunt would take you for chocolate cake, which was presumably a calculated psychoanalytic strategy on Frau Diski's part to stop her customers from getting rowdy: they had all been nice boys once and there were some deep bourgeois instincts that even a barrel of beer couldn't drown.

'You seem to be in low spirits, Herr Loeser.'

'I haven't had a fantastically good evening.'

Frau Diski sat down beside him. 'Why don't you tell me about it?'

'There's no point.'

'I want to know.'

'Well . . . I was after a girl, of course. And I should have got her. But someone else got her instead. And what makes it really intolerable is that it was my fault that he did.' He meant that he'd handed Adele over to Rackenham, but now he remembered that he'd also been too stubborn to let her believe he was a writer. Would that have made a difference? Did writers really get more sex just because they were writers? Presumably writers hoped and prayed that they might. He'd read somewhere that Balzac only took up writing because he thought it might help him meet women. And it worked, of course: he married one of his fans. But that was after he'd written ninety-two novels, and they were married for just five months before Balzac died of a lung complaint. Even assuming they'd fucked every day since the wedding, that meant Balzac had written about half a book for every wheezy sexual encounter. Not a very efficient rate of return. Still, it was better than nothing, and if Countess Ewelina Hańska was as good in bed as Marlene Schibelsky, it might just about have been worthwhile.

'Who is she, this object of desire?' said Frau Diski.

'Oh, I used to tutor her when she was about fifteen. But naturally she's older now,' he added hastily.

'What's her name?'

'Adele.'

'What does she look like?'

'Ravishing long black hair like nobody has any more except peasants. Huge innocent eyes. Perfect pale skin. Musical laugh. So slender you just want to reach out and stroke her collarbone and her shoulderblades and her spine and her hips and her spine and all the rest.' He wondered if it was possible to vomit with lust.

'You needn't say any more, Herr Loeser. Come this way.' Frau Diski got up again and led him down the carpeted corridor towards the bedrooms.

'But I haven't chosen a girl yet. Have I?' He realised he was staggering a bit.

'There's no need to bring them all out on parade as usual when your description is so evocative. You should be a writer.'

'I mean, not that I really mind. Just as long as it's not Sabine again. Not that there's anything wrong with Sabine.'

'Here you are, Herr Loeser.' They stopped, and Frau Diski opened the door to the bedroom before them. Inside, a girl sat on the bed brushing her hair with her back to the doorway. She wore nothing but lacy white underwear, and in the gaslight her skin looked as soft as water, the vertebrae of her spine a row of pebbles half submerged in a stream. The room smelled of clean linen. For a dilated instant Loeser felt as if he were looking at

44

something unreal behind glass, like a photograph in an old locket, but then Frau Diski said, 'This is . . . Anneliese,' and the girl turned and Loeser felt his heart leap into his mouth.

'Frau Diski, I think you must have misunderstood me,' he stammered. 'Just now, I wasn't trying to explain the sort of girl I wanted, I was only trying to explain what had happened to me tonight. Like you asked me to. I'm not – I don't . . .'

'I'll leave the two of you alone,' said Frau Diski with a smile. She gave Loeser a gentle push into the room and then closed the door, trapping him inside the locket.

'Anneliese', who could not have been more than fifteen years old, looked like Adele, but she did not look like Adele at fifteen, nor did she look like Adele at eighteen. Rather, she looked just as Adele would have looked at fifteen if she had already been beautiful, if she hadn't been pudgy and half finished. She had the hair, the eyes, the skin, the bones, but she also had the youth – she was the old Adele he had once known so well, combined with the new Adele he had met only for a few minutes. The likeness was uncanny, but it was a likeness to somebody who had never existed, a loan from a parallel world.

He knew, though, that this was not a job that anyone should be doing at this girl's age. Even his own atrophous moral faculties could tell him that. He tried not to look at her body because he knew he'd feel so guilty if he got an erection. Naturally he'd seen very youthful harlots on street corners before, but he wouldn't have known that there were any to be found here in the cosy Zinnowitz Tearooms.

Loeser stared at the girl, and the girl smiled shyly back at Loeser. Cries of synthetic pleasure seeped very faintly through the wall to his left.

He couldn't, of course. He couldn't.

Could he?

2

BERLIN, 1933

When Loeser awoke he realised at once that a mistake had been made: he had been sent the wrong hangover. Somewhere in northern Rhodesia there was a bull elephant who had got drunk on fermented marula fruit, rampaged through a nearby village, and fallen asleep in a ditch, and was now pleasantly surprised to find itself greeting the day with only the mild headache that follows a couple of bottles of good red wine from the Fraunhofens' cellar. Perhaps if Loeser got in touch with the relevant authorities he could get this unfortunate little mix-up corrected, but he would have to do so without moving his head or opening his eyes. Otherwise he would die from the pain.

After twenty minutes of lying there motionless as he pondered his strategy, he heard his landlady come up the stairs to slip a letter under his door. Probably it was from Achleitner, which wasn't worth getting up for. But at least it must be quite early. There was still most of the day left to be ruined. Except then he remembered about Adele and the waiters from the Schwanneke, and he decided to go back to sleep, wondering if it was possible to set his alarm clock to wake him up when everyone he knew was dead. He thought of Hecht's recent play about the legend of Urashima Taro, the Japanese fisherman who rescued a turtle from some children, discovered that the turtle was the daughter of Ryujin the sea dragon god, was rewarded with a trip to Ryujin's palace, and returned to his village to find that somehow three hundred years had passed. What bliss that would be.

By early 1933, even the most heedless and egotistical Berliner – so, even Loeser – couldn't help but notice that something nasty was going on. At parties now, optimism had given way to dread, and yells to whispers – the really good times were never coming back, and to think what might come next was just too horrible. Of course, it was mainly young working-class toughs who had propelled this awfulness at the beginning, but now people of every generation and every class had joined the brainless charge. They seemed to think that, just because the civilised solutions of the 1920s had begun to falter, that was a reason to dash headlong in the opposite direction. Most of Loeser's friends agreed that something urgently needed to be done, but no one had any idea how to fight what was somehow already so dominant. Some had even begun to talk about leaving the country, at least until sanity was restored. German history was at a turning point.

Loeser could still remember the first time he had heard of this new drug ketamine. Everyone had taken the train up to an estate north of Ritterbrücke that belonged to somebody's absent parents. It was one of those country parties where it felt as if no matter where you went you were always being watched by either a live horse or a dead stag, until you found yourself lingering by the washbasin after a piss just to escape this weirdly oppressive ungulate panopticon. At about midnight, bored with playing hide-and-seek, Loeser had wandered out to the back lawn where the jazz band was performing, hoping to find a girl to dance with. Instead, he nearly tripped over a boy who lay flexing and humming in the grass, and looked around to see several others in the same state. So when he spotted Hildkraut he went over to ask him if there had been a mustard gas attack, since they couldn't all be so drunk already, and Hildkraut explained that they'd taken a black-market horse tranquilliser called ketamine, at which point Loeser began to feel as if he had slipped into some sort of Dada world.

'Why on earth would anyone voluntarily take horse tranquilliser?'

'Because they can't get good coke any more.'

'They can't get good coke any more, so this is the logical alternative?'

'Yeah. Started with scummy kids from the suburbs, then it got to the art schools, and now everyone takes it.'

Vanel wandered past looking for a cigarette lighter and they both ignored him. 'What does it do?' said Loeser.

'You feel as if you're being sucked down this fathomless, gloomy tunnel. Or to put it another way, it's as if all the different weights and cares of the world have been lifted from your shoulders to be replaced by a single, much larger sort of consolidated weight. Your limbs stop working and you can't really talk. If you take enough then it can last for hours and hours, but it seems like even longer because time slows down.' Hildkraut smiled wistfully. 'It's fantastic.' At their feet, somebody groaned softly as if in enthusiastic assent. 'And it makes Wagner sound really good.'

'I'm sorry to be obtuse,' said Loeser, 'but has everyone gone insane? I take coke because it's fun. I take coke because it makes me feel confident and talkative and full of energy, or at least it used to, when it wasn't mostly brick dust. If I want to feel as if I'm being sucked down a fathomless gloomy tunnel for hours and hours then I have a complete set of Schopenhauer at home.'

'Well, anyway, the story is that Brogmann once took so much that he blacked out and then woke up in a stables surrounded by actual horses. Explain that.'

After interrogating several other people at the party, Loeser concluded that he was the last person in Germany to have heard of ketamine. But nobody offered him any. And after that episode, as the months passed, fashionable Berlin night-life distorted into an unrecognisable parody. Nobody seemed to laugh or dance or kiss any more, they just lay around slurring and drooling, vanquished until morning. Certainly, most of his worthwhile friends didn't bother with ketamine – why would they, when they still remembered what proper drugs were like? But they were twenty-five or twenty-six now. And it was the nineteen- and twenty-year-olds who had all the clout. For the first time in his life Loeser had a sense of what the early days of Expressionism must have felt like to the prior generation of Realists. Not only did he almost begin to miss the exhausting and obnoxious conversations he used to have with people who were inconsiderate enough to have done more coke than him, he also almost began to envy Achleitner, off in the mountains with his new Nazi friends, far away from all this tranquilliser nonsense that had a real chance of ruining what was otherwise quite a promising decade.

The triumph of ketamine had coincided with the triumph of another dark horse, to use an unfortunate phrase – a certain pretty girl called Adele Hitler, who was now among the first rank of those all-too-influential foals and fillies. At that first party in Puppenberg, she'd been a novelty item, but by the end of 1931 she was getting more invitations than Brecht, and it wasn't hard to see why: she could be relied upon to look stunning, she could be relied upon to get entertainingly drunk, and above all she could be relied upon to fuck some-one worth gossiping about. Rackenham was just the begin-ning. When you heard about who Adele Hitler had gone to bed with after a particular party, it was like reading the solu-tion to a really elegant murder mystery: you'd never for a moment suspected that it might be x, but now that you'd found out it really was x, you realised that it could never have been anybody other than x. She fucked Brecht because everybody did, she fucked Brogmann because nobody did; she fucked Littau because he was queer, she fucked Hannah Czenowitz because she was straight; she fucked Hecht because he had a girlfriend, she fucked Klein because he was known to be impotent; she fucked clarinet-playing Negroes and one-legged war veterans, drug dealers and ambassadors' sons. And this was Adele Hitler's legend: that in two years of astonishing promiscuity, she hadn't ever fucked anyone more than once, and she hadn't ever fucked anyone who could not, in one way or another, be considered a little bit of a coup.

There was something about beautiful, sexually prolific women that made Loeser feel as if his soul were being pelted with sharp flints. If they were being sexually prolific with him, then of course it was fine. But with anyone else it was agony. He couldn't stop thinking about that occult moment of surrender, that critical turn when all their softnesses were redispersed, when their limbic electorate voted in some new and unfamiliar tyrant. How did it happen? Did those girls really enjoy these fleeting encounters with men they barely knew? There was no satisfactory answer, because if they didn't, then their beauty was being exploited and despoiled, which was a tragedy, and if they did – well, they couldn't. They just couldn't. For eyes as dizzying as Adele's to exist in the same body as a banal urge to get stoked over a desk by an unwashed playwright was a paradox as imponderable as the indivisibility of the Trinity.

Loeser himself, meanwhile, hadn't had sex for a very long time. He had worked hard to erase all mental records of the night of the corset factory, but if he assumed, in the interests of supplying his own biography with at least a minimally sympathetic protagonist, that he hadn't laid a finger on that fifteen-year-old prostitute, then the last time was with Marlene Schibelsky, and that was nearly two years ago. When he'd said to Achleitner that he might never manage it ever again, he hadn't believed his own words, but now he retrospectively detected in them a vibration of plausibility. So intense was his sexual frustration that it had begun to feel like a life-threatening illness: testicular gout, libidinal gangrene.

His dispiriting conversation with Adele had turned on this

very subject – sexual abundance, that is, not its opposite. The previous night he'd arrived at a party at Zinnemann's flat in Hochbegraben to discover that Zinnemann, always a domineering host, had invented a new game.

'We're at that age now where everyone's slept with everyone else,' he had explained to his assembled guests. 'There might have been royal dynasties of Persia that were more incestuous but I think apart from that our social circle is just about the limit. The phrase "permutational exhaustion" wouldn't be out of place. Now, some people say it's tiresome and we should all make new friends. I think it should be celebrated.' And he started handing out bundles of coloured string. 'Look around the room. If you see somebody you've gone to bed with, then you tie yourselves together at the wrists with one of the ten-foot pieces of string. And if you see somebody you've gone to bed with repeatedly on some sort of joyless *petit bourgeois* pseudo-marital basis – if you see someone you've "gone out with", in other words – then you tie yourselves together at the wrists with one of the five-foot pieces of string. The result will be no more awkward in practice than any other party – just rather more tangible. And after tonight, every other party you ever go to will seem carefree in comparison.'

There was a baffled pause. Then, to Loeser's disbelief, everyone started to do as they were told. They must have realised it would be a good story the following day. Before long, Zinnemann's drawing room was a great rainbow spider's web. The point of the colours was to make it easier to trace a string from its beginning to its end, and indeed several liaisons were revealed that had not previously been public. Every guest was dragged this way and that by their past loves, held in quivering strummable tension by their old conquests, so thoroughly entangled in a universal net of erstwhile romance that they would have to duck under somebody else's heartbreak just to cross the room for a drink. There was such a

thing as symbolism that was too bespoke, thought Loeser –
but the real problem was that Marlene wasn't here, and nor,
as it happened, were any of his other four, so he had no string
around his wrists and he looked like a eunuch. He couldn't
tolerate that, even if it was virtually true. So he crawled out
of the room on his hands and knees and got a cab over to the
Fraunhofens' in Schlingesdorf.

Herr Fraunhofen was a machine-gun manufacturer whose
wife Lotte thought she was cultured, so every month she invited
writers and actors and artists and their auxiliaries to her house
for an evening salon. (It was one of those houses where even the
tassels on the tassels had tassels on their tassels, which might
have sounded like a trite joke if it hadn't in several cases been
literally true.) Of course, no one of interest bothered to turn
up before midnight, by which time the boring bit was over but
there was still lots of wine left and often some food. And indeed
Loeser was standing in the dining room with a mouth full of
cold sausage when he felt a tap at his shoulder. He turned. It
was his former pupil, wearing a black dress with a spray of
peacock feathers at the hem. These days most of her clothes
were borrowed from fashion designers she had befriended.

'Hello, Egon.'

Loeser swallowed a cumbersome bolus of veal. 'Hello,
Adele.' They exchanged some gossip about Herr Fraunhofen's
recent gambling losses and then he said, 'I would have thought
this party would be a bit elderly for you. I don't think I've
seen a single person giving themselves a subcutaneous injection of panda laxative or whatever the latest thing is.'

'I was in a cab with John and Helga and we couldn't think
of anywhere else to get a free drink,' Adele explained. 'Also,
that Sartre fellow is here.'

'The Frenchman? I met him. He has a face like a four-year-
old child's drawing of its father.'

'They say he's very brilliant, darling.' She called everyone
'darling' now. 'He's studying under Husserl.'

'Don't tell me you want to sleep with him? Imagine waking up in the morning to find that monstrous dead eye staring fixedly at your tits. And anyway, you don't know who Husserl is.'

'I do: author of *Transcendental Phenomenology*. And anyway, why don't you shut up?'

This was the only way Loeser knew how to socialise with Adele Hitler, the object of the greatest erotic obsession he'd ever had in his life, without bursting into tears: he made bitter jokes about her sexual itinerary. Not very heroic. But at least she seemed to find him funny sometimes, and quite often they behaved almost like old friends. In fact, he probably could have kept it up indefinitely, as one somehow sometimes did in these situations, and there wasn't any good reason why he should have chosen this conversation, out of all the conversations they'd had since that night in Puppenberg, to be frank with her for the first time – the thumbscrews of his desperation were no tighter than usual – but he was drunk, and there was something about Zinnemann's game that had exhausted his patience, and he just found himself saying, 'Why do you do it, Adele?'

'Do what?'

'Why do you waste yourself on all these people? Why do you go to bed with Sartre and Brogmann and . . . and . . .' He tried to think of a sufficiently damning example.

'And the waiters at the Schwanneke?' offered Adele.

'Yes, exactly,' said Loeser. Then: 'Sorry, what?'

'You want to know why I go to bed with the waiters at the Schwanneke.'

'Actually just at this moment I want you to reassure me that you don't, in fact, go to bed with the waiters at the Schwanneke.'

'Well, I don't go to bed with all of them.' Loeser just stared at her, nauseated, so she added: 'Darling, everyone goes to bed with the waiters at the Schwanneke. The proprietor's queer so they're the most handsome in Berlin.'

'God in heaven. My most febrile paranoid fantasies . . . are they all true?'

'What can I say, Egon? It's not as if I did it specifically to annoy you. Is this a class neurosis?'

'You'll fuck the man who brings your coffee just because he's handsome, and yet I chase you for nearly two years and—'

She waved her hand as if to swat him away. 'Oh, please let's not get into that again. "Love is the foolish overestimation of the minimal difference between one sexual object and another."'

'Who said that?'

'I saw it on the wall at a party.'

'Oh, so it must be true! And all my devotion means nothing?'

'I'm flattered, but there'd be no point in us even trying. You're the sort of man who couldn't stand it if I were unfaithful, but you're also the sort of man I couldn't help but be unfaithful to. You're that type. You're an apprentice cuckold.'

An apprentice cuckold! Was he truly? As Loeser lay clammy in bed he couldn't remember how the rest of the conversation had gone. What a joke on mankind, he thought, these random deposits of beauty, like random deposits of gold, an arbitrary and purposeless desideratum, the stipulation at the start of a philosopher's or a mathematician's tract – 'Let x be what you want most in the world'; 'Suppose y is worth killing for' – that condemns all that follows to the status of ornamented tautology. And then he thought of what she'd look like if she were next to him now, a creature of blinking eyes and tangled hair, regrowing limbs with each yawn but still so slight that the shape of her body could hide among the rumples in the sheets. He went back to sleep and had a series of dreams in which he was drinking glass after glass of ice water but he never got any less thirsty, and then was woken up again at eleven by the usual shouts of 'Jump!' and

'Stretch!' and 'Kick!' This, at least, was worth getting up for, so he pried open his eyes like two stubborn oysters and then somehow got himself to the window. Diagonally across Kannerobertstrasse there was a big music box factory that had reopened after a period of bankruptcy, and three times a day the girls who worked there were all obliged to assemble on the roof for twenty minutes of productivity-boosting exercise. For Loeser, this cabaret was both a torture and a more wholesome alternative to *Midnight at the Nursing Academy*, and he rarely missed a performance. One day he planned to go down and wait outside the factory door at the end of a shift, begging for autographs.

Afterwards, moving around his flat as if he'd been beaten by prison guards, he took mercy on his mouth under the kitchen tap and then opened the letter his landlady had delivered, which was indeed from Achleitner. Loeser hadn't seen his best friend in nearly three months, ever since Achleitner had met a leonine fifty-two-year-old Nazi aristocrat called Buddensieg at an art exhibition and Buddensieg had taken Achleitner off to his castle in the Black Forest, where he apparently played host to a sort of never-ending homosexual jamboree. Achleitner, in his letters, raved about the food, the wine, the rooms, the countryside, and, above all, the boys. The Nazis, he had written in his latest, 'are wedded to a sort of aesthetico-moral fallacy, which is that if a man has blond hair, blue eyes and strong features, then he will also be brave, loyal, intelligent and so on. They truly believe that goodness has some causal kinship with beauty. Which is idiotic, yes, but no more idiotic than you are, Egon. When you see a girl like Adele Hitler with an innocent, pretty face, can you honestly tell me you don't assume she must be an angelic person? Even though it makes about as much sense as astrology. Queers do it too, of course, but not so much, because we were all boys once ourselves, so boys aren't mysterious to us in the same way that girls will always be mysterious to you, and we we can be a bit more sceptical. Or take any fairy tale – Cinderella must always be beautiful, and her sisters must always be ugly, even though the story would surely have a great deal more force if it were the other way round. All the Nazis have really done is make a cult out of this romantic faith in physical loveliness – there's something almost touching about how childish it is. As aesthetes, they don't even have the ruthlessness of a Gilbert Osmond. Anyway, the result is that there are more exquisite boys in this castle than there are in all of Berlin put together. I woke up this morning with three in my bed. I am absolutely drunk on it. Although I must remember not to neglect old Buddensieg or he might kick me out.'

What Loeser hadn't been able to understand was how Achleitner didn't get bored. With the exception of a few tolerable communists like Hecht who had the good sense not to bring up Marx every five seconds, any fee-paying member of a political party was certain to be petrifyingly dull. Even a castle full of stamp collectors or football supporters would be better because at least they wouldn't be so self-righteous all the time. But Achleitner insisted that he hadn't heard one word about politics since he arrived in Spunk Olympus. 'Lots about diet and exercise and sunbathing and lots about the lost holy city of Agartha and lots of very tired Jewish jokes, but nothing on Versailles or unemployment or electoral reform, thank goodness. We get the papers delivered but nobody reads them.'

Loeser, like most people, had from the age of fourteen regularly concluded that he didn't have any real friends in the world, and like all fatuous melancholic generalisations this was wonderfully comforting because it so drained the lake of one's responsibilities. But to realise that it might actually be true was a different matter. For a few weeks, Loeser had tried to persuade Achleitner to come back to Berlin, but he knew it was no use. No one would give up paradise for a Berlin of ketamine and coloured string. And without Achleitner, who was left? Yes, if Loeser went to a party, there were always dozens of basically interchangeable people with whom he could have a drunken good time. But if he woke up the next morning in need of a companion for a rueful breakfast, there was almost nobody he could telephone. These days, the individual he saw most often was probably Klugweil. Not long after the Teleportation Accident, Blumstein had shamed his two collaborators into apologising to each other so that they could get back to work on *Lavicini*, and in fact they now got on better than they had before their rift. Loeser had even started to confide in Klugweil about his loneliness, going so far as to ask whether Klugweil thought it was a sign of hermitical derangement that one afternoon he had absent-mindedly said 'Thank you' out loud to a chewing-gum machine on a U-bahn platform. But the actor, who had finally come to his senses about dull Gretel the previous summer, never seemed to answer the telephone any more, so one could only assume he'd found some new girl he didn't want to tell anyone about. The result was that Loeser might actually have to resort to – but, no, the thought was too terrible. He'd just have breakfast at home.

Except that, upon further inspection of his kitchen, it appeared that he had eaten all the food in the flat when he got home from the party last night. In fact, a few minutes' forensic reconstruction seemed to suggest that he had attempted to make jam doughnuts from scratch, using mostly raw cabbage and angostura bitters. Indeed, since the results were gone, there was no reason to suppose he hadn't succeeded. If only he'd kept some record of the experiment.

So he would have to go out after all. And he would either have to go out on his own, or he would have to call Ziesel. He knew Ziesel would be free. Ziesel was always free. In Berlin there were typhoid bacteria more socially in demand than Ziesel.

He cast around his flat for some means of putting off this horror. On his desk were a dirty wineglass, an unpaid tailor's bill, a few notes for *Lavicini, Berlin Alexanderplatz* with its bookmark at page 202 and an attempted letter to his great aunt in Cologne, which so far stood at two sentences in length. All of them looked back at him imploringly.

He called Ziesel.

'Hello?' In the background there was some chatter.

'Dieter. It's Egon. Have breakfast with me at the Romanisches.'

'I can't.'

'See you in about twenty minutes.'

'Egon, I can't.'

'If you get there before me, order the double ham and eggs.'

'I'm very sorry, Egon, but I just can't join you. I'm already in the middle of breakfast. Some of the fellows from the brass band are here.'

'What?'

'I'd be free for lunch.'

After a long pause Loeser said, 'You, Dieter Ziesel, are too busy to have breakfast with me, Egon Loeser.'

'Yes,' said Ziesel.

'I, Egon Loeser, am assumed to be so eager to share a jolly repast with you, Dieter Ziesel, that I will just hang around for two hours until you are free.'

'If that's how you want to put it,' said Ziesel.

'This – this! – is what my life has come to.'

'I wouldn't like to say,' said Ziesel.

After another long pause Loeser said, 'Right, I'll see you at one,' and put down the telephone.

Since he was still unwilling to pass the time with any of the orphans on his desk, Loeser decided he might as well get dressed and go out to Luni's, a second-hand bookshop on Ranekstrasse next door to an antique shop with medieval suits of armour standing vigilant in the window like militarised fashion mannequins. This would be his seventh visit in two weeks, and the elegant girl at the counter was treating him ever more warily; she had obviously concluded that he'd developed some sort of forlorn romantic preoccupation with her, since if anyone was really that desperate to read *The Sorceror of Venice* by Rupert Rackenham they would just pay twelve marks for a new copy. But in fact Loeser would have drunk a pint of toothbrush-mug run-off before contributing one pfennig to the royalties of the man who'd first fucked Adele Hitler, and he couldn't just borrow the book, even though every passenger on every tram seemed to have it, because he didn't want anyone else to know that he was so desperate to read the thing. Rackenham's novel was by all accounts a very thinly disguised sketch of the Berlin experimental theatre scene circa 1931, and since nobody had been willing to answer Loeser's oblique enquiries about the way he had been portrayed – even Brogmann had been too tactful to take the piss out of him – Loeser could only conclude that his fictional analogue was a golem of spite and libel, the sort of character assassination where they have to have a closed casket at the wake. He felt quite excited to have been the victim of the kind of affair you read about in interesting people's biographies, and he was already looking forward to confronting Rackenham about it. For two years he'd been trying to persuade everyone that Rackenham was a bastard, but he'd never been willing to explain why he thought so. Now he'd have a proper reason for his hatred that did not involve getting tripped up in pursuit of a kittenish female.

On the way to Luni's, he made a bet with himself that he would see Drabsfarben, who for some reason seemed always to be passing by the shop; and indeed he did, but as usual Drabsfarben looked so distracted that Loeser didn't try to say hello for fear of scaring off some rare harmony that was grazing in his compositional rifle sights. Inside, the girl at the counter tensed visibly at the sight of him.

'Do you have it yet?' he said, working so hard, as usual, to exclude all emotion from his voice that he slid a long way past casual and in the end sounded more as if he were barely suppressing some *grande passion.*

'Yes. Someone came in with a review copy yesterday.'

When he paid for the book she dropped the change into his hand from about eleven inches up to avoid brushing his palm. On his way out he reflected that in spite of it all there was something nice about knowing, for once, precisely where you stood with a girl. Then he sat down on a bench to skim through *The Sorceror of Venice*, hiding the cover against his knees in case anyone he knew walked past. At first, although no one was watching, the flick of his fingers was ostentatiously unconcerned, but as not one but two outrages arose from the text, it became involuntarily furious.

First outrage: theft. The novel began in 1677 with the arrival in Paris of the great Venetian set designer Adriano Lavicini. Loeser should have guessed as soon as he heard the title, but after all Rackenham's talk in that taxi to Puppenberg about the pointlessness of historical fiction, it never would have occurred to him that the Englishman might help himself to the very same shank of the seventeenth century that Loeser, Blumstein, and Klugweil had been trying to turn into a play for nearly three years. (Three years! Einstein's equations said that time slowed down on a merry-go-round or ferris wheel because of the relativistic effect of the angular momentum. Was that why, in Berlin, which never stopped whirling, you could work for season after season on just one play and still feel as if it was all right that you'd barely got anything done?)

In Rackenham's travesty, Lavicini fell in love with a young ballet dancer he met at the Théâtre des Encornets, who was actually Louis XIV's rebellious daughter Princess Anne Elisabeth in disguise. She spurned his advances because she was worried he might uncover her identity, so he built the Teleportation Device as an expression of his love, loading the scene changes in *The Lizard Prince* with little winks and curl-icues that only she would understand. In the final chapter, when she saw it all for the first time during the première, she was won over at last, and feigned a fainting fit so she could hurry backstage into his arms. As the performance contin-ued, they made love on a couch, giving a jealous stagehand the opportunity to smash the Teleportation Device's controls, sending the (otherwise reliable) machine haywire and conse-quently killing all three of them. Rackenham seemed to be making some point about how some of the greatest art in the world is created to impress girls, and that's rather sweet in its way, but the artist musn't lose sight of his moral responsibili-ties or chaos might ensue.

In the Loeser–Blumstein–Klugweil production, by contrast, there would have been nothing so glib, and no romance: instead, Lavicini became so maniacal about his Teleportation Device that he lost all humanity, refused to acknowledge the machine's many defects, and in the end was literally consumed by it. What that might have symbolised would be left up to the audience. To Loeser, it was about how politics, business, and all other such bourgeois social contraptions had a tendency to turn anyone who got involved in them into an insufferable prick.

Second outrage: insult. And this one was much worse. *The Sorceror of Venice* did not contain, as predicted, a brutal parody of himself. Nor did it contain some unexpectedly warm tribute. Nor did it contain even the most innocuous incidental likeness.

There was no character based on Loeser at all.

There were characters recognisably based on Achleitner, Blumstein, Brecht, Drabsfarben, Grosz, Heijenhoort, Klugweil, Ziesel, and Zuckmayer. There was even a character based on Brogmann. Charming Lavicini, needless to say, was based on the author, and Princess Anne Elisabeth seemed to be Adele. But Loeser was nowhere. In a book that was being read all over Europe as the most scandalously detailed document of the young Berlin artistic classes that had ever been produced – a book that specifically centred on a fucking *set designer* – he was nowhere. To appear in *The Sorceror of Venice* was to go to bed with posterity, and everyone was allowed to go to bed with posterity but Loeser: Adele all over again, except that this wasn't posterity's fault, because posterity was getting pimped out by Rupert Rackenham, of all people. And of course it wasn't even possible to complain about his negation, because that was the one response that would make him look even more pitiable than he already did – except perhaps to sink his life savings into the staging of a baroque opera called *Rupert Rackenham is a Worthless Cunt*, music by J. Drabsfarben, libretto by E. Loeser, which was what he urgently wanted to do by the time he finished skimming the book. Instead, he set off for the Romanisches, and upon arriving twenty-five minutes late to meet Ziesel, the first person he saw was Rupert Rackenham himself, drinking coffee with Klein.

The Romanisches still had its separate sections for artists, actors, writers, directors, film producers, art dealers, fashion designers, Marxists, philosophers, right-wing journalists, left-wing journalists, doctors, psychiatrists, and all the rest, but by the end of the 1920s the territorial negotiations had become even more complex because of the defeat of movements like Dadaism and Expressionism and the consequent power vacuum. One might have expected a sort of Versailles, with one faction taking their western Prussia, another their northern Schleswig, another their Alsace and Lorraine, and so on, but in fact there was always an initial reluctance to sit down where the tablecloths were still stained with obsolescence. So those seats were occupied in their first weeks of availability by the sort of insignificant newcomers who could otherwise only get a place near the entrance and were happy to penetrate further into the café, until the real customers decided that, well, if anyone was going to sit there, it shouldn't be these packs of stray dogs, and briskly moved in, sometimes pausing to inform the head bouncer, with his greying beard and pierced lip, that these latest arrivals shouldn't be let in at all. For the last year or so, Loeser, Klugweil, and their fellow New Expressionists had been waging a campaign to recover the section of the terrace that had once belonged to the original Expressionists and was now given over to theatre critics. But none of them had had much luck – what they needed, Loeser often thought, was a strong leader.

Rackenham and Klein were in the middle of a conversation about boxing when a copy of *The Sorceror of Venice* was slapped down on their table with such force it made the coffee cups flinch in their saucers. They looked up. 'What the fuck made you think you could do this?' said Loeser. He hadn't seen Rackenham in person since the première of *Urashima the Fisherman*.

'I'd already spent the advance so I didn't really have any choice,' said Rackenham.

'No, I mean, what the fuck made you think it was all right to steal our plot?'

'I'm not sure what you mean. Lavicini was a real individual. Nobody can own him. I did all the research myself.'

'But you know perfectly well you never would have thought of writing a novel about him if I hadn't told you about our play.'

'Yes, like most of us I like to continue my education through conversation.'

Loeser was trying to keep in mind that he couldn't admit to being offended over the lack of a Loeser character. 'It wouldn't be quite so bad if you didn't get everything wrong!'

'What do you mean?'

'I don't know where to start. Among the twenty or thirty historical celebrities with whom Lavicini just happens to cross paths in your ridiculous plot is his old friend Leonardo da Vinci.'

'Yes, he helps with the Teleportation Device.'

'Leonardo died a hundred and twenty-nine years before Lavicini was born.'

'Bad timing on his part.'

'You also have somebody referring to Leonardo as Signor da Vinci. Da Vinci means "of Vinci". That's like referring to Joan of Arc as "Mademoiselle of Arc". "Telegram for Mademoiselle of Arc!"'

'All right, I feel a bit sheepish about that one.'

'And da Vinci carries a pocket watch and calls people "rotters".'

'You're such a pedant, Loeser. It's a novel, and I wrote it in a hurry. If my public want historical rigour they can refer to the Domesday Book or *Wisden*.'

'But for God's sake, why even bother to write a historical novel if you're not interested in history as it actually was? Your Venice is worse than Kempinski's New York.'

'You must understand, I don't have much imagination,' said Rackenham. 'Every one of my novels is a *roman à clef*. It's just a question of whether I bother to hide the *clef* under a flowerpot. And I was getting bored with doing nothing but changing the names each time. I had a nasty experience with my last one. In *Steep Air*, when it's implied that the judge's daughter goes to bed with three rugby players at once after a party – that story is true in almost every detail. It happened to a university girlfriend of mine. She confided it to me in a tender moment, not long before our untender disunion. When I wish to enact a private sexual humiliation, I'd much rather the girl's face was buried in a pillow at the time than buried in a book, but since this one wasn't quite stupid enough ever to let me fuck her again, I had no choice but to use my publisher as an intermediary. And I assumed it would remain private, because obviously rugby players can't read and obviously my old flame couldn't complain about what I'd done, even to her dearest friends. When she read it she would have felt so angry, and so powerless, and it would have guaranteed me the upper hand every time I saw her for the rest of our lives. Ideal in every way.'

'What happened?'

'One of the rugby players had a chum who knew about the episode and was literate. He told all three of them about the book. They came down to London in search of me. Luckily I was in someone else's flat that night. It's one of the chief reasons I ended up in Berlin.'

'So what difference does it make if you settle your scores in seventeenth-century Venice? It's still quite obvious who everyone is supposed to be.'

'Yes, but my theory is that people will feel so absurd about coming to me and saying, "This syphilitic gondolier in a carnival mask is transparently my good self" that they won't want to do it. History is a sort of fantasy, and fantasy softens the blow. So far it seems to have worked. But of course, whatever precautions one takes, excuses can always be found for fury, as you've just demonstrated.' Rackenham drained his coffee. 'Anyway, Loeser, I should have thought you'd still be in a cheerful mood after what happened with Adele last night.'

'Are you taking the piss? It was awful. She called me an apprentice cuckold.'

'But you kissed her.'

'What?'

'You kissed her,' said Rackenham. 'I didn't see it myself, but you came up to me afterwards and told me about it. I've never seen you so happy.'

'I don't remember anything of the kind.'

'I'm not surprised. You were as glazed as a sash window. You were trying to hang on to your own wineglass for balance.'

'You're sincerely telling me I kissed her.'

'Yes.'

'Rackenham, if this is a joke, I will stuff this book so far down your throat that your duodenum will autograph it in bile.'

'It is not a joke. You said you had just kissed her.'

And then Loeser remembered. He really had.

'You're an apprentice cuckold,' Adele had said in the Fraunhofens' dining room.

'And you're an aspiring joke,' Loeser had replied.

'How do you mean?'

'I estimate you have about three more weeks until this conquering trollop routine loses its novelty and people start talking about something else. After that you will pass out of gossip and into mere signification. The only time anyone will mention your name is when they need a simple way of referring to a specific pattern of social behaviour. You will be living shorthand for something out of date. A ghost. A statue. A joke.'

'And how exactly can I avoid that fate?'

'Stop being so predictable. For instance, you might try being old-fashioned just for a night.'

'That sounds tiresome. What does it involve?'

'I'll take you to dinner and there'll be no absinthe and no ketamine and you can decide whether to sleep with me on the basis of my intelligence and my charm instead of my notoriety and my jawline.'

'How boring. Where would you take me?'

'Borchardt's.'

Adele smiled and raised an eyebrow. 'What about the Schwanneke?'

'Don't be silly.'

'If it's the Schwanneke, and you're nice to the waiter and give him a big tip, then I will condescend to eat with you.'

'Honestly?'

'Yes. I won't go home with you afterwards, though. That wouldn't be very old-fashioned.'

'But you might kiss me, at least?'

'I suppose.' She frowned. 'I shouldn't have said that. Now you will just spend the whole evening calculating how you can coax me that far.'

'Probably.'

'Well, if we get it over with now you shan't be distracted.' Adele stood up on tiptoe and kissed him in a way that was both utterly passionless and staggeringly potent. 'Eight o'clock tomorrow, then?' she said afterwards.

Loeser wanted to respond but he felt as if both his tongue and his penis were likely to end their days among the shell-shocked in a rural mental institution.

'Well, anyway, I'm going to find Sartre,' said Adele. 'Just because I'm seeing you tomorrow it doesn't stop me making his acquaintance tonight. Have a nice evening.' And she was gone.

When all this came back to Loeser in the Romanisches Café, he nearly bent down to give Rackenham a hug, but then he reminded himself that the Englishman hadn't actually had any part in this victory. Instead, he just picked his book, apologised for the interruption, and went over to sit down with Ziesel.

'Dieter! How have you been?' he said, and generously permitted almost an entire phoneme to venture out of Ziesel's mouth before cutting him off: 'I've been pretty fucking well myself, since you ask. I'm having dinner with Adele Hitler tonight. Adele Hitler. And she kissed me last night.'

'Oh yes?'

'She said she won't sleep with me but, come on, we all know her. And after that I feel fairly sure she'll be my girl-friend. I'll be the first to tame the beast. You wouldn't know about this, of course, but there's normally something a bit distasteful about going out with someone who's fucked a lot of other men. "If a woman is good at sucking cock, it can only be because she's sucked a lot of cocks. That is man's eternal tragedy." Somebody said that ... Goethe, no doubt ... And sometimes I think it's only the replacement of the cells of the body that makes sex even conceivable: there's no way I could kiss a girl's clitoris if on a molecular level it was the same clitoris that other men had kissed instead of on a mere Ship of Theseus level. But this time I won't care about any of that. If she's mine, I'll be operating on a new plane. Oh my God, Dieter, this is probably the best thing that's ever happened to anyone. To think – for two years the highlight of my romantic life is flirting with an elderly dental nurse, and now this. Oh, yes, a ham sandwich, some gherkins, and a glass of champagne please – thanks. And I've even beaten Marlene! It had never occurred to me that she might take even longer to find a new squeeze than I would, but look at me now. I've got Adele Hitler and she's still got no one. No one!'

Ziesel took the pause for breath that followed as a cue for corroboration and said, 'Well, no, quite, I mean, Klugweil hardly counts, does he?'

Here it was: the equal and opposite reaction.

'What on earth has Klugweil got to do with this?' said Loeser.

Some sort of rapid mental computation clicked across Ziesel's face. 'Nothing. He doesn't have a girlfriend either. That's what I meant.'

'You said he "hardly counts". He hardly counts as what?'

'Whatever we were talking about. I wasn't really following.'

'You were following perfectly well. It sounded almost as if you were trying to express some sort of connection between Klugweil and Marlene.'

'Not at all.'

'Don't try to lie to me, Ziesel.'

Ziesel cringed. 'I thought you must already know.'

'That my best remaining friend in Berlin is fucking my ex-girlfriend? Is that what you're trying to tell me?'

'Well—'

'No, I did not already know that.'

'But you dumped her. Two years ago. It's not as if he stole her from you.'

'Are you now dictating what I am or am not allowed to be angry about? I will be as angry as I fucking like. I don't need to be issued a licence. Jesus, I am generous enough to let you have lunch with me and this is what I get in return.' The waiter arrived with his glass of champagne. Loeser knocked it back and then rushed out of the Romanisches to catch a tram.

Sometimes psychology could be very straightforward: Loeser's parents had died in a car crash, and ever since he had hated cars. He had never learned to drive, and he refused even to be a passenger in a private vehicle. Taxis were all right because a taxi was essentially a very specific bus. And trains were relaxing. But trams were best. Loeser, as an expert judge of character might have noticed after a lot of close observation, was not a man who shed tolerance and camaraderie in every flake of skin. But somehow, as soon as he stepped on a tram, his usual sensibilities would vanish and he would look around at the other passengers with their mysterious lives and find himself powerfully grateful that he had been born in a big twentieth-century city. He delighted in the tram network's indifferent generosity: who else would ever work so hard to help you achieve your desires without pausing even for a moment to enquire what those desires might be? Wasn't that an attitude about one stop short of love? Even a doctor would only do what you asked if he thought it would keep you healthy, while a tram would unhesitatingly take your fare even if you were on your way to jump off a bridge. Loeser couldn't stand it when his friends complained that the trams were too expensive or too crowded or too erratic. That was so spoiled. Hecht had told him that if he extended this sentiment to the entire brotherhood of man, he would realise

69

he was a communist at heart, but Loeser wasn't interested. No Party was ever going to get him to a party. To Hecht, he liked to quote from *Politics*. 'There is only one condition in which we can imagine managers not needing subordinates, and masters not needing slaves,' Aristotle had said, 'and this condition would be that each instrument could do its own work,' like the golden robotic handmaidens in the *Iliad* that Hephaestus had built to help out in his workshop. (Or like a tram with no conductor.)

Marlene answered the door in a fetching green silk kimono that she hadn't owned when she was going out with Loeser. She smelled of vanilla perfume under a thick baste of sweat.

'Oh, Egon,' she said, 'are you really standing here in front of me or is this just a wonderful dream?'

'What the fuck is this about you and Klugweil?'

'You've finally heard.'

'Finally heard?'

'Everyone else already knew, of course, but we've been making half an effort to keep it from you because we knew you'd be such an unwarranted arsehole about it.'

'Try as I might I just can't believe the two of you would do this to me.'

'It's been two years, Egon. In any case, I could quite justifiably have fucked Adolf the day after you dumped me – but it's been two years.'

'You must be thrilled you've caught up with him at last.'

'I am, actually. And I'll tell you why. Do you remember, after what your idiotic gadget did to his arms, the doctors told him they'd never quite go back to normal?'

'Vaguely.'

'The doctors were right. And guess what that means.' She leaned forward to whisper in his ear. 'He can do it with both hands at once.'

'Do what?' Marlene smiled and raised an eyebrow. Then Loeser realised. 'No!'

'Yes.'

'No one can do that with both hands at once! I tried half a dozen times! There isn't room! Arms just don't do that!'

'Adolf's do. We ought to thank you, really. But the neighbours might disagree. It's frightful how it makes me wail.'

'So you're trying to tell me you've climbed the carnal ranks? All right, good, well, so have I. It so happens that I'm having dinner with Adele Hitler tonight.' He had not intended to mention that.

Marlene laughed. 'Really? You're actually wasting the price of a meal on the biggest slut in Berlin? Good grief. Are you also under the impression that you have to bribe the librarian every time you want to get a book out of the public library? Adolf, did you hear that?' she called back into the flat. 'Egon's having dinner with that filthy Hitler girl tonight. He's very proud of it.'

'Klugweil's here now?' said Loeser.

'Indeed he is.'

'Let me in. I want to talk to him.'

'Sorry. I want to make the most of the afternoon. Adolf's on very good form. Goodbye, Egon. And good luck tonight. I do hope she's worth it.' She started to shut the door.

'Wait. Please. Just one more thing.'

'What?'

'Have you ever slept with any of the waiters at the Schwanneke?'

'You're disgusting.'

'Oh, Christ, I know that blush! You have!'

Marlene slammed the door in his face.

He trudged back down the dusty staircase for which he'd once had such affection, resenting every familiar creak of every floorboard for its new allegiance to his former friend. Blumstein's house was half an hour's walk away, but this time Loeser was too angry to wait for the tram, so he went on foot. The director and his wife lived not far from the Fraunhofens in a sort of giant trophy case that had been designed for him in 1923 by a young architect from the Bauhaus called Gugelhupf. Its glass walls killed something like a thousand birds a year, and ever since its construction the neighbours had complained of an unmistakable quality of mourning to the dawn chorus in Schlingesdorf. That glass of champagne had postponed Loeser's hangover but he still hadn't had anything to eat and he began to feel as if the ballast of his rage was the only thing that was stopping him from floating away like a balloon.

'We can't work with Klugweil any more,' he said as soon as Blumstein opened the front door.

Blumstein sighed as if he were estimating how much of his afternoon he was going to lose to this. 'Good afternoon, Egon,' he said. 'Come in. I'll ask Emma to make us some coffee.'

'Don't bother about coffee,' said Loeser, following him into the expansive sitting room. From a shelf in the corner stared out some of the obscene painted masks from Blumstein's notorious student production of *The Tempest*, which everyone always claimed to have seen even though it had run for two nights twenty years ago in a theatre the size of an igloo. 'I just want to get this over with.'

'This is hardly the first time you've come here to gripe about our mutual friend,' said Blumstein. 'If you could forgive each other for the "Teleportation Accident" then you can forgive each other for whatever it is that's happened now.' He lowered himself into one of Gugelhupf's black rectilinear armchairs and gestured to another one for Loeser but Loeser stayed standing.

'I'm not just here to whine this time. I mean it. He's stabbed me in the back.'

'How so?'

'There's no use telling you the whole sordid story. The point is, we can no longer be collaborators. But on the way here I realised that it's for the best, anyway. Have you heard him these last few months? All of a sudden he's determined that *Lavicini* should be all about the Nazis. Our play is not about the fucking Nazis. The New Expressionism doesn't waste its time with politics. We agreed on that.'

'We agreed on that in 1929,' said Blumstein.

'And?'

'With all due respect to Equivalence, things do change. Do you even realise they shut down the Bauhaus last month? It's very hard to have a conversation with you about this because you don't read the newspapers, but at a time like this it seems to me that an artist has certain responsibilities.'

'I agree. At a time when the atmosphere of Berlin is even more polluted with political talk than usual, we ought to give our audience a few breaths of clean air.'

'If you had heard what's being said about the Jews—'

'Then what would I think? That you're all going to be rounded up by thugs tomorrow morning?'

'No, of course not, but . . .' Blumstein paused and gave his left shoulder four or five unhappy taps with his right hand. 'I had not planned to tell you this yet, Egon, but Adolf and I have been working on a small project of our own.'

'What do you mean?'

'Just a simple piece about what's happening in Germany. What's happening today, not what happened in the late seventeenth century. Something that we can write and rehearse and stage in a few months and that people will actually want to come and see.'

Loeser was so shocked that all he could think to ask was, 'Who's going to do the set?'

'There won't be a set. Nothing but black drapes. Like we used to do it right after the war.'

Loeser thought of all that he'd learned from the older man, and all that he owed to him. That excused nothing. 'So after three years of work we're abandoning *Lavicini*.'

'There's no reason why we can't return to *Lavicini* in the future but just now—'

'Oh, to hell with this.'

Blumstein jumped up and followed Loeser out of the house. 'Egon, please try to understand. I might be wrong about all this, I hope I am – but at the moment I don't feel as if I have any choice.'

But Loeser hurried away without looking back, so the only reply Blumstein got was the soft double thump of a young sparrow shattering its skull against the glass wall of his house and then dropping into the bed of petunias behind him.

When Loeser arrived at the Schwanneke that evening, the restaurant was crowded but luckily there was almost no one there he knew. He wondered if Adele would let him feed her ice cream off his spoon. On the way back to his flat, he'd told himself that nothing that had happened today really mattered – not Rackenham, not Marlene, not Blumstein – because he was having dinner with his prize tonight. But then he remembered the party in Puppenberg, and the canyon of his disappointment, and he reached the irrational conclusion that the only way to ensure that she really would turn up was to convince himself that she wouldn't. So as he bathed and dressed and changed his month-old sheets he had told himself again and again that she wouldn't come, she definitely wouldn't come, she absolutely definitely wouldn't come.

And then she didn't come.

Loeser waited an hour and a half, pulling threads from the hem of the tablecloth, counting the punctuation errors in the menu, watching the staff at their duties in an attempt to work out which ones had fucked Adele and which ones had fucked Marlene. At last, numbly, he gave up hope, and paid for the bottle of wine he'd drunk. As he was putting on his coat he noticed three waiters conferring near the door. All he could think about was how these cunts could apparently have any woman they wanted without even trying. He found himself

74

veering towards them, and on the way he snatched a fork from a vacant table. He didn't know what he was going to do.

'Excuse me,' he said.

'Yes, sir?' said one of the waiters.

Any woman they wanted, he thought. These cunts.

There was a long pause.

'Are there any job openings here?' Loeser said at last.

'I'm afraid not, sir.'

'I see. Fine. Thank you. Goodbye.'

Outside, Loeser hailed a cab to take him to the Hitler residence in Hochbegraben. To arrive uninvited at Adele's house would represent the final collapse of his dignity, but he didn't know what else to do. The door was answered by the Hitlers' maid, who recognised him from when he used to tutor Adele. He realised he missed those boring, luxurious afternoons in the Hitlers' drawing room, and he was reminded of a business plan that Achleitner had once suggested for the newly established Allien Theatre:

1. Put on plays ferociously satirising the sort of people who live in nice houses in Hochbegraben.
2. Sell a lot of tickets to the sort of people who live in nice houses in Hochbegraben.
3. Make enough money to move into a nice house in Hochbegraben.

'Herr Loeser!' said the maid. 'What a lovely surprise!'

'I'm sorry to call so late. Is Fräulein Hitler at home, please?'

'I'm afraid not, Herr Loeser.'

'Do you know where she is?' he said. For the first time he wondered where Adele's parents thought she went when she didn't come home night after night. Dance lessons?

'She left for the train station a few hours ago.'

'The train station?'

'Yes, Herr Loeser. Fräulein Hitler has gone to Paris.'

'Paris? For how long?'

'I don't know, Herr Loeser, but she did pack quite a lot of suitcases to be sent after her.'

'Did she leave a note for me? Anything like that?'

The maid looked embarrassed. 'Not that I know of, Herr Loeser.'

'I see. Fine. Thank you. Goodbye.'

He reached into his pockets to see if he had enough cash on him for another cab and found only the fork from the Schwanneke. He would have to walk. Above him the moon over Berlin shone bright as a bare bulb in a toilet cubicle. When he got to the swimming pool on Sturzbrunnenstrasse he crossed the road, and off to his left was the library of Goldschmieden University, in front of which about fifty students seemed to be holding a bonfire. They were all cheering. Probably it was some sort of silly art performance, but still, out of curiosity, Loeser decided to see what was going on. As he drew closer, he saw that what they were burning was books, tossed one by one into the middle of a square framework of logs. Several boys and girls held placards that were difficult to read in the flickering light. The smell of the smoke was surprisingly caustic for such a stolid fuel.

'What are you doing?' he said to the nearest youthful biblioclast. Every time a heavy book landed it threw off a cheerful spittle of cinders, and shreds of stray paper danced in the wind like fiery autumn leaves.

'This is degenerate literature. We are destroying it in the name of Germany. Would you like to join in?'

Loeser chuckled. The student was playing his part with an almost Expressionist rigidity. There was, Loeser had to admit, something quite amusing about acting out this medieval folk magic just outside the doors of fashionable, modern Goldschmieden. It was the sort of thing that Loeser himself might have come up with at that age. He was about to ask whether they were affiliated to a particular company or collective when the student pressed a novel into his hand. He looked down. *The Sorceror of Venice* by Rupert Rackenham. Straight away, all thought of objective theatrical evaluation forgotten, Loeser turned and hurled the book into the bonfire with a delighted yell. Next, the student handed him a script for Brecht's *The Threepenny Opera* and a torn copy of *Berlin Alexanderplatz*. Loeser happily sent Brecht and Döblin after Rackenham. Then some Kafka and Trotsky and Zola, against none of whom he had anything in particular, but he was too much in the swing of it to stop. At last, the heat started to get a bit uncomfortable, so he gave the student a grateful slap on the back and continued on his way.

But as soon as he left the glow of the bonfire, all his troubles settled back on to him like a swarm of photophobic midges. Adele gone, Achleitner gone. Blumstein betraying him with Klugweil, Klugweil betraying him with Marlene. Ketamine, politics, boredom. No sex for two years. This sticky film of disappointment and frustration over everything. Berlin was hell. He thought of that essay Nietzsche had cobbled together in the last sane year of his life after he fell out with Wagner. *Nietzsche Contra Wagner. Loeser Contra Blumstein. Loeser Contra Omnes.*

How did Lavicini feel when he left Venice? How long did he think he'd be gone? Did he have the slightest fear that he might die in a foreign land?

All right, Loeser decided. Fuck it.

Paris.

3
PARIS, 1934

'Dear Mother and Father. Good news: I am rich. I have cornered the market in foreskins.' Scramsfield sat outside a café on the Rue de l'Odéon, trying to convince himself that, really, it was a blessing that the plan had failed, and the first of his consolations was that he could never have told his parents. 'I have given up literary ambitions for ever now that the tender hatbands of newborn boys have brought me a different sort of fame. I can walk into any bar in Paris and straight away there is a shout of, "Ho, drinks on the house for the snozzle tycoon of the Champs-Élysées!"' No. Impossible.

But of course he needn't have been so explicit: he could just have said he was in the medico-cosmetic supplies business. Which would have been true. According to the Armenian, half the foreskins were going to be mashed up into a skin cream and the other half used as grafts to heal burns and pressure sores and venous ulcers. The reason that old women and private hospitals would pay thousands of francs for an ounce of penis carpaccio was that apparently the cells of a fresh baby were still so vague that they'd melt benignly into any old forehead or thigh. It sounded like voodoo, like medieval popes drinking infants' blood to put off death, but after some consideration Scramsfield had decided he believed it: he only had to think of himself in 1929, getting his first sight of Le Havre from the deck of the *Melchior*, to remember that as a new arrival you would shake hands with anyone you met as if they were your best friend. The Armenian had explained that there was no particular reason it had to be the foreskin; it could just as well be the belly fat, except that of course the foreskin was normally the only disposable part of the kid, whereupon Scramsfield had wondered what he meant by 'normally'; but anyway, that was what distinguished it from the famous monkey gland racket, where the idea was that you couldn't sew just any part of the monkey into a man's sac, it had to be the inventory of the monkey's own sac, so you'd get all the relevant endocrinal juices.

Perhaps 'racket' was the wrong word. Scramsfield had a friend called Weitz who was a dentist. (He often left his consonants half formed when he spoke, as if his mouth were wide open; Scramsfield had once asked him about it and he said it was the same as how if you lived in a foreign country for long enough, you started to pick up the accent.) Last year Weitz had published a short but influential article in the *European Journal of Anaesthesiology*, and as a result he'd been invited to dinner with the famous Dr Serge Voronoff up at the Château Grimaldi, where an animal trainer from a bankrupt circus was employed to run the monkey-breeding operation that took up most of the grounds. Weitz reported that Voronoff truly believed in what he was doing: he truly believed that he could give a man an extra twenty or thirty years of life – and ruffian sexual prowess – by hiding a monkey testicle like a contraband package between the man's own pair. 'You are only as old as your glands,' he would say. For years, the patients had queued up: he'd grafted presidents and maharajahs and the Duke of Westminster's dog and even, it was rumoured, Pope Pius XII, which made you wonder just what it was about that particular job that made you so desperate to postpone the big meeting you had scheduled with your boss. And now that everyone else had finally realised the whole thing was nonsense, and its inventor was getting mocked in all the newspapers, Voronoff himself still believed in it as wholeheartedly as he ever had. Well, why not? They couldn't take away his money. They couldn't take away his pretty twenty-one-year-old wife.

In any event, the prepuce game wasn't like the primate game. Scramsfield could never have had a monopoly like Voronoff, or not for long. And that was his second, more practical consolation: within three or four months, either the rabbis or the Armenian would have got bored with splitting their cut, so to speak, and Scramsfield would have been quietly circumvented. Still, for those three or four months, he could have lived like a Guggenheim. He could have put out another issue of *apogee*, sixty-four pages with half-tone illustrations on coated paper, contributors paid on time at five cents a word; he could have put down a deposit on that old boot shop in the Latin Quarter that he'd told everyone he was going to turn into a gallery; he could have redeemed his long-suffering blue Corona from the pawnbrokers; he could have given back this borrowed suit and bought one for himself that didn't cut into him under the arms. He wouldn't have wasted it all at the Sphinx this time. And right now he wouldn't be sitting here watching the door of Shakespeare and Company, knowing that if nobody who might want to make his acquaintance turned up by the time the shop opened again after lunch, he would have to go in to steal some more books to sell to Picquart. He hadn't eaten since breakfast the day before and hunger kept barging his thoughts out of the way.

But Scramsfield's third and supreme consolation was Phoebe. She had sent him to Paris to be a writer. And with the Armenian in jail because of those cheques, he was free to be a writer again. No money and no distractions was better than money and distractions. His father had money and distractions. Anyone could have money and distractions. That was the important thing.

Just after one o'clock on this clement April day, two women walked up to the door of Shakespeare and Company, stood for a minute looking at the books in the window, and then tried the door. It was locked, but they kept trying it, as if they thought it might realise its rudeness and change its mind.

After wiping his front teeth with a napkin, Scramsfield got up, hurried towards the women, slowed to a saunter before he got near enough to be noticed, and then carried on past. A few steps further on, as a considerate afterthought, he paused, turned, and said, 'Looking for Sylvia? She's closed until two.'

And there it was on their faces, as always, the moment of relief so deep it seemed almost carnal: the tourist's hopeless gratitude for a friendly American voice, an honest American face, an ally against this conspiracy of waiters and concierges and policemen and taxi drivers and beggars and shopkeepers and train conductors. One of the women was young, blonde, pretty enough, but all her features a little askew somehow, like paintings haphazardly hung; the other was older, greying, not similar enough in the face to be the mother, perhaps the aunt but more likely the governess. 'Oh,' said the older woman. 'Thank you. Who is Sylvia?'

'Don't you know Miss Beach? She runs the store. She's an American, but the French close for lunch, so she does too.'

'That's awfully irritating. We'd hoped to buy a copy of *Ulysses*.' She had an upper-class Boston accent not unlike Scramsfield's own.

'You picked a good week. The fifth edition's just out. Jimmy's over the moon about it. He says they've finally chased out most of the typographical errors. He's punctilious about those typographical errors.'

'Jimmy?'

'Jimmy Joyce,' said Scramsfield, as if it were obvious.

The older woman exchanged a glance with the younger one. 'You know Mr Joyce?'

Scramsfield shrugged. 'Sure. Everybody in Paris knows Jimmy. I had dinner with him and Sylvia just last night. He still hasn't found a single restaurant in France he can tolerate.' Then, in an accent that was Irish or at least Scottish: ' "I've eaten headache pills with more blood in them than this steak!" ' Both women laughed delightedly, which was when

Scramsfield saw the younger woman stroking the head of a poodle she had in her handbag, except that the poodle was tiny and green and hairless and wore a white lace bonnet and, in conclusion, just wasn't a poodle, even though he knew he wasn't nearly hungry enough yet to be hallucinating. 'Well, say hello to Sylvia for me when you see her,' he said, doffing his hat as two curly-haired boys in sailor suits ran past rolling bicycle wheels with sticks.

'We will,' said the older woman. Then, as Scramsfield turned to walk on, she called after him, 'Oh, but I don't believe you told us your name.'

Scramsfield turned back for the second time, smiley and mechanical as a chorus girl. 'You're right. How blockheaded of me. Herbert Wolf Scramsfield.'

'How do you do, Mr Scramsfield? I'm Margaret Norb and this is my niece Elisalexa Norb.'

'And this is Mordechai,' said Elisalexa, grabbing her iguana by the throat, pulling it out of her handbag, and holding it out in front of him. 'He'd like to shake your hand.'

The reptile was sprinting in the air, and in its eyes was a plea for rescue, but Scramsfield still reached out and took one of its clawed feet between finger and thumb. A long yellow dewlap hung from its lower jaw like a monkey's vacant pouch. 'How do you do, Mr Mordechai?' he said solemnly.

A short while later they were all sitting down for lunch at Le Beau Manchot on Rue des Saules, and Scramsfield was telling the Norbs about his time as an ambulance driver in the Italian army, where he first met Hemingway. 'You can't believe anything Hem tells you about those days. He says he saved my life at Schio. I know it was the other way around. But the only reliable witness was Sidney Howard and he's dead now.' When the undercooked trout arrived Scramsfield made sure it wasn't obvious how famished he was from the way he ate, recalling one particularly desperate occasion here when in his haste he had swallowed half a baked lemon and surprised the whole restaurant with a high wail of shock like an operatic *lamento*. They soon got on to the subject of their common home town, and Scramsfield was relieved when it became clear that the Norbs did not know his parents. 'And you don't know Phoebe, either? That's a shame. She's my wife. She's coming out here to join me in a few weeks.'

Elisalexa's father made industrial chemicals: sulphuric acid, hydrochloric acid, nitric acid and so on. He'd got through the first years of the Depression by cutting his workforce right down, Margaret explained, and although a few poor souls did make for the vats after the first round of firings, Mr Norb had made sure to install safety nets by the time of the second. That sort of logical leadership, and his preference for government bonds over corporate stocks, had left the family's fortune almost intact after the crash, which was how the Norb women were able to afford their educational trip to Europe.

Over dessert, Scramsfield told the Norbs about *apogee*, his literary magazine, which had been the first to publish T.S. Eliot, and *The Sorrowful Noble Ones*, his debut novel in progress, which Jimmy Joyce simply wouldn't be allowed to look at until it was finished. Elisalexa had not spoken at all during the meal, except to Mordechai, and she now occupied herself stuffing morsels of cake into the lizard's mouth with the back of a spoon before holding his jaws shut to make sure he swallowed. He had chocolate all over his bonnet and some in his eyes. Everyone was getting on very well. Afterwards, Margaret wouldn't let Scramsfield pay any share of the bill, despite all his protests. She spent a short while trying to calculate the tip before Scramsfield told her it ought to be at least a hundred francs.

'That sounds like quite a lot.'

'That's just how it works here, I'm afraid. The only reason they can sell the food so cheap is because they know we'll pay the waiter's salary ourselves.'

'Well, the food *was* awfully cheap.'

In fact, twenty francs of that would go to the waiter, thirty francs would go to the manager, and fifty francs would go towards paying off Scramsfield's tab here. The only reason he'd brought the Norbs to Le Beau Manchot was this arrangement, which was replicated in half a dozen establishments around Paris.

As they were leaving, Scramsfield happened to mention that if they should want to meet Hemingway, he was almost certain to be found at the Dingo. Margaret said they'd planned to go shopping at Lanvin and Molyneux this afternoon but she would much rather meet Hemingway and she was sure Elisalexa would too. So they went to the Dingo, but Hemingway wasn't there. Scramsfield said they should wait, so while they were waiting they made a list of the other notables that the Norbs would like to meet: Fitzgerald, Joyce, Picasso, Chanel, and above all Diaghilev, because Margaret was a great lover of ballet. Scramsfield assured the Norbs that these introductions could hardly be easier for him to arrange. After a few rounds of drinks – whisky for Scramsfield and *citron pressé* for the Norbs, who paid the bill again – Scramsfield decided that perhaps they ought to try the Dôme. Hemingway wasn't at the Dôme either, so next they tried the Rotonde, then the Closerie des Lilas, the Coupole, Lipp's, the Strix, and finally the Falstaff Bar, by which time they were all hungry again, so they went to dinner at Le Maison d'Or. After a few glasses of pinot noir it became clear that Margaret Norb had something to confide.

'As it happens there is one other gentleman I'd like to meet, Mr Scramsfield.'

'Yes, Miss Norb?'

She leaned in closer. Her face had soaked up the red wine like blotting paper, and there was a large dark mole on her forehead that seemed to Scramsfield to be staring directly at him. 'I'd be awfully eager to meet this Dr Voronoff. I've heard he can take thirty years off your age, you know. I don't understand quite what it involves but it's something to do with glands. Monkeys' glands. Very scientific.'

Scramsfield was somewhat taken aback until he remembered something Margaret had said about how Mr Norb didn't care to have newspapers in the house because even the *Wall Street Journal* was full of socialism. He'd drunk a lot of whisky and at this stage he had to be especially careful not to say anything which might give the mistaken impression that he wasn't absolutely on the level. 'I know Dr Voronoff quite well, Miss Norb. I'm sure a free consultation for a friend of mine would be no burden at all.'

'Good heavens, Mr Scramsfield, is there anyone in Paris you don't know?'

'There is one man in Paris I don't know, Miss Norb, and that's the man who can give me a decent American haircut!'

Laughter.

After he'd coaxed Margaret into leaving another two hundred and fifty per cent tip, he tried to get the Norbs to the Flore for just one more drink, but the aunt was already visibly stewed, and kept burbling about how they needed to get back to their hotel so that Elisalexa could be put straight to bed. They agreed to reconvene for lunch at Le Beau Manchot the following day, where Scramsfield intended to make a proposal to the Norbs: merely to shake hands with Hemingway or Fitzgerald or Joyce or Picasso or Chanel or Diaghilev might be enough for the average gabbling sightseer, but what about if they could tell their friends and relations back in Boston that they'd hosted a stylish and historic dinner for all six at once? They need simply advance a little cash – say five thousand francs – for the food, the wine, the staff, and the hire of the dining room, and Scramsfield could get it all ready for the day after tomorrow. And he would do his honest best. He always did his honest best. He wasn't some sort of con man. But if by any chance it turned out that the guests weren't all available, so the dinner couldn't go ahead, and he'd lost the ticket stub on which he'd written down the name of the Norbs' hotel, so he couldn't return the money, then he would have more than enough in his pocket to bail out both the Armenian and his typewriter.

On his way out of Le Maison d'Or, Scramsfield felt a hand on his shoulder and flinched. 'Excuse me?' With some reluctance, he turned – but was pleased to see that the author of this intervention was nobody he knew. Before him was the sort of man who could, when necessary, adopt an easy posture and receptive face, but the moment he was given permission to relax would fall back gratefully into his natural configuration of hunched shoulders, cocked head, folded arms, locked knees, knotted brow, narrowed eyes, pursed mouth, gritted teeth, clenched fists, and curled toes; the sort of man with blood pressure so high you could send him to the bottom of the ocean without a diving bell. A few years younger than Scramsfield, he was quite thin and quite pale, with black hair parted at the side and a dark grey suit that fitted him well but was beginning to emancipate its threads. He spoke with a German accent and had a distracted, impatient intelligence that seemed to hover a few inches to his left.

'Yes?' said Scramsfield.

'I know I shouldn't have eavesdropped, but I was eating alone at the table next to yours and I heard that woman saying something about how you know everyone in Paris. Is that true?'

This fellow had presumably also heard Scramsfield's barber joke and he couldn't immediately think of a substitute, so he just shrugged.

'I'm looking for a girl called Adele Hitler. Do you know her?'

Scramsfield tried to remember if he'd ever heard the name. Nothing came to him. 'Sure, I know Adele. She usually drinks at the Flore. I can take you there if you like.'

'I don't want to trouble you.'

'I was going anyway. Maybe you can buy me a drink when we get there.'

'I'd be pleased to. My name is Egon Loeser.'

'Herbert Wolf Scramsfield.' They shook hands.

Adele Hitler wasn't at the Flore but, as he had with the Norbs, Scramsfield said they ought to wait, so they each had a brandy. Lucienne Boyer sang from a gramophone. The bar was still packed with the early crowd – so different from the late crowd – still so full of optimism, exuberance and youthful good looks – still so unburdened by nostalgia for their distant and irrecoverable salad days of four hours earlier.

'Did you really come all the way to Paris just to find this girl?'

'Yes,' said Loeser.

'She must be a knock-out.'

'Yes.' He'd hoped to arrive several months earlier, he elaborated, but he'd had difficulty extracting from a family trust some money without which he couldn't afford to travel.

'What do you do in Berlin?' said Scramsfield.

'I'm a set designer for the theatre.'

'Terrific. A man devoted to his muse. I'll drink to that.' Scramsfield told Loeser about *apogee* and *The Sorrowful Noble Ones*. Loeser didn't look very interested, so he changed the subject to local restaurants, but Loeser didn't look very interested in that either, so he asked Loeser what was in the brown-paper parcel that he carried under his arm. The German unwrapped the parcel to show him. Inside was a very old edition of Dante's *Inferno*, bound in dark red leather, so saggy and crinkled that it looked almost viscous, like cured strawberry jam.

Scramsfield allowed his attention to wander during the explanation that followed, since any story that began with a dead man's book collection was unlikely to end with a dirty punchline, but the basics were as follows. Because Loeser didn't think he had much chance of bumping into Adele Hitler before the bars filled up at night, he'd been spending his afternoons finding out what he could about a hero of his called Adriano Lavicini who'd once lived in Paris. And by good luck he'd discovered that there was a rare-book dealer in the Marais who had acquired in an auction several books that had once belonged to this fellow. By now, though, only one of those books was left in the shop, and it was the least desirable of the whole lot, not just because at some stage in its long life it had spent several months drinking from a leaky roof but also because there was no reason to think that Lavicini had ever even parted the covers: it had originally belonged to a friend of Lavicini's called Nicolas Sauvage, and when Sauvage died, he left Lavicini some of his books, but then Lavicini himself died only a few months after this inheritance. Loeser bought it anyway, and when he examined it over dinner at Le Maison d'Or, he was thrilled that he had. Evidently neither Lavicini nor, centuries later, the book dealer had noticed that about halfway through the Eighth Circle, Sauvage had stashed a letter that Lavicini had sent him in January 1679.

'What's in the letter?' said Scramsfield.

Loeser took a blank envelope from his pocket and slid out the old folded letter. ' "Dear Nicolas" ,' he read, going slowly so that he could translate as he went, ' "I could not sleep at all the night after we parted because I was so concerned that you had not taken my warnings with . . . due serious-ness. I do not know what good it will do to repeat them but I cannot think of any other recourse. So allow me once again to be plain: if you proceed with your plans, you ought to fear for your life, and the lives of your family. You know what happened to Villayer when he tried to match himself against forces he could not help but underestimate: he met his death in the Cours des Miracles" – Court of Miracles. "I do not pretend I am a wiser man than Villayer. But the choices I have

made have brought me closer to the heart of this malevo-
lence than any man should ever have to come. Therefore, I
know its power, and its reach. I hesitate to say any more
in a letter, but please, Nicolas, my dear friend, mark this: if
you persist in your intention to conquer those . . . dark lower
depths, then you will soon find yourself entombed in them. I
know it is your proud belief that man should be free to make
these" – I haven't been able to work out quite what this next
phrase means – "unprecedented travels"? Anyway: "to make
these unprecedented travels, just as Villayer believed that he
should be free to make his unprecedented communications,"
or whatever that is, "but until our own strength can match
that of those who oppose us – and until the current order
of things is utterly upset, we both know it never will – it is
a . . . doomed and desolate aim. Blaise is sensible enough to
comprehend this – why can you not?" I think that must be
Blaise Pascal – he and Lavicini knew each other. "For the
hundredth time, I beg you to desist. Pray write back as soon
as you receive this letter. Adieu." Then a postscript at the
bottom: "I neglected to enquire at dinner: de Gorge is looking
for a good barber for his dog – do you know of one?" '

They ordered some more brandy. 'Who was Sauvage?' said
Scramsfield.

'He was a carpenter. But a very good one. He helped
Lavicini with some of his mechanical stage designs. Villayer
was a politician. And you know Pascal, of course.'

Scramsfield nodded. He didn't. 'What was the Court of
Miracles?'

'Gringoire the playwright goes there in *The Hunchback
of Notre Dame*.' The broad, unpaved cul-de-sac next to the
Filles-Dieu convent, Loeser explained, had become a sort of
criminal sovereign state, a Vatican City of misrule, full of
burglars, pickpockets, highwaymen, and prostitutes, who
had their own laws, their own king, and even their dialect.
The Court of Miracles got its name partly because as soon

as the beggars went home there at the night, the crippled would 'miraculously' walk again, the blind would 'miraculously' see, the pustulent would 'miraculously' wash off their sores, and so on; but also partly because it was supposed to be full of fortune-tellers and witches and devil worshippers. 'There was one cult that would eat parts of an animal while the animal was still alive in order to become like that animal.' Scramsfield thought of Voronoff. 'Later on Louis XIV got the police to clear it out and then ran a boulevard straight through it.'

'So what do you think the letter means?'

'I don't have a clue. Apparently I would not have gone far in *grand-siècle* Paris because when I write a letter I actually like to specify whatever it is that I'm talking about. Regardless, what's strange is that Lavicini, Villayer, Sauvage . . . they all died these odd accidental deaths in 1678 or 1679. At the time, lots of people thought that Lavicini had got involved in . . . well, it's almost too ridiculous to say. And I wasn't aware that anyone suspected the same of Villayer or Sauvage. But here's Villayer meeting his death in the Court of Miracles, where the fish cults were, apparently. And here's Sauvage trying to make "unprecedented travels" in "dark lower depths". I've no idea what to make of it all. Tomorrow I want to go and see where the old Théâtre des Encornets was, where Lavicini died. And I want to find out more about Villayer and Sauvage.' Loeser replaced the letter in its protective envelope and wrapped up the book. 'Well, there's no sign of her here. Don't you think we should go somewhere else?'

So they went to the Strix and then to Zelli's. But they still didn't find Adele. By now it was after midnight. 'Isn't there someone we could ask?' said Loeser. 'You must know someone who knows.'

'That's a fine idea.' They got up and made a tour of the bar. These days, Scramsfield's pals didn't greet him with quite the warmth that they once had, but he knew there was less money than ever coming from America now, and even bonhomie did have overheads.

After they'd made five or six enquiries Loeser said, 'So far we've only been talking to Americans.'

'So?'

'I still don't know exactly what made Adele decide to come to Paris. But I have a theory, because I remember the last thing she did before she left: she had a dalliance with some strabismic philosophy student from Paris. I think she must have enjoyed it so much that she came straight here in search of more French kisses.'

'I don't see your meaning.'

'What I mean is, she'll probably be hanging around the French, not the Americans. I don't want to be gratuitously difficult about this, Scramsfield, but do you actually know any Gauls?'

'Of course I do.' But Scramsfield had hesitated just for a moment, and he could see that Loeser had intercepted the hesitation.

'How long have you been here?' said Loeser, now giving him a harder look.

'Five years.'

'And you don't have a single French friend?'

'I do. An old man called Picquart. But apart from that . . . Americans here don't really have French friends. They might have French mistresses, but they don't have French friends.'

'That's contemptible. In Berlin all the foreigners were desperate to make friends with us. I think they knew we were better than them.'

'It's different here.'

'Do you even really know Adele?'

Scramsfield felt a squirt of panic. 'Yes! You wouldn't take me for a liar? Good old Adele! You know what she's like! Always flitting around. Always disappearing.' He shook his fist in mock fury. 'Isn't she? Ha ha! But we'll find her in no time. Let's get another drink and then we'll work out a plan.'

'I think I'd better go back to my hotel.'

Scramsfield grabbed Loeser's arm. 'Don't be a fool. I was just joking about not knowing any of the French. I was being satirical ... Like Mencken ... Look, that's Dufrène over there. He's a dear friend of mine and he'll know where Adele is. He's certain to.' Scramsfield didn't like Dufrène, and he didn't want to talk to him, but it didn't seem that he had any choice. They went over to the back bar where Dufrène was standing with a Pernod. The milliner had moist white skin, he smelled of peppermint, and his head, neck, shoulders, and waist were all of more or less the same diameter, which in sum could not help but produce the impression that he had been squeezed out of a tube of toothpaste. They'd been introduced at a poker game by the Armenian. Scramsfield wondered if Dufrène had heard anything from the Armenian since the Armenian went to jail. He hoped not. There was some chance the Armenian might blame Scramsfield for the trouble over the cheques. That was absurd, of course, and they would sort it out when Scramsfield got together the money for the Armenian's bail.

'Fabrice, my old pal! How are you?'

'What you want?'

'I'd like to introduce you to a marvellous new friend of mine. Fabrice, this is Egon Loeser.'

Dufrène regarded Loeser but didn't shake his hand. 'What does he offer you?' he said to the German. 'Is Ernest Hemingway reading your novel? Or is Coco Chanel sucking your cock? Whoever they is, he does not know them.'

Scramsfield laughed loudly. 'Very funny, Fabrice,' he said. 'But nothing like that. Loeser is looking for a lady acquaintance of his called Adele Hitler. We can't find her. I saw you and I thought, if anyone knows where she is, Dufrène knows. I thought, Dufrène knows every beautiful girl in Paris. Yes? If anyone knows, good old Dufrène knows.' He was afraid to stop talking because of what Dufrène might say next.

Rightly, as it turned out. 'What I cannot understand about you, Scramsfield, is why don't you go home? Why don't you go back to America? Why don't you go home since five years with the rest of them? Paris is not wanting you. Paris is maybe wanting him for a week so we can take his money but is not wanting you.'

Scramsfield had known Dufrène was a risk but he hadn't expected this. 'I can see you're a little bit under the influence, Fabrice, so perhaps we'd better just leave you in peace.'

'No, you are the one who is "under the influence". I am sober compared. How many drinks does this gullible imbecile buy you tonight already? You are pathetic.'

'Listen here, Dufrène, a joke's all right between pals but you must still be polite to my friend. He's new in town and I bet you don't want him to think that Frenchmen are as rude as everyone says, ha ha! Do you?'

'Do not have any more to do with this man,' said Dufrène to Loeser. 'If you are determine yourself to give your money to a fraud I have a friend who sells you an excellent forge Monet. Then at least you have something to show for your trip.'

'Let's be going, Loeser. Fabrice is obviously embarrassed that he can't tell us anything about Adele. I'll see you another time, Fabrice.'

Dufrène smiled. 'Do you know what I hear the other day, Scramsfield? I hear a small rumour about your "fiancée".'

That was when Scramsfield hoisted a right hook at Dufrène's jaw. The milliner pulled off a languid dodge before punching Scramsfield in the stomach with the disinterested efficiency of a clerk stamping a passport. Scramsfield dropped immediately to his knees and his dinner dropped immediately out of his mouth, splattering his shirt and the floorboards and Dufrène's polished black shoes with half-digested steak frites in a casserole of red wine and whisky. He tried to get to his feet but his knees took no notice and then he felt Loeser grab him under the armpits. A few people sarcastically applauded, and as he was dragged out of Zelli's, his heels drawing a translucent railway line of bile, he found himself howling, 'I've boxed with Hemingway! I'll tear that son of a bitch apart! I've boxed with Hemingway!'

Outside, Loeser propped him up against a lamp-post and then turned to leave. 'Where are you going?' Scramsfield moaned. 'Are you going to find a cab?'

'I'm going back to my hotel.'

'How am I going to get home? I don't think I can walk.' His vomitous white shirt was steaming in the cold night air as if freshly laundered.

'You just need to sober up for a few minutes. Get your breath back. Maybe someone will bring you a glass of water.'

'But Loeser, you're my best pal.'

'I only met you three hours ago.'

'You're my best pal and you can't leave me here like this.' Then Scramsfield started to cry. Loeser made an angry remark in German and then walked as far as the street corner. After what seemed like hours, he could be heard in negotations with a gruff cab driver, who wanted an extra twenty francs to help lift Scramsfield into the back seat and an extra thirty francs for puke insurance. Scramsfield managed to communicate his address between seaweed breaths, and then they were rattling unbearably over the cobbles, and then Loeser was helping him up five flights of stairs to his apartment, and then he was in bed.

'Undress me,' Scramsfield said. 'I think I've shit my pants.' He felt as if someone were stirring the room with a wooden spoon.

'Definitely not,' said Loeser. Then he seemed to remember something, looked around for a moment, and stamped his foot. 'I left the *verdammte* book at the bar!'

'Yeah, it was under your chair.'

'Why didn't you remind me? I'm going back for it.'

'No. Don't leave. You can't leave. I'll die if you leave. You're my best pal.' He wanted to take his shoes off but they were too far away.

'I want that book. It'll be gone by the morning.'

'There's a bottle of champagne under my desk. Real good stuff. Real expensive. I was saving it for when I finished my novel but you can drink it if you stay.'

Loeser found the champagne and popped the cork. No grey vapour spooled out. He took a swig and then crumpled his face. 'That is infernal,' he said when he could talk again. 'It's as if they've decided to incorporate the eventual hangover directly into the flavour as a sort of omen.' He examined the label. 'And they've spelled "champagne" wrong on here.'

'You can't leave now you've opened it,' said Scramsfield in undisguised triumph. 'That was my special bottle. You've opened it now and you can't leave.'

Loeser sighed, sat down in the chair by the desk, and forced down another mouthful of champaggne. On the desk was nothing but a framed photo of Phoebe, a pair of underpants, an empty bottle of grenadine, and a lumpy knoll of cigarette ash that presumably still concealed a stolen hotel ashtray somewhere at its base, but between the desk and the wall were three stacked parcels, each containing two hundred copies of the first issue of *apogee*, minus the four he'd posted back to Boston and the two he'd folded into a flotilla of paper boats when he was bored last weekend. Loeser picked up one of the remaining five hundred and ninety-four and started to leaf through it.

'Is this your literary magazine?'

'Yes.'

'Why are all these copies still in your apartment?'

'A wop poet called Vaccaro says he'll shoot me dead if I circulate it in Paris. He doesn't realise I never really planned to in the first place, which is funny, I guess.' Scramsfield explained that he had a homosexual school friend from

Boston called Rex Phenscot whose highest ambition had been to publish a story in some influential avant-garde journal printed in Paris because that was how so many of his heroes had got their start in the 1920s. So Scramsfield had written Phenscot a letter suggesting he ask his lawyer father to invest some money in the first issue of *apogee*. The money duly arrived, and he'd used half to pay the 'editorial board' and the other half to print the magazine (he could have forged the printers' receipt and kept the entire payment for himself, but he wasn't some sort of con man). Phenscot's story about an incident in a rural diner only took up a few pages, so Scramsfield had manufactured enough Dada poetry to fill up the rest of the magazine by copying out random sections of a boiler repair manual into irregular stanzas, knowing that this should be sufficiently confusing to satisfy his patron; but then Vaccaro had got hold of a galley proof and angrily accused Scramsfield of ripping off his best idea. So apart from the two copies he'd sent to the Phenscots and the two copies he'd sent to his parents, *apogee* had to cower in his apartment. All those popinjays like Vaccaro thought they were so brave and exciting. Well, Scramsfield knew a girl called Penny who'd gone to bed with a succession of prominent Dadaists and Surrealists the previous winter, and she'd now quit that gang to become the mistress of a psoriatic Lutheran mortgage accountant from Grindelwald; not for the money, she said, but because she wanted a more imaginative sex life.

'So was this really the first magazine to publish T.S. Eliot?' asked Loeser.

'I never even read T.S. Eliot. You?'

'No.'

'You read Joyce?'

'I look forward to starting *Ulysses* as soon as I finish *Berlin Alexanderplatz*. Did you really box with Hemingway?'

'No. I only met him once. I didn't even have time to tell him my name.'

'Why is everyone here so obsessed with this Hemingway anyway? In Berlin nobody reads him.'

'Who do they read?'

'Of the Americans? I don't know. I read Stent Mutton.'

'I love Stent Mutton!' said Scramsfield, delighted. Then his face fell: 'Oh Christ, none of this would ever happen to Stent Mutton. Stent Mutton would never get beaten up by a designer of expensive hats for rich French ladies. Stent Mutton would never get beaten up by the fucking toothpaste man.'

'No. I've always imagined him as a sort of grizzled ex-drifter. Still carries a rusty blade even when he goes into the Knopf offices to sign a contract for a radio adaptation. Just in case.'

'Yeah, me too. He probably couldn't ever tell his criminal buddies he'd become a writer because they wouldn't understand. I'm in the opposite fix.'

'What do you mean?'

'I've been writing *The Sorrowful Noble Ones* for six years. I've never got past the first paragraph. I don't even know what it's going to be about, apart from, I guess, some rich gadabout fellows who are noble but also – well, you know.'

'Sorrowful.'

'Yeah. I did write a book once, a real one, about facts, under a different name, but it was just for the money. It only took three days and I never even saw a copy. And I can't tell anyone I don't really have a novel. Any more than I could tell those ladies that I don't know Hemingway or Joyce or Fitzgerald or Eliot or anyone.'

'You're as bad as Rackenham.'

'Who?'

'A writer I used to know in Berlin. He wrote a book about Lavicini and it was meant to give you the feeling that you were being taken around Venice and Paris and introduced to all these exciting luminaries. But the truth is, he can't introduce you to anyone. He doesn't know anyone either. It's all nonsense.' Loeser paused to peer down the neck of his bottle as if it were the barrel of a microscope. 'This is starting to taste not so bad. And I can't really smell you any more.'

'So who's this girl?' said Scramsfield. 'Is she young? Oh, why even ask? Of course she's young. What else?'

'I've been aspiring to fuck her for – *Gott im Himmel*, it's been three years now. But I still feel the same way now as I always have – that if I did fuck her, just once, then, somehow, everything would be all right. Even everything in the past. Everything – everyone – I ever missed out on. Can you understand that?'

Scramsfield understood. 'You fucked any French girls since you been here?'

'No. I haven't slept with anyone since I started chasing Adele. It's not that I'm trying to be faithful to her, that would be cretinous, it's just that – I don't know. It hasn't happened.'

'You haven't got laid in three years?'

'No.'

'Boo hoo,' said Scramsfield. 'That's nothing. I haven't got laid in five.'

'Why not?'

'I can't get it up. I go to whores sometimes, to try, and I just end up sucking on their tits.'

'Didn't you say you had a fiancée? What are you going to do when she comes here and you get married?'

There was a time when Scramsfield could get drunk and it was like excusing himself from a party and he would go into the next room and his guests would have the politeness not to follow him and he would be alone in the quiet. Now when he went into the next room they all just crowded in there with him. 'She isn't coming,' he said. 'Phoebe isn't coming to Paris.' There was a long pause in which all they could hear was the distant grind and clatter of the horse-drawn pump wagon that came past every night like a coprophagic ogre to empty the district's septic tanks. Then Scramsfield told Loeser about Phoebe.

They'd met in the summer of 1927, just after Scramsfield was expelled from Yale. He'd been accused of cheating in three different exams, and the Dean had made it clear that if he simply wrote a letter of apology he would be allowed to come back for his sophomore year, but despite all the urgings of his mother and father, who had evidently decided to take the Dean's word over their own son's, Scramsfield would not surrender to an accusation he still maintained to be false. One hot Saturday afternoon in August, when a frost of ill feeling still lay thick on the family's tongues, his mother suggested a visit to the Isabella Stewart Gardner Museum. Scramsfield didn't want to go, but he also didn't want to look as if he were sulking, so he accompanied his parents.

In the Titian Room, with its raspberry wallpaper, they happened to see the Kuttles, another rich Back Bay family. Scramsfield had never before set eyes on the Kuttles' blonde daughter, and standing with her in front of *The Rape of Europa* he felt so panicked by her beauty that after she made an enthusiastic comment about the painting he just stared at her, silently, like some sort of sweating inbred elevator attendant. Only later did he find out that she'd assumed he felt such scorn for her unsophisticated commentary on the Titian that he hadn't even bothered to reply.

And that was how their courtship glided on for several months afterwards. Phoebe would say something about art or poetry or music or philosophy, and either Scramsfield wouldn't listen because he was lost in the orchards of her face, or he would listen without understanding what she meant, but either way he would put on his stern thoughtful expression, and Phoebe would conclude that she still wasn't quite clever or knowledgeable enough to impress him. Sometimes he liked to imply that he'd deliberately engineered his departure from Yale because he'd decided he had nothing left to learn from such a stuffy institution. Phoebe began to worship Scramsfield, just as Scramsfield began to worship Phoebe, but the difference was that he had to keep his worship a secret, a heresy inside their love, an impermissible inversion. She couldn't know how far beneath her he felt. He was soon bored with all the exhibitions and readings and recitals and salons, but he would go anywhere with her. And it was inevitable, really, that they should soon start to talk about going together to Paris.

('Are we still in the prologue?' asked Loeser. Scramsfield ignored him.)

All their heroes were in Paris. Art was there, and love, and truth. They could go there and get married and be poor and happy and free. Scramsfield could write a novel and Phoebe could paint and anything they did there would be so much better and more real than anything they could do in America, which was nothing now but a dry goods company pretending to be a nation. They were so certain.

He couldn't remember when he'd first suggested that if they couldn't go to Paris they ought to kill themselves. He must have been drunk. He might even have meant it as a joke. But then almost without debate it became a basic doctrinal premise between them: that it would be better to evaporate over the flame of their own love than to be trapped for ever in awful Boston with their awful families, doing awful jobs and having awful children.

When they'd sworn all that to each other, however, it had felt abstract, because they were still confident that they could get to Paris. No one else seemed to have any trouble. But as 1928 went by they worried more and more about the money. They knew that if they eloped their parents would cut them off straight away. Once they were out there, they were sure they would find the rent somehow – for a good bohemian, money was something that just came into your house at odd intervals like a one-eared tabby until you scared it off by fussing over it too much, so that in their elastic fantasy they were to go hungry sometimes, in a romantic and inspirational way, and they were also to employ a cook – but as it was they didn't even have enough for two tickets on a steamship. Scramsfield thought of stealing some antiques from his parents' house and selling them (to whom?), but Phoebe wouldn't let him take the risk, because if he were caught and went to prison they'd be separated for years. If he were in Boston now and he needed two hundred and seventy dollars, Scramsfield often thought, he could be wearing blackface, leg irons, and a sandwich board that read DO NOT UNDER ANY CIRCUMSTANCES GIVE MONEY TO THIS MAN, and he could probably still find it a dozen ways. But back then he knew how money worked in the same way he knew how electric lighting worked.

Phoebe and Scramsfield had both agreed that they couldn't tell anyone what they planned to do, not even their friends. But in the end, when they'd thrown away every other possibility, they decided that Scramsfield had better talk to his Uncle Roger. Scramsfield had heard rumours from his cousins that twenty years ago there had been some epochal scandal about Uncle Roger and a Cushing daughter and a week's disappearance and a cheap hotel in New York. Uncle Roger was now a bachelor who spent about a hundred hours a week playing golf, but that story was still enough to suggest that he might, once, have had at least a smear of passion in his soul, and might understand why it was so important that Phoebe and Scramsfield should be able to run away together to the city where their future was impatiently waiting.

It was in Uncle Roger's drawing room with an unaccustomed tumbler of bourbon in his hand that Scramsfield realised for the first time that he didn't actually want to go to Paris very much. He hated foreigners, he loved American plumbing, and he was pretty certain that writing a novel didn't pay, even if you had a good idea for one, which he didn't. And out there he would presumably have to buy a lot of drinks for all these people he kept pretending to have heard of, and be grateful for the chance to buy drinks for them. He wanted to be with Phoebe for ever, sure, but he'd forgotten what was supposed to be so gruesome about being with her for ever in a nice big Boston townhouse full of servants. The great revelation took place at precisely the instant he opened his mouth to make his case, and he was never sure, later on, whether it had been this that had guaranteed his failure. While Uncle Roger sat frowning in his armchair, Scramsfield paced the room, mumbling about art and love and truth like a salesman who had never sampled his own product. Then he asked for a loan.

After a slow, regretful shake of the head, Uncle Roger said it was insulting even to have speculated that he might sanction such a damned childish escapade, let alone fund it. He said he was going to have to think very seriously about telling Scramsfield's parents, and Phoebe's too. Scramsfield's plan, if this happened, had been to bring up Uncle Roger's infamous youthful transgression, and appeal to him to remember what those torrid years had felt like – but he didn't have the courage. Instead, he apologised incoherently, begged his uncle not to say anything to anyone else, departed the house, and had walked a mile before he found a drugstore from which to call Phoebe. They were going to have to kill themselves. It was urgent now, because if Uncle Roger did tell their parents, then they would probably be forbidden from seeing each other ever again. Something inside Scramsfield was banging with split knuckles on the inner walls of his head and screaming at him to end this folly; but something else was telling him that if he backed out now, it would prove that he didn't love Phoebe as much as he had always told himself he did, and she would know it, too.

The two sweethearts had cut out several newspaper articles about suicide pacts and saved the clippings in a secret scrapbook, so they knew that the usual procedure was for one party to kill the other and then turn the weapon on themselves. But given that each of them found it painful even to wake the other up from a nap, neither of them could possibly imagine murdering the other, by consent or not – their love was too strong. So they would have to do it separately but synchronously, which meant taking not one but two pistols from Phoebe's father's gun collection.

They did this the following Sunday afternoon, when all four of their parents were at a charity picnic in the Kelleher Rose Gardens. Phoebe had pretended to feel faint and Scramsfield had pretended he was going birdwatching with Rex Phenscot. He had to wait for nearly half an hour on the sidewalk opposite the Kuttle house before Phoebe signalled from her bedroom window that the servants were all playing cards in the kitchen and it was safe for him to come in; and in that time several automobiles came down the quiet street but only two individuals on foot. The first was a girl in a blue dress walking a dog, around the same age as Phoebe and blonde like her too, but with a plate-like face rinsed clean of any crumb of intelligence. Scramsfield thought wistfully about how this girl would never want to go to Paris, except perhaps for shopping. The second was a bearded man in a filthy overcoat and bare feet, shuffling along with his head down, holding a dog leash in his hand like the girl but with only an obedient invisible animal attached. Scramsfield wondered what harm it could possibly do the world if he simply sent this man into the house to die as his proxy.

Phoebe let him in. They went quietly into her father's study, took a key from his desk drawer, opened the cabinet in which he kept his guns, and took out two pistols – a little derringer with a pearl handle and a Colt revolver that must have been nearly as old as the house – along with a box of bullets. Then they went upstairs to Phoebe's bedroom, where Scramsfield loaded the guns according to instructions he'd memorised from an old book in the library.

He couldn't get the safety catch on the derringer to work. And after a minute of fiddling he began to wonder if he could turn this into an excuse to call the whole thing off. But then Phoebe took the gun from him and unlocked it straight away. Her father had given her a lesson about safety catches when she was younger in case she ever came across a gun that someone had forgotten to put back in the cabinet. Still, now that escape had brushed his ankle, Scramsfield wouldn't let it slip away again. He decided he would say something forceful about what a waste this would be, and how Baudelaire (or somebody like that) wouldn't want them to do it. Phoebe worshipped him and she would listen. He started to speak but just then she started to speak too, and they both halted like two polite strangers.

'What were you going to say?' Phoebe said.

'No, you first,' he said. Phoebe looked nervous. Maybe she didn't want to go through with it either. And if she tried to renege first, he thought, then he could just keep silent, as usual, and look as if his resolve had never failed him, and not make a mistake about Baudelaire, because now that he thought about it, maybe Baudelaire actually had shot himself, unless that was Rimbaud?

Phoebe swallowed. 'Shouldn't we ... I mean, I always thought we'd wait until we were married but now that we won't ever be married I don't see why we should wait.'

Scramsfield's heart stumbled against his lungs. He'd kissed Phoebe a lot, of course, and felt her breasts through her clothes and seen her once in her underwear, but never anything more. Losing his virginity felt real and gigantic in a way that dying did not, even now.

'What were you going to say, before, darling?' Phoebe said.

'Nothing,' said Scramsfield. 'I think you're right. I think – I think we should.'

They undressed without looking at each other, then Phoebe lay down on her bed and Scramsfield climbed on top of her.

What followed did not last more than a minute and a half, and afterwards he was disappointed to realise that somehow the act had contributed not even one iota of detail to his inadequate understanding of the structure and mechanics of the human vagina, despite his having made such a diligent investigation with the most sensitive part of his own body – there was nowhere on the outside of a man that was ever soft in quite that way, he thought, except perhaps the gum still healing after the dentist took out a molar – but it was all still fantastic enough to make him wonder: if you could do this right here in Boston whenever you wanted, at no expense, what the hell was the point of going to Paris? Or anywhere else at all?

Afterwards, without speaking, they both got dressed and sat down cross-legged on the floor, facing each other, knees touching. Scramsfield knew that this was his last chance to rescue himself, but he also knew that if he spoke up now, it would look as if the whole thing had just been a plot to filch Phoebe's virtue. She would despise him. He couldn't stand that.

Phoebe picked up the revolver and held it to her right temple. Scramsfield did the same with the derringer. If they both collapsed backwards, he thought, their corpses, observed from above, would present the neat rotational symmetry of royalty on a playing card. The room was fluffy with sunlight.

'I love you,' Phoebe said. Her knuckles were white on the grip of the revolver. 'I don't regret anything.'

'Same to you,' said Scramsfield.

Did something in Phoebe's eyes flinch in bafflement at the banality of his words and the casualness of his tone? He wasn't sure. But she still leaned forward to kiss him. Then she nodded ready and he nodded back. 'Three,' she said, and Scramsfield's finger tightened on the trigger. 'Two,' she said, and a tear rolled down her cheek. 'One,' she said, and Scramsfield felt a firework of panic soar inside him as he realised for the first time that this was actually going to happen.

Then Phoebe shot herself.

His ears ringing, Scramsfield took the derringer from his temple, slid the safety catch back on, and put it on his pocket. Then he got up, left the bedroom, hurried down the stairs to the front door, and got out of the house before any of the servants had interrupted their card game to investigate the noise. When he got home, he looked in the mirror and found that he didn't have a speck of blood on him. That night, after receiving a telephone call, his mother poured him a gin and tonic and then told him that Phoebe Kuttle had been killed by accident when handling one of her father's guns. Scramsfield burst into tears.

He never worried about getting in trouble. Nobody remembered to enquire about his fictional birdwatching expedition with Rex Phenscot (although someone mentioned that twenty years ago the Phenscot family had lost a beautiful daughter of their own) and as far as he knew nobody noticed the disappearance of the derringer, which he threw into the Charles one night. A coroner did investigate Phoebe's death, as a formality, but he correctly concluded that the gunshot could not have been anything other than self-inflicted. Still, because Phoebe hadn't left a note – they had decided suicide notes were pretentious and egotistical – a police officer was sent to speak to a few of her friends. In the drawing room of his house, the grandfather clock ticking like a bone chisel, Scramsfield was asked how long he'd been one of Miss Kuttle's suitors. Then the police officer said: 'The coroner tells me that Miss Kuttle appears to have been party to some sort of . . . improper transaction shortly before her death.' That was how he put it. He had an Irish accent. 'Would you know anything about this?'

Scramsfield shook his head. 'That's a very disturbing thing to hear,' he said solemnly, leaving it deliberately ambiguous whether he even knew what the police officer meant or was just bluffing along. 'I guess it could be a clue, though. You know, to what Phoebe was doing with that gun. Maybe you should ask Mr and Mrs Kuttle about it?' The police officer nodded, although they both knew no such discussion would ever take place.

At the wake, Uncle Roger took Scramsfield aside. 'Look here, Herbert. I am beginning to see now that I may have been a little harsh when we talked the other day. I think after a shock like this, a good long trip is just what a young man needs. I've talked to your parents and they agree. The money's yours if you still want it. A return ticket and plenty more for hotels and so forth.' Scramsfield didn't think Uncle Roger had any idea that his earlier refusal had led indirectly to Phoebe's death – rather, he just felt guilty for having been uncharitable to a relative who was now bereaved. That night, Scramsfield dreamed that while he was kissing Phoebe in a hat shop he stole a coin out of her mouth with his tongue. Someone had put it there to pay for her steamship ticket but he needed it to pay for his own.

The *Melchior* was full of young men and young couples, and to Scramsfield every single one of them seemed to be auditioning for the roles of Phoebe and himself in some inept small-town musical-comedy production of their intended life together. Insincere and ugly, they gabbled enough about all the things that Phoebe had loved to make Scramsfield hate those things; they used words like 'art' and 'love' and 'truth' and 'poor' and 'glad' and 'free' and 'real' and 'good' – words in which he had come to believe even though he didn't know what they meant – in ways that made Scramsfield realise that what they meant was nothing at all, that earnest monosyllables had nothing to do with life. The older couples were the worst, because they were the ones who could easily have gone to Paris in 1922 or 1923 if they'd wanted, when it was still new, but had not had the imagination to go until everyone else had already been. They all read *The Sun Also Rises* like an instruction manual, and of course they were all rearing novels of their own. Scramsfield kept to himself until he met a girl from New York who was thrilled when he told her how his fiancée had shot herself because she couldn't be with him. One night they were both drunk in her cabin and she asked him to make love to her. But as soon as she lay down on the bed he thought of Phoebe on the floor and his erection fell down. It only took her two days to find another man who said he had a dead girlfriend. After that he didn't see the point of admitting that Phoebe wasn't still alive.

Paris was a trial. He didn't want to be friends with any of the new arrivals, he wanted to be friends with the genuine exiles, but they were hard to find, and when he did find them, he didn't know how to talk to them. He knew it would have been a lot easier if he'd been half of an attractive couple. He spent all of Uncle Roger's money too fast out of boredom. Then in the autumn came Black Tuesday. Later on, people who wanted to be dramatic would say it had been like a bomb going off at the American Express on the Rue Scribe, but in truth the result was not immediate: lots of companies raised their dividends to 'restore confidence', and there were more Americans in Paris in the summer of 1930 than at any time in the 1920s. Soon, though, the dividends fainted away again, and everyone went home – first the poor, then the rich, and then all those in the middle who had depended on the rich: bank clerks and portrait painters and reporters for English-language newspapers. Scramsfield's parents wrote asking him to come home too. But he'd been there less than a year, and he hadn't conquered the city like he was supposed to.

'So I stayed,' Scramsfield said. 'That was five years ago. I don't like it here, but I'm not leaving until I finish this novel and publish it. That's what Phoebe would want. You don't think I should go home, do you?'

But there was no response from Loeser. Scramsfield looked up. The German had passed out in his chair, his fingers still curled around the neck of the champaggne bottle. Out in the street, a woman was singing.

Some time later, Scramsfield fell asleep too.

The next morning they were both awoken by the determined slamming against the apartment's front door of what sounded like a gravestone, jewellery safe, bust of Napoleon, or similar object of medium size and considerable mass, but what turned out – upon Scramsfield's displacing himself from his bed by a sort of gastropodous undulatory motion, rising to his feet, and reluctantly unbolting the portal – to be nothing but the dainty gloved fist of Miss Margaret Norb. Just behind her stood Elisalexa Norb, and in the crook of Elisalexa's elbow squirmed little Mordechai. The aunt looked angry, the niece looked angry, and even the iguana had a kind of resentful squint.

'Good morning, Miss Norb, and to you too, Miss Norb,' said Scramsfield. Because he'd comprehensively vomited, his hangover wasn't as ruthless as it might have been, but his mouth still tasted as though he'd been tonguing Mordechai all night, and yesterday's clothes were now stuck to him in various places by muck's cruel tailor. 'To what do I owe the pleasure of this—'

'Mr Scramsfield!' said Margaret Norb, interrupting him with a stinging emphasis on the initial syllable of the honorific. 'I must ask you to explain yourself.'

'Uh, yes?'

'This morning we made sure to get to Shakespeare and Company before it closed for lunch. While we were there we found ourselves in conversation with a very agreeable clergyman from Philadelphia, and we confessed to him our excitement about the prospect of being introduced to so many of your celebrated "friends". But this clergyman was a cultured fellow, and he was able to tell us that Joyce sees no one,

Hemingway isn't even in Paris any longer, and Diaghilev . . .'
She swallowed. 'Diaghilev is dead! Thank goodness he wasn't
more tactful otherwise we still mightn't know.'

'Miss Norb, I assure you—'

'Let me finish, please. As luck would have it, our conversation was overheard by a third party. This other man, from
Chicago, told us that he had a cousin who came to Paris and
had a very similar experience with a scoundrel who drank a
lot of whisky on his tab. The cousin actually went as far as
to put up money for a dinner party that never took place. He
also bought a signed first edition of *Ulysses,* which a book
dealer later informed him was a very poor fake – for one
thing it was only fifty-eight pages long, including woodcuts
and glossary. The man from Chicago gave various other
details that led us to believe that you were the souse involved.
The shop had your address in its lending library records and
the proprietress was happy to give it to us after we explained
that you had told lies about her for personal profit. Unless
you can satisfy us that an improbable mistake has been made,
we are going to report you to the *gendarmerie* as a confidence
trickster.'

As if to throw her support in with all this, Elisalexa Norb
stuck her tongue out at him.

Scramsfield smiled. 'I'm so glad you're giving me the chance
to clear all this up, Miss Norb. To start with, I can tell you
that I've never had anything to do with anyone's cousin from
Chicago, and I've certainly never tried to sell anyone a sham
Ulysses. As for the introductions I promised: sure, Joyce
normally sees no one, but he will make an exception for my
dear friends. If Hem has left Paris then I'm a little offended
he didn't tell me but we'll have it out as soon as he gets back.
And Diaghilev—'

'Yes?'

'Oh boy, you can't have thought I meant Sergei Diaghilev,
Miss Norb? Your clergyman pal from Philadelphia was right,

110

of course, we lost him to tuberculosis a few years ago. I still remember the funeral – Cocteau gave such a moving elegy. No, I was going to introduce you to his brother Fyodor. Every bit as talented.'

'And I suppose you have similar alibis for Fitzgerald and Picasso and Chanel?'

'I think you're being a tad unfair, Miss Norb, but let me say that if I have wandered away from the scientific truth once or twice . . .' He shrugged and spread his hands, contrite and self-effacing. 'Well, I'm a writer, Miss Norb. My imagination is my forge. If you stay in Paris much longer you will find many others like me.'

'Not good enough, Mr Scramsfield. We are going to the police. Goodbye.'

'No,' said Scramsfield. 'Wait. Please! Don't be rash.'

'Nothing you say can persuade me,' said Margaret Norb, turning away.

'I can get you an appointment with Voronoff.'

She stopped. 'The real Dr Voronoff?'

'Yes.'

'In a week, I suppose? And we'll be buying you dinner until then.'

'No. Not in a week. This afternoon. I can hardly lie about that, can I? If you haven't had the operation by six o'clock today then you can tell the *flics* anything you like.'

He had her. He could tell. He did not have the remotest idea what he was going to do next, but he had put off calamity.

Then she sniffed.

'What in heaven's name is that smell?'

The effluvium from his bed and his clothes had reached her. Even knowing that most American tourists learned to shutter their olfactory epithelia as soon as they left their hotels, Scramsfield was surprised it had taken so long. 'I don't smell anything,' he said.

'It's revolting.'

111

'Might be the people downstairs. I believe they're French.'

'Mr Scramsfield, you can hardly expect me to believe that you are a close associate of an important man like Dr Voronoff when your own apartment smells like a sewer.'

'It must be the monkeys,' said Scramsfield, and involuntarily squeezed his eyes shut for a second, as if he was thirteen again and had just thrown a baseball that would either win the afternoon's game or break a neighbour's window.

'The monkeys?'

'Yes. Until the day before yesterday, Dr Voronoff was keeping some stud monkeys here that he had just imported from Morocco. Now they're at the Château Grimaldi. But the stink does linger, ha ha!'

'You mean to tell me that Dr Voronoff sometimes uses this very apartment as a base of operations?'

'Quite often,' said Scramsfield, on a roll now. He pushed the door open wider, so that the Norbs could see into the apartment, and pointed at Loeser, who was still sprawled in Scramsfield's wooden chair. 'In fact this is Dr Voronoff himself.'

Loeser went white.

'This is Dr Voronoff?' said Margaret Norb.

'Yes. I'm afraid he was up very late last night operating. And he speaks very little English.' He gave Loeser a significant look that meant 'Get up and introduce yourself in a Russian accent'. But Loeser must have misunderstood this because instead he just performed something resembling a palsied military salute and then looked down at his feet. 'The operation won't take place here,' Scramsfield hurried to add. 'We will come to your hotel with all the equipment. Shall we say four o'clock?'

'He'll carry out the operation? For no charge? On both of us?'

'Both of you?'

'Elisalexa is young, Mr Scramsfield, yes, but I believe there's no such thing as being young for too long.'

'Of course not. Both of you, then. Absolutely. For no charge.'

'In that case we shall await you this afternoon at the Concorde Sainte Lazare. If you do not appear as promised, you know what will happen. Good day, Mr Scramsfield. Good day, Dr Voronoff.'

The Norbs made their exit and Scramsfield shut the door. He turned to Loeser. 'That went damned well, I thought.'

'Do not ever do that to me again,' said the German.

'Sorry, pal, but I knew you'd pull it off.'

'You can't sincerely expect me to go through with what you have just set in motion.'

'I can't have them go to the cops.'

'It's not my problem you're on the run because you murdered your fiancée.'

'What? I did not murder my fiancée and I am not on the run!'

'You told me last night you pushed her off a steamship and she drowned,' said Loeser. 'That's why you can't go home to New York. Something like that.'

'Were you listening at all?'

'You rambled on for so long that I may have passed out a short while before the end. But I got the fundamentals.'

'Phoebe tragically took her own life and it wasn't my fault. I can go back to Boston whenever I like.'

'Yes, all right, you're welcome to type up the footnotes and I'll give them my careful attention.' Loeser levered himself out of the chair. 'You know, when I woke up, I looked around at these squalid and unfamiliar surroundings and for a moment I really thought I might have met some wonderful floozie last night.' He went to the sink and began to splash his face with water.

'Come on, old pal. You'll do this for me, won't you? Look here: if you do, I'll take you to see Picquart.'

'Your French friend? Why should I want to meet him?'

'He's a historian,' said Scramsfield. 'A scholar. There's nothing he doesn't know about Paris. He'll be able to tell you the truth about Lavicini and . . . all those other fellows. The dog barber. The Castle of Mystery.'

'Court of Miracles,' said Loeser. He looked around for a towel to dry his face, but there was none, so he made the most of his arm hair.

'Yes. He hates Germans, there's no way he'd see you otherwise, but if I call in my very last favour with him, he will.'

'If I believed you, wouldn't that make me as gullible as the Norbs?'

'He's not Hemingway. He's not Picasso. He's just an old man I happen to know. Why would I bounce you about that?'

'I don't see how you expect this to work, anyway. We don't have a monkey.'

'We could use a little black boy,' said Scramsfield. 'One of those Algerians.'

'I think there is some chance the ladies will penetrate that ruse.'

'Well, if we bring a cage with a sheet over it, it doesn't matter what's inside. They'll never see. They'll be under anaesthetic.'

'How are we going to manage that?'

'I know some Cambodian medical students who will sell us barbiturates.'

'Barbiturates?'

'Yes.'

'Do you think they'd have any good cocaine?'

'I don't know. Probably.'

Loeser went to the window and looked out. 'This is going to take up the whole afternoon, isn't it? I was going to visit the site of the Théâtre des Encornets today.'

'You still can. I won't need you for the preparations. Just be back here by three o'clock.'

'You'd better have bathed. Get at least a gallon of carbolic acid from the Cambodians.'

So a few hours later, Herbert Wolf Scramsfield and Sergei Voronoff arrived at the Hôtel Concorde Sainte Lazare wearing white doctor's coats, carrying brown doctor's bags, and wheeling a trolley on which rested an enshrouded birdcage, like the agents of some sinister and incomprehensible room service delivery. After they told the concierge their cargo was primatal he tried to throw them out, but they insisted he telephone up to the room and enough of a fuss was made that he had no choice but to let them into the service lift.

The Norbs were staying in two bedrooms connected by a small drawing room. 'Mordechai wants to see the monkey,' said Elisalexa Norb as soon as they were through the door.

'I'm afraid that's out of the question.'

'Why?'

Scramsfield thought for a moment. 'Patient confidentiality,' he ventured. This seemed to satisfy the Norbs. You could pump this suite full of coal tar until there was only an inch of air beneath the corniced ceiling, he thought, and it would still, on balance, be nicer than his own apartment.

'Will you require us to undress before surgery?' said Margaret Norb.

'No,' said Dr Voronoff before Scramsfield could reply.

'But where will you put the glands?'

'Zyroid,' said Dr Voronoff, gesturing at his neck.

'You will at least need to roll up your sleeves for the anaesthetic, however,' said Scramsfield.

He took two needles out of his doctor's bag and carried out the injections. Then he guided Margaret Norb to an armchair and Elisalexa Norb to a chaise longue. Within a few minutes they were both asleep, the latter with her tongue poking out of her mouth. Behind them, a folding Japanese screen of painted cedar wood showed a bearded man lifting a turtle into a fishing boat.

'Why did you tell them not to undress?' Scramsfield asked Loeser.

'I've sunk pretty low in my time, but I am not yet at the stage where I will pose as a doctor to molest unconscious women. Not quite yet.'

'Who said anything about molesting them?'

'You would definitely have molested them.'

'I wouldn't, but in any case we'd better get a move on. I didn't give them much of this nembutal stuff so I don't know when they'll wake up.' If only Weitz were here, thought Scramsfield. He took a small brown paper parcel out of his doctor's bag and emptied its contents on to the shiny top of the Boulle writing desk.

'What are those?' said Loeser.

'What do they look like?'

'Armoured raspberries.'

'Haven't you ever seen a lychee before?'

'No.'

'Good. Let's hope the Norbs haven't either. They're delicious, by the way. The Cambodians go crazy for them. Surprisingly good in a martini, too.' Scramsfield tossed one to Loeser. 'Peel that.'

With some difficulty, Loeser did so. Scramsfield peeled a second.

'Perfect,' said Scramsfield. 'One hundred per cent convincing raw monkey balls.'

He returned to his doctor's bag and took out a small tube of glue.

'That's your plan?' said Loeser incredulously. 'Glue these things to their necks?'

'What else are we going to do? We're not surgeons. We could have glued them somewhere more discreet if you hadn't interfered.'

He was about to get to work when out of the corner of his eye he saw Mordechai sitting on the mantelpiece next to the clock.

'Loeser,' he hissed.

'What?'

'The lizard.'

'What about it?'

'It's watching.'

'So?'

'What if it tells the girl what we did?'

'How would it do that? It doesn't talk.'

'I think they have some sort of . . . some sort of *connection*. Catch it and put it in your bag.'

Loeser made a grab for the iguana, but it leaped from the mantelpiece and fled through the doorway into Elisalexa Norb's bedroom. That was enough to put it out of sight, so Scramsfield began the operation. '*Das ist ein Tiefpunkt,*' muttered Loeser several times to himself after that. '*Das ist ein echter Tiefpunkt.*'

Within an hour, the Norbs had begun to stir. Margaret was lagging behind so Elisalexa kept pinching her aunt's calf until she woke up properly. Both then tottered over to the mirror to examine their ripe gemmeous xeno-transplants.

'They do rather stick out,' said Margaret Norb. 'The glands.'

'Yes,' said Scramsfield, 'but they'll soon be absorbed into your body.'

'Can I touch it?'

'If you like.'

She hesitantly brought an index finger up to the little moist bulb, then stiffened in shock. 'It's so sensitive.'

Elisalexa Norb did the same, then licked her finger. 'It tastes sweet,' she said.

'Please don't do that, dear, it's disgusting,' said Margaret Norb. She turned to Voronoff. 'This is wonderful, Doctor. Mr Scramsfield, perhaps you'd be so good as to telephone down for a bottle of champagne.'

A few minutes later an olive-skinned boy arrived with a bottle of Veuve Cliquot and four glasses. He looked at

Margaret Norb, then he looked at Elisalexa Norb, then he squinted in puzzlement and raised his hand to his own neck as if he were about to point out a minor oversight in the guests' toilette – but of course he thought better of it. On his way out, Margaret Norb gave him fifty francs, which he nodded at philosophically as if somehow it explained everything.

Margaret Norb led a toast to Dr Voronoff. 'How is the health of our donor?' she said after her first sip of champagne. Scramsfield couldn't work out what she meant until she nodded at the birdcage on the trolley under its black sheet.

'Still under sedation,' he said. 'But stable.'

'They lead comfortable lives, do they? After their . . . sacrifice?'

'Luxurious, yes,' said Scramsfield.

Elisalexa Norb gave a small burp. Scramsfield looked over and saw that she had already drained her glass.

'Purhayps zay lady should not bay dvinkink so soon aftur hur anayzaytic,' said Dr Voronoff with genuine concern. But his warning was too late, because Elisalexa Norb almost immediately staggered backwards and bumped against the writing desk.

'Oh dear,' said her aunt. 'Elisalexa, you must be put straight to bed to recuperate.' She stepped forward with the intention of carrying this out, but was almost as unsteady herself. Dr Voronoff caught her arm as several ounces of champagne hopped from her glass to the carpet. 'Or – goodness – well – Mr Scramsfield, might you be kind enough to . . .'

'Certainly, Miss Norb,' said Scramsfield. He guided a giggly Elisalexa into her bedroom. She was quite pliant, but as they went through the doorway she grabbed for the brass knob so that the door swung most of the way shut. This didn't worry Scramsfield until he was helping her down on to her bed and he realised she was pulling him down with her by the lapels of his doctor's coat. He lost his balance.

'Miss Norb!' was all he had a chance to say before her mouth was on his. Somehow she got his tongue between her lips and began to suck it down like a steamed mussel that wouldn't slip out of its shell. With one hand she was unbuttoning her dress and with the other she was bullying his crotch. Her whole body was quivering like a nervous poodle. At last she gave up the kiss and he got his tongue back. He felt as if he'd been punched in the mouth. 'For Christ's sake stop this,' he whispered. 'Your aunt is in the next room.' But by then her girdle was half unlaced, and he got a glimpse of a cranberry nipple.

Elisalexa Norb flung her head back against the pillow. With his mouth on her breast, the lychee glued to her neck was only inches from his eyes, and there was something soothing, almost spiritual, about its smooth pale surface, so that by meditating on it he could almost forget that at any moment they might be caught. He switched to the girl's other nipple. He would not have thought that anything could possibly improve on the first breast, but the second breast was, somehow, even more sensational, and he was enjoying this so much that he was beginning to think he might be able to support an erection for long enough to make love to her.

Then there was a daub of green in his peripheral vision.

Scramsfield couldn't believe how fast the reptile could move. Already it was crouched beside its mistress's neck, sniffing the lychee, flicking its tail. He tried to shoo it away with his hand, but Mordechai just gave him a contemptuous glance and then went back to the fruit. He wondered if he ought to say something, but he decided it was better not to. And he was still fiddling with his belt buckle when the iguana opened up its jaws, fit them somehow around the counterfeit genital, ripped it away with one jerk of its head, and leaped from the bed with its prize.

Elisalexa Norb screamed. Her hand shot to her neck. 'My gland!' Looking to the door, she was just in time to see Mordechai escaping into the drawing room, so she pushed Scramsfield off her with surprising force and made after the pet. He lunged to catch her wrist. 'Miss Norb, you're not dressed! What will the others think? Please just—' But she broke free and rushed out of the door, bare breasts bouncing. Scramsfield, not knowing what else to do, followed. Beyond, he was expecting to find his doom. What he found instead was Margaret Norb bent forward over the writing desk with an expression of anticipatory ecstasy and Dr Voronoff manoeuvring himself into position behind her.

'Elisalexa!' shrieked Margaret Norb. She hurriedly and ineffectually rearranged her petticoats, then turned and slapped Dr Voronoff so hard in the face that he nearly fell over sideways.

'Where is he?' said Elisalexa Norb, totally uninterested in what her aunt was doing. Scramsfield had just caught sight of the lizard in the opposite corner of the room, so, like an idiot, he pointed. The girl hurled herself towards the iguana, but her legs were still muddled, and she tripped, bounced off an armchair, and collided finally with Dr Voronoff's trolley, knocking it to the ground with a crash and sending the bird-cage flying through the air. It slipped its black sheet, landed by the Japanese screen, and rolled to a stop.

The silence afterwards was so total that you could hear the little brass creak of the empty cage's door as it fell slowly open.

'Perhaps we'd better be going,' said Scramsfield to Dr Voronoff. And, with some haste, they were going.

The two men were out of the Concorde Sainte Lazare and around the corner before Loeser said, 'What the hell were you doing with her in there?'

'I could ask you the same question,' Scramsfield panted, making a dance step to avoiding getting tangled in some-body's dog leash.

'I said no but she insisted.'

'Yes. Mine too. Champagne and nembutal. Must remember that. "Scramsfield's Patent Aphrodisiac Serum".'

'Oh God, don't talk like that, we sound like rapists.'

'Rapists? We're not rapists. They're the rapists.'

'I'm not going to debate free agency with you, Scramsfield.'

They passed a pharmacist with an unsettling window in which nine plastic pelves each demonstrated a different herniary bandage. 'Come on, buddy, I've heard how you all do things in Berlin. Are you telling me you never used dope and booze to get a girl to go to bed with you?'

'I've never done that.'

'And you never tried?'

Loeser coughed. His right cheek was still pink. 'When are we going to see Picquart?'

'We can go now if you want. He's always at home.'

Picquart lived on the fifth floor of a dirty building in the Latin Quarter with a staircase so hellishly steep and narrow that halfway up you began to wonder if it wouldn't have been easier to try your luck with a drainpipe. Scramsfield knocked on the door.

'*Quoi?*'

'It's Scramsfield.'

'*Bien.*'

They went inside.

Heraclitus taught that all is change. Scramsfield knew this from his first semester at Yale, and he was sure Picquart's three cats would agree with the Greek. The entire apartment was crammed with piles of old books, often with only the narrowest of pedestrian corridors between them, and these piles were continually being rearranged, relocated, or removed, so that after every nap the cats woke up to an entirely unfamiliar topology, like a tribe dwelling in some impossible mountain range that rumbled every hour with random, hyper-accelerated geological convulsions. Yesterday, they might have found a nice ledge, hidden between two volumes of a dictionary, which caught the morning sunlight through the window; today, it would be gone, or it would be too high to reach, or it would topple as soon as they set paw on it. The cats didn't seem to leave the apartment very often, and Scramsfield imagined it was because they found the great city outside to be eerily, almost unbearably static. However, Picquart said they did sometimes go outside to mate. Heraclitus taught, also, that all things come into being through strife, and Scramsfield hadn't believed this in Boston, but he believed it in Paris, because the sound the local cats made when they fucked on the roofs in the middle of the night was really enough to persuade anyone.

Picquart himself was a wiry and warty old man with a nose like an eroded cathedral gargoyle. They'd met in a prison cell when Scramsfield had been arrested for running away from a restaurant without paying the bill and Picquart for swearing at a policeman. The next morning they both got out and Picquart now sometimes bought stolen books from Scramsfield. They didn't particularly like each other.

'What do you have for me? Who is this?'

'I don't have any books today, Marcel. This is Egon Loeser. He's an old pal of mine.'

'*Un Allemand?*'

'Yes.'

'What does he want?'

Loeser took out the letter from Lavicini to Sauvage, along with a box of cigars they'd bought on the way, and gave both to Picquart. 'Scramsfield said you might know what this character Sauvage is talking about there,' he said.

Picquart read the letter, then looked up. 'What do you think he's talking about?' he said.

'I don't know. But I wondered if it might be . . .'

'*Oui?*'

'Some sort of black magic.'

Picquart laughed. 'Black magic? *Non.* You're an imbecile.'

'What, then?'

'This isn't about the devil. This is about Louis XIV. Do you know what Villayer was doing in the Cours des Miracles?'

'No.'

'He was trying to build a post office.' Villayer, Picquart explained, was a politician, a shrewd and particularly disloyal member of Louis XIV's Council of State. Every day, as a consequence of his position, he sent his servants out to deliver hundreds of messages and pick up hundreds of replies: political, commercial, philosophical, social, and sexual. But the bigger Paris grew, the more expensive and complex this network became, and the more obsessed Villayer became with its failures, drawing diagrams and annotating maps late into the night – many of his friends grew used to receiving notes that just read 'This is a test' – until at last he realised that the only constituency with which he now spent any real time was the pulsatile village of his own couriers. He decided that the capital needed a universal postal service, if only so that he could go back to being a real politician. Around that time, the journalist Henri Sauval was working on the Sun King's behalf to make every respectable citizen of Paris believe that the Court of Miracles was full of criminals and cultists. Really, it was just an impoverished square like any other, but Louis was in the process of reshaping the city by finding excuses to evacuate and demolish every section, no matter how small, that wasn't under his power. And Villayer saw that if he put Paris's main post office in the middle of the Court of Miracles, he could expose Sauval's manipulations, and perhaps save the Court's inhabitants from losing their homes. He not only signed his own death warrant, therefore, but countersigned it too: Louis didn't want a postal service in Paris, because he didn't know if he could control it, and he especially didn't want a post office in the Court of Miracles. So he had Villayer snatched on his way home from a banquet and beaten to death.

Lavicini learned all this because through de Gorge he'd met several of the King's closest advisors. And when Lavicini warned Sauvage in the letter, it was because Sauvage was about to make a very similar mistake. The first public transport in Paris was a fleet of carriages that Sauvage himself had installed. Half a dozen strangers could ride together and they only had to pay five sous each. He'd paid Blaise Pascal to design the routes, working from some of Villayer's old maps, so that they would be optimal down to the yard, an endeavour that Pascal later spent an unsuccessful week trying to adapt into a strategic board game. But the carriages were still slow. The streets of Paris were too crowded. So Sauvage had the idea of using the abandoned quarries under the city for the world's first underground public carriage system. Once again, Louis didn't want that because he didn't know if he could control it. 'Lavicini was warning Sauvage that if he carried on with the plan, Louis would have him killed just like he had Villayer killed,' concluded Picquart. ' "If you persist in your intention to conquer those dark lower depths, then you will soon find yourself entombed in them." *Comprends?* And that is just what happened. A hundred years later, de Crosne started burying our dead in the Catacombs, but Louis and his assassins were avant-garde in that respect.'

There was something about the eyes of Picquart's biggest cat had always made Scramsfield feel sick, and at that moment he realised for the first time that they were the same pale yellow-green as a medicine he'd been given for an ear infection as a child.

'*Erstaunlich*,' said Loeser. 'May I ask one more question?'

'If you wish.'

'What happened to Lavicini? What was the Teleportation Accident, really?'

'You suspect that was "black magic", too?'

'I don't know.'

'No. It was an assassination attempt. Gunpowder. When the Théâtre des Encornets collapsed, it was nothing to do with Lavicini's machine. It was because Louis was in the audience that night. After he moved the court to Versailles, he hardly ever came to Paris. So if you wanted to kill him, you had to take every chance you could get. Even if you killed a lot of others in the process.'

'Who was it?'

'*Aucune idée*. Could have been the English. Could have been the Spanish. Could have been anyone. Louis had a lot of enemies, even more than the average tyrant. Sauvage had a son who disappeared around that time. Sons are vengeful. Does that answer all your questions?'

'Yes. Thank you.'

'Loeser, Picquart and I have a bit of business to do,' said Scramsfield. 'You may as well go.'

'All right. See you at Zelli's, Scramsfield.'

After Loeser had left, Scramsfield said, 'Was all that true? What you told him?'

Picquart shrugged. '*Bof*. All theories. Villayer, Sauvage, Lavicini – it was all three hundred years ago. *Personne n'en saitrien*. But he didn't want theories, he wanted facts. So I gave him facts.'

A few days later, just before one o'clock, on one of those cruel April mornings that are spread out across the sky like a Norb etherised upon a hotel chaise longue, Scramsfield sat outside the café on the Rue de l'Odéon writing a letter to his parents. A blond man walked up to the door of Shakespeare and Company, but instead of trying the handle, he just took out his watch. After wiping his front teeth with a napkin, Scramsfield got up, hurried towards the man, slowed to a saunter before he got near enough to be noticed, and then carried on past. A few steps further on, as a considerate after-thought, he paused, turned, and said, 'Looking for Sylvia? She's closed until two.'

Scramsfield watched for the gratitude in the man's face, but there was none. 'I'm not, actually,' the man said. 'I'm meeting someone here.' That explained it: he was English. 'Who are you?' he added.

'Just a friend of Miss Beach's.'

'And you make it your business to loiter outside the shop, informing every potential customer of its opening hours? Does she pay you for that? Odd sort of friendship.'

'I just happened to be walking past—'

'No, you weren't. I saw you in that café. Are you about to sell me something? You have that air.'

Scramsfield was taken aback. 'I'm not some sort of confidence man, if that's what you're implying.'

'I wasn't implying anything so glamorous. But perhaps that is how you regard yourself. I suppose you were hoping I was a rich American?'

'Look here, I'm very well respected in Paris—'

'Oh yes?'

'Yes.' Scramsfield drew himself up to his full height. 'In fact, the one man in Paris I don't know is the man who can give me a decent American haircut.' But this time he didn't get the tone of the joke right, so that it sounded as if he were affirming the existence of a specific individual of that description whose acquaintance he believed it morally unsound to make.

'I see. In that case, did you ever meet Adele Hitler?'

Scramsfield did remember the name, but for once he was afraid to exaggerate. 'I don't think so. Who is she?'

'A rich girl I know from Berlin. Pretty little beast. She ran off to Paris, so I arranged to be introduced to her parents, and then I talked them into paying for me to come out here and hunt her down and bring her home like Urashima Taro.'

'Have you found her?'

'After about three minutes of asking around, I found out she's not in Paris any more. Apparently she decided to go on to Los Angeles. But I haven't told the parents yet because they're paying my expenses. I think I can string it out here for about another week. Then I might see if they'll send me to America. You see, I'm a parasite of sorts too. It's not so shameful, if one plays the game with some conviction. Which I'm afraid you don't.'

'If you know where she is, why are you still asking about this girl?'

'I'm told she didn't have enough money to have her luggage sent on after her,' said the Englishman. 'So it's still in Paris. But no one seems to know where.'

'Why do you need her luggage? To send back to the parents?'

'No. At the Strix the night before last I met a certain scion of the House of Grimaldi who became friendly with Miss Hitler while she was in Paris but couldn't persuade her to stay here with him. He's offering several thousand francs for a parcel of her unlaundered underwear.'

Scramsfield scratched his ear. 'Is that right? Well, nice to meet you. I'd better get back to . . . uh, I'd better get back.'

Relieved that the encounter was over, Scramsfield returned to his table at the café. After a few minutes he saw a second fellow walk up to Shakespeare and Company and greet the Englishman he'd just spoken to. They embraced and then ambled off together, just as Scramsfield remembered where he'd first heard the name Adele Hitler.

After they'd parted at Picquart's apartment, Scramsfield hadn't particularly expected ever to see Egon Loeser again. He didn't like to stay friends with people who had seen him at his worst. But if he found Loeser and told him about Adele Hitler going to Los Angeles, then surely the German would have to buy Scramsfield a steak. Or at least a few brandies. And for once Scramsfield wouldn't even have to lie.

The first place he looked for Loeser was the Flore. But the bar was nearly empty, and he was about to make for Zelli's when he felt a tap on the shoulder. The scent of peppermint was so strong that even before he turned he knew it would be Dufrène.

'Hello, Fabrice.'

'Scramsfield, *pauvre con*, what is this the Armenian says about you and the cheques?'

'The Armenian?'

'Someone bails him. He comes looking for you. He says it's your fault he goes to jail in the first place.'

'That's ridiculous. It was just rotten luck. I did everything I could.'

'You should tell him, then. Because he's angry. He says he's killing you. He says he's ripping your balls off.'

How apt, thought Scramsfield. 'Just a misunderstanding. Thanks for letting me know, buddy. I'm going to go and find him right now and tell him what really happened and then we'll both be laughing about it. Simple as that.'

'I hope so. For your sakes.'

Outside the Flore, Scramsfield looked around, but to his relief there was no sign of the Armenian, just two curly-haired boys in sailor suits poking a dead tabby cat with sticks. He decided it might be best if he got out of Paris for a while. A nice impromptu countryside vacation, just a month or two, working on the novel, until the Armenian calmed down. (Or got taken back to jail.) In principle, there was nothing to stop him leaving a message for Loeser about the girl before he got on the train. But then there would be no way for Loeser to buy him that steak. No, he'd give him the news when he got back. Paris was a joy this time of year. It wouldn't do Loeser any harm to wait a little while.

Part II

Ten pins in a map

4
LOS ANGELES, 1935

The Chateau Marmont

The splinter of reflected sunlight in the drop of water that clung trembling in the breeze to the thin blue nylon of a swimming costume just at the spot where it stretched tautest over the apex of the mound of Venus of a redhead in tortoiseshell sunglasses who lay smoking a cigarette on a reclining chair beside the oval swimming pool of the Chateau Marmont on Sunset Boulevard: that was Loeser as he stood in his underpants at the window of his hotel room on the morning after his arrival in Los Angeles. He, too, hung in that drop of water, every parameter of his lust encoded in the coefficients of its surface tension, quite ready, if it dried up in the sun-doubled skin-heat, to dry up with it. Then the redhead noticed him and he dived out of sight so fast he nearly twisted his ankle.

Had Loeser ever had sex? He supposed he probably had, but the memory was by now so dim that he almost wondered if in fact someone else had just described sex to him once and he'd gradually come to miscategorise it as an experience of his own, as one sometimes does with incidents that took place in childhood. At this point he couldn't quantify his sexual frustration any more than he could weigh his own brain. Perhaps it directed everything he said and did. There was no way to be sure. It was too much a part of him. Unlike his penis, which he now regarded as a sort of ungrateful hitchhiker, a fatuous vestigium.

He sat down on his bed. Since he couldn't go back to the window for a while, he decided he might as well set the clock to *Midnight at the Nursing Academy*. Although he hadn't intended to stay more than a short time in Paris, he didn't like to be separated from the photo album even for a day, so he'd taken it with him when he left Berlin and now it had unexpectedly come with him all the way to America. Last night he'd checked into the hotel so late that he hadn't bothered to unpack, so it would still be in the suitcase, which lay unfastened on the floor beside the bed like a drunk passed out with an open mouth, hidden there between his second-favourite white shirt and his third-favourite white shirt.

Except he soon found that it wasn't.

In a state of overflowing panic not unlike the one that had accompanied his loss of Adele Hitler at the corset factory all that time ago, he flung item after item out of the suitcase until there was nothing left to fling, and then he started clawing idiotically at the suitcase's inner corners. It was gone. But he was sure he'd packed the book that last afternoon in his steamship cabin. And he was sure he hadn't taken it out of the suitcase since then. The only time he'd lost sight of his travelling companion was when he was going through customs at New York Harbour, just before asserting in a questionnaire that he was not insane, leprous or syphilitic, that he did not live by prostitution, and that he had no intention of assassinating the President of the United States.

They'd stolen it. The custom officers had rooted through his luggage like organ harvesters through a torso, just as they were entitled to do, and found the book, and then instead of reporting it as contraband, they'd stashed it in a locker, to take home or sell on. He should have bribed someone. And now it was too late.

Loeser had owned *Midnight at the Nursing Academy* for nearly seven years. He'd had a far longer relationship with the delightful women in that book than he'd ever had with any human female. He knew, by heart, like a poem, every beckoning expression, every obliging pose. He often felt he owed it his sanity. The loss of it was unthinkable, somewhere on the scale between a wedding ring and a first-born child. He would definitely be willing to assassinate the President of the United States over this. Or at least forcibly infect him with syphilis.

Trying to stay calm, he smoked a cigarette, got dressed, and left the hotel. Outside, on Sunset Boulevard, a bungalow sat in the middle of the road. At first, Loeser couldn't work out what he was seeing, and then he realised that the house had been jacked up on to a steel frame and attached to a flatbed lorry. As the lorry turned a corner, one corner of the house's beige tiled roof had snagged on a telephone pole, and now two men in overalls stood beside it, arguing about what to do, as a queue of cars built up behind the surreal blockage. What were the penalties, Loeser wondered, for being drunk in charge of a family home?

Even in this part of Hollywood, where exhaust fumes hung thickly around the palm trees, Los Angeles smelled unnaturally good. Loeser didn't understand it. The whole city felt like an apartment for sale, which the estate agent had sprayed with perfume just prior to a viewing. The sun here was strange, too. You found yourself locked in a staring contest with the daylight, waiting for it to blink, but it never did. Meanwhile, there was both a remarkable clamour of signs and advertisements on every building and a remarkable proportion of pedestrians mumbling to themselves as they went past, as if nothing in this nation was capable of holding its peace.

Cut-Rate Books

In rebellion against its habitat, the shop was gloomy, malodorous, and almost as disordered with books as Picquart's apartment in Paris. A short-wave radio hummed jazz as if it had forgotten the tune. By the door was a rack of magazines:

Broadway Brevities, Smokehouse Monthly, Police Gazette, Captain Billy's Whiz-Bang, Artists and Models, Spicy Romances, Jazza-Ka-Jazza, Hot Dog, Paris Nights. Loeser picked up a paperback at random from a pile: *An Encyclopedia of the Carnal Relations Between Human Beings and Animals* by Gaston Dubois-Desaulle. He picked up another: *Women in Love* by D.H. Lawrence.

'You looking for anything in particular?'

Loeser looked up. The man behind the counter had a strong jaw like an actor but also a mesh of acne scars on both cheeks. He wore glasses with thick black frames and a wool tie. 'Yes. A book called *Midnight at the Nursing Academy.*'

'Publisher?'

'I can't remember,' said Loeser, realising that this was like knowing someone for years and never bothering to ask where they grew up. 'It's French. Hardcover. Twenty-eight photographs.'

'Never came across that one.'

'Where do you think I could get it, then? I'll pay anything.'

The man took a sip from a cracked mug of coffee. 'You might have some trouble. Stores like this can't carry books like that. Anything "deemed flagitious by general consent", you got to take your chances with the international mail. Might be a few copies in private collections but that's probably about all.'

'Private collections?'

'Yeah. Plenty around. But people don't tend to advertise them. There's a few everybody knows about, like the Gorge library, but those ain't a hell of a lot of use.' He had one of the most brutally cacophonous American accents Loeser had ever heard; no one who spoke like this, surely, could ever have any success in life.

'What's the Gorge library?' said Loeser.

'Wilbur Gorge. The automobile-polish guy. His collection's supposed to be the biggest in the country – maybe the biggest in the world. Up at his mansion in Pasadena. I don't know anybody who's ever seen it, though. Might be bullshit. But if anybody has your book, he probably has it.'

'I see. Thank you for your help.' Loeser was about to depart when he noticed a copy of *Stifled Cry* by the cash register. 'You stock Stent Mutton?'

'Very popular with our customers.'

'What's his latest?'

The man took down a title called *Assembly Line*.

'What about Rupert Rackenham?'

'Nothing by him, no.'

'I'm glad to hear it.' It wasn't yet noon, but Loeser hadn't had breakfast, so he said, 'In addition, I want to try an American hamburger sandwich. Which is the best?'

'The best in Hollywood or the best in Los Angeles?'

These two designations were not yet quite distinct in Loeser's mind, but he had an idea that the latter was more comprehensive. 'The best in Los Angeles.' Should he have said the best in California?

'For my money, that's Nickel's over in Pacific Palisades.' The man took a business card out of his jacket pocket, wrote on the back with a pencil, and handed it to Loeser.

'12203 Sunset Boulevard,' Loeser read. 'And I'm on Sunset Boulevard already. So it's just further on west from here?'

'Yeah, it's a pleasant drive.'

Drive! Loeser had heard about this: the bizarre American hatred of travelling anywhere on foot. They would think nothing of getting in their car even if their destination was on the very same street. 'I shall walk,' he said.

'Wouldn't do that. It's a long way.'

'Don't worry, I'm from the Old World. I'm used to walking.' As he strolled whistling out of the shop, Loeser heard the proprietor shout something after him, but he ignored it. The business card was still in his hand, so he turned it over to read the other side: WALLACE BLIMK – BOOKSELLER. Before he had lunch, he thought, he would work up a decent appetite. Four hours later, he collapsed by the side of the road.

Sunset Boulevard

As a result, no doubt, of some bureaucratic oversight, Sunset Boulevard had a beginning and a middle but no end. The coast was not far now, but Sunset Boulevard probably just rolled on down the beach and into the water and onward to Shanghai. Quite early on, Loeser had realised that the numbers he could see on the buildings were nowhere near 12203, but since they seemed to rise every block in random increments, that hadn't, unfortunately, been enough to discourage him. So he had carried on, more determined with every step to eat the best hamburger in Los Angeles, and by the time he fainted, just next to a sign advertising a pet cemetery, he had already walked further than he'd ever walked in his life. For long stretches, there had been houses but no pavement, or not even houses, just orchards and an occasional petrol station or diner, and he'd trudged over grass or gravel, as cars zoomed mockingly past. The sun beat like a gin hangover, and on his right the mountains had caught the afternoon light, dandled it, and released it again. Who had designed this set and why had no one told them they were going much too far?

'Are you all right?' A spaniel-eyed woman in a gingham dress was touching his shoulder. 'Do you need a glass of water? My house is just here. I think you dropped your book.'

Embarrassed and unsteady, braised in his own brine, Loeser got to his feet, picked up *Assembly Line*, and followed the woman to her porch.

'Where's your car?' she said when he was gratefully seated. As well as the glass of water, she'd brought him a chocolate chip cookie.

'I don't drive.'

'You lost your licence?'

'No. I never learned.' She gave him a look of concern as if she were wondering whether he was defective or just poor, so he added, 'I'm from Germany.'

'Oh. How do you like America?'

'It's preposterous.'

On his forced march, Loeser had realised that the great advantage of living in this senselessly stretched-out place would be that you would never bump into anyone ever again. Years before, as an optimistic recent university graduate, he had thought that the best thing about Berlin was that you couldn't so much as go out for a coffee without coming across half a dozen people you knew. Within a few months, he had concluded that this was actually the worst thing about Berlin. There, if you humiliated yourself trying to get someone to go to bed with you, you would then have to see them twice a week for the rest of your life – a welt on your world. Here, they would just vanish. Every ex-girlfriend, rival, creditor, parasite: avoiding them would only be a matter of not specifically seeking them out. It would be such a secure, logical way to live, fortified by dispersion against coincidence. He was proud enough of this observation that he had begun to compose a paragraph about it for his next postcard to Achleitner. Unfortunately, it was about to be ruined. 'Is that a Stent Mutton you've got there, by the way?' the woman said. 'I'm nuts for Stent Mutton.'

'Me too!'

'My husband knows him a little. They met at the Athletic Club. I hear his wife is awfully pretty. Their house isn't far from here.'

'Really?'

'Sure. Down there just this side of where the canyon meets the beach. You can't miss it. Looks like a sort of greenhouse.'

Loeser didn't know what he expected to find at Mutton's house, but just visiting the holy site would be enough to justify the day's ordeal. He drained his glass of water and looked out to sea.

The sun was in Loeser's eyes as he walked west, so it wasn't until he was quite near by that he got a good look at his destination, and beheld an implausible snag in the ontology of this foreign land. There, on a rise that sloped affably down to the beach, was the Blumstein residence in Schlingesdorf – tugged all the way from Berlin, it seemed, by some tireless amphibious cousin of the lorry he'd seen stuck on Sunset Boulevard. In every dimension it was identical, and yet the weird light of this land had done something to it, parsed it as a homonym, the same structure with a different result: back in Berlin, even in summer, the house was a jar for pickling clouds, but here in the glare the glass walls looked aqueous, unsolid, a cage of refraction. On the patio, next to the swimming pool, a blonde woman sat at a redwood dining table writing a letter. She looked up as Loeser approached.

'Is this Stent Mutton's house?' he said.

'That's right. I'm his wife.'

'My name is Egon Loeser. I'm from Berlin. I've come to see Mr Mutton.' Which was not quite a lie, thought Loeser, because he would very much have liked to meet the author, but was also not quite honest, because it rather implied he had an appointment, perhaps that he had crossed the Atlantic expressly for this long-scheduled colloquy.

'You should have called ahead. I'm afraid he's not seeing anyone today. He's resting inside. We just got back last night and the journey was a horror.'

'Got back?'

'From Moscow.' Mutton's wife took off her sunglasses in an interrogative sort of gesture. When the woman in the gingham dress had said she was awfully pretty, that had been an almost slanderous understatement. And there was a sugary, heliotropic ripeness to her body that made her look as if she couldn't have been cultivated in any other climate. 'You're from Berlin, you said? How long do you plan to stay in Los Angeles?'

'No more than two weeks.'

'You're an artist of some sort. Or a writer, maybe.'

'I work in the theatre. How did you know?'

'You have that look. My husband and I know only a little about the situation in Germany, Mr Loeser, but we know it's very difficult.' What did she mean? Difficult to get laid unless you were Brecht? Was she about to invite him to pillage her quietly in the bushes? 'I don't know what kind of welcome you've had out here so far, but I can assure you we're both very sympathetic to exiles. Especially those of you who simply want to continue your creative work in peace. I wonder if you've heard of an organisation called the Cultural Solidarity Committee of California?'

'I'm afraid not.' Loeser was feeling a bit insulted about being described as an exile.

'My husband and I are founding patrons. And that's not because we're saints, by the way.' She smiled. 'We have ulterior motives. I can't count how many fascinating men and women we've met through the Committee. As it happens, we're having a small reception here this evening. Perhaps you'd like to join us. You could see my husband then. I'm sure we'd both love to hear about your escape. Each story we hear seems to be more exciting than the last.'

'I'd be delighted,' said Loeser. (Escape from what?)

'Until tonight, then. A pleasure to meet you, Mr Loeser.'

'Before I go: I'm curious about your house.'

'Yes, aren't we lucky? We've only just moved in. It was finished while we were in Russia. The architect is a compatriot of yours named Gugelhupf. We brought him to Los Angeles last year so that he could adapt the design precisely to the terrain and the climate. He's very scientific.'

'I see.'

'And afterwards he decided to stay in America. We took that as a compliment! You may be able to meet him later.'

Instead of walking back up to Sunset Boulevard, Loeser decided to go for a stroll along the beach. The tide was going out and big spaghetti clods of yellow seaweed lay drying on the sand. After a while he came to a hotdog stand from which he bought three hotdogs and a bottle of Coca Cola, and then he took off his shoes and sat down just beyond the limit of the waves to read *Assembly Line*, salt foam snapping at his feet like a tethered animal.

Holidays to Moscow, cultural charities, afternoon naps in an auto-plagiaristic Bauhaus villa: Loeser had begun to worry that Mutton's gorgeous wife might have neutered him. But he was reassured by this latest novel, which was Mutton's most savage yet. His industrialists and aristocrats had never been so grotesque, nor his narrator so remorseless. Loeser read it through twice, by which time the sun had started to slump into the sea, and he spent the next hour watching the sky like an opera, hardly able to believe that he'd been reduced to slack-jawed tears by something as trite and self-congratulatory as a Pacific sunset.

By the time he'd recovered his composure it was nearly nine. He'd heard parties started early in America, so he walked back up to the luminescent fishtank. Sure enough, there were a handful of people standing on the patio, and as he approached he caught a few sentences of the nearest conversation. '. . . And I told the man, I don't want synthetic violets in my cologne any more than I want synthetic lemon juice in my gin fizz! I don't give a damn if it smells the same and I don't give a damn if "everyone uses it", I'm not spraying myself with something called methyl heptin carbonate, it sounds like poison gas. Then I gave him that line from *Midsummer Night's Dream* – you know, "but earthlier happy is the rose distilled", and so on – but he didn't know what I was talking about. I don't think I'll be going to *that* store again.' The man talking wore a powder-blue three-piece suit with pearl buttons; a white shirt with a collar pin; a bow tie, pocket handkerchief, and socks that were all red with white polka dots; and black patent leather brogues with perforated uppers. He spoke in a professorial and mildly self-mocking drawl. When he caught sight of Loeser coming up the slope, he broke off and said, 'Now, what do we have here? A beachcomber?'

'I'm a guest of Mrs Mutton,' said Loeser. 'Do you know where she is?'

'Oh, you're one of my wife's charming pet Europeans! I believe she's in the kitchen.'

'Actually I'm looking for Mr Mutton's wife.'

'Yes, as I say, Dolores is in the kitchen.'

'I mean Stent Mutton, the writer.'

The man exchanged a bemused glance with the elderly Japanese fellow he'd been talking to. 'Is this the start of a radio comedy routine? I am "Stent Mutton, the writer". Who are you?'

'I'm Egon Loeser. But you can't be . . .'

'I can't be what?'

'But where's your knife?' Loeser blurted.

'If you want to cut a cigar there's a guillotine in the drawing room.'

Stent Mutton was a scarred, hulking ex-criminal who only scratched out his raw narratives to exorcise the horrors through which he'd lived. Loeser knew this. But he was now trying to remember how he knew it. He was trying to remember whether he'd really read it somewhere, or whether he'd just promoted an assumption to fact.

'I see you've brought one of my penny dreadfuls,' said Mutton, pointing at the paperback that Loeser had forgotten he was still holding in his hand. 'Did you want me to sign it?'

Loeser took a step back. He didn't want this man defacing his book. A signature from the real Stent Mutton would have been marvellous. But not a signature from this impostorous dandy. He shook his head and hurried on into the house. Whereupon:

141

'Egon! What an unexpected pleasure!'

'No,' said Loeser in German. 'No, no, no, no, no, no.'

'Aren't you happy to see me?' said Rackenham, who was holding a martini and looked almost parodically tanned and healthy.

'What the fuck are you doing in Los Angeles?'

'I'm supposed to be finding Adele Hitler and persuading her to go back to Berlin. But I haven't got very far. And what are you doing here? Don't tell me you've come for Adele too? I can see by your face that you have. But I presume you're not getting paid by her parents, like I am. Have you really come six thousand miles just to have sex with her?'

'Do you know where she is?'

'Not yet. Were you in Paris, too?'

'Yes.'

'What a pity we didn't cross paths.'

'What a pity. How did you end up at this party?' The gathering reminded him of an evening at the Fraunhofens' before anyone got drunk.

'I know Mutton from the Hollywood Cricket Club. He's the only Yank on the team but he bats so well we can hardly make an issue of it. We're playing the Australians next month.'

'You're already in a cricket club? How long have you been out here?'

'Two or three months. No, it hasn't taken me too long to find my feet, if that's what you mean.'

'Where are you living?' said Loeser, because that, after all, was the sort of thing people asked at parties.

'I'm now the Sorceror of Venice Beach. What about you?'

'The Chateau Marmont.'

'I presume you don't intend to live in a hotel indefinitely?'

'I like it there,' said Loeser, thinking of the women around the swimming pool, 'and anyway, I'm not going to stay in Los Angeles long enough to need a house of my own. I'm just going to find Adele, seduce her, and take her back to Berlin with me.'

'Well, when that plan fails, I can recommend Pasadena. It's heavenly.'

'Where's that?'

'East of Hollywood. It's where the millionaires live. And, more importantly, their wives.'

'Like Wilbur Gorge?' said Loeser, remembering what Blimk had said earlier.

'Yes. How do you know Gorge?'

'I don't. Do you mean to say you do?'

'Yes. I have the sort of easy, genial relationship with the Colonel that you can only have with a man you're vigorously cuckolding.'

'Could you introduce me?'

'Why?'

'I just want to meet him,' said Loeser. 'It doesn't matter why.'

'I could get you an invitation to dinner, but what would I get out of it?'

'I'll owe you a favour. All right?'

'I suppose so. By the way, you know Hecht's here?'

'In Los Angeles or in this house?'

'Both. He's got a contract with Paramount. You might see Drabsfarben, too. And Gugelhupf.'

'I already knew about Gugelhupf. But the others? You can't be serious.'

'Half the Romanisches Café is here, Loeser. Or at least on its way.'

Loeser felt a heavy squelch of dismay. 'But the only thing I like about this place is that I don't have to see anyone I know!'

'Nonetheless.'

'Fucking hell, this is like going to the Alps for a tuberculosis cure and finding out everyone else in the sanatorium is determined to reinfect you. Well, as long as Brecht doesn't turn up, I won't have to jump into the ocean. Thank God I'm going home soon.'

'Mr Loeser! I'm so glad you could come.' Mutton's wife was radiantly at his side. 'I see you already know Mr Rackenham.'

'Yes. Mrs Mutton, before I forget, I don't have a car and I'm staying at the Chateau Marmont and I'm not quite sure how I'm going to get back to my hotel . . .'

'Oh, don't give it another thought, we'll have the butler drive you. Now, you must meet Mr Gould. He's a recent arrival from Berlin, like yourself.'

She led Loeser back out to the patio, where Gould turned out to be one of the men he'd passed on his way in. A tall fellow with a smile as big as an almond croissant, he was talking to Stent Mutton and two women. Dolores Mutton introduced Loeser to everyone. 'Yes, Mr Loeser and I have already met,' said her husband, raising an eyebrow.

One of the other women said, 'Mr Gould was just telling us about how he got out of Berlin.'

'Yes. As I said, the Nazis had tried to ban my latest book of poems. So, like a fool, I went to the police station to insert a complaint. They told me if I waited a few minutes I could see the police chief. So I sat down. Then, by luck, I overheard another policeman mention my name to one of his comrades. There was an order out to arrest me. But they did not realise yet that I had just walked right into their clutchings. So I waited until no one was watching and then I fled straight to the train station. I did not even go home to pack a bag, I just purchased a suitcase on the way and carried it, vacant, so I would look like a realistic tourist.'

'You sound so calm about it all,' said Dolores Mutton.

'Actually, never have I been so frightened!'

'Knowing that you can have everything taken from you just because you happen to be Jewish . . . I can hardly imagine what it must have been like, Mr Loeser.'

'Sorry?' His attention had wandered during Gould's boring anecdote.

'Tell me, how did you get out?' said her husband. 'Was it just as perilous?'

Loeser's old rule against lying about himself to impress had not formally been repealed. So he was about to inform the woman that he was not Jewish; that he 'got out' on a tourist visa, which had taken him ten minutes to acquire; and that never, in Berlin, had he felt himself in jeopardy, nor had he detected that anyone else was. But then he remembered Scramsfield. What punishment had ever befallen Scramsfield for his almost hallucinant level of dupery? Why should Loeser come all the way to Hollywood, where half the population punched their time cards every morning at the 'dream factory', and still stubbornly persist in correcting every flattering little misapprehension, while right now Scramsfield, a man who had shot his fiancée dead during sex and got away with it, was probably cheating his rent out of some tipsy dowager? Scramsfield swam in his lies like a penguin. Loeser waddled around damp and pretended to be dry. No more. Also, Mrs Mutton was far too beautiful to disappoint, and he'd already decided he didn't like Gould and didn't want him to win. So: 'Yes,' said Loeser. 'My escape was quite dramatic.'

'Go on.'

'They'd been tipped off that I was going to try to get across the border into France. But, you see, I'm a designer of theatrical effects. So I used an invention of mine called the Teleportation Device. From one side to the other as easily as an actor circling around from stage left to stage right without being seen.'

'How did it work?' said one of the women.

'I'm afraid I can't say anything about my invention while there is still a chance it may be in use. My first loyalty must be to my tribe.'

'Oh, yes, of course.'

The butler came to tell Dolores Mutton she was needed inside.

'So you were in the theatre?' said Gould. 'What was your last production before you left?'

'*Lavicini*,' said Loeser, even though it had never actually been performed.

'Oh. I did not see that. Still, I knew a lot of theatre persons – we must have crossed roads at some point. Were you at Brogmann's party with all the stolen brandy?'

'No.'

'What about when Vanel directed the nude ballet at the beach?'

'No.'

'I do not remember you coming on the big camping trip that Klein organised.'

'No.' Not only did Loeser not take part in any of these things, he didn't even remember getting invited to any of them. Who was this prick and why did think he could make Loeser feel as if he'd missed out on all this fun back in Berlin?

'How extraordinary that the two of you had to come all the way to the edge of another continent to meet for the first time,' said Stent Mutton.

'And now you are out here you will work for the movies, I assume, Herr Loeser?' said Gould.

'Why?'

'You are a set designer.'

'Yes. For the theatre. Not for the movies. I despise American movies.'

'That does not mean you will not be slurped in,' said Gould. 'I do not know why but the studio bosses seem to have a lot of respect for Germans. Like it or not, there is no better way for us to earn some livings in California. Look on Hecht. He is working for Goatloft.'

'Who's Goatloft?'

'He directed *Scars of Desire*. Very powerful. So Hecht is making five hundred dollars a week now. That is fifteen hundred marks, almost. He certainly has not been making that in Berlin.'

'Is it hard there, for writers?' said Stent Mutton.

'Sometimes. Especially if you do not get an allowance from your parents and you do not like living on credit. I used to work as a waiter.'

How fucking self-righteous, thought Loeser. 'Where?' he said.

'The Schwanneke,' said Gould.

To the assembled witnesses, what then happened was that somehow Loeser tripped over from a stable standing position. What actually happened, as only some sort of careful Muybridgean analysis could have made clear, was that he tried to thump Gould in the nose and instead threw a punch so inept that even its intended recipient could not confidently identify it as such. The problem was his legs, which were just beginning their slow transmutation into the elongated pine cones that can be found glued to the pelvis of anyone with Loeser's desultory level of physical fitness who wakes up the morning after a four-hour hike, and were therefore in no condition to perform a sudden vengeful charge. Neither, really, was Loeser himself, who hadn't had any warning that he was about to make an assault on Gould – he just heard 'Schwanneke' and without a word of internal debate he was forward, lunging, off balance, hand barely reconstituted into a viable fist. Scramsfield at Zelli's was Max Schmeling in comparison. And what would have been really regrettable for Loeser here was if he'd fallen into the nearby swimming pool as a result of his botched left hook. But he didn't, because Gould grabbed his shoulder to steady him. Then Loeser, confused, embarrassed, not wanting Gould's help, tried to push him away, overcompensated, slipped on a slice of lime that had defected from someone's gin and tonic, and fell into the swimming pool as a result of that instead. He hadn't even had a drink yet.

After he'd climbed out, Mutton suggested he go to the bedroom for a change of clothes. 'Take anything you want.'

'There's no need.'

'At least borrow a shirt.'

Loeser went dripping into the house, trying to ignore the stares and chuckles, and through into the main bedroom, where he selected a shirt and slacks from Mutton's enormous wardrobe. Just as in Blumstein's house, there was a bathroom off the main bedroom, and he decided to go in there to change so he could lock the door behind him. As he dried his hair with a towel, he noticed a pair of expensive pistachio-green French knickers lying on the floor next to the bath, and with all their lace and frills and bows they looked comically out of place, a pathogenic gland transplanted into this functionalist cuboid, ready to infect the whole structure with blisters of purposeless ornamentation unless it was annihilated first by some swift Loosian immune response. Loeser, who dearly loved underclothes with lace and frills and especially bows, and sometimes came close to tears when he saw some on a washing line because of the way they made his sexual longing twinge like an old bone fracture, found himself mesmerised for a while by the thought that this silk had only recently been soured and sweetened by the loins of a woman as ravishing as Dolores Mutton, and because of this unavoidable delay he was still buttoning his collar when he heard that same woman's voice through the door.

'No. You're asking too much this time. He's still my husband. What if he found out? I know you think he won't, but he's smarter than you'd like to believe. He might. He easily damn well might. And I'm not going to put him through that. It would finish him. I know you don't care, but what if he divorced me? Where the hell would we be then? You don't want that any more than I do. I'm not saying we have to stop this, of course I'm not, I know better than that, but there have to be limits. It's no good making threats, Jascha. I just can't. I'm sorry.'

'Jascha'! Could it really be Drabsfarben? Loeser pressed his ear to the door, but if there was a reply, it was too low to hear.

'Well, you picked a fine time to tell me that,' said Dolores Mutton after a while. 'It's crazy that we're even talking like this. You're always saying I need to be more discreet. Come here on Thursday morning, Stent's going to be out at the *Herald* offices most of the day. Now go. I'll follow you in a few minutes.'

Loeser heard the bedroom door open and close. Then the handle of the bathroom door turned until it clicked against the lock. 'Is somebody in there? Hello?' Loeser considered waiting until she went away, but that might turn into a siege. He unlocked the door. 'Oh, hello, Mr Loeser,' said Dolores Mutton. There was enough ice in her voice for a serviceable daiquiri. 'Perhaps I should have mentioned that we prefer our guests to use the other bathroom.'

'I'm sorry, Mrs Mutton, I was just changing my shirt.'

As he walked past her into the bedroom, she caught his arm, gripping hard. 'I don't know what you may have heard just now, but . . .' She paused. Part of him was mindlessly excited that her warm skin was on his. 'I don't care for gossip, Mr Loeser, and neither does my husband. Not at our parties, not in our home. I hope you will think about that before you say anything you may come to regret.' Then she released his arm, went into the bathroom, and slammed the door behind her. Loeser, shaken, decided to leave the party and walk down to the beach so he could think.

How could Jascha Drabsfarben have allowed himself to get tangled up with Dolores Mutton? In Berlin, a lot of girls had lusted after the composer, and, as far as Loeser could tell, it was because they knew that nothing they did could ever make him lust back. Hannah Czenowitz had once drunkenly confessed a fantasy in which she was on her knees sucking Drabsfarben's cock while he was composing at a grand piano and he was so absorbed in some complex non-standard key signature that he didn't even notice. There was some debate over whether he masturbated, and the consensus was that he probably did, about once a month, for reasons of psychological tidiness, but quickly, so he could get back to his music. Therefore occasional utilitarian intercourse didn't seem out of the question – but a furtive affair with a married woman would be far too distracting. Drabsfarben would never tolerate the drain on his time.

Then again, Loeser had heard that a lot of foreign writers found themselves blocked when they came to Hollywood. So perhaps Drabsfarben had lost his inspiration out here too, and for the first time he was trying to use a woman as a muse. You could certainly write symphonies about Dolores Mutton; you could write at least a scherzo about her cleavage alone. And however implausible it all seemed, Loeser knew what he'd just heard. The real question was whether to tell Stent Mutton. Yes, the man was a loathsome fraud. He'd lied to Loeser, albeit in a way Loeser couldn't really explain. But Loeser still loved his books. Knowing the truth about Mutton didn't make Mutton's characters feel any less real; in fact, maybe they seemed more real now, because if they couldn't be understood as mere analogues of their creator, then they could only be spontaneous births with a sort of mystifying independent life. And there was no question about what a Stent Mutton hero would do about all this. He would just walk over. Say what had to be said. In very short sentences.

Loeser went back to the house and found Stent Mutton on the patio next to the big barbecue grill.

'I see you found something to fit you all right.'

'Yes. Look here, Mr Mutton, I need to talk to you in private.'

'About what?'

'It's very important.'

Mutton followed him a short distance up the hill, away from the guests, into a forum of crickets.

'Well?'

'Just now, while I was changing, I overheard a conversation in your bedroom. It was between your wife and Jascha Drabsfarben, who's an old friend of mine from Berlin. I think they're having an affair.'

'What?'

Loeser was already beginning to realise that this was going to cause even more trouble than the last time he'd eavesdropped on Drabsfarben, but it was too late to turn back. Also, there was something about a conversation of this kind that made him feel enjoyably authentic and masculine. 'Your wife is being unfaithful to you with Drabsfarben,' he said. 'I heard enough to be sure and I thought you deserved to be told.'

'Is this another comedy routine?'

'No, Mr Mutton. I'm perfectly serious.'

Mutton sighed. 'This is the trouble with marrying a girl like Dolores. Most men realise they wouldn't know what to do if they had all that beauty to themselves, so they can't believe I do, either. They think I must let her share it around a little. But actually, Mr Loeser, my wife is devoted to me. She's not perfect and neither, goodness knows, am I. But we love each other as deeply today as we ever have. Nothing, and I mean nothing, could persuade her to betray me sexually with another man. If I know anything, I know that. You're wrong. And I strongly suggest you leave this party before you do any more eavesdropping.'

Probably Wilbur Gorge was just as confident, thought Loeser, and meanwhile Rackenham was ploughing his wife. If life up to this point had taught him anything, it was that everyone else was having sex with anyone they wanted, all the time, and it was naive ever to hope otherwise. 'If you'd heard what I heard—'

'I don't care what you think you heard. Please get off my property. I'm perfectly serious, too.'

Loeser hesitated.

'What now?' said Mutton.

'It's just that I don't have a car and your wife said your butler could drive me back to the Chateau Marmont.'

'Goodbye!' Mutton growled. Then he turned and went back to his party.

It was nearly ten. Loeser knew he couldn't walk back to Hollywood, unless he wanted to spend the rest of his life confined to a wheelchair, so he decided to go up to the corner of Sunset Boulevard and hail a cab. He'd left all his cash in his wet trousers, which were still hanging over the towel rail in the Muttons' bathroom, but he could pick up some more at the Chateau Marmont. However, after a long wait, he still hadn't seen a single vacant taxi, and anyway the traffic here was probably going too fast for anyone to see him and pull over. He would just have to cross the road to the diner he could see on the east side of Sunset Boulevard and ask them to telephone a cab company for him.

Loeser made several attempts at this, and each time he got less than halfway across the moat of tarmac before he saw some diesel-powered megalodon bearing hungrily down on him and he had to hurl himself back to safety on the shore. And of course there was no crossing visible in either direction. But what else was he supposed to do? Sleep under a bush? He was standing there on the grass, feeling a rising crepitation of despair, when he saw an unthreatening green car coming east up the perpendicular road. He stuck out his thumb and tried to look respectable.

The car stopped beside him, and the driver rolled down his window. 'Need a lift?'

'I'm trying to get to Hollywood.'

'I'm going all the way to Los Feliz.'

The driver leaned over to unlock the door on the passenger's side.

Loeser cleared his throat. 'Actually, I need to sit in the back.'

'What?'

'I can't ride in a private car unless I pretend it's a taxi.'

'Are you going to pay me?'

'No.'

The driver shrugged. He had the cleftest chin that Loeser had ever seen. 'Suit yourself, pal.'

So Loeser got in the back of the car. Even with this indulgence, he felt too uncomfortable to make conversation, so he just looked out of the window. They were soon passing the same roadside totems that Loeser had seen on the way here, great papier-mâché lemons and sausages and rabbits and candy canes and cowboy hats advertising various drive-in amenities for the easily pleased. In the afternoon sunlight they'd seemed flat, primitive, ridiculous, but now, at night, illuminated from below by bright bulbs, looming into view at forty miles an hour, they achieved a sort of fuzzy megalithic grandeur. Perhaps Achleitner had been right, Loeser thought with disgust. Kempinski's Haus Vaterland really was the future. California itself was nothing but a Kempinski colony, an amusement complex propagated into a republic. But then it occurred to him that if all your potential customers were whizzing by in their automobiles, then of course you had to make sure that your function could be apprehended from a distance in an instant. Hence this childishness. He remembered what Wagner had written to his wife on a visit to Venice a hundred and fifty years after Lavicini's death: 'Everything strikes one as a marvellous piece of stage-scenery. The chief charm consists in its all remaining as detached from me as if I were in an actual theatre; I avoid making any acquaintances, and therefore still retain that sense of it.'

Loeser shut the door quickly behind him to avoid contaminating the shop with sunlight or fresh air.

'You make it to Nickel's yesterday?' said Blimk.

'No. I met Stent Mutton, however.' Last night, by the time he got into bed, he'd been so tired that just closing his eyes had produced a plunging sensation, like the leg of a stool snapping beneath him. This morning he'd woken up late. He'd wanted to read for a while, but the only novel he'd brought with him to America was *Berlin Alexanderplatz*, and although after three hundred and nine pages it really felt like it might be about to get going, he thought he might need something more potent to distract him from the women around the swimming pool, so he'd come back to the shop.

'What's the guy like?'

Loeser was about to tell Blimk the awful truth about Stent Mutton when he noticed a pocket book on a pile near by and found himself drawn almost involuntarily to pick it up. It was called *Dames! And how to Lay them* by Clark Snable, and the cover had a childlike drawing of a woman lying naked in a bed, rumpled sheets exposing one enormous breast with a nipple that pointed upward and outward as if it were tracking the position of the moon. 'Tired of feeling like a cast-iron chump?' enquired the back cover. Loeser was definitely tired of feeling like a cast-iron chump. 'Want to learn all the famous secrets of sexually romancing huge quantities of toasty eager dames with real class any night of the week even Monday like it was easy?' Loeser definitely wanted to learn all the famous secrets of sexually romancing huge quantities of toasty eager dames with real class any night of the week even Monday like it was easy. He started to read. The paper stock was so cheap it felt almost moist, in the same way that dollar bills could feel moist, as if the book itself were gently sweating. After a while Blimk said, 'You want to sit down with that?'

'I promise I'll pay for it,' said Loeser.

'Don't mean to hassle you. Honestly, buddy, it's just nice to have somebody in here who isn't trying to jerk off all surreptitious.'

So Loeser sat down next to Blimk in his nest behind the counter. 'Have you read this?' Loeser said.

'No,' said Blimk.

'It's amazing. Apparently you can seduce any woman in under five minutes if you tell her a story about eating a peach on a rollercoaster, which makes her unconsciously think of sex, and then imply she's fat while touching her knee.'

'Bullshit.'

'No, it's proven. This man Clark Snable says he's done it four hundred times.'

Blimk grunted. He sat with his elbows on the counter and his head resting so heavily in his palms that his whole face was smeared into a melty grimace of total engrossment, so Loeser asked what he was reading. Blimk held up a magazine. It was called *Astounding Stories*, and on the cover was a lurid painting of a big green blob with lots of eyes and tentacles chasing two explorers through an icy cave, above a banner advertising a serial called 'At the Mountains of Madness' by H.P. Lovecraft.

'Who's H.P. Lovecraft?'

'Fella from Rhode Island. Writes stories about monsters from other dimensions. Cults. Human sacrifice. Alien gods. They're pretty good.'

'Really?'

'Sure. And some people think it ain't just fiction.'

'What do you mean?'

'Some people think it's all true.'

'But he writes for a magazine called *Astounding Stories*.'

'Yeah, but they think that's 'cause what he says is so shocking no newspaper will publish it in case it causes a panic. So the only way to get the truth out is to dress it up in a cheap Hallowe'en costume.'

'Who could possibly think that?'

'People in high places, I heard. Cordell Hull, the Secretary of State. He trusts Lovecraft more than he trusts his best military intelligence. He really thinks America is being menaced by ancient beings from beyond Euclidean space. That's the scuttlebutt.'

'That is absurd.'

'Yeah, maybe, but you can't blame a fella for wondering if there ain't more things in heaven and earth, et cetera et cetera. And I don't mean what you read in a Bible. Other things. Worse things.'

Loeser thought of Lavicini and all the mysteries of the Teleportation Accident. 'I suppose not.'

Blimk took out a pack of cigarettes and offered one to Loeser. 'Smoke so much these days I need a chimney in here.' He nodded up at a brown discoloured patch on the ceiling above his nest. 'Think I'm growing a stalactite.' They both lit up. 'Where you from, don't mind me asking?'

'Germany,' said Loeser.

'Oh yeah? What took you to Hollywood? Nazis kick you out?'

Loeser decided if he could be honest with anyone, he could be honest with a pornographer. 'Nothing to do with that. I'm looking for a girl.'

'She run off with somebody?'

'We were never actually attached.'

'You just like her a lot?'

'Yes.'

'You came all the way to America 'cause you had a crush on a girl? My mother'd call that sweet.'

'I'd never thought of it like that before. Yes, I suppose it is sweet. In a manner of speaking.'

'Romantic.'

'*Genau.*'

'Find her yet?'

'No. They have a whole shelf of California telephone directories at my hotel, and I went through all of them this morning. She's not listed. But she might have changed her name. Especially if she's going into the movies.'

'Think that's likely?'

'She's certainly pretty enough. And she's ambitious. I may have to ask around at the studios. I don't know what else to try.'

'You should hire a private dick. I know a fella down the block, you give him a week, he can find anybody in LA.'

Blimk wrote the address on another business card and Loeser paid him for *Dames! And how to Lay them.* 'Do you have anything by that Lovecraft fellow?'

Blimk went into the back room, looked through a filing cabinet, and returned with a magazine. 'This one's my favourite. "The Call of Cthulhu". You can borrow it but I need it back after.' It was a tattered copy of *Weird Tales* from 1928. This time, Lovecraft's name was only listed in small type on the cover, the editors apparently having been more excited about an opus called 'The Ghost Table' by Elliot O'Donnell, which was illustrated with a picture of a man with a pistol protecting a woman in a blue dress from a malevolent clawed heirloom. They would never have stood for that sort of thing at the Bauhaus, thought Loeser.

The Bevilacqua Detective Agency

The detective, whose office was above a cigar shop, had a smile that looked as if his mouth were being pulled back at the corners by fishing hooks. 'Take a seat,' he said. 'What can I do for you?'

'Wallace Blimk recommended you,' said Loeser. 'I'm trying to track down a girl. She only arrived in Los Angeles a few months ago.'

As Loeser spoke, Bevilacqua had unwrapped a cherry lollipop and put it in his mouth. When he wasn't sucking it he rested it carefully in an ashtray. 'She making any special effort not to be found?' he said.

'I doubt it.'

'Should be straightforward, then. Cost you twenty dollars a day plus expenses.'

'Is this mostly what you do? Missing persons?'

'About half that. And about half adultery. Someone thinks their spouse is having an affair and I find out for them.'

'You do a lot of that?'

'Plenty,' said Bevilacqua, in a tone suggesting there was barely a marriage west of the Rockies he hadn't helped to snuff out.

'Tell me: when you tell a man that his wife is sleeping with someone else, what's his reaction?'

'Furious,' said Bevilacqua, making an emphatic gesture with his lollipop. 'But only until they see the proof. After that, they're just grateful. Real grateful. It's pathetic, sometimes. Embarrassing. The women, they just go quiet, in my own personal experience. Now, let's get down to business. What can you tell me about this girl?'

'Her birth name is Adele Hitler. She's twenty-two. Black hair, blue-green eyes. Speaks good English with a heavy German accent.'

Bevilacqua looked up from his notebook. 'Cute?'

'Pardon me?'

'Is she good-looking?'

Loeser was silent for a moment, then he got up. 'I'm sorry. I've changed my mind. I hope I haven't wasted too much of your time.'

'What's the matter?'

'Goodbye, Mr Bevilacqua.'

Loeser hurried out of the office. There had been something in the expression on Bevilacqua's face just then that had made Loeser certain that if he found Adele he would fuck her. After all, in Stent Mutton books, private detectives always fucked every single woman involved in the case, from the client's daughter down to the nearest hat-check girl. After what had happened with Rackenham, he wasn't going to hand Adele over to another blithe predatory male if he could possibly avoid it. Unless he could enlist a private detective who was certified by three reliable doctors as impotent, he was just going to have to find her without help. He looked around at the bustle of Sunset Boulevard. Just as a past drought would show for ever in the rings of a tree, the Depression was still there in Berlin under the new bark if you knew where to look, but Los Angeles did not feel as if it had ever gone thirsty.

The Mutton House

Carrying his new camera on a leather strap around his neck, Loeser cut diagonally across the prosperous scrubland at the side of the road so that he would be at least partially occluded by bushes as he approached the patio of the house. At first, there was no sign of Dolores Mutton, but when he got closer he saw her through the glass, in the kitchen, eating an orange; all of a sudden the Gugelhupf design seemed as if it were specifically intended for easy surveillance. Drabsfarben evidently hadn't arrived yet, so Loeser sat down in the shade of a tree, brushed the dust from his trousers, and waited. Dozing emeraldine on a rock a few feet away was a lizard not unlike Mordechai. The smell of the ocean came in on the breeze, such a mild musk for such a huge animal.

Just before noon, a car drew up outside the house and the composer got out and went into the house. Crouching very low, Loeser moved towards the patio. Drabsfarben and Dolores Mutton stood in the sitting room, both already in postures of anger as if they had never interrupted their argument from the party two nights ago. Loeser took a few photos, but he needed them at least to kiss if he was going to

159

force Stent Mutton to admit he was wrong and then luxuriate in the gratitude that Bevilacqua had insisted would follow.

'What the heck are you doing?'

Loeser's heart bounced like a tennis ball. He turned. A stocky boy in a denim shirt stood there with a big brown paper bag under one arm.

'I'm a friend of the Muttons,' said Loeser.

'Sure you are,' said the boy. Then he grabbed Loeser by the collar with his free hand and led him roughly down the slope towards the house, shouting 'Mrs Mutton! Mrs Mutton!'

Dolores Mutton came out on to the patio. 'What is it?'

'I was on my way here with your groceries and I saw this creep hiding up there taking pictures. He's a prowler or something. He sounds foreign.'

'Thank you very much, Greg. I know this man. He's bothered us before. You did just the right thing.'

'Want me to wait here while you call the cops?'

'No, there's no need. I'll deal with him. Just leave the groceries.'

Greg put down the bag and she took five dollars out of her purse and gave it to him. When he was gone, Loeser whimpered, 'I just came for my shirt and trousers.'

'Why were you taking photos of us?'

'The house. It's such an architectural—'

'Like hell.' She snatched the camera from him, then hurled it against the barbecue grill. It hit with a clang and then dropped to the tiles. The sunlight writhed in her blonde hair like a trapped thing. 'Let me tell you something, Herr Loeser. I have watched Jascha end a man's life. Have you ever cut a pomegranate in half and turned the halves inside out to get at the seeds? Do you remember the sound that it makes? Jascha can end a man's life with a sound not too different from that, and certainly no louder. I was there once and I heard it. If you ever try anything like this again – if you speak one more word out of turn to my husband – Jascha will kill you and

160

make it look like an accident. I wouldn't be able to stop him even if I wanted to. That camera is going in the trash with your clothes, and I don't want to see you within a mile of this house as long as you live. Got that?' Loeser was too shocked to reply, so she repeated, louder, 'Have you got that?'

'Yes. I see. Fine. Thank you. Goodbye.'

Loeser turned and ran.

He was terrified, but he knew he shouldn't be, because what he'd just heard from Dolores Mutton was only a figurative threat. Surely. A vivid, detailed, persuasive, and chilling but still one hundred per cent figurative threat. Drabsfarben wasn't a murderer. Loeser was certain of that. Then again, he'd been certain that Drabsfarben wasn't a fornicator. He didn't know anything. Still, what kind of lunatic would risk the electric chair to cover up a transgression as minor as infidelity? Maybe a Stent Mutton character. But no one in the real world. If only he could ignore the piano wire he'd heard tightening in her voice. 'For beauty is nothing but the beginning of terror, which we are still just able to endure, awed because it serenely disdains to destroy us. Every angel is terrifying.' That was Rilke. Obviously at some point old Rainer had crossed Dolores Mutton.

The Gorge House

By now Loeser was all too familiar with California architecture and its vacuous hybrids of Gothic, Tudor, Mission, and so on, but the enormous red-roofed Gorge mansion was such an arbitrary and oxymoronic pidgin of styles that it might have been assembled as part of a game of Exquisite Corpse. Everywhere there were columns, turrets, arches, trellises, balconies, arabesques, and gargoyles, none of which seemed to have any reason for existence beyond making you thirsty for a tall glass of iced Gugelhupf. Still, it did have a strange charm, and the garden at the front of the house was elated with flowers. Waiting on the verandah after he rang the bell, Loeser thought for a moment that he saw someone watching him from the driver's seat of a black Chevrolet parked at the end of the street, but before he could be sure the front door swung open and he was shown into the house by Gorge's personal secretary, an epicene fellow called Woodkin.

'Colonel Gorge is in his study, but he will be down in a moment. Please come through to the parlour.'

The previous afternoon, on his return to the Chateau Marmont, Loeser had been given a telephone message from Rackenham: 'I'm having supper with Gorge tomorrow night and I've told him I'm going to bring a guest. Short notice but you have no friends here so I assume you're available. Come at seven and try not to be too dour.' Partly because of that last instruction, and partly because it would justify having accidentally packed the absurd item, he was wearing a tie his great aunt had given him, which had an ugly repeated pattern of clock faces. He didn't really have a plan for the evening. ('Yes, Colonel Gorge, I should be delighted to have a tour of the house. Will it by any chance include your legendary giant vault of "rare books"?') 'Am I the first to arrive?' he said.

'No, Mr Rackenham is already here. Would you like anything to drink?'

'Whisky, please.'

'I'm afraid Colonel Gorge does not allow liquor in the house.' Woodkin's diction was so gracefully servile that it didn't sound like he was speaking out loud so much as just drawing your attention to a particular combination of semantic units that he wondered if you might find appealing.

'What do you mean?' said Loeser.

'No alcohol whatsoever. He's very strict.'

'O brave new world. Well, I mean, do you have any cologne? Surgical spirit? Cooking wine? Anything of that kind?'

'I'm afraid not.'

'What do people normally drink here?'

'The Colonel prefers ginger ale.'

The 'parlour' was about the size of a cathedral nave. Rackenham stood at the opposite end, practically out of earshot, studying a portrait of a muscular grey-haired man with a grim, almost demented gaze and the sort of moustache that could beat you in an arm-wrestling contest. There were ten such portraits hung around the room, and as he waded through the thick golden carpet to join Rackenham, Loeser happened to pause and look around him, and realised that the steel spokes of their regard converged on an invisible axle precisely where he stood. He let out an involuntary squeak of fear and hopped out of the way, then hurried on. Rackenham nodded hello, and Loeser saw that the engraved brass label on the frame of the nearest portrait read 'HIRAM GORGE: 1854–1911'. He glanced at its peers on the left and right. 'I don't understand,' he said. 'The face in all of these paintings is the same. I mean, it's not just a family resemblance – they're identical.'

'I'm sure you can guess the explanation,' said Rackenham.

Loeser gasped. '*Mein Gott*, you mean Gorge is some sort of immortal undead being like Dracula?'

'No, not quite. Our host can trace his ancestry back to the seventeenth century, but no original portraits survive. So he had all these commissioned when he built this house. He sat for all ten of them in different period costumes. The artist was rather good – you'll notice the physiognomy does become subtly more atavistic as they go back in time. Of course, there's also no hint here that his grandfather's mother was a Mexican girl. Or that he has some Creole blood from a generation or two before that.'

Loeser trudged across the room to look at the portrait next to the door, the 'oldest', which showed Gorge in a powdered wig and lace cravat, with the label 'AUGUSTE DE GORGE: 1638–1739'.

'No! Gorge is descended from Auguste de Gorge?'

'Yes,' said Rackenham. 'Most of us are, probably. De Gorge had an extraordinary number of children. Mostly illegitimate, however. Wilbur Gorge's branch of the family tree was almost the only one to retain the family name.'

'How can he have lived to be a hundred and one?' said Loeser, trudging back again.

'Old for his era, yes, but still no Dracula.'

'I thought he was ruined after the Teleportation Accident.'

'He was. It didn't kill him, though. Very little did, it seems.'

Woodkin came in with Loeser's ginger ale. When he'd gone out again, Rackenham took a pewter flask out of his pocket, unscrewed it, and poured a few measures of gin into Loeser's glass. Loeser thanked him, sipped, winced, and gave the improvised highball a stir with his little finger. 'This house is *erstaunlich*.'

'It's not even the biggest on this street. This is Millionaire's Row.'

'Still. Did he inherit the money?'

'No. Gorge's father died penniless in Albuquerque. Sky-Shine paid for this monstrosity.'

'But how rich can you possibly get selling – what is it? Car polish?'

'Of every ten tins of car polish that are sold in this country, Gorge's firm makes seven, under various different brand names. "You doll up your wife, why let her ride in a shabby car?" And each tin sells for a dollar but costs ten cents to make. That's what his wife told me. You can get unbelievably bloody rich selling car polish. But there's no heir. The Colonel and his wife only have a daughter, and they haven't shared a bed in a decade. No male cousins, either. The last one went down on the *Lusitania*. So ten generations after Auguste de Gorge, the name dies in this house.' If Gorge's wife wouldn't fuck him, thought Loeser, that was obviously why he'd started his famous collection. Rich and powerful as he was, the sort of man who drank ginger ale at dinner was probably too morally squeamish for physical infidelity, so, like Loeser, he'd devoted himself to the only release that was still available to him. Loeser found this at once depressing and comforting. No doubt it gave Gorge the sort of 'satisfaction' that a man might feel after being fitted with the world's most advanced and expensive catheter.

'So what's it like? To "cuckold" him?' He had never used the word in English before.

'Have you ever persuaded anyone to betray their husband or wife with you?' said Rackenham.

'No.'

'There's really nothing more satisfying than the first time you manage it. I was fourteen, I think. After that it's routine, of course, and Pasadena is a long drive for me. But the boys on Venice Beach don't have any money, the cocaine trade here seems to be run by surprisingly circumspect Mexicans, and I'm not about to take a job for the first time in my life. Gorge's wife likes to buy me things, but unlike the other women of Millionaire's Row, she won't ever give me cash, because she's worried I'll feel like a gigolo. As if I'd be measly-minded enough to give a damn. So I just pawn everything. She won't come down tonight, by the way. Amelia doesn't like to see her husband and me in the same room. She always counterfeits a headache.'

'What's the daughter like?'

'Mildred? One of the most disagreeable females I've ever met in my life.'

'Ugly?'

'No, in fact she has rather a cud duck, as we used to say at school. It's not that. You'll understand if you ever meet her. Now, I may as well warn you, there is one other thing about Gorge,' said Rackenham. 'He's not all there.'

'What do you mean?'

Rackenham was about to explain when Woodkin ushered two more guests into the drawing room, so instead he just smiled at Loeser and murmured, 'You'll soon see.'

Woodkin introduced the new arrivals as Ralph Plumridge, Assistant Public Utility Liaison at the Los Angeles Traffic Commission, and Wright Marsh, Vice Chairman of the Executive Council at the California Institute of Technology. Loeser's heart sank. In Berlin he'd always gone out of his way not to socialise with people with real careers. They were impossible to talk to.

'We just happened to arrive at the same time, you understand,' said Plumridge to no one in particular. 'We're not a couple of queers!' In fact, the two bureaucrats' mutual aversion was obvious from the absurd way they had positioned themselves not quite side by side but instead angled slightly outward, like two secret agents confining each other to peripheral vision.

'Hey, Marsh, I heard one of your biologists got his tenure revoked last week.'

'Not that I'm aware of.'

'Yeah, he did. The other fellows at the department said he was faking his fieldwork. He submitted a paper describing something that none of them had ever heard of in their lives.'

'What was it?'

'It was like a man, he said, but with these two big lumps on its chest, and no dick! Ha ha ha!' Plumridge slapped his thigh.

When Wilbur Gorge came in, he looked just like all his portraits, although they hadn't been able to capture his bisontine bulk. Before acknowledging anyone else, he circled the room, greeting all nine patrilineal ancestors by name, then apparently checking the symmetry of his moustache in the final portrait of himself as if it were a mirror. At last he joined his three-dimensional companions. 'Marsh,' he cried. 'Plumridge. Rackenham.' Then he glared at Loeser.

'Colonel, this is the fellow I was telling you about on the telephone,' said Rackenham. 'Herr Loeser from Berlin. He's an old friend of mine.'

Gorge shook Loeser's right hand in a way that made Loeser glad he wrote with his left, and then said, 'All wrong, your clocks.' Loeser looked down at his tie and smiled dutifully at the joke. But Gorge's expression was oddly serious. 'Hours out. Can't stand a bitched clock. Wind 'em for you if you like. Don't know why you've got so many. Just need one, most cases.' Loeser hesitated, and Gorge reached out and started to scratch at his tie. 'Can't seem to find the knob,' said Gorge. 'Bolted on, are they? Glued?' His eyebrows were so bushy they looked almost tumorous.

'That is merely the pattern of Mr Loeser's necktie, sir,' said Woodkin, handing him a glass of ginger ale.

'Necktie! Right. Beg your pardon. Marsh! Wife?'

'Her sister called just before we left. Some minor emergency. Sends her apologies.'

'I didn't know you were married, Marsh,' said Plumridge.

'Yes. Last month.' Marsh took a photo out of his wallet and passed it around.

'Congratulations, pal, she's just your level,' said Plumridge.

'Hello, Mrs Marsh,' said Gorge politely. But then when Marsh made to put the photo back in his wallet, Gorge grabbed his wrist. 'God's sake, man, don't stuff her back in there! No air. Sure to suffocate. Don't you care a snap about your wife?'

'It's only a photograph, sir,' said Woodkin.

'Photograph! Right. Pardon me.'

'Will the Gorge ladies be joining us?' said Plumridge to Gorge.

'No. Upstairs with her skull. Off at Radcliffe. Stag tonight.' After a moment's analysis, Loeser took Gorge to be referring respectively to his wife, his daughter, and the occasion. Gorge turned to Woodkin. 'Tell Watatsumi nix the tuna. No need for damsel food.' Woodkin nodded and went out. 'Nazi, Loeser?' said Gorge.

'Pardon me?' said Loeser.

'Nazi?' repeated Gorge, as if he were offering Loeser some sort of hors d'oeuvre.

'No, Loeser is not political,' interceded Rackenham. 'He is very happy, I'm sure, to have escaped all the unpleasantness going on in Berlin.'

Loeser thought of Brecht and nodded.

'When Professor Einstein last came to the Institute, he told me he thought it might be a very long time before he could go home,' said Marsh.

'What's he like?' said Rackenham.

'Fascinating. You know, last year, a woman donated ten thousand dollars to the Robinson Laboratory in exchange for meeting him. Worth every cent, I should say.'

'Talk much, him and Bailey?' said Gorge.

'They did, yes. Which is unusual. Professor Bailey is normally quite secretive about his work.'

'Why would a CalTech physicist need to be secretive?' said Plumridge. 'He's juggling atoms, not patenting a toaster.'

'I believe he's just reluctant to disseminate even the first hints about his researches until he's quite sure they will develop into something worthwhile.'

'Field?' said Gorge.

Marsh hesitated. 'Physics.'

'Know that! Branch?' Marsh didn't answer. 'Theoretical or applied?' said Gorge. Marsh still didn't answer. 'Don't know or won't tell us?'

'I don't know,' said Marsh at last.

'You mean to say you don't have even the faintest idea what your top scientist is working on?' sneered Plumridge. 'Except that it's "physics"? Doesn't he talk to anyone about it?'

'He does have one research assistant,' said Marsh. 'But he chose someone from outside the faculty – a non-specialist, in fact – so as to cut down on departmental gossip. All I know is that he's in touch with some top men at the State Department. Quite a lot of our physicists are, to tell the truth. Although I shouldn't say any more than that.'

'Weapons,' said Gorge.

'Perhaps,' said Marsh. 'As you know, Dr Millikan is normally very much against federal involvement in the sciences, but he believes an exception should be made for defence research.'

'Made an investment, why I ask. Take an interest.'

'Of course.'

'The Colonel just gave CalTech a lot of money,' explained Rackenham to Loeser.

'Million dollars for the Gorge Auditorium,' said Gorge. 'Put on some plays. Can't stay in labs all the time, the students. Ran an opera house in Paris, my great-great-great-great-great-great-great-grandfather. Ran a dirty puppet show in New Orleans, my great-great-great-great-grandfather. Family tradition. Not my own game but damned proud of it.'

'When it's finished, the Gorge Auditorium will be one of the finest buildings on campus,' said Marsh.

'Oh, what an achievement,' said Plumridge.

Woodkin came back into the drawing room. 'Watatsumi tells me dinner is about to be served, sir.'

'Mess hall!' said Gorge, and the five of them followed him to the dining room, in which a crystal chandelier hung galactically over a long table. They all sat down except Woodkin, who stood behind his employer like a valet. Two maids brought in five silver serving dishes, inside each of which was a cheeseburger and a china bowl of frenched potatoes.

Loeser saw that Rackenham, who was seated next to him, had taken out a fountain pen and was sketching some sort of spotty cucumiform entity on his napkin. He then gave the napkin to Loeser and whispered, 'Say to Gorge you don't like pickles so does he want yours.'

'Why?'

'Just say it. You don't like pickles so does he want yours. He'll like it. I promise. You don't understand American table manners yet.'

Loeser cleared his throat. He didn't want to do this but he was only here because of Rackenham so he wasn't sure he could refuse. 'Colonel Gorge, I'm afraid I don't happen to care for pickles, perhaps you'd like to—'

But Gorge had already snatched the napkin out of his hand. 'More for me!' he cried cheerfully, and stuffed it into his mouth. Then as Loeser watched in horror the tycoon began to chew.

Woodkin stepped forward. 'That is not a pickle, sir, that is only a drawing of a pickle in black ink on a napkin.'

Gorge spat out the sodden wad of cotton. The action of his jaw had been so powerful that it was already frayed at the edges. 'Napkin! Right. Beg your pardon.' He laughed industrially. 'Fine prank, Krauto. Damned fine prank.'

Woodkin, who had presumably observed Rackenham's guilt and Loeser's innocence, said: 'Actually, sir, it might be that not everyone at this table is quite familiar with the details of your condition.'

'Oh? All right – explain: can't tell the difference between pictures and the real thing. Got it? Just can't. See the difference, not blind, just don't realise it. Damned confusing. Have to get Woodkin to remind me. Used to be all right, but it's the polish. Sky-Shine. Huffed too much of it over the years, working on the formula, testing the product, sleeping in store rooms. Polished part of the noggin clean away. Don't know what to do, the doctors. Don't blame 'em. Why I can't drink: makes it even worse. Get by all right, though. Still whip smart at everything else. Except spelling. Never could spell, though, since I was a cub – nothing to do with the polish, that. Waste of time, anyway, spelling. Waste of fucking time!'

'As Colonel Gorge says, his severe visual agnosia has not affected his business acumen,' added Woodkin. 'He is simply required to work in an office with no photographs, diagrams or figurative art of any kind.'

'Right. Can't have pictures of anything. Just like the damned Musselmans! Can't go to the movies, either. Went to see *Shanghai Express* couple of years ago. Shouldn't have, but Dietrich. Tell 'em what happened, Woodkin.'

'When the film started, Colonel Gorge assumed he must have been drugged, kidnapped, and taken to China. He assaulted one of the popcorn boys, fled, and found himself outside on Hollywood Boulevard. Thereupon he observed an advertisement for a depilatory product that made comical use of an image of a mountain gorilla, and attempted to wrestle the animal to the ground before it could endanger a nearby lady.'

'Saw my mistake pretty soon after that, of course. Felt like a fool. Paid for all the damage.' Gorge applied seven or eight spoonfuls of mustard to his hamburger and then turned to his newest acquaintance. 'Living whereabouts, Krauto?'

'The Chateau Marmont,' said Loeser, who had hoped he might have misheard the first time Gorge called him 'Krauto'.

'I don't know how you can stand to live in a hotel,' said Marsh. 'There's no privacy.'

'Yes, he should certainly move. Don't you have a few properties near here, Colonel?' said Rackenham.

'Think so. Woodkin?'

'Only one at present, sir. You own a house in that inconvenient triangle of land between your tennis courts and the Sprague mansion. It is currently untenanted.'

'Why the hell untenanted?'

'It's quite small, sir, and there is nowhere to a park a car.'

'Want it, Krauto?'

'Sorry?'

'Want to rent it? Work out a price with Woodkin. Needn't pay much. No use letting it sit empty.'

'Hold on, Colonel, not everyone wants to live in Pasadena,' said Plumridge. 'You haven't even asked him.'

'Good point. Want to live in Pasadena, Loeser?'

'It's nice here, but a bit out of the way,' said Plumridge.

'Not if you work at the Institute,' said Marsh.

'But he doesn't,' said Plumridge.

'Loeser, may I say this,' said Rackenham. 'Everyone else who arrives in Los Angeles from Berlin seems to be settling in Pacific Palisades. And there is hardly any part of Los Angeles further from Pacific Palisades than Pasadena.'

Just then Loeser began to make out something now that he had first glimpsed in the shadows as he fled Bevilacqua's office: the fear that he wasn't going to find Adele tomorrow, or the day after, or the day after that – that dispersion fortified you not just against coincidence but against serendipity – that two blind men wandering in a village square might die before they collided – that no amount of desire or determination could overcome the sheer brainless size of this place – that even though he'd extracted more than enough from his parents' trust for a holiday to Paris, if he stayed on at the Chateau Marmont he would soon run out of money and have to go home with nothing to show for his sojourn.

All this was probably true. But he didn't care. There was no way he was staying out here in this nonsensical country for one day longer that he had to. 'I'm sorry, Colonel Gorge,' he said, 'but as I've already told Rackenham, I won't be in California long enough to require a house of my own. I'm going back to Berlin soon.'

'Tell me, Herr Loeser, what are the streetcars like in Berlin?' said Plumridge.

'Fantastic,' said Loeser with some fervour. Apart from Nerlinger, who made paintings of the S-Bahn, no one at home ever seemed to want to talk in detail about public transport.

'You fellows had the first electric trams in the world, of course.'

'I didn't know that.'

'Sure. Siemens. Beautiful engineering. I used to have one of their radios. Had to throw it out, though. They're bank-rolling the Nazis and my wife's family are Jewish.'

'I rode one of your American streetcars this morning,' said Loeser. 'It was adequate.'

'Where did you go?'

'Hollywood to Pacific Palisades.'

'On the Santa Monica Air Line, I guess? Second oldest line in California. Used to run all day, Red Cars, USC to the coast. Now it's just for rush hours, and barely even that. Damn shame. You know, Los Angeles used to have the finest public transportation system in the whole country. Now we've got squat, practically.'

'I heard it's General Motors who are killing the streetcars,' said Rackenham. 'Some sort of conspiracy.'

'Red propaganda!' said Gorge, slamming the table so hard with his fist that Loeser thought he saw his half-eaten burger separate momentarily into its constituent vertical sections.

'Our host is just about correct,' said Plumridge. 'The street-car companies are dying for plenty of reasons, but a conspir-acy's got nothing to do with it. The main point is, people hate them. And so they should. Those companies run the minimum number of cars they can get away with. They don't give a thought to safety or hygiene. They cheat and bribe. A lot of them only got started to manipulate real estate values, anyway. And even if they were a consortium of saints, they couldn't last much longer. The traffic's the problem. Who's going to take a streetcar when it has to wait in downtown jams like any other jalopy? You can't turn a profit like that. Hard enough before, and then the Depression came. No, we can't leave anything to the streetcar companies. The city has to do it. Pittsburgh just bought up all their private railway companies, and they're going to run them at a loss for as long as it takes to turn them around.'

'How can the city afford to buy up the streetcar lines?' said Rackenham.

'It can't. The streetcar companies overstate the value of their assets to keep the banks and the shareholders happy. But even if they'd give us a fair price, it wouldn't be worth it. We'll just let them fail. Meanwhile, we start fresh. Los Angeles isn't Pittsburgh. We have to be a hell of a lot more ambitious. First and foremost, the lines have to be elevated to beat the traffic. We would have gotten elevated lines in twenty-six if it weren't for Harry Chandler.'

'Who's that?' said Loeser.

'The tyrant of the *LA Times*. Back then, the railroad companies wanted to build the new Union Station at Fourth and Central. They had right of way there in every direction, so it could have been a terminal for the elevated lines. But Chandler had real estate holdings at the Plaza, by the old Chinatown, so he wanted Union Station there instead. He put the *Times* to work, and now Union Station's at the Plaza, which nobody can run streetcars into.' A land deal, Loeser thought, just like Louis XIV murdering Villayer so that Villayer's post office couldn't redeem the Court of Miracles. Perhaps that was just what cities were: land deals built on top of land deals built on top of land deals, with a few million warm bodies as mortar. 'Anyway, this time, we won't let Chandler kill the plan. Rackenham, can I borrow your pen? Thanks.' Plumridge unfolded his napkin on the table. 'We won't try to build the terminal downtown, we'll build it up in north Hollywood, at the foot of the hills. And then we'll connect up every suburb in Los Angeles.' He sketched out a map of the city, with a big box at the junction of Sunset Boulevard and North Kings Road, and routes looping off in every direction. 'For instance, Rackenham, you could get from Venice Beach to Pasadena in thirty minutes if you took an express. How long did it take you today in the traffic? Sixty minutes? Ninety minutes?' Then Marsh, reaching across the table to point out an error, knocked over Loeser's ginger ale so that it splashed across the napkin.

'Flesh of Christ!' screamed Gorge, jumping up from his seat. 'Telephone, Woodkin! Newspapers! Ambulance! Thousands drowned!'

'It's just a map, sir. It's not really Hollywood itself.'

Gorge coughed and sat down. 'Map! Right. Pardon me. More ginger ale for Loeser.'

'We'll make it fast and cheap and modern like nobody's ever seen,' said Plumridge. 'We've got all kinds of ideas. Some of the cars, the roof will come off when it's sunny, like a convertible. Fit them out with soda fountains and magazine racks, like a drugstore. Coffee. Maybe cocktails in the evening. Jazz bands. Soon enough, people get used to going out without their Packards. They know that wherever they end up, they can catch a streetcar home, and they won't be stranded. So they try walking. And then they start to realise how goddamned cracked it is that they'll get in a car and drive an hour in traffic just to eat a steak. Maybe they'll go to the place on the corner instead. You know, my wife comes from New York. She used to walk everywhere, since she was small. She can't stand it here. Maybe one day we can make Los Angeles feel like New York.'

'New York is a filthy, old-fashioned city,' said Marsh as the maids cleared the plates. 'New York was built for the horse and cart. We have electricity now. Telephones. Automobiles. Proximity is no longer a relevant parameter. The modern city is like water. It finds its own level in the volume it has available.'

'But if that's the case, why did we ever need to make a law against tall buildings in downtown? If people here want sprawl so much, why do we expressly have to forbid them to build skyscrapers and penthouses?'

'Because next time there's an earthquake we don't want the same carnage as San Francisco had. Or Lisbon, for that matter. The lesson is not new. You've read Rousseau's letter to Voltaire? "It was hardly nature that there brought together twenty thousand houses of six or seven storeys." '

'Hundreds of years go by between earthquakes like that. The law is draconian. All it proves is that people crave density! The truth is, the "modern city" isn't like water, it's like oil. It spreads and slicks and stains. You know, if we don't do something about it, in a few decades' time, four fifths of downtown will be parking spaces. Four fifths! What kind of human being will be willing to live in a city like that? I know there's plenty of space here. I know people love their cars. I know it seems like there's no other way it can go. But think about how Los Angeles got started. There's no reason for a town here. There's no harbour, there's no river. There's not even enough water to drink. It's nuts. But the place just willed itself almost arbitrarily into being. And if it can do that, it can do whatever it wants. This place is still a kid, after all. If it wants to grow up to be like New York, it can. Like New York, but with avocado groves.'

Marsh shook his head scornfully. The maids returned with pudding, which was strawberry pancakes with vanilla ice cream and maple syrup. Loeser had never encountered this delicacy before in his life, and the sheer rushing pleasure he got from the first mouthful was so great that it seemed to overflow the aqueduct delimited for it in his brain's hedonic plumbing and slop sideways into the dried-up sexual reservoir that was adjacent, giving Loeser what felt like the closest thing he'd had in four years to a non-self-administered orgasm. He ate the rest so greedily it was only afterwards that he realised he'd been audibly grunting, and his stomach felt like wood. He had always hated the period towards the end of a meal when long gaps opened up between utterances: there was something repulsive and undignified about that shared awareness of the human animal's basic inability to think and digest at the same time. The conversation torpidly returned to Marsh's work at the California Institute

176

of Technology, where, he said, he was being distracted from his proper administrative duties by a problem so unpleasant that he couldn't bring it up over dinner. Then Gorge forced him to, of course. So: 'We keep finding dead dogs all over the place,' he said. 'Six now. Mutilated and, uh, disembowelled.'

'Is the cafeteria food that bad?' said Plumridge.

Marsh ignored him. 'The heck of it is, we know who's doing it. We have a janitor called Slate. Odd fellow. Can't look you in the eye. And he's always sneaking around at night. Once, somebody even found a bloody rag in his mop cart. But we don't have any positive proof.'

'Find some pretext,' said Gorge, passing out cigars from a box. 'Fire him that way.'

'I want to, but Millikan won't have it. He knew Slate's father, or something like that. And Slate does his job pretty methodically. So unless we actually catch him standing over a dead beagle with a linoleum cutter in his hand, there's nothing we can do. A lot of the students are very frightened. And I have to worry about it all day – when I should be concentrating on the Gorge Auditorium.'

Too late, Loeser realised that a dinner without wine was not likely to last long after the last course, and he was still no closer to *Midnight at the Nursing Academy*. He could excuse himself to go to the lavatory, but the house was far too big to search. For all he knew, Gorge's collection might be down some secret tunnel. The only plan he could think of was to wait awkwardly until all the other guests had left, then find some way of raising the subject with Gorge. Could he bring himself to do that? Before he made up his mind, Marsh and Plumridge had finished their cigars and were making their excuses, and then Rackenham said, 'You know, Colonel, Loeser doesn't have any way of getting home.'

'Woodkin: sled.'

So Loeser got a lift back to Hollywood in the back of Gorge's limousine, which he made sure to think of as a taxi. As they were turning off Palmetto Drive, Loeser said, 'Colonel Gorge seems to be in remarkably vigorous health for a man of his age.'

'Yes,' said Woodkin. 'He attributes it to an operation he had a few years ago.'

'What sort of operation?' said Loeser, with the feeling that he already knew the answer.

'It was the invention of a French surgeon. He passed through California in twenty-six and the Colonel engaged his services. Perhaps you've heard of him? Dr Sergei Voronoff.'

'No. I don't believe I've ever heard that name.'

'The operation normally involves the transplantation of certain primate glands into the human body. But the Colonel didn't believe anything that came out of a "little chimp" would be of any use to him.'

'Where did he get the glands, then?'

'From a coyote. The Colonel shot it himself.'

Loeser decided that this was his last chance to get anything useful out of the evening, so he needed to be bold. 'Is hunting one of Colonel Gorge's hobbies?'

'Yes. He is very proficient with a rifle. And a bow. And a tomahawk. And his hands.'

'Does he have any other hobbies?'

'Several.'

'Do they include . . . A mutual acquaintance told me that Colonel Gorge has a very impressive collection of . . .'

'Yes?'

'Of specialist incunabula, I suppose you might say.'

'I'm afraid I'm not sure what you might be referring to. The Colonel is not a particularly keen reader. His hobbies are mostly of the outdoorsman type. By the way, Mr Loeser, if you change your mind about the Pasadena house, you only need to telephone. Mr Rackenham comes by the mansion often, so I can give him the keys and he can drop them off with you on his way back to Venice Beach. I won't have time to show you the house myself, I'm afraid, but you can go and inspect it whenever you want. If you like it, you can simply move in. If you don't, you can bring the keys back, no harm done. We could let you have it for thirty dollars a month. As Colonel Gorge says, it's wasteful to leave it empty.'

Even Loeser, with his tenuous grasp of the value of the American dollar, knew that was a cheap rent. Still: 'That's kind of you, but it won't be necessary.' He could tell he wasn't going to get any further with Woodkin, and for the first time he wondered if Blimk's gossip might be baseless after all. Perhaps he'd been wasting his time tonight. But then, all at once, he made the connection that he should have made an hour ago. If Gorge and his wife didn't sleep together any more, the neglectful party wasn't necessarily female. A man with Gorge's neurological defect would have an extraordinary appreciation for certain types of photographic stimulus. In fact it rather dizzied Loeser to think of quite how much you could enjoy a book like *Midnight at the Nursing Academy* if you were lucky enough to have a disorder like visual agnosia. Of course you would start a collection. Of course you would keep adding to it until it was the biggest in the world. Of course you would be distracted from your wife. Loeser almost wanted to snort a gallon of polish himself. He'd never have to worry about rejection again.

Not that anyone ever really said no in this city, he'd noticed. Probably even if you came right out and begged a girl to let you fuck her, she'd say, 'I'm awfully sorry but right at this time we just don't have a suitable vacancy. However, we'll keep you in mind, and something may develop shortly. And we do appreciate your applying and are aware of your fine qualifications.' As they paused for a minute at some traffic lights, he could see by the side of the road, just next to a school playground, a copse of oil derricks in those black wooden frames like lifeguard towers on the beach. They were everywhere in this city, always nodding, nodding, nodding, an endless dumb affirmation. Perhaps when the big earth-quake was about to come, they'd all finally start shaking their heads.

The Chateau Marmont

Loeser was awoken by the telephone. Every night that he'd slept in California, his eyes had produced almost geological quantities of dried rheum, like a waste product of his body's slow adjustment to the climate. He rubbed them clear and then reached for the receiver. '*Hallo?*'

'This is Dolores Mutton.'

'I have not been nowhere near of the house!' screeched Loeser, so alarmed that his grammar started to tilt.

'Yes, about that. I'm calling to apologise, Mr Loeser. I can't tell you how rotten I've been feeling about how I behaved yesterday. You'd only come to pick up your clothes and take some pictures and I treated you like some sort of vagrant. And I was just as bad before that at the party. I can be a real ogress when I'm in the wrong mood, and I don't come to my senses until it's too late. You can't imagine how many friends I've lost over it. Poor Stent bears the brunt, of course. If you'll ever forgive me, then I want you to know that you're welcome at the house whenever you like. It goes without saying that I'll replace the camera and the clothes. By the way, I suppose you're wondering why your friend Jascha was at the house that day. I should have explained. Jascha is on the board of the Cultural Solidarity Committee. We were having a little meeting over coffee. And in fact, Mr Loeser, your name had already come up that morning. There is an empty seat on the board, which we'd very much hoped to fill with someone of your race. Not to be too blunt about it, but most of the refu-gees coming to America are Jewish, and yet we don't have one Jewish board member – it's a real embarrassment. I don't suppose you'd be interesting in joining the Committee? We can't offer much money – just a token stipend, about thirty dollars a month – but the duties are very light and we'd be honoured to have such a distinguished artist among us. What do you say?'

Loeser was excited to realise he was being bought off. Evidently, Dolores Mutton had conferred with Drabsfarben, and they'd decided that bribes would be safer than threats. He hoped they wouldn't go back to the threats when he turned down the bribe. 'I'm grateful for the offer, Mrs Mutton, but I won't be in Los Angeles nearly long enough to take up any kind of job.'

'Are you quite sure?'

'Yes. So let's just consider the whole matter permanently closed, shall we? The whole matter,' he repeated significantly.

There was a pause on the other end of the line. 'I see. Thank you, Mr Loeser. Goodbye.'

Loeser decided to have breakfast in the hotel restaurant. He dressed and went downstairs, picking up a copy of the *Los Angeles Herald* from the sideboard as he found a table. There was a story about some musicologists who had measured the wave frequency of traffic noises at various spots throughout the city and discovered that the tonal pitch of Los Angeles was F natural.

Flipping past the international politics and the Hollywood gossip, he came to an article by none other than Stent Mutton, who had a long account of his trip to the Soviet Union. The prose was so different to his novels that it was almost hard to believe that this was the author of *Stifled Cry* and *Assembly Line*. He explained that he had arrived a sceptic but after a fortnight he was a convert. 'The citizens of Moscow joke about minor inconveniences, usually if not always with complete good humour, but they never think of allowing these shortcomings to blind them to the big things that life in the Soviet Union alone can offer. How sturdily and with what calm confidence do they face life, feeling that they are organic parts of a purposeful whole. The future lies before them like a well-defined and carefully tended path through a beautiful landscape.' Mutton had toured a prison, which he found clean, comfortable and humane. 'So well known and effective is the Soviet method of remaking human beings that criminals occasionally now apply to be admitted. An eventual disappearance of wrongdoing is expected by Soviet authorities as the mental habits produced by the socialist system become established in Soviet life.' He'd even had a short audience with Stalin. 'A lonely man, he is not influenced by money or pleasure or even ambition. Though he holds enormous power he takes no pride in its possession. His demeanour is kindly, his manner almost deprecatingly simple, his personality and expression of reserve, strength and poise very marked. His brown eyes are exceedingly wise and gentle. A child would like to sit on his lap and a dog would sidle up to him.' Loeser felt he ought to cut the article out and send it to Hecht. Except that Hecht couldn't be a communist any more if he were out here making five hundred dollars a week at a film studio. Could he?

He finished his breakfast and went out on to Sunset Boulevard, where a hearse was inching down the street so slowly that it looked as if someone had merely forgotten to put on the handbrake. The air smelled of pasteurised honey. He planned to spend the day talking his way into casting agencies to find out if they had anyone matching Adele's description on their books. If he hadn't found her in thirty days, he would give up and go home. He couldn't bear to stay here any longer than that. Nothing could be allowed to change his mind. One month, and then back to Berlin.

5

LOS ANGELES, 1938

The Loeser House

When Loeser came inside and saw the lipstick on his writing table, it struck him that he had been living with his ghost for nearly three years now and, like the husband in an arranged marriage, he still didn't really know her. He put down the three letters that he'd taken from the mailbox outside, picked up the lipstick, and took it over to the antique wooden chest where he kept everything the ghost left in his house. Only once had the ghost ever taken anything back: a pearl necklace that he'd found underneath the sofa. Perhaps she'd changed her mind about him keeping it – if, after all, these things were indeed gifts, and not, as he was coming to believe, merely droppings, secretions.

His ghost was making him gullible. Last year, wandering along the beach near the Muttons' house before a party, he'd seen a strange white scattering in the distance like a flock of baby seagulls come to rest on the sand. When he got closer he saw that they were condoms, thousands of them, every one still slimily tumescent as if stretched around an invisible penis. Here was all the sex he ever hadn't had in his life, he thought, the counterfactual rubber wraiths of every stolen chance and near miss, come here to haunt him, as mocking as the lingerie brought to him by the lodger in his house. Next time he tried to talk to a pretty girl, there they would be, squelching around his shoes, wriggling up his trouser legs, bellyflopping like giant maggots into his glass of wine. He stamped on one angrily and it collapsed with a fecal burp. Surely his domestic ghost didn't look so ugly, if she had a form at all. Only later, at the party, did he find out from Stent Mutton that there was a sewage line hidden further up the beach, and every few months, after a Saturday night, a glob of used condoms would get trapped in a pipe then washed out all at once on to the sand, inflated by methane and ammonia. So in fact Loeser had only one prophylactic spectre in his entourage – the Trojan in his wallet that had expired the previous April. He decided to bury it in its wrapper.

No, Loeser still hadn't got laid. He'd mostly given up hope. Time, like space, could rush so peremptorily past. The monasteries of Mount Athos in Greece, he had read, were supposed to be the holiest places in the world because no women had set foot on the island for a thousand years, and by that odd criterion he felt his penis should be venerated as a relic on a par with the incorrupt cadaver of Saint Athanasios the Great. In the Greek Orthodox Church to which those monasteries belonged, there were bishops who said that Hell was just being without God's love; Loeser could never take seriously the idea of hell as a mere privation, but life without sex did feel like hell, and either way at this point he would have swapped an eternity of God's love for one middling blowjob. He had developed a habit of clenching his left hand into a fist whenever he saw something that made his frustration jolt: a bare shoulder, a giggling couple, a swimwear advertisement in a magazine. Then one morning he was looking at himself in the mirror before getting into the bath and his left forearm seemed visibly more muscular than his right. Horrified, he took out a tape measure, and found a difference at the thickest point of nearly half an inch. He went to his desk, searched through his papers, found an example of his signature from 1935 on a carbon copy of an immigration form, and wrote his name again next to it. His new 'Egon Loeser' slumped broad and clumsy compared to the old. Lust had deformed his body. He couldn't sign a cheque without confessing it. There was a Venetian proverb from around the time of Lavicini: 'The first sin is to be born desperate.'

After seven years, he still thought about Marlene Schibelsky a lot. The memory of his last girlfriend seemed to have chased him around the world as doggedly as Loeser himself had chased Adele. This was partly, of course, because she was the last woman he'd slept with, and the most enjoyable ever, but also because Loeser, unlike the reader of a biography, did not have the luxury of referring back to an earlier chapter to remind himself of the circumstances of his parting from Marlene, and so he had allowed himself to patch the narrative into something a bit more – well, sorrowful and noble, to use Scramsfield's conjunction. All memories, after all, were implausible ghosts, bad historical novels, as tawdry and convenient as Signor da Vinci in *The Sorceror of Venice*, as dank and dead as the giant sloths dredged out of the tar pits south of the Chateau Marmont. And so Loeser had decided, in squinty retrospect, that he'd loved Marlene, and he hadn't really wanted to break up with her, but he'd hoped it would be best for the both of them. (Or something like that.) Since leaving Berlin, he'd thought often, inexplicably often, of the men she'd fucked before and after their time together, Klugweil and the waiters at the Schwanneke and all the others. The thought of it hurt him, although the pain, at least, had begun to lose its spikes, plotting a curve of much the same shape that certain greater pains once had. He found it odd, in fact, how dispassionately, how empirically, he could verify its continued presence by calling on specific recollections, as if his nostalgia were a doctor tweaking a dislocated joint and asking, 'Does that hurt? What about that?' And the pain really did feel as if it were located somewhere in the torso, although Loeser would not really have placed it in the heart, as in the anatomical doctrine of cabaret songs, but just behind the lungs, snuggling there like an unwanted gland transplant from some especially dolorous species of mollusc (a ghost condom with a shell). Once Marlene had told him an anecdote about where she'd taken 'boys' when she still lived with her parents and it was difficult to find a place to make love. He was supposed to find it funny, and at the time he had, but now all he could think of was that word she used, 'boys'. She probably just meant two or three, but he had no way to know, and, as it was, Cantor himself could not have conceived of an infinity big enough to enfold that plural. All those boys. Them instead of him. He thought about that and it made the gland throb softly, reliably, and sometimes he had to clench his fist, even though he was trying to give that up.

Loeser's favourite book in Blimk's shop, where he spent most of his afternoons, was still *Dames! And how to Lay them*. He referred to it constantly, like a psalter, with an inexhaustible excitement at the notion that it was possible to seduce a woman just by following a rigorous system of instructions. The problem was, there wasn't much in it that he felt he could put to practical use. 'Want to impress a dame the morning after the night before? Run to the kitchen while she's still snoozing fit to bust, and come back with what I like to call the Egg Majestique. That's one of every type of egg on a tray: a soft-boiled egg, a hard-boiled egg, an egg over easy, an egg sunny side up, a poached egg, a devilled egg, a pickled egg, a coddled egg, a scrambled egg, a one-egg omelette, and a shot of egg nog for the hangover. No dame will be able to believe you know so many ways to cook eggs. Egg protein is good for the manly function, and after you've pulled off the Egg Majestique, you'll probably need it, if you know what I mean.' This sounded pretty authoritative to Loeser but he just wasn't quite sure.

His amity with Blimk was of an unfamiliar kind. They'd never been drunk or hungover together; they had no one to gossip or complain about; and they were of such different backgrounds that they didn't feel even secretly competitive. In other words, they had brought together none of the essential constituents of a friendship, and yet the result was still recognisably a friendship, which to Loeser was by definition an avant-garde achievement, like Duchamp's urinal. When he was still living back at the Chateau Marmont, it was only really out of boredom that he had first got into the habit of visiting the shop, but Blimk had seemed to appreciate the company. Now, they often sat reading together for hours at a time inside a companionable silence so sturdy that customers looked almost apologetic when they had to interrupt it to buy a book. On Sundays, to Loeser's faint disbelief, they played tennis.

In April the previous year, word had reached Blimk that H.P. Lovecraft had died of intestinal cancer at his aunt's house in Providence. By that time, diligent as a seditionist, Blimk had collected nearly all the fiction Lovecraft had ever published, swapping decade-old issues of *Weird Tales* and *Amazing Stories* in the post with a network of eight or nine other Lovecraft obsessives. Often Loeser would read out a story from beginning to end so that Blimk, who couldn't type without glaring at the keys, would still have a copy after he was obliged to pass on the original magazine. One of his correspondents was a Professor of classics at Harvard, another was an inmate at Attica prison in New York, and another was a congressional aide in Washington, from whom Blimk had first heard that rumour about the Secretary of State's complete faith in the scientific accuracy of these 'stories'. To Loeser, Lovecraft's work seemed to be in flight from its own unlikelihood. How on earth could one plausibly account for the presence of ancient evil in a country as young as the United States of America? In New England and Rhode Island, Lovecraft could just about sustain it, but if he had lived in sunny, modern Los Angeles, Loeser sometimes felt, the man could never have become a writer.

But of course it was wrong to assume that, as with some obsolete make of spark plug, the production of ghosts had been discontinued. There could be ghosts in new places, in airports and automats and amusement parks. Loeser had become aware of his own ghost within a week of moving into Gorge's spare bungalow in Pasadena. In the middle of the night, he had been awoken from a dream about pencils by a thumping and scratching above his head, loud and wild as if something was about to smash through the ceiling. Terrified, he pulled on a dressing gown, got a torch from the kitchen, and went out on to the patio to see what was on the roof. But there was nothing there. When he went back to his bedroom, the thumping had stopped, but a few hours later, just as he'd finally calmed down enough to doze off, it started again, even louder. He slept on the sofa that night, hearing only the snores of the icebox motor. The following morning, he decided he ought to venture out as usual – this was when he hadn't yet run out of ideas for how he might find Adele – so it wasn't until he got home that evening, and made a thorough investigation of his bedroom, that he discovered what the ghost had left for him: a pair of dark stockings, expensive ones, stuffed down behind the headboard of his bed like the discarded cocoons of two great pedigree silkworms. Doing his best to be sceptical, he tried to think of other ways they could have got there. But all the doors and windows had been locked when he went out and they still were when he got home. The house had no secret tunnels. There was no way any human being could have got in. And ever since then, he had heard the same thumping and scratching about once a week, and found a physical deposit from the ghost in some odd hidden place about every few months. They were almost always feminine in nature, which is how he'd decided the ghost itself was a woman. He didn't want to bring it up explicitly with Woodkin in case Woodkin thought he was a lunatic, but he had at least managed to ascertain that the house had never had any female tenants, murdered or otherwise.

Were ghosts moored to structures, he sometimes wondered, or to spatial coordinates? If he had his house jacked up on wheels and towed to Venice Beach like that house he'd once seen on Sunset Boulevard, would the ghost be dragged with it, or would it continue inanely to haunt the same triangle of land even after it was empty? If you could have a ghost ship, could you have a ghost tram? Could the ghost be Scramsfield's fiancée, the one he'd strangled to death in that Boston art gallery, passed on to Loeser by some ritual invocation over the champaggne?

He decided to open his post. The first letter was his monthly cheque from the Cultural Solidarity Committee of California. The second was from Achleitner. And the third was from Blumstein. He hadn't heard from the director since he'd left Berlin.

Dear Egon,

Perhaps you are surprised to find me writing to you. It has been so long now since our friendship was interrupted. After you dismissed my first & only attempt at reconciliation, it would have been unpleasant for both of us if I had pressed the matter. So I decided, unhappily, to respect your wishes. If I am to explain why I have altered that policy now, I want to do so without using a melodramatic phrase like "last chance". I will only say that I truly believe that we in Germany are approaching some sort of rupture, some sort of chasm, in our history. From this side of the chasm, I can still speak to you. From the other side of the chasm, there is no way of knowing. So I write to you now, hoping you will indulge my letter.

Perhaps you are already sceptical. I know you never believed in politics, or in history. For a long time, I didn't either. So there is no point repeating the bare facts that you must already have read in the newspapers, because I know it won't make any difference. I think the only way to persuade

you that my concerns are real may be to tell you about some-
thing that happened to me yesterday. It was what finally
inspired me to write to you.

I was on a tram to Schlingesdorf. It was the middle of
the afternoon & the tram was quite empty. Everyone had
distributed themselves evenly among the available seats, as
they always do, so that nobody had to share an armrest with
anybody else. There was also a man in Nazi uniform, I think
he must have been a member of the Schutzstaffel, who was
standing up near the front of the tram even though there
were all those seats available.

We came to a stop & a man got on. He wore a shabby
overcoat & shoes with the soles almost falling off, & he had
one of those faces that, even to another Jew, seem so char-
acteristically Jewish that they almost approach caricature.
He gave the Schutzstaffel man an uncomfortable glance,
then carried on past him, twisting his whole body so that
he couldn't even be accused of brushing against the man's
uniform. He sat down next to an old woman with some
shopping bags. The Nazi watched him for a while, sneering,
& then said 'Jew. Why do you assume that a good citizen
like that will be willing to sit next to you?' The Jew shrugged
& asked the woman if she objected. The woman shook her
head. Then the Nazi said 'Jew. You are intimidating her into
silence. Unless she specifically tells me that she is willing to
sit next to a dirty Jew, I cannot allow you to sit next to her.'
The Jew obviously didn't wish to make life difficult for the
old woman, so he got up & moved to another seat, next to a
businessman. The Nazi said 'Jew. Why do you assume that a
good citizen like that will be willing to sit next to you?' But
the Jew didn't want to be made to move a second time, so
he looked at the businessman in hopes of support. The Nazi
said 'Sir. You must say "I am willing to sit next to a dirty
Jew." Unless you say those exact words, I will conclude that
he is intimidating you into silence, & I will insist that he

find another seat.' The businessman hesitated & then looked
down at his newspaper. The Nazi said 'Jew. Find another
seat' but the Jew didn't move, so the Nazi said 'Jew. Unless
you find another seat I will arrest you.' So the Jew asked
where he could sit, & the Nazi said 'Well, I don't know. Is
anyone on this tram willing to sit next to a dirty Jew like
this?' I raised my hand.

The Nazi turned to me & said 'Say it out loud.' I said 'I
am quite willing to sit next to that Jewish gentleman.' The
Nazi said 'Is that because you are a Jew yourself?' I said 'I
am Jewish, yes.' So the Jew came & sat next to me. He didn't
thank me & I didn't want him to. For a few minutes, there
was silence on the tram – silence like you've never heard on
a Berlin tram! And then the Nazi began the second act of
his production. He said 'Do you two Jews realise that young
couple sitting opposite you now have no choice but to look
at the two of you? You are right in front of them.' Neither of
us answered, so the Nazi continued 'Why do you assume that
two good citizens like that will be willing to look at you?'
Again, neither of us answered. 'Unless they specifically tell me
that they are willing to stare at two dirty Jews, I cannot allow
you to sit opposite them.' Egon, I have dealt with bullies
before, and I decided I had had enough. I got to my feet and

Loeser crumpled up the letter and tossed it into the waste-
paper basket. It went on for pages and pages and frankly he
had better things to do. It was just like his former mentor
to tell some long, convoluted, implausible anecdote about
public transport because he thought it would get him some
sympathy – undignified for a man of his age. He started on
Achleitner's letter.

Egon,

Sorry I haven't written for so long. I'm back in Berlin
now and you wouldn't believe how hectic things are here.
You were right – my long holiday in the castle couldn't last

for ever (although it did seem to last about nine tenths of for ever). We've been expelled from paradise. Buddensieg's been called back to the city and he insisted we all come back with him. It's all right, though, because he's given me a job, so I can pay my rent. And I reveal the following in confidence, Loeser, because I deduce from the tone of your last letter that you need a bit of cheering up, but you'd better not tell Hecht or Gugelhupf or Ophuls or any of the others out there with you: I have to wear a uniform! Have you ever heard anything so ridiculous? But at least I don't really have to do anything – much the same as your cushy post on that committee, or so it sounds. Oh, you'll never guess who I saw in the street the other day. Blumstein! Yes, the old bore's still around. I went up to say hello but after he saw the uniform he wouldn't even look me in the eye. Probably still wishing the November Group years had never ended. Well, they have. They really have. So how are things in the Golden State? Have you found Adele yet? No, I thought not. I hope you've at least found somebody willing to reset your stopwatch, as it were. I'm surrounded by vigorous men in riding boots so as you can imagine I couldn't be happier. Well, I suppose I should go, we've got a reception in a minute for some lunatic who says he can see psychic runes or something. Stay out of the sun, it never agreed with you.

Hugs!

Anton

The Gorge House

Over the huge Georgian fireplace in Gorge's billiards room was the stuffed head of a grizzly bear, its jaws fixed open in a way that made it look not so much ferocious as just very impressed. 'Sit down, Krauto,' said Gorge, who reclined in an armchair with a glass of strawberry milkshake. 'Anything to report?'

'Not that I can think of.'

'Still German?'

'I believe I am, yes.'

'Can't be helped. Job for you, if you'll take it. Should damn well take it. Reek of idleness, Krauto, don't mind me saying. No room for idle men on Gorge land. Now, Marsh – remember him? From CalTech. Building my auditorium.'

'The fellow from the Executive Council. Yes.'

As he spoke, Gorge kept glancing over Loeser at the bear's head. He had an expression as if some kind of turbid struggle was going on in his brain. 'Heap of delays, but theatre's finished now. This Christmas, first play. Needs a director. Want to put you forward to Marsh. Couldn't refuse you, Marsh, if I did.'

'First of all, Colonel Gorge, I'm not a director, I'm a set designer, and second, even if I were to direct for the first time, a Christmas play at a university theatre . . .'

'Doesn't matter. Not about the play, this job. Look here: gave a million dollars for that theatre. Enough to get invited to the banquets at the Athenaeum Club, all that horse-shit. But doesn't get me any closer to the scientists. Need to find something out about this man Bailey. Met him, but he's zipped up. Need a party on the inside. Scrape up some intelligence.'

'In other words,' said Woodkin, whose telephone call had summoned Loeser to the mansion, 'Colonel Gorge hopes that if you are accepted into the community of the Institute, which is only three miles from here, you may have a good chance of harvesting some information about Professor Bailey and his activities. Colonel Gorge is very interested in these—'

But then Gorge jumped from his seat with a roar and ran out of the room. Before Loeser even had time to give Woodkin a puzzled glance, he had returned carrying a double-barrelled shotgun with an engraved bronze stock.

'No, sir!' cried Woodkin.

Gorge stopped, raised the weapon, and took aim. Loeser dived to the floor. There was an explosion and the bear's head tumbled from the wall.

'Got the fucker!' said Gorge in triumph, barely audible over the ringing in Loeser's ears. Then he looked at the perforated trophy on the carpet and blinked several times in confusion. Motes of cotton stuffing swirled in the air. The wall above the fireplace was speckled with a halo of buckshot. One of the bear's glass eyes lay like some sort of ominous cocktail olive in a puddle of pink foam where Gorge's half-drunk milkshake had been knocked over. 'How do you think he got in the house?'

'That was not a live bear, sir,' said Woodkin, calm again. 'That was merely the head of a bear that you shot once before in Montana.'

'Head! Right. Beg your pardon.' He looked at Loeser, who was returning tremulously to his seat. 'Should have explained, Krauto. Noggin's gotten worse. All sorts of trouble. Tell him, Woodkin.'

'Colonel Gorge's condition has deteriorated further. Some of the doctors are now calling it an "ontological agnosia". As well as confusing representations with the objects of those representations, he now has difficulty distinguishing, for instance, the living from the dead.'

'Won't even tell you what happened at McGilligan's funeral the other day. Almost as bad as the time I met that fellow with all the tattoos.'

'I can only apologise, sir,' said Woodkin. 'It should have occurred to me to remove all items of taxidermy from the house the moment the doctors informed me of your condition's progress.'

'Well, matter in hand: what say, Krauto? Want to take on this play?'

Loeser didn't. But although he'd had dinner with Gorge regularly since moving into the house near by, he still hadn't reached the level of intimacy with his landlord where he could ask about Gorge's collection. And he still missed *Midnight at the Nursing Academy* like a lost love. He'd experimented with literally hundreds of different publications borrowed from Blimk's shop, some of them with contents that alarmed/baffled even him, but nothing had ever satisfied him in quite the same way. If he did this job for Gorge, then perhaps he could finally ask for the reward he really wanted.

The California Institute of Technology

Explore this university in a few thousand years' time like the narrator of Lovecraft's 'The Nameless City', thought Loeser as he approached on his bicycle, and you might take it for a grand complex of temples and mausolea: although he knew from Woodkin that almost no part of CalTech was more than two decades old, these buildings were the first he'd observed since he'd come to Los Angeles that one could plausibly imagine as ruins. The laboratories and libraries and lecture theatres – delineated with the clarity of architectural drawings under the noon sun by the hard black shadows of their own cornices and pilasters, lushly interspersed with paths and lawns and fountains and rows of cypresses – had a gravity that made them seem far more sacral than, say, the typical Californian Methodist church. Also, the campus, like most of the surrounding city, felt almost deserted, except of course CalTech did not have the excuse of everyone being locked up in their cars, and the proportions of its halls seemed to redouble its emptiness. No necropolis was ever so quiet. If it was term time, where were all the students? Not working, surely?

Loeser had arranged to find Marsh at the entrance of Throop Hall, an imposing domed administrative building in the local Spanish Colonial style. The breeze nuzzled an American flag on a tall pole not far from its portico, and the sky above was full of ribbons and ruffles and loops and bows and threads and all the other clutter of a dressmaker's table. He waited in the shade next to his bicycle for twenty minutes before giving up and going inside.

'I'm looking for Dr Marsh,' he said to a woman behind a desk. 'I'm supposed to be meeting him here.'

For a moment she looked reluctant to answer. 'I'm afraid Dr Marsh isn't available.'

'What do you mean?'

'He's missing. He didn't show up for his eight o'clock budget meeting this morning. We called his wife, and she said he never came home last night. We think he may still be somewhere on campus. There's a search going on. What did you need him for?'

'My name is Egon Loeser. I'm going to be directing a play at the Gorge Auditorium. Dr Marsh was going to give me a tour of the university.'

'Well, in the circumstances, I'm sure we can find another member of the faculty who'd be happy to show you around. In fact . . .' She waved to somebody behind Loeser. 'Excuse me, Dr Ziesel? Do you have a minute?'

This time, Loeser wasn't even that surprised. Although his duties as the only 'Jewish' committee member of the Cultural Solidarity Committee of California had turned out to be pleasantly non-existent, he still went to receptions at the Muttons' house about twice a year, and every time there were half a dozen anxious new arrivals from Berlin, most of whom he recognised. He'd almost resigned himself now to this toxic seepage of his old life into his new one. Still, Dieter Ziesel – that was going too far. Loeser noticed that he'd put on even more weight.

'Egon!' said Ziesel, before continuing in German. 'What a delight. I'd heard you were in Los Angeles but I wasn't sure when we might meet.' He switched to English. 'This is my colleague Dr Clarendon.' Loeser shook hands with the scientist at Ziesel's side, who was a tall gaunt man with small narrow eyes set deep in his skull like two old sisters trying to spy out of the windows of their house without being noticed themselves. His hair was steel grey and his palm was very smooth and cold. 'What brings you to the Institute?' asked Ziesel.

Loeser repeated what he'd told the woman at the desk.

'I wondered if you might fill in for Dr Marsh, if you have time,' said the woman.

'I have always time for an old friend. Would you like to join us, Dr Clarendon?'

'I'm afraid I ought to get back to the lab.'

'Oh, shucks,' said Ziesel, confusingly. He said goodbye to Clarendon and then switched back to German. 'Now, Egon, is there anything in particular you want to see?'

Loeser didn't want to take a tour with Ziesel, but he could hardly turn round and demand that the woman at the desk find him a less odious replacement. 'I need to see the Gorge Auditorium. Obviously. And—' Loeser hesitated. He couldn't be too obvious about Gorge's agenda for sending him here. On the other hand, Ziesel was probably too doltish to be suspicious. 'I'd very much like to meet Professor Bailey.'

Ziesel grinned. 'I bet I know why!'

'What do you mean?' How could he possibly know?

But Ziesel just winked and then led Loeser back out of Throop Hall. 'Up here's the Athenaeum Club,' he said, pointing, as they walked north along the path. 'It's supposed to look like something out of an Oxford or Cambridge college – a bit pretentious if you ask me. Over there's the Dabney Hall of the Humanities. And that's the Guggenheim Laboratory of Aeronautics.'

'How long have you been in America?' said Loeser.

'Nearly a year. Back in Berlin I published a paper on the subatomic properties of thorium that caused a bit of a stir – perhaps you came across it?'

'Funnily enough, I did not.'

'Well, anyway, I owe my job to that paper. They offered me a research fellowship out here and naturally I jumped at it – you of all people don't need me to explain why! It's supposed to be temporary, but they've told me in confidence that I can stay as long as I like. I would rather have gone to Princeton, but the weather here is better, and of course if I'd gone to New Jersey I never would have met Lornadette.'

'Who's Lornadette?'

'We do have a lot to catch up on! Lornadette is my wife.'

Loeser stopped dead. 'Your wife?'

'Yes.'

'You're married?'

'Yes.'

'To a living, human woman?'

'Yes.'

'Is she physically or mentally deformed in any way?'

'Quite the opposite.'

'Did any money change hands? Was it anything to do with a visa or a work permit?'

'No! We met and we fell in love and . . . it all just happened very fast. I've never been so happy in my life.'

'Does she let you have sex with her?'

Ziesel blushed. 'Egon, I mean to say—'

'You're married. You're actually married. I, Egon Loeser, haven't got laid in half a decade and you, Dieter Ziesel, come out here and straight away you find a wife.'

'Been a bit arid lately, has it?' said Ziesel, and chuckled. 'Well, we've all gone through periods like that.'

'Firstly, Ziesel, it is not funny. I know that, to people who have regular sex, the thought of someone else not having sex always seems like an amusing trifle incapable of inducing any genuine sympathy, but if I tell you that the closest I've come to sex in seven years is half undressing an erogenously narco-tised maiden aunt, you should react as if I've just told you I've got stomach cancer. All right? Because that's what it's like. It's the worst thing in the world. It attacks you on every level of your being. It is not fucking funny. And secondly, "we" haven't "all gone through periods like that". Don't say that as if we're the same. We are not the same. I deserve to be having sex. You, on the other hand, should be grateful you've ever had sex in your life. You must have got used to chastity a long time ago. I am not used to it and I never will be.'

Ziesel pursed his lips. 'Look, Egon, do you want to go to Professor Bailey's laboratory or not? I should have thought you'd be excited. Especially after what you've just said.'

'Meeting some physicist is not going to make up for this fucking unspeakable injustice, and I don't see what it's got to do with anything I've just said. But, all right, we may as well hurry along. Lead the way, uxorious Dieter. Oh, by the way, did Heijenhoort come with you?'

'No, he stayed in Berlin.'

Bailey worked in the Obediah Laboratories. This was a building, Loeser's favourite yet, that resembled a sort of stone dam built by Aztecs trained at the Bauhaus.

'Where are all the white coats?' said Loeser as they went inside.

'That's chemistry,' said Ziesel. 'Physicists don't wear white coats.' He led Loeser down a corridor to a room that was labelled only '11'. The door was ajar, so he knocked softly and then pushed it open. 'Professor Bailey? May we come in?'

'He just just just left.'

Loeser looked inside. The man who had spoken was standing at the laboratory's sink, soaping the taps with a washcloth. Loeser could see him in profile, except that he didn't have a profile, which is to say, his face was a flat plane – his chin and forehead murally vertical, his nose squashed back against his skull, his mouth lipless, his eyes pasted on so far forward that they could have winked at each other sideways. The configuration was unnatural enough that it could surely only have been the result of some grim natal mishap involving a steel table or a concrete floor. He wore baggy grey overalls and had straggly black hair that looked as if it had spent a few days hexagonally loomed across a shower drain before he even grew it.

'Oh, hello, Slate. Do you know where he went?'

'Him and Miss Miss Miss Miss Miss—'

'His assistant, yes.'

'They went to the the the the the basement to get get something from a supply cupboard.' Slate didn't look up from the taps as he spoke. Around him, the laboratory seemed surprisingly neat – lots of electrical instruments, lots of notebooks, and a large shape in the centre of the room concealed by a dust sheet, but none of the clutter that Loeser associated with science – except that on one of the desks there was for some reason a toy steam engine.

'Thank you, Slate,' said Ziesel.

'Christ, he's the sort of person that haunts your dreams,' said Loeser in German as they went downstairs.

'He's a decent fellow, really.' They turned a corner. 'Oh, yes, here is Professor Bailey. Are you forgetting your keys?' Ziesel asked in English.

'No, the door's jammed.' Bailey must have been around forty, but he already had the tinge of late middle age: short, balding, and pot-bellied, he also swayed a little on his feet, reminding Loeser of one of those round-bottomed wooden toys that it is impossible to knock over. He wore a bushy moustache and the lenses of his glasses were so thick that, like an astronomer observing Neptune, he was probably seeing several minutes into the past. 'Thankfully some younger, nimbler hands have taken over.'

His assistant, a girl with short black hair, had her back to them as she rattled the lock. 'I think I've nearly got it, Professor,' she said. Her voice was familiar from somewhere.

'Well done, my dear.'

'Egon, this is Professor Bailey, one of our most distinguished physicists,' said Ziesel. 'Professor Bailey, this is Egon

Loeser, an old friend of mine from Berlin. He is very keen to meet you.'

Bailey smiled and shook Loeser's hand. 'And why is that?'

'Well—' Ziesel started to say.

Just then Bailey's assistant cried, 'There!' as the lock finally submitted. But the steel cupboard door swung open with twice the force she must have been expecting, because there was a weight leaning against it from the inside. She tumbled backwards, and the weight tumbled down, and Loeser saw simultaneously that the girl was Adele and the weight was the man he'd dined with more than once at Gorge's house. Marsh was dead, and Adele was here, and there was a great messy gash in his chest like an apricot with the stone gouged out, and she'd cut off her beautiful long hair, and the hole was so deep that part of his ribcage must have been demolished, and she looked almost like a grown-up now, and his mouth had drooled a rivulet of blood, and her skin was still as pale as a Berlin winter, and his eyes were wide and unblinking and dead and ghastly with terror, and her eyes were wide and unblinking and alive and gorgeous with shock, and someone shouted, 'Dear God!' and it was Adele, it was Adele, it was Adele, it was Adele, it was Adele.

She got unsteadily to her feet, and for a long moment all four of them stood there, silent, as if in a gallery, studying a sculpture they did not understand. Finally Bailey said, 'Dieter, take Miss Hitler away' – except it sounded like he'd mispronounced her name – 'and tell Slate to go for help.'

'I'll go too,' said Loeser. If everyone thought he wasn't man enough to stay there with the body, then so be it. He couldn't let Adele out of his sight. So they trooped upstairs, and Ziesel went to find Slate in Bailey's laboratory, and Loeser went out into the sun with Adele.

'When I was living in Hollywood,' she was saying, 'there was an accident right outside my apartment, I didn't see it happen but I ran to my window, and some guy had gone through his windshield and into this parking meter and he was wrapped around it like he was hugging it, and then they pulled him off it and . . .'

'Adele, it's me. You can speak in German.' She didn't seem to hear him. Slate ran out of the Obediah Laboratories and on past them towards Throop Hall. His gait was lopsided, as if the lawn were sloping steeply under him. 'There's so much I want to ask you.' Loeser himself had never seen a dead body before, but none of this felt real yet – they were all just theoretical particles on a blackboard.

'Jesus, Egon, not now! Didn't you see him? How could someone do that to Dr Marsh?'

'I've been looking for you for five years.'

'You shouldn't even be here now. You're nothing to do with CalTech. They'll want to find out what happened and you'll get in the way.'

'But I've only just found you!'

Finally, irritably, Adele switched to German. 'Listen, Egon, if you really want to talk, come back at eleven o'clock tonight. I'll be in the laboratory.' Three boys in baseball jackets walked past, laughing as they swapped impersonations of Slate's stutter.

The Loeser House

'*Hallo, hier ist Loeser?*'

'Oh, Mr Loeser, it's Dolores Mutton. Did you have a pleasant morning at CalTech today? It's such an interesting institution.'

'It was not a pleasant morning for anyone. How did you know I was at CalTech?'

'A little bird told me. I was wondering if you might have been introduced to a particular member of the faculty – Professor Bailey? The physicist?'

'Yes, I was, actually.'

'My husband and I would be so keen to meet Professor Bailey. We're told he's a magnificent intellect. I know he's not an exile, but we'd love to have him at one of our receptions. Perhaps you could bring him along next time?'

'But I've only just met the man. We're not friends.'

'Still, we'd be so grateful.'

'I really don't know, Mrs Mutton. As I said, I've only just met the man.' Loeser could smell his lamb chop beginning to char.

'I see. Well, perhaps we'll have a chance to discuss this further. Goodbye, Mr Loeser.'

The California Institute of Technology

At night the paths were lit by old-fashioned-looking street-lamps on tall black posts, and sometimes one of these was close enough to a cypress that from a certain angle the post could hardly be seen and the white bulb shone out through the crush of leaves like some hot lactescent fruit the tree had borne. Leaving his bicycle at Throop Hall again, Loeser wandered lost for a while until he found the entrance to the Obediah Laboratories. The door wasn't locked. He was planning to go straight to room 11 to find Adele, but then something drew him to the basement. Until he went back to where Marsh's body had been and confirmed that it had been taken away, part of him would feel as if it were still lying there.

At the bottom of the stairs, not far from the storage cupboards where the corpse had fallen, Loeser had the sense that he was not alone. 'Hello?' he said, wondering if he should turn back. What took place after that, he could only recall later as a sequence of terms in a geometric progression of sheer terror. First, the curl of light reflected off a glass-fronted firehose cabinet on the wall near by; second, the abrupt disappearance of that light; third, the snipping sound that made Loeser think of an insect with sharpened steel mandibles; fourth, the humanoid shape coming forward out of the gloom; fifth, the light shining from that shape's eyes and casting jagged shadows across the ceiling; sixth, the claw that the shape had at the end of its left arm. Loeser raised a hand, half to block the glare and half to shield his face from attack. And then:

'Mr Loeser, if I remember correctly?'

Loeser realised that the shape was not Marsh as a monstrous revenant but rather Dr Clarendon, the colleague of Ziesel's that he'd met earlier. He was wearing a miner's torch on a strap around his head and in one hand he held a big pair of wire cutters. 'I'm sorry,' Clarendon added, 'is this too bright?' He pulled off the miner's torch and held it dangling in his other hand so that it poured out a more diffuse downward glow. Loeser looked past him and could see now that he'd apparently been installing some sort of machine, with a metal case and lots of dials and and switches and exposed wires, about the size of a radio set.

'What are you doing down here?' Loeser said, his heart still spinning in his chest like the rotor in a gyroscope.

'An experiment,' said Clarendon, as if nothing could be more natural. He had that odd conversational manner of some scientists and mathematicians that is so doggedly awkward that it sometimes seems to verge upon the flirtatious.

'Why are you doing an experiment in the dark?'

'We don't know much about ghosts, Mr Loeser, but we know that they don't care for the light.'

'Ghosts?'

'Yes.'

'Are you doing a seance?'

'No. Seances are unscientific. I'm testing my phasmatometer. There aren't many deaths on campus, so I don't often have the opportunity. It may take me a few days to calibrate it, but if the phasmatometer is working properly, I will soon be taking precise measurements of the residual presence of Dr Marsh.'

'To find out who murdered him?'

Clarendon raised an eyebrow as if he hadn't even thought of that. 'Not in particular. If any direct communication takes place, that will only be an accident. Still, I expect Dr Marsh will be very pleased to be the subject of such an important experiment – an apt conclusion to his career. Eventually I hope to refine the phasmatometer to the point where I can turn my work over to the State Department.'

'What do they want with it?'

Clarendon replied with a shake of the head. 'Anyone could be listening, Mr Loeser,' he said softly.

Loeser wondered who could possibly be listening. He also wondered why the State Department should care about ghosts. Perhaps the hope was that, when a communist passed into the next world, whether he was a NKVD Colonel or a double agent from Michigan, he would switch his allegiance to a more godly nation, and the phasmatometer would allow him to be thoroughly debriefed. The defector might even be able to reduce his time in purgatory, like a plea bargain. Or if he were unwilling, you could set the machine to wallop the ghost with a Bible and then dunk his head in a bucket of holy water. 'So it would work anywhere?' he said.

'Yes.'

'Because I happen to have a ghost in my house.'

'Really? Well, if you wish, I could bring the phasmatometer and take some readings. Some fieldwork under less controlled circumstances might be a useful supplement to my experiment with Dr Marsh.'

Perhaps Clarendon could finally reveal what his ghost wanted, Loeser thought. 'Can you come tomorrow evening? I live in Pasadena. Not far.'

'Yes. Seven o'clock. Leave your address at Throop Hall.'

'They already have it. Thank you, Dr Clarendon.'

Loeser went back up the stairs and turned right down the corridor towards where Bailey worked. On the way, he passed a room with its door ajar, lit only by the cellophane glow of the moon, and he felt himself horripilated by the strange tension, the negative hum, of a physics laboratory at night: all these machines – all these precise little lanterns whose job it was to shine into the cracks between atoms, between moments, between universes – caught, after hours, enjoying the dark; inert as anvils until you flipped just one switch and turned just one dial and then they'd probably slurp enough electricity to cut the power in Gorge's mansion. Nonetheless, the bite of this atmosphere, even in aggregate with the scare he'd just got from Clarendon, could barely stand comparison with the cosmic intensity of finding himself, after all this time, alone in a room with Adele, who stood beside one of the larger instruments in room 11, making notes on a clipboard. 'Back to work already?' he said in German, trying to sound casual.

'It takes my mind off things.' She put down the clipboard and boosted herself up on to a table to sit down. 'You didn't say what you're doing in Los Angeles.'

'I was looking for you.'

'But I've been here nearly four years.'

'You're not in the telephone book.'

'I am. But I changed my name. I got bored with people asking me if I was related. I'm Adele Hister now. Did it really take you this long to hunt me down?'

'I didn't. Hunt you down, I mean. This was just chance. How did you end up here? You never even studied science.'

'I got thrown out of my apartment in Hollywood so I moved in with my friend Dick. He's the most darling queer boy from Wisconsin, and he's a graduate student here. One day he took me to a party at the Athenaeum Club, as his "date", and I met the Professor. We talked all evening. He was looking for an assistant – someone from outside the Institute. And I still don't quite know why but he gave me the job.'

'Even though you don't know anything about physics?'

'Dick gave me some lessons. It's not so hard. And the Professor wanted a non-specialist. He says most of the students here have too many prejudices about reality.'

Loeser remembered his assignment from Gorge. 'What is Bailey working on?'

'I can't tell you.'

He could tell she wanted to brag. She always did. 'Adele. Come on. I'm your oldest friend in this country.'

'Well, you musn't say anything to anyone.' She leaned forward. 'The Professor is building a teleportation device.'

'What? Like Lavicini?'

'No, a real one, not a theatrical effect. You put an object in the chamber, you set the controls, it disappears, and it reappears somewhere else. He's very close to completing a prototype.'

'What sort of lunatic believes that teleportation can really happen?'

'Jews call it *Kefitzat Haderech*. Muslims call it *Tay al-Ard*.'

'But that's mysticism. It can't be scientifically possible.'

'It is, Egon. It's happened in this building. Of course, it's difficult. I don't think anyone but the Professor could have done it, not even Einstein. The point is, you can't just delete the subject in one place and create a copy in another. If you did that to a human being, all you'd be doing is murdering someone and replacing them with a clone a few minutes old. That way, no one who believed in a soul – like my parents, for instance – would ever be willing to set foot in a teleportation device. So instead you have to move the object itself, really move it. But it can't move through the intervening space. It has to be in one place, and then, snap! Suddenly in another. It has to change its position all at once. Well, what's position, anyway? It's not a function of space. There's no more such a thing as space than there's such a thing as the ether. Space is just objects, and position is a function of those objects. So if you can – the Professor always warns me against the Pathetic

Fallacy, but it's so hard to avoid sometimes – if you can make an object *forget* its old position, and then *persuade it* of its new position, then that's teleportation. But how do you do that? Well, the Professor once said to me, "Adele, what's the one thing in the world that can uproot almost anything?" '

'What is it?'

'He wouldn't tell me the answer. He's secretive sometimes. But I know. I worked it out. It's love, Egon. Love can uproot almost anything.'

'You think love makes the Teleportation Device run?'

'Yes. The reason it works is that . . . Oh, Egon, I love him!'

'Who?'

'The Professor, of course. I love him! He's the most wonderful man I've ever met. He's so clever and kind and honest and dedicated.' Just talking about it seemed to make her squirm into herself with pleasure like someone trying on a new fur coat for the first time. 'And now I know he's brave, too! You saw how he was, after what happened. And then after you left I started crying and he came upstairs and he knew exactly what to say. I love him so much. I go to bed thinking about him and I wake up thinking about him and then I'm allowed to spend all afternoon with him. I'm so lucky he works here at the weekends, too – I can't stand my days off.'

'So you're fucking him?'

She snorted. 'No, I am not, you reptile! We've never so much as exchanged a significant glance. He doesn't even suspect how I feel.'

'Why don't you tell him?'

'I couldn't. I'd be too humiliated. I know a genius like him would never be interested in a girl like me. He'd be nice about it, of course, but if he ever found out, I'd just wither away.'

'But, Adele, you're the most exquisite girl I've ever met. He's only a boring scientist.'

'That shows you shallow you are, Egon. He's a great man. He's invented a teleportation device.'

'So have I, as it happens.'

'But this one is going to change history.'

'And it works because you're so in love with him. So who is *he* in love with?'

'No one,' replied Adele, showing a crackle of hypothetical jealousy. 'He's too wedded to science.'

'So how does it work for him?'

Adele bit her lip. 'It doesn't.'

'It doesn't work for him?'

'No.'

'But if it runs on love, and he doesn't know that you love him, how does he explain the fact that it works for you and not for him?'

'He doesn't know.'

'What do you mean?'

She couldn't meet his eyes now. 'He thinks it does work for him. I always perform the experiments for him and he's so adorably absent-minded so sometimes when he's not paying attention I . . .'

'You fake the results?'

'Yes. Oh God, Egon, don't look at me like that. I coax the results along a bit because I couldn't bear him to be discouraged. I'm not deceiving him, really. He thinks the Teleportation Device works, and it does. I know it does because I test it myself every night. I put things in it and they disappear, just as they're supposed to.'

'How do you know someone else isn't meddling with it while your back is turned?'

'That wouldn't be possible. I'll show you.'

She got down off the table, led him to the back of the room, and swung open a heavy steel door that looked as if it had been installed more recently than the lab's other fittings. The chamber beyond was about the size of a lavatory. Its walls, floor and ceiling were all lined with grey rubberised panels, and in the centre was a small platform.

'Can I go inside?' said Loeser.

'Just for a minute.'

He stepped through. 'What's the point of all the rubber?'

Adele followed him in. 'Electrical insulation. And behind the rubber there's lead. The Professor still has no idea what the radiation in there might do to a human body. That's why the door's on a time lock.'

'Like a bank vault?'

'Yes. Once it's closed, it can't be opened until the cycle is over. So no one can blunder inside.'

A prototype teleportation chamber would be a pretty memorable place to fuck someone, it occurred to Loeser. 'So if someone were to shut it now, we'd be trapped in here together for hours?'

'The time lock's synchronised to the ultramigration accumulator, and there's no experiment running, so it won't operate. I just wanted you to see how I can be sure that no one else is interfering with the things I put in here.'

'What sort of things do you mean, by the way?'

'Just . . . things. It doesn't matter. But it works. It's only a question of making it work for the Professor as often as it works for me. And that will happen, I know it will, if he just carries on a bit longer without getting put off by these petty shortfalls.'

'But if these things disappear, aren't they supposed to reappear as well? Isn't that the point of teleportation?'

'They do reappear. Somewhere. I'm certain. But at the moment, I can't quite control it, so I don't know where. I think it's because I can't control my heart, either.'

'You used to be such a little demon and now you talk like somebody's simpering chattel. If Bailey is Hephaestus, you're one of his robotic handmaidens.'

'Well, at least I don't go to bed with other men any more. Isn't that what you always used to object to so much?'

'Yes, I suppose there is that. Still, you've changed so much. I don't like it, Adele.'

'That's the promise of this country, isn't it? To come here and reinvent yourself? I'm always reading that in the editorial column of the *Herald*.'

'Why would I want to reinvent myself? I'm happy as I am.'

'You don't seem very happy.'

'That's temporary.' Except, he realised, it was supposed to be temporary because he hadn't found Adele yet. And now he'd found her, and she wasn't exactly pole-vaulting into his arms. Still, if she wouldn't fuck him in the teleportation chamber, maybe one day he could at least do a few lines of coke off the platform.

'You shouldn't be in here,' said Adele, perhaps presciently.

Loeser followed her back out to the laboratory. 'Do the police know who killed Marsh?' he said.

'No.'

'Because I've been thinking about it. It's Ziesel.'

'What?'

'It must be. Ziesel is a man to whom terrible things are destined to happen. It's intrinsic to his character. Yet here he is with a job and a wife, loved and respected. It can't be as simple as that. There must be something else going on that we don't know about, to spoil things. And this fits perfectly. He obviously has some compulsion to murder. The only reason he has such a perfect life at the moment is so that it will be all the more painful when he gets dragged off to some verminous lunatic asylum.'

'You sound as if you positively long for his life to be a catastrophe.'

'No, I don't, I've got nothing against him, I just mean that there are some people for whom things must always go wrong, or the universe isn't working properly. Ziesel is one of those. You can tell as soon as you meet him. So unless he's got some other disturbing secret, he must be the Monster of CalTech.'

'But, Egon, everyone knows it was Slate.'

'Just because of his two-dimensional face and his speech impediment?'

'No. He murdered all those dogs. There was never proof, quite, but everyone knew it was him. And they were found in just the same way – chests torn open, hearts missing.'

'Jesus Christ, Marsh's heart was missing?'

'Yes. Slate has no alibi. And I know better than anyone, because I'm always here at night, and Slate's always here too. He's not cleaning. He's just stalking around. He's not even supposed to work after six, but I've seen him here at two in the morning. He tries to hide from me sometimes.'

'Aren't you scared?'

'No. It sounds absurd, but the way he looks at me – I can just tell he wouldn't hurt me. He might hurt anyone else, but he wouldn't hurt me. I'm sure of it.'

'I saw Dr Clarendon in the basement.'

'Yes, he often works late too. I can't understand why he's not more afraid, after this morning – alone down there in the dark.' She looked at her watch. 'Egon, I need to take some more readings. You should go home. You're not safe here either.'

'Has Ziesel gone home?'

'Yes.'

'Then we're both safe. Don't be silly. It can't be Slate. That would be too obvious. I'm definitely not going home yet. What is it? What are you looking at?' Loeser turned, and then let out the sort of noise a Pomeranian makes when you tread on its tail. Standing there in the doorway of room 11 was Slate himself, who for some reason gave a long, slow shake of the head and then hobbled on down the corridor and out of sight.

'I think I might go home after all,' said Loeser hoarsely. He waved goodbye to Adele, hurried out of the Obediah Laboratories, and sprinted to his bike.

As he cycled back down Del Mar Boulevard, he thought about Bailey's Teleportation Device. Could it really run on love, as Adele claimed? He found the idea insipid. Loeser himself hadn't been 'in love' since he was at university, and he'd long since forgotten what it felt like; the notion was as abstract to him now as it had been when he was a child. But desire was another matter. It was desire, not love, that had uprooted Loeser, that had brought him all the way to California. Desire, he believed, could uproot almost anything. Adele had probably just confused the two, as people did. But if the Teleportation Device ran on desire, then that implied that Adele felt some tremendous voltage of lust for wobbly old Professor Bailey. And that was just as implausible. Still, if she really did, did that mean he'd got to her too late? Something leaden settled in his stomach at the thought. What use was *Dames! And how to Lay them* now? Perhaps, as they said in English, 'that ship had sailed'. Or perhaps, with Adele, the ship had never even docked. Perhaps there was no ship. Perhaps there was no harbour. Perhaps there was no sea.

China City

At the corner of Ord and Spring a huge iron gate led to a winding street calling itself Dragon Road. Past the gate, every roof had a pagoda, every surface was painted red or gold, and every nail held up at least one long string of paper lanterns or silk flags. Men in conical straw hats pulled rickshaws back and forth, shouting for business.

'What is this?' said Loeser as he stepped down from the bus.

'China City,' said Blimk. 'It just opened and I been wanting to see it.'

Last night, after he got home, Loeser hadn't been able to sleep. Marsh's disheartened corpse had jigged in his mind with Slate hunched in the doorway, so that he found himself almost wishing for the familiar scuffling of his ghost over his head. So that morning – having tossed and turned for so long that his sheets had cycled through every possible permutation of rumple and were somehow actually neater when he got out of bed than when he got in – he dressed, abolished a pot of coffee, and took an early streetcar to Blimk's shop. By the time he arrived, a plumber was already at work on a leaky pipe next to Blimk's desk, and he was making too much noise for either of them to concentrate on their reading, so they decided to close the shop for a few hours and take a bus downtown. Blimk did have a car, but he was considerate about Loeser's transport anxiety.

One of the consequences of Harry Chandler using the influence of the *LA Times* to make sure Union Station was built at the Plaza, Blimk now explained, was that the old Chinatown with its brothels and opium dens had been demolished in 1933 to make way for it, and for five years now the Chinese population of Los Angeles had not had anywhere in particular to live. But now there were two neighbourhoods competing for their favour: China City, built by a wealthy San Francisco socialite (and friend of Harry Chandler) called Christine Sterling who'd already converted nearby Olvera Street into a 'Mexican' tourist attraction, and New Chinatown, a few blocks north-east, built by a businessman called Peter Hoo Soo who was President of the Chinese American Assocation. Sterling's development was a good deal more ornate: she'd leased studio props from Cecil B. DeMille and she'd had the town hall decorated by a set designer called Wurtzel to look like a Chinese pirate junk.

'I knew him in Berlin!' said Loeser.

'He works on a lot of Goatloft's movies now,' said Blimk.

'But I can't actually see any Chinese people here. Except waiters and rickshaw drivers.'

'Would you live here, if you were a Chink?'

'No, I suppose not.'

At the Muttons' parties, the most recent Jewish arrivals always complained about how first they'd been dismissed from their jobs and then they'd been forced out of their homeland. They said it had broken their hearts, and they claimed to miss every little thing about Berlin. Loeser now imagined stuffing them all into Germany City: a square mile of freshly painted beer halls and art galleries and cabarets, with its own miniature Potsdamer Platz and and its own miniature Romanisches Café and even its own miniature Kempinski's Haus Vaterland (which like the real one would have its own USA-themed bar, which would have its own Los Angeles, which would have its own Germany City, and so on ad infinitum). They'd probably like it better than Pacific Palisades. Christine Sterling's China City, he saw, was as if Paris had been rebuilt by a set designer who'd only heard about it from Herbert Wolf Scramsfield and *The Sorceror of Venice*; and yet it still didn't feel any more obviously artificial than the rest of Los Angeles, even though Los Angeles wasn't imitating anything except itself. A man with a gentle case of Gorge's agnosia could walk down Dragon Road and believe he was really in Peking. What if that literalist walked down Sunset Boulevard? Would he understand this cosmopolis better than anyone, or would he be trapped in a recursion? When Loeser heard the exiles whine, he sometimes thought to himself that he, too, had been dismissed from his vocation and forced out of his homeland. His vocation was sex. His homeland was the female body. He felt just as lost as they did, but no one was ever sympathetic. And as he turned left down Lotus Road with Blimk, it occurred to him that China City was to China exactly as *Midnight at the Nursing Academy* was to a living, breathing girlfriend. The simulation might seem laughable at first, but perhaps after seven years away from home, an immigrant from Guangdong would come here and weep with guilty relief, because it was the nearest thing he had left to what he remembered. They passed a restaurant that advertised its chef as knowing '100 Different Ways to Fix a

Chicken' (but did not explain how the chicken was faulty), and Loeser said to Blimk that they should stop for chop suey because he'd never had it before. Blimk told him that chop suey didn't even exist in China. And Loeser decided that Chinese food invented by Americans was exactly what he wanted to eat that morning.

'Couple of fellas came into the store yesterday,' said Blimk after they'd sat down and ordered. Loeser had nearly asked for a starter of turtle soup but then he had thought of Urashima Taro. 'Wanted to know what rent I paid, how long I'd been there. Asked them who they were and they said they were from the Traffic Commission, just wanted to check some facts. Can't see what my rent's got to do with the traffic. Didn't know better, I'd be worried about Eminent Domain.'

'What's the Eminent Domain?' said Loeser. It sounded like an old-fashioned euphemism for the afterlife.

'When the government buys your property out from under you without asking, for a highway or a railroad or some-thing. That's how they got the Chinks out of Chinatown to build Union Station. I ever lost my store like that, think I'd just go back to Brooklyn and live with my sister. Not even worth relocating, amount I make. Can't be Eminent Domain, though. I'm up in north Hollywood, and they already got a Union Station. Asked my landlord and he doesn't know shit about it. Probably just want to put a tax on parking or something.'

'Probably,' said Loeser. And it wasn't until their bowls of chop suey arrived, and Loeser unfolded his napkin on his lap, that he noticed the dragon embroidered on it in black thread, and was reminded by its shape of the map that Plumridge had drawn on one of Gorge's napkins at that dinner in 1934: the network of elevated streetcar lines conjoining in Hollywood at the corner of Sunset Boulevard and North Kings Road. He hadn't heard anything of the plan since, and he'd assumed it had come to nothing. But just then, for the first time, he realised that Plumridge's proposed terminal would occupy the very same block as Blimk's bookshop.

'What's the matter?' said Blimk. 'Ain't hungry now you've seen the food up close?'

The Gorge House

Gorge's cigar gave off a smell like a village being razed by retreating infantry. 'Sit down, Krauto,' he said. 'Got to CalTech?'

'Yes.'

'And?'

'It seems that . . .' The sentence was so absurd that Loeser almost couldn't finish it. 'It seems that Professor Bailey is trying to build a teleportation device.'

Gorge waved his hand impatiently. 'Know that. Known that since thirty-six.'

'Then why did you send me?'

'Want to know if the fucking thing works, of course.'

'Why?' said Loeser. And then all at once it seemed obvious. 'You think that if Bailey completes his Teleportation Device, it will replace the car. You want to destroy Bailey because you think Bailey will destroy your car polish business.'

'Destroy Bailey? Never heard such horseshit! Say Bailey's Teleport Gizmo is real. Say I destroy him. Next year, have to do the same thing to some other son of a bitch. Next year, dozen more. Invented one place, soon be invented everywhere – general rule. Can't do a fucking thing about it.'

'But what about your car polish business?'

'1948: Teleport Gizmo in every house. Millions of 'em, all over the country. Think people won't want their Teleport Gizmo shiny? Think people won't want to buff 'em up every day? Sell just as many tins as before. Won't cost me a dollar, the Teleport Gizmo.'

217

'So you want to know if Bailey's Teleportation Device is real' – another sentence, this, that jammed its elbows in the doorframe until it could be dragged outside – 'so that you can pre-emptively corner the market in teleportation device polish?'

'Woodkin: mongoloid?'

'On the contrary, sir, I believe Mr Loeser is of above average intelligence,' said Woodkin.

'Hard to believe. Listen here, Krauto. Remember Plumridge?'

'Yes. He wanted to build an elevated streetcar network,' said Loeser.

'Can't have it. Tell him, Woodkin.'

'Colonel Gorge believes there are two reasons why an elevated streetcar network would be undesirable for Los Angeles,' said Woodkin. 'The first is that mass transit of any kind tends to promote authoritarian socialist leanings in its users, whereas drivers of automobiles tend to be committed free market capitalists. New York's subway, which carries more passengers than all the other heavy rail systems in America combined, is only one example of how ubiquitous mass transit can pervert a city's political tendencies. The Marxian uprising in this country, if it ever comes, will begin on a crowded commuter carriage. The second reason is that Colonel Gorge believes the wars of the future will be fought with weapons so mighty that at present we can hardly imagine them. Think of a bomb so big it could vaporise a whole town, perhaps by harnessing cosmic rays, or some other new spark from Vulcan's forge. Drop that bomb in the centre of New York, and you would kill millions. Drop that bomb in the "centre" of Los Angeles, and you might only kill a few thousand. In any given urban area, high-capacity mass transit promotes concentration. Automobiles promote dispersion. If America is to win its next war, perhaps against Russia or China, without being crippled by a single surprise attack against its civilian population, it must spread its urban areas out as evenly as it can. Mr Plumridge may only be an Assistant Public Utility Liaison at the Traffic Commission, but that title belies his true significance. He has some very powerful interests behind him.'

'If you hate his plan so much, why did you invite him to dinner?' said Loeser.

'Friends close, enemies so close you can see right down their throats,' replied Gorge. 'Saying goes.'

'And what's Bailey got to do with Plumridge?'

'Teleport Gizmo works, no need for streetcars. Redundant. Bad for Plumridge, bad for Reds, good for America. Teleport Gizmo doesn't work, have to save Los Angeles myself. No choice. But can't just have Plumridge stomped. Same principle as Bailey: queue of other bastards behind him. Spend every cent I had, thought it would help, but no use with this kind of government horseshit. Delay it, best I can do. Piece of cake if I owned a newspaper, but don't, and Harry Chandler hates my guts. Have to go straight to Norman Clowne.'

'The Secretary of the Traffic Commission,' interjected Woodkin.

'Only bureaucrat powerful enough to sink these fucking streetcars for good. Says he'll do it, Clowne. But wants my girl.'

'What do you mean?' said Loeser.

'Wants to marry my daughter. Doesn't deserve her. No other way, though.'

'You're going to hand over your daughter to Clowne in exchange for him sabotaging Plumridge's elevated streetcar plan?'

'Duty as a patriot,' said Gorge. 'Doesn't mean I have to like it. Why I need to know if Bailey's a shyster or not. Teleport Gizmo's real, can tell Clowne to fuck himself. Teleport Gizmo's a flop, have to start sewing Mildred's trousseau.' He leaned forward. 'So?'

A line came into Loeser's head from Lovecraft's *The Shadow Over Innsmouth*, Blimk's favourite of the late author's stories and the only one that had ever been published in its own bound edition instead of in a monthly magazine: 'I had no car, but was travelling by train, trolley, and motorcoach.' That, really, was what got the narrator into trouble in the first place. Still, Loeser knew that a new public transport system, like an orthopaedic brace to correct the city's bad posture, was the only thing that was ever going to make Los Angeles a tolerable place to live. He should just tell Gorge what Adele had told him: the Teleportation Device worked. Whether or not it really did, it would mean Plumridge could go ahead with his plan, without Gorge bothering to defeat it through Clowne.

But that would also mean that Blimk, Loeser's only real friend here, would lose his shop and probably move back to Brooklyn. The streetcars might make Los Angeles tolerable for every other Berliner, but they would make it intolerable for Loeser.

Plus, Plumridge had seemed like a total prick at that dinner.

'Well, Krauto?' barked Gorge.

'I'm sorry but I don't know yet,' said Loeser. 'I went to Bailey's lab and I met him and I met his assistant. But I didn't see any of his experiments myself. So it's still too early to say.'

Gorge leaned back. 'Good. Hoped you'd say that. Don't want you pretending you're sure when you're not. Come back when you're absolutely fucking certain. Not one minute sooner. Daughter's pussy at stake.'

The Loeser House

Clarendon began to unpack his heavy combination-lock briefcase full of phasmatometric apparatus. 'Are your houseguest's manifestations concentrated in any particular part of the residence?' he said.

'Not really,' said Loeser, 'although I mostly hear her in the bedroom.'

' "Her"?'

'Oh, that's a hunch of mine. Did you have any luck with Marsh last night?'

'I haven't yet made any precise kinetic measurements,' said Clarendon, bending to plug part of his ghost hardware into the electrical socket by the door. 'But the readings I took gave unmistakable signs of his presence.'

'I'm still intrigued as to what the State Department has to do with your experiments. I shouldn't think anyone can eavesdrop on us here. Well, except the spectre, of course.'

Clarendon looked up at him. 'How fast is this house moving, Mr Loeser?'

Loeser glanced at the window and thought of the bungalow on Sunset Boulevard. 'I'm not sure that it's moving at all.'

'Incorrect. Add together the rotation of the earth, the motion of the earth around the sun, the motion of the sun through our galaxy, the rotation of our galaxy, and the motion of our galaxy through the universe, and relative to a certain arbitrary framework this house is moving at nearly two million miles an hour, or five hundred miles a second. The reason we are not left behind in space is that fortunately we are all moving at the same speed. The most important gift your mother ever gave you was momentum. However, there can be no transfer of momentum between a fresh corpse and its affiliated ghost, otherwise all energy would eventually leak out of our plane of existence into the ghost's plane of existence, which would in some novel sense violate the first law of thermodynamics. Therefore, in order to keep pace with the locus of its haunting, a ghost must have its own means of accelerating to two million miles an hour – and, indeed, maintaining that speed, if the substrate of the ghost's plane is not frictionless – by drawing on some massive, perhaps infinite source of energy. My hope is that it will one day be possible to build a machine to trap this energy – something between a treadmill and a turbine, existing half on our plane and half on the ghost's. The machine will exert friction on the ghost, but since the ghost cannot be slowed down, the ghost will continuously pass energy into the machine. Even if it is only possible to drain a tiny fraction of the ghost's terajoules, I estimate that a few hundred ghosts would be enough to power the entire continental United States, leaving our annual production of oil, gas, and coal available to our armed forces, and our cities smogless. As you will no doubt already have noted, my calculations rely on the assumption that in the afterlife ghosts retain considerable mass. My evidence for this is that victims of decapitation carrying their own severed heads have been observed to complain about the weight.'

'I see.' Loeser's main concern about the Eminent Domain was that he would arrive to find all his ex-girlfriends there and there wouldn't be any drugs to get him through it. 'Do you think everyone gets an afterlife, even if they don't believe in it?'

'God will allow no man to escape the reward or the punishment that he deserves,' said Clarendon, putting an odd stress, Loeser thought, on the word 'punishment'. 'On earth as it is in heaven. Now, if you'll excuse me, I need to concentrate for a few minutes while I calibrate the equipment.'

'Take your time. Do you want a drink?'

'No, thank you.'

Loeser made himself a whisky and soda. Outside a fire engine screamed down Palmetto Drive. He thought about Marsh. Was there really a laboratory ghost haunting the California Institute of Technology? And then he realised that Marsh wouldn't quite be the only one of that species. The whole state of California was a laboratory, a room for testing new theories, measuring new forces, designing new gadgets.

So Loeser himself – uneasy and pale, detached and misplaced, a spilt drop of something old and cold – what was he, while he lived here, but another laboratory ghost?

After a while, Clarendon frowned and said, 'There's no ghost here.'

'What do you mean?'

'According to my readings, there is no ghost in this house.'

'But I've been living with her for three years. I'm sure of it. Couldn't your equipment be unreliable?' Then the telephone rang. Loeser made an apologetic gesture and went to answer it. 'Hello?'

'It's Adele.'

He switched to German. 'Adele! I don't remember giving you my telephone number.'

'I got it from Mrs Jones at Throop Hall. Egon, I think I know who killed Marsh.'

'I thought you were sure it was Slate.'

'It wasn't Slate. It can't have been. There have been other murders.'

'What?'

'Last year, one of the cooks from the cafeteria. And the year before that, one of the gardeners. Hearts gone, same as Marsh. Millikan covered it up each time so there wouldn't be a panic. But he couldn't do that with Marsh because there were too many of us there when we found the body. And now the rumours have got out. I heard about it from Dick. When the cook was killed, Slate wasn't even in California. He was visiting a sister in Alaska. He'd already been gone for a week and the corpse was only a few hours old when they found it.'

'I was right! It was Ziesel!'

'No, not Ziesel,' said Adele, and then said the inevitable three syllables.

'Clarendon?' repeated Loeser without thinking, and then bit his lip. The phasmatometrist presumably didn't speak German but of course he could recognise his own name.

'Yes. He's building a machine powered by ghosts, and he's under pressure from the State Department to finish the machine before this war in Europe starts, and he needs to test it first, and he can't just wait for people to die in accidents. I think he's killing people himself! He's breeding ghosts like biologists breed mice!'

'How do you know so much about his research?'

'The Professor told me. And listen to this: Dick said all the bodies have turned up in or near the Obediah Laboratories. That's where Clarendon works. Ziesel is all the way over in Robinson.'

'Adele, he's in my house.'

'What do you mean?'

'He's here. Now. With me.' Loeser didn't dare look round.

'God, why?'

'He's testing for a ghost here.'

'So he has all his machines with him? And the two of you are alone? Loeser, what if he's there to kill you and capture it on the phasmatometer?'

'Adele, for Christ's sake, call the police! Tell them to come here!'

'I will, but they may not get there in time. Egon, you have to get him out of your house.'

Loeser put down the phone and turned to find Clarendon standing there only a few inches away, holding the same big pair of wire cutters that he'd had in the basement last night. 'I was wondering if you might unlock that window,' Clarendon said. 'Sometimes I use an aerial to detect possible electromagnetic disturbances from the Heaviside Layer. It's the most accurate way to compensate for them.'

To unlock the window, Loeser would have to turn his back on Clarendon again. Just the thought made the nape of his neck wrinkle with fear. He thought he saw Clarendon's grip tighten on the handle of the tool. 'I thought there was no ghost here.'

'It's worth a second try. I'm confident that my apparatus is reliable, but in any experiment there are unanticipated factors.'

'Dr Clarendon, I really don't want to take up any more of your evening. I'm sure your apparatus got it right the first time. I must have been wrong about the ghost. I've always been a bit jumpy. Now, as it happens I have two dozen people coming to dinner so I'm afraid—'

'It will take just a few more minutes, Mr Loeser, if you'll just oblige me by unlocking that window. I can't seem to work the catch.'

For a long moment, Loeser stared at Clarendon, wondering if he could possibly overpower him without losing a finger. The rhythm of his heart seemed to be drumming out, 'Please/don't let/him eat/me please/don't let/him eat/me.' Then, for the second time that day, the doorbell rang.

Drunk with relief, Loeser dashed to the door and flung it open, hoping that it was burly policeman with a revolver, a nightstick and perhaps for good measure some sort of medieval halberd.

But it wasn't. It was someone even more formidable than that. It was Dolores Mutton.

'Mrs Mutton!' he cried joyfully. 'Hello! Hello!'

'Good evening, Mr Loeser.' She walked past him into the house and looked Clarendon up and down. 'Oh, I see you have company.'

'This is Dr Clarendon.'

'A pleasure to meet you. Now, I assure you I wouldn't usually interrupt like this, Dr Clarendon, but I have some very important Cultural Solidarity Committee business to discuss with Mr Loeser. It's awfully kind of you to cut your visit short.'

'In fact I was hoping to stay and take a few more—'

'Awfully kind of you,' repeated Dolores Mutton, combining a perfectly gracious smile with a voice that suggested she

225

wouldn't need to resort to a pair of wire cutters to relieve him neatly of his thumbs. Clarendon blanched and then with some haste started packing up his equipment. Nobody spoke until he'd finished, after which he scurried out without saying goodbye or picking up his hat. Loeser was pleased but unsurprised to observe that the terrifying angel had the same efficient effect on other men that she'd once had on him. As soon as the door was closed, she said, 'I don't think you understood me on the telephone last night.'

'About Professor Bailey?'

'Yes. You're going to start bringing him to our parties.'

'I told you, Mrs Mutton, I don't know him well enough.'

'I'm not giving you a choice, Loeser. You'll do it, or Jascha and I will destroy you. And because of your predictable greed, we won't need to resort to violence to do that. You've been embezzling from the Cultural Solidarity Committee of California for the last three years. Unless you do as we say and arrange for us to become friends with Professor Bailey, we'll give the evidence to the cops, and you'll be tried and convicted, after which you'll serve time in jail and then be deported back to Germany.'

'Embezzling? What do you mean?'

'You've siphoned over a thousand dollars out of the Committee's funds.'

'But that was my salary.'

'For what?'

'I'm on the board. You said you needed a Jewish board member.'

'But you're not Jewish, are you, Mr Loeser? And you've never been to a board meeting. In fact, there's no record of your ever being offered any type of post on the Committee. You just used your friendship with my husband and me to betray us by stealth.'

'You sent me those cheques every month.'

'You may never have noticed, but those cheques were made out in your own handwriting. Apart from "my" signature on them, which you are obviously not very good at faking. Any good graphologist will confirm that.'

Dolores Mutton's unpredictable alternation between friendly and aggressive over the past three years had been like a slow version of one of the advanced procedures from *Dames! And how to Lay them*, and Loeser could hardly take all this in, but nonetheless he was struck just then by a triumphant thought. 'So you copied my handwriting. Or Drabsfarben did. What did you copy it from?'

'Several years ago, in Berlin, you sent Jascha a letter about a play. You wanted him to write the score.'

'*The Teleportation Accident*. He said no. But he brought that old letter all the way to America?'

'Jascha maintains an extensive library of handwriting samples. It often comes in useful.'

'Well, you're not as clever as you think, Mrs Mutton! My handwriting has changed since then. "Any good graphologist" will confirm that, too. Your cheques won't fool anyone.'

'Actually, that will make them all the more convincing, because it will look like you tried to contrive a different scrawl, but didn't succeed in masking your real one.' She shrugged. 'In any case, if our preparations don't work out, that will be a pity, but it won't be a problem. We'll just go back to how we would have done it before. We'll run a risk.'

'What do you mean?'

'Jascha will kill you and make it look like an accident. Goodnight, Loeser. You know what you have to do.'

'Wait – how long do I have?'

'Like you told me, you've only just met the Professor. And we're reasonable people. We can give you six months.'

'Why is this so important? What are you going to do with him? Is this about the Teleportation Device?'

'Don't worry about that. Just get us Bailey.'

After she shut the door behind her, Loeser stood there paralysed for so long that he still hadn't shifted when his doorbell rang for the third time that night. He opened the door to a policeman in uniform.

'Are you all right, sir?' said the policeman. 'We had a report of an intruder at this residence.'

'I'm fine. There's no one here.'

'So you didn't call us?'

'No. I'm sorry. Perhaps it was a nuisance call.'

'So there's nothing wrong here at all?' said the policeman.

'No,' said Loeser. 'There's nothing wrong here at all.' And at that moment, as the policeman peered past him into the house, Loeser watched two young deer running down Palmetto Drive, nacreous in the twilight, ghosts on a frictionless plane.

Part III

This is your life

6

LOS ANGELES, 1939

The final dying sounds of their dress rehearsal left the California Institute of Technology Players with nothing to do but stand there, silent and helpless, blinking out over the footlights of an almost empty auditorium. They hardly dared to breathe as the slim, solemn figure of their director emerged from the naked seats to join them on stage, as he pulled a stepladder raspingly from the wings and climbed halfway up its rungs to turn and tell them, without so much as a preparatory clearing of his throat, that they were a damned talentless group of people and a terrible group of people to work with.

'We are going to start again,' he said. 'From the beginning. And carry on until we get it right.'

No murmurs of dismay followed these words, nor even the briefest eye contact between the Players. Like slaves who had been whipped so many times they had forgotten how to flinch, they just moved numbly back into their places for the first scene. Loeser got down off the stepladder, pulled it back into the wings, and returned to his seat in row F.

'Ready, Ziesel?' he shouted.

'Ready!' shouted Ziesel from his technician's box.

'*Auf geht's.*'

Ziesel cut the footlights so that the auditorium was in total darkness. Dr Pelton, CalTech's best amateur pianist, struck a series of eerie dissonant chords. Then a spotlight lanced across the stage, revealing Adele Hister standing on a dais in the centre. She wore a tight black gown with a sort of asymmetrical cheongsam collar and spiky shoulders.

'Look, Grandma,' she howled, raising a lump of magnesium ore high above her head, 'I caught a snowflake in my hand and it isn't melting!'

Another spotlight came on, this time revealing Mrs Jones, a secretary from Throop Hall, as she rolled a rusty wheelchair down a long steel ramp.

'But, precious,' Mrs Jones howled back, 'it's not even snowing outside.'

'I know, but look!'

'Well, precious, I hope you know what that means. My own dear old grandma told me when I was just a little girl. If you catch a snowflake when it isn't snowing, you get one wish. And if the snowflake doesn't melt, you get three wishes.'

'Three wishes!' At this point a row of three more lights came on, these ones shining intensely into the stalls as if there were escaped prisoners among the audience.

'Yes, precious. What will they be?'

'Gee, Grandma, first of all, I wish that we get a real white Christmas. Real snow on Christmas Day, like in stories.' One of the three lights shut off, and Dr Pelton, in the orchestra pit, tolled a deep, funereal bell.

'And?'

'Second of all, I wish that Ma and Pa find the money to buy medicine for poor old Nigger.' A second light shut off, and a second bell tolled. At the same time, a different light came on, revealing the huge aluminium model of a dog's skull, ferocious jaws agape, that was suspended on chains from the ceiling to represent the family's ailing pet.

'And?'

'And third of all, I wish that mean Mr Parker doesn't make Pa work in the factory on Christmas Day.'

A third light shut off, and a third bell tolled. At the same time, a hydraulic machine press that had been installed at the front of the stage started up, producing a hammering noise that left much of the dialogue that followed almost inaudible.

232

' "Mean"? That's no way to talk about your future father-in-law, precious,' shouted Mrs Jones.

'What do you mean?'

'Everyone knows you're sweet on Chip Parker, precious. Just yesterday, you were necking with him at the soda fountain.'

An obscene pink light began to strobe.

'I was not! How did you know?' Adele still held the magnesium over her head and her elbows were starting to quiver.

'Don't worry yourself about that. Grandmas always find these things out. Now, here's your Ma coming back from town.'

The strobe shut off and a long blast of dry ice befogged the stage as Dr Pelton's wife Martha entered on a conveyer belt. She wore wooden conquistador armour.

'Ma!' screeched Adele.

'Hello, little one.'

'Isn't it chilly today, Ma?'

'It sure is, little one, but nothing more warms me up faster than coming back to this wonderful cosy house.' Many more lights came on, revealing the rest of the set, which was mostly composed of ladders, pulleys, dustbins, and broken mirrors.

'Oh, Ma,' said Adele, flinging out her arms as if crucified as Dr Pelton scraped a steel protractor across the strings of his piano, 'isn't Christmas just the loveliest time of year?'

There had been some concern among the faculty that *The Snowflake* by J.F. McGnawn, Dr Millikan's choice for this year's California Institute of Technology Christmas play, might not be quite compatible with Egon Loeser's particular style of direction. Neo-Expressionism was apparently the term, and if you wanted to be equitable about last year's inaugural Gorge Auditorium production of *The Little Match Girl*, you might say that it had provoked a quantity of bracing debate. Nonetheless, the university's president had his

233

heart set on *The Snowflake*, and Loeser was still the only real theatre man with any connection to the faculty, so the two of them had reportedly made the bargain that if Millikan could have the play he wanted, then Loeser could direct it, not to mention write the music and design the costumes, without any interference at all.

Bailey, who sat at the very back of the auditorium, had slipped into this morning's dress rehearsal to see how his young assistant was getting on. When the Players were most of the way through their second run-through of the first scene, he decided he'd watched as much as loyalty to Adele demanded, so he got up and went back out into the December sunshine. The light in Los Angeles was not by any means a hibernant beast but sometimes just for a few days in winter it did get fat and furry and slow.

Bailey was walking towards the Obediah Laboratories when he noticed a small crowd of students gathered near the Dabney Hall of the Humanities. They were staring up at something on the roof. He looked up himself, and what he saw ripped away his breath. There was an old black Model T Ford up there, parked as if it were about to drive suicidally off the edge.

'*Dad*,' *he said*, '*how did that get up there?*'

'I don't know, son,' his father said.

As was their deferential habit when they came to an unfamiliar place, they had got down off their bicycles to wheel them on foot. The ground here was sticky and there was a sweet smell in the air, like walking under a mulberry tree in late summer, except there were no trees by the side of the road. He must have been twelve or thirteen by then and they had already been through so many small towns on their way to Tiny Lustre that Bailey had gone from treating each one like an exciting new frontier to treating each one like some friend of your uncle's to whom you might be introduced at a family function – you knew that you were probably never going to see them again and that they were therefore not worth any investment of your finite curiosity. This particular town was called Scarborough, and they only had to walk a short distance further up Main Street before they saw that something ghastly had happened here.

Splintered wood and broken glass and torn awnings; human shapes lying on porches, unmoving, covered by sheets, or in one case not even a sheet but an old patchwork quilt; a horse thrown head first through the window of a saloon, its back legs still weakly kicking like a dog in a dream; an over-turned cart with blood and hair stuck to one of its wheels; from all directions, the sound of whimpering or crying; and that insistent sickly odour, getting stronger and stronger as they walked. At the north end of the town was some sort of factory, and up there the disarray was at its worst, with nurses and firemen and policemen running back and forth among gawpers like themselves. Bailey thought at first that a tornado must have scrambled the town, but then his father stopped a man in a butcher's apron to ask what had happened, and they found out about the accident.

The factory was the Scarborough Ginger Ale Company bottling plant, the town's biggest employer, and beyond it was a branch of the Atlantic Coast Line Railroad. About an hour ago, a circus train from the Mockton-Piney Circus, heading east towards Florence, had made an emergency stop to check an overheated axle bearing on one of the flatcars. The driver of an empty Atlantic Coast Line train behind it had missed the signal posted by the brakeman – he must have been drunk or asleep, but no one would ever know now because he was dead – and had sped straight into the back of the circus train. The caboose and the rear four sleeping cars had all been pulverised, and the car that held the circus's elderly performing elephant had snapped off its couplings and rolled south down the incline into one of the Scarborough Ginger Ale Company's half-a-million-gallon steel storage tanks.

The tank had burst and sent a mighty wave of ginger syrup rushing like an apocalypse down Main Street, high enough to sweep that Model T Ford on to the roof of that bank. So far they'd counted more than thirty dead and more than a hundred injured, too many to fit in the town's hospital. As the man said this, Bailey caught sight of a headless body being taken out of the bottling plant in a green wheelbarrow, basted in its own gore, the tips of its fingers dragging on the ground. All Bailey could think about was that as they'd gone past Florence he'd been begging his father to let them take a train, just a slow, unpopular rural train, just once.

' "When many a great shipwreck has come to pass," ' said his father softly after the man in the butcher's apron had moved on, " 'the great sea is wont to cast hither and thither benches, ribs, yards, prow, masts and swimming oars, so that along all the coasts of the lands floating stern-pieces are seen, giving warning to mortals." Carry on, son, please.'

' "Even so," ' said Bailey, ' "if you suppose that the first-beginnings of a certain kind are limited, then scattered through all time they must needs be tossed hither and thither by the tides of matter, setting towards every side, so that never can they be driven together and come together in union, nor stay fixed in union, nor take increase and grow." ' His father had been teaching him Lucretius for two years now, and he knew most of the first two books of the Cyril Bailey translation of *De Rerum Natura* off by heart. Soon he would be ready for Walt Whitman and William James.

'Exactly right.'

'Those poor people,' said Bailey.

'Poor people?' repeated his father, and straight away Bailey knew he'd made a mistake. He still made mistakes so often. 'There was a much bigger train wreck in Washington just a few months ago. Are the men and women here worse off than the men and women there?'

'No, Dad.'

'Is there any reason why we should feel any more pity for the men and women here just because we happened to be near by when it happened?'

'No.'

'What fallacy would that be?'

'Propinquitous Conceit.'

'Exactly right. And what fallacy did the people of Scarborough commit?'

'I don't know.'

'Well, I expect most of them thought that just because something like this had never happened before, they didn't need to worry that it would ever happen, and so they didn't need to take precautions.'

'Inductive Normalism.'

'Exactly right.'

They watched the rescuers work for a few minutes longer. The activity was so disciplined and repetitive by now that it was almost as if this factory had been deliberately adapted for some new and unspeakable purpose – as if all these people would go home at five and come back tomorrow at nine and carry on working here until they retired.

'Dad?' Bailey said hesitantly.

'Yes?'

'Did They do this? Did They think we might have been on one of those trains?'

'I don't think so, son,' his father said. 'Remember, They want us alive.' And as they turned to leave Bailey heard yet again the squeak of the green wheelbarrow . . .

Moving like a clockwork automaton, Bailey approached the crowd of CalTech students so he could hear what they were saying about the car on the roof of Dabney Hall.

'They must have lifted it up there with a crane,' someone suggested.

'Where would they get a crane that tall?'

'Maybe they had a teleportation machine.'

Bailey glanced with suspicion at the originator of this last remark, but he saw that the boy had been joking – he didn't know anything.

'You're all dumb-asses,' someone else said. 'They took it to pieces, lugged it all up the utility staircase, and put it back together. There's no other way to do it.'

'That would have taken all night.'

'Anything worth doing takes all night. Don't you remember when they bricked up that door in Page and then painted it over like it was never there?'

'Where would they even get a car like that? It must be fifty years old.'

So it was just another student prank, thought Bailey. The boys here loved pranks – once, before his death, Marsh had decreed that they must wear jackets and ties for evening meals, and that night they had all arrived for dinner in jackets and ties but no trousers or shoes. He should have known, of course, but for a moment the car on the roof had seemed to him like some sort of malevolent lesion in time. It had been a long while since anything had reminded him of that day. By now some of the students had noticed Bailey standing there, so he nodded at them curtly and walked on towards Throop Hall. On his way past the front desk, Mrs Stiles waved to him. 'Oh, Professor Bailey, I've been calling your lab.'

'I'm sorry about that, Mrs Stiles, I was at the Gorge Auditorium.'

'How are the rehearsals coming along?'

'Very well, I think. Was it anything urgent?'

'There's somebody here to see you.'

Bailey couldn't see anyone waiting. 'Who?'

'An old coloured woman. She just went to powder her nose. She says she's a family friend.'

That wasn't possible. 'Did she give her name?'

'Lucy,' said Mrs Stiles.

Bailey stared at her.

'Lucy,' said his mother again from the doorway. 'Mrs Phenscot wants to talk to you about tomorrow's luncheon. She's in the orchid house.'

'Yes, ma'am,' said Lucy.

She put down the knife with which she had been boning a chicken and went to wash her hands. It was only then that Bailey's mother noticed Bailey's father sitting on a stool by the kitchen window.

'Tom,' she said sharply, coming forward into the kitchen. 'I didn't know you were down here.'

'Oh, sweetheart, Lucy and Franklin and I were just having a little tongue wag – weren't we, son?'

Bailey didn't look up from his toy steam engine. He was inside the train as well as above it and the great black oven beside him was its coal furnace. With Lucy gone he would have to stoke it himself. His mother waited until the cook had gone out and then said, 'I wish you wouldn't do this.'

'Do what?' his father said.

'All these "discussions" with Lucy.'

'I treasure our discussions.'

She tutted incredulously. 'I grew up with her, Tom, I love her as much as anyone, but we both know the only reason you keep coming down here is so you don't have to talk to my father. I'm sorry you think he's so unbearable.'

'I don't see why—'

'In fact, no, I'm not sorry you think he's so unbearable. I don't care what you think of him. I'm only sorry you take such pleasure in being rude to my family. Do you think I like apologising for you all the time?'

'Oh, sweetheart, you know I don't mean to offend your daddy any more than necessary. I come down here to talk to Lucy because I like talking to Lucy. Have you ever discussed God with her?'

'No, Tom, as it happens I haven't ever discussed God with the cook.'

'You know she believes in everything? I mean it. Everything. African deities, Red Indian spirits, Catholic saints – they're all the same to her.'

'And that's fascinating to you?'

'Yes. Because she doesn't see any contradiction. The priests on Hispaniola taught her grandparents that there's one god and all different kinds of angels. It's a sort of cheerful, omnivorous credulity.'

'It sounds like a child's religion.' His mother took off her glasses and folded them up, which was how she showed she was resigned to seeing a tiresome conversation through to its end. Bailey wondered what it would feel like to run the wheels of his steam engine over the raw flesh of Lucy's chicken.

'It does have a child's honesty. The other religions dissemble. Everything that's in Lucy's faith is in your parents' Catholicism too, sweetheart. The difference is that your parents' Catholicism has to suppress the parts it doesn't like. Lucy told me that back on Hispaniola her grandparents used to sacrifice livestock, and every so often, if things got desperate, someone might sacrifice a cripple. Her family didn't take part, she says, but it happened. Don't you think that's in Catholicism? All that bloodshed? But it's hidden. Not very well hidden, though – you've seen that crucifix they have on the wall that frightens Franklin so much. And who knows what goes on in that chapel of theirs?'

'Nothing "goes on" in there. That's where I was christened.'

'Then why won't they let me inside?'

'You're an atheist. It's the family chapel and no atheist has ever set foot in there before. You know that. You're lucky they even let you into their house. Especially when you behave like this.'

'No atheist? What about you?'

'Tom . . .'

'You're not telling me you've changed your mind again? That you believe in their god after all? Next you'll decide you want to let them put him through that initiation ritual.'

'Confirmation is not an initiation ritual.'

'Confirmation is bullying our son into joining their cult when he's still too young to understand why he might not want to.'

'Our son is right here and when you talk like that you probably scare him a lot more than that trinket on the wall. I don't want to have this argument again.'

'Come along, sweetheart, you promised me. You're going to help me make sure they don't put him through that. You're going to talk to your mother about it. Why don't you go now? She's always in a good mood when she's with her orchids.'

That was three weeks before his mother disappeared and his father took him away in the middle of the night . . .

'Are you all right, Professor Bailey?' said Mrs Stiles.

'I'm sorry, Mrs Stiles, but I don't have any family friends named Lucy and I won't have time to see her today.'

Bailey turned and strode away as fast as he could without quite breaking into a jog. He'd come here to pick up some typing from one of the girls but instead he carried on until he was out of Mrs Stiles's range of vision and positioned himself behind a pillar so that he could observe whoever came out of the women's bathroom near the reception desk. And then, sure enough, there she was, this shadow out of time. She was old, now, of course, probably almost seventy, walking with a stick, but she didn't look all that different. Hurrying out of Throop Hall by the doors at the other end, he tried to pretend to himself that he hadn't seen her, but this was a rupture in his history far harder to deny than that Model T on the roof of Dabney Hall. Some sort of storage tank had been broken open in his head and now he couldn't seem to stop the memories from gushing through him.

'Professor Bailey? Might I importune you very briefly?'

Bailey stopped. Why could he not be left alone today? The intervention here was from a blond man with an English accent who seemed to have been waiting there for him beside the steps up to the door of the Obediah Laboratories. 'Yes?' he said.

'My name is Rupert Rackenham. I live over in Venice Beach and I'm an old Berlin friend of Adele, your assistant. I've been given a freelance commission to write about you for the *Daily Telegraph* in London. They've heard you're very eminent in your field. I'd hoped to set up an appointment in advance but the lady at Throop Hall told me she's been instructed not to pass on any messages of that kind.'

'She has indeed. I'm afraid I'm much too busy.' That name, Rupert Rackenham, was familiar to Bailey from somewhere, but even more familiar was that voice: not just the accent but the false, practised, opportunistic charm. And yet he knew he'd never met this man. 'There is all sorts of interesting work going on at CalTech. Perhaps you could talk to one of my colleagues instead. Dr Carradine, for instance.'

'What does Dr Carradine do?' said Rackenham.

'He is building a machine for making eel congee out of electric eels that is itself powered by electric eels. An elegant design.'

'I'd much rather talk to you, Professor Bailey. It need only take an hour. The *Telegraph* will pay for lunch. I've cleared it with Dr Millikan. He thinks it will be good publicity for the Institute. We would begin with your family background and then—'

'No. I'm afraid not. Not this year.' And he tried to hurry on into the Obediah Laboratories, but the Englishman, undiscouraged, put a hand on his shoulder to slow him.

'*Don't touch my son, please,*' said Bailey's father.

'Oh, I'm terribly sorry,' said the Englishman with a smile, withdrawing his hand not quite straight away. 'It's just that I think your son dropped his toy. Wouldn't want him to lose it. Handsome little object.'

Bailey felt a cold tickle of embarrassment, knowing that at fifteen he was several years too old now to be carrying around a toy of any sort, and he couldn't look the Englishman in the eye as he took back his steam engine. Nonetheless, he recognised the Englishman, and the Englishman recognised him, because they had seen each other three times before, in other Wisconsin towns. For their itinerary to intersect more than once with some other traveller's was not that unusual – there were only a limited number of logical routes, for instance, up the western shore of Lake Michigan. Looking out across the empty planes of this state from his bicycle, Bailey had often thought of Lucretius. 'Space spreads out without bound or limit, immeasurable towards every quarter everywhere. No rest is allowed to the bodies moving through the deep void, but rather plied with unceasing, diverse motion, some when they have dashed together leap back at great space apart, others too are thrust but a short way away from the blow. Many, moreover, wander on through the great void, which have been cast back from the unions of things, nor have they anywhere else availed to be taken into them and link their movements.' Bailey and his father had not truly linked their movements with the Englishman, but they had wandered on together for a few days, and at first Bailey assumed it was this featherweight acquaintance that the Englishman had taken as a permit for the immediate camaraderie of his demeanour here in the hotel corridor. Only later would he deduce that the Englishman adopted that same demeanour with everyone he met.

'I see we're in adjacent lodgings,' said the Englishman. He held out his hand. 'Bertram Renshaw. Archaeologist.'

But his father ignored the hand and hurried Bailey into their small double room. After the door was closed he said, 'Don't talk to that fellow.'

'Why, Dad?'

'There's something not right about him.'

'Is he working for Them?'

'He could be. We'd better leave early tomorrow. We'll double back towards Madison.'

His father's criteria for identifying a stranger as an agent of either the Phenscots or the Catholic Church were mysterious to Bailey. Sometimes they wouldn't even have to encounter a person in multiple towns, as they had the Englishman: just one sighting at a distance would be enough. But this time, Bailey couldn't disagree with his father. There was indeed something not right about Renshaw. Most likely, his father would have preferred them to make their escape straight away, but for nearly two weeks now he had been wriggling on the hook of an abscessed tooth, and Sheboygan Falls had a good, cheap dentist. So at three o'clock, after setting Bailey his algebra problems for the day, he went out. As usual, Bailey was not to leave the hotel room for any reason, unless his father had not returned within six hours, in which case Bailey was to assume his father had been captured and carry on alone to Tiny Lustre.

The sky was overcast that day and through the window of the hotel room Bailey could see crows flying high up in it like punctuation lost on a blank page. He waited fifteen minutes, then went out into the corridor and knocked on the door of the Englishman's room. When Renshaw opened it he said, 'I sure am sorry to bother you, sir, but I was wondering if I might borrow a pencil sharpener. I can't find mine.'

Renshaw looked pleased. 'Certainly. Come inside and I'll look for one.'

For the first few years that he had travelled with his father, Bailey had been very afraid of their pursuers. But lately he had thought more and more about what it might actually be like to meet one of these dark entities. And this was the first chance he had ever had. He knew he ought to feel frightened but he didn't.

'Why don't you sit down, my boy?' said the Englishman. 'It might take me a moment or two to find.' He started rummaging around in a suitcase. 'Where are you and your father from?'

'Philadelphia.'

'That's a long way to come on a bicycle.'

'He took me out of school for a year so I could see a little of our country.'

'A magnificent notion. I come from London, but I've been all over this continent. Always something new to see. Mostly travel by motor car myself.'

'You're an archaeologist, you said, sir?'

'Yes.'

'And you go around looking for bones?'

'Sometimes. But these days I'm more of an educator. Science isn't any use, you know, if we scientists keep it all to ourselves.'

'So you give lectures?'

'Not often. I've found that the general mass of the American public is seldom prepared for the latest discoveries. I prefer to arrange meetings with interested individuals with progressive sensibilities. They, in turn, can use their influence to sow the seeds of this new knowledge.'

'What knowledge is that?'

Renshaw smiled. Somehow he had still not located the pencil sharpener. 'Oh, I'm not sure a lad of your age would be far enough ahead in your education.'

Bailey gave the invited response. 'I'll bet I am far enough ahead, sir.'

'Are you quite certain?' said Renshaw almost coquettishly.

'Yes, sir.'

'In that case, my boy, have you ever heard of the Troodonians?'

'No.'

'I should have been surprised if you had. Come and assist me with this.' Another of his cases was almost as big as a tenement stove, and Bailey had to help Renshaw lift it on to the bed. Then Renshaw snapped open four heavy brass catches to bisect the case vertically, and Bailey saw that the left side held the top half of a skeleton and the right side held the bottom half, each bone pulled snugly against the thick black velvet lining by leather loops, so that the case could be used as a sort of display cabinet when it was swung all the way open. Most of the skeleton looked unmistakably humanoid – the feet and the ribs and pelvis – but the skull looked more like a bird's or a lizard's. Also, it had a tail, and only four long digits on each hand.

'What is this?' said Bailey.

'I expect you've been told that the Red Indians were the first civilisation to inhabit North America,' said Renshaw. 'Well, they weren't. The Troodonians were far more advanced. While the Red Indians were still living in caves and eating worms, the Troodonians were herding livestock and trading goods.'

'What did they look like?'

'They evolved from dinosaurs, my boy. So they had scaly skin and serrated teeth. They laid eggs, and had no mammary glands, because they fed their young on regurgitated food. They worshipped a benevolent creator and lived according to his wishes. Their language would probably have sounded like birdsong, but they were also strongly telepathic, so they communicated mostly by thought. Unfortunately, although they were a cunning, acquisitive race, they were also a peaceful one. There is no such thing as a Troodonian weapon. So when the Red Indians decided to take over the Troodonians' lands, they met with very little resistance. In the end, almost the whole race was destroyed, and all we have left now are disjected remains. Some biologists do argue that a few surviving Troodonians might have undergone some sort of evolutionary reversion to a more primitive lizard form – small, quadripedal and robust – but I don't find that theory very credible.'

'Did you dig this one up yourself?'

'One of my colleagues found it in Arizona.'

'And you carry it around to show to people?'

'Not just to show, my boy. That would be selfish.' Renshaw explained that he placed discreet advertisements in small regional newspapers announcing an archaeological breakthrough of epochal magnitude, with an address to which interested parties could write for more information. He then toured the homes of the respondents with a Troodonian skeleton, and once he'd found a good home for that skeleton with a keen gentleman scholar, he telegraphed to his colleague in Arizona to despatch a replacement by rail so that he could continue his trip. And since his purpose was primarily educational, he practically gave away each skeleton, asking only enough in return to help cover some of the costs of the excavations. Never more than a thousand dollars. In fact, he could tell that Bailey and his father were both of a cultured, enquiring temperament. Perhaps they might be interested in a purchase themselves? You couldn't take a Troodonian skeleton on a bicycle, of course, but they could send it back to Philadelphia to await them on their return. And it was at this point that Bailey finally realised what Renshaw really was.

According to his father, the confidence man wasn't quite the most contemptible type of human being on the planet. That was the confidence man's victim. But the confidence man himself was still pretty bad. Ever since they left Boston, Bailey's father had been working on his manuscript, *The Complete Taxonomy of Anthropic Cognitive Unsoundness.* The epigraph was from Lucretius: 'Just as in a building, if the first ruler is awry, and if the square is wrong and out of the straight lines, if the level sags a whit in any place, it must needs be that the whole structure will be made faulty and crooked, so that some parts seem already to long to fall, or do fall, all betrayed by the first wrong measurements; even so then your reasoning of things must be awry and false, which all springs from false senses.' And the introduction promised that any man who trained himself rigorously using the book would be invulnerable to the predations of confidence men, hotdog vendors, sales clerks, politicians, moralists, aesthetes, beggars, cheap newspapers, sentimental novels, tearful women, and, above all, priests.

'Where is your father at present?' said Renshaw. 'Is he next door?'

'He's at the dentist,' said Bailey. 'I don't know when he'll be back.'

'I see.' Renshaw coughed and turned back to the skeleton. 'You know, my boy, the Troodonians had internal genitalia. Everything would have been tucked up inside a little vent called a cloaca.'

'Oh.'

'Whereas mammals like you and me are lucky enough to have been given external genitalia.' He put a hand on Bailey's thigh, its fingers quivering as it rested there like the legs of a nervous animal. 'Everything is . . . everything is just . . .' He didn't seem to be able to finish his sentence. 'Perhaps you might like to . . .'

There was a hammering at the door. 'Franklin?' his father shouted. The door was on a latch so Bailey had to get up and run over to open it from the inside. 'I knew I could hear you,' his father said, glaring at the Englishman. 'What are you doing in here?'

'Your son came to borrow a pencil sharpener.'

'He's got a pencil sharpener.'

'I couldn't find it, Dad.'

'Come on, Franklin.'

They went back into their room.

'I told you not an hour ago that there was something wrong about that fellow. You shouldn't have gone in there.'

'But he's not a detective or anything, Dad.'

'That may seem so obvious now that you feel as if you knew it at the time you made the decision. But you didn't. What fallacy is that?'

'Retrospective Reassurance.'

'Exactly right.'

Bailey's father never punished him, because for the last five years it had been his responsibility to train his son to behave rationally in every circumstance, and he believed that the failure of a pupil was by definition just as much the failure of a teacher. However, he didn't speak to his son for the rest of the evening, except to report that the dentist had been too busy to see him that afternoon so he would have to try again tomorrow. The next morning, Bailey went with him to the dentist and waited in an armchair while his father had his tooth pulled. They left Sheboygan Falls straight afterwards, his father's mouth still stuffed with bloody cotton, and Bailey never saw the Englishman again . . .

The ultramigration accumulator was already warming up, so he must have come into his laboratory and turned it on. He couldn't even remember how he'd disengaged himself from Rackenham. It was possible, he thought calmly, that he was having some sort of dissociative episode, and that he ought to go home before it got any worse. Where did it come from, this compulsion to tumble always back into the past? But the latest phase of his experiments was reaching its conclusion, and something about the sight of the Ford on the roof had made him determined to see it through as soon as he could. He set to work. After about an hour, Adele came in.

'How was your rehearsal, my dear?'

She grimaced. 'Don't ask.'

'I saw a few scenes and I was very impressed.'

'Back in Berlin, people used to say Egon had quite a bit of talent and he might do something important one day, except you couldn't ever tell him so because his head would get so big. I don't know what they'd make of *The Snowflake*.'

'Speaking of Berlin, I met a fellow just now who said he was an old friend of yours.'

'Oh, you mean Rupert?'

'That's right. Rupert Rackenham. How did you guess?'

'I ran into him just now on my way here.'

'He's still out there loitering?'

'I'm afraid so. All the same, it's nice that you met him at last.'

'Why do you say "at last"? Who is he?'

'You remember. He wrote that book you liked.'

'Book about what?'

'Lavicini,' said Adele.

'Who's Lavicini?' said Bailey.

Someone shouldered past him on their way to the bar, and he spilled some of his grapefruit juice on the carpet, but he was so dismayed he hardly noticed. Could it be that teleportation had already been achieved in Germany and the news had not made its way to the United States? Could it be that some Italian engineer working for Siemens had beaten him to it? He hadn't even meant to mention teleportation to this singular girl in the first place, and indeed he wasn't at all sure what she was doing at an Athenaeum Club cocktail party – you could tell just by looking at her that she wasn't one of the undergraduates' girlfriends, and she had a German accent. But then Adele explained about the Teleportation Accident of 1679.

'How do you know all this?' he said when she'd finished.

'A friend of mine published a novel about Lavicini. And I was in it. I was the ballerina who died, except I was really a princess.'

Straight away, with the irrefutable force of a religious revelation, Bailey was certain of two things. The first was that Lavicini's story was the key that would unlock the final door in his teleportation research, the door on which he'd been knocking for so many years. And the second was that this girl – the ballerina, the princess, the herald – would have to become his assistant. She probably didn't know anything about physics, but that didn't matter. She seemed bright. She could learn.

Teleportation as a fantasy had come to Bailey when he was still travelling with his father. They couldn't take trains or streetcars or steamboats because their faces might be recognised; they couldn't hire an automobile because their licence plate might be tracked; and they couldn't even take a direct route from east to west on their bicycles because their next stop might be anticipated. As the years wheeled on, Bailey began to wonder if they would ever get to California. And yet in his dreams he would look out of a window and he was already there. Lucretius made it seem as if anything was possible if you understood the nature of things. Couldn't there be a machine that could hurl a body across a continent as a telephone could hurl a voice?

But Bailey hadn't had his first revelation of how teleportation might actually work until he arrived alone in Los Angeles in 1915. Boston and Chicago and New York, the cities he'd seen with his father, were bodies with organs, but this territory, like space itself, was still just a giant bag of cytoplasm. It had almost unlimited capacity and its inhabitants were willing to drive almost unlimited distances. If you were trying to decide where to build a house or a restaurant or an ostrich farm, therefore, you had no substantive grounds on which to do so: here, location was a meaningless and arbitrary property. All spatial coordinates were equivalent. And that was how teleportation would function. A teleportation device would have to convince the object in the chamber that it just wouldn't matter if it were somewhere else. (Only a few months before this party at the Athenaeum Club, he'd been driving back from Venice Beach when he'd got stuck in the most infernal traffic jam he'd ever encountered. There must have been an accident up ahead, because he didn't see anyone make an inch of progress for twenty minutes or more. Horns quacked pointlessly. Bailey had been reminded of Lucretius: 'All things are not held close pressed on every side by the nature of body; for there is void in things. For if there were not void, by no means could things move; for that which is the office of body, to offend and hinder, would at every moment be present to all things; nothing, therefore, could advance, since nothing could give the example of yielding place.' And then he saw the driver of a dented green Chevrolet up ahead open his door, get out, and simply saunter off down the street, something in his bearing making it obvious that he did not intend to return. He was chased by curses, because if his car sat there driverless then the jam would take even longer to clear, but he never looked back. And all Bailey could think about was that this was teleportation. A particle's spatial coordinates were the steel chassis in which that particle was trapped. To escape from them, the particle merely had to get out and walk.)

Bailey wasn't, of course, the only physicist to be interested in teleportation. Over the years he'd met quite a few who'd read *The Disintegration Machine* by Arthur Conan Doyle when they were boys, or *The Man Without a Body* by Edward Page Mitchell (the author also of *The Clock that Went Backward*), and had never forgotten about it. But he knew they would never get anywhere, because they hadn't thought about it hard enough. They didn't seem to realise, for instance, that when an object departed the teleportation device, it couldn't just leave a vacuum behind, and when it arrived at its new destination, it couldn't just displace the matter that was already there. The laws of physics wouldn't allow that. Teleportation would have to be an exchange. If you set the device correctly, a human body would be swapped for a volume of air of exactly the same shape. But if you were off by a few feet, the subject might find himself embedded part of the way into a wall, like that horse thrown through the window of the bar in Scarborough, and in the chamber of the teleportation device you would find a sort of bas-relief. Indeed, if you teleported a naked corpse right into a block of marble, you could produce a sculpture accurate to every pimple.

The Monday after he met Adele at the party at the Athenaeum Club, Bailey sent for a copy of *The Sorceror of Venice*, and when he'd finished it he went to the Los Angeles Public Library to find out everything else he could about Lavicini. Each new detail made him more certain that the secret of teleportation was here. So when that same week a soft-spoken man from the State Department came to tell him that on the orders of Cordell Hull he was now to direct his scientific work according to the recent discoveries of an obscure author from Rhode Island called H.P. Lovecraft, Bailey was not nearly as surprised as the man seemed to expect him to be. When he looked over the State Department summaries of Lovecraft's stories, what he heard was a chord of recognition. Lovecraft understood everything. Bailey quoted Lucretius to the man: ' "For even as children tremble and fear everything in blinding darkness, so we sometimes dread in the light things that are no more to be feared than what children shudder at in the dark and imagine will come to pass. This terror then, this darkness of the mind, must needs be scattered not by the rays and the gleaming shafts of the day, but by the outer view and the inner law of nature." ' The man nodded and then told Bailey that there was only one small obstacle remaining: it had been impossible to obtain a proper security clearance for Bailey because for some reason State Department investigators had not been able to find any trace of his existence before 1915, when Bailey had enrolled at what was then called the Throop College of Technology. Presumably, the man said, there was a simple explanation? But Bailey just stared in silence at the man until at last he coughed and got up to leave. The question of a security clearance was never brought up again, although he was told that he was now so valuable to the American government that he could no longer be permitted to travel on aeroplanes.

From then on, the State Department sent Bailey every new story that Lovecraft published, and also typed extracts from his letters, which they often intercepted and steamed open. He soon began to feel that in other circumstances he could have been good friends with Lovecraft. To learn that Lovecraft, too, had read Lucretius in his youth did not surprise him: even Lovecraft's dread gods were sternly materialist, and it took a Lucretian belief in the illimitable reach of empirical enquiry to write that 'the sciences, each straining in its own direction, have hitherto harmed us little; but some day the piecing together of dissociated knowledge will open up such terrifying vistas of reality, and of our frightful position therein, that we shall either go mad from the revelation or flee from the deadly light into the peace and safety of a new dark age.' Bailey thought Lovecraft would have taken some pleasure in *The Complete Taxonomy of Anthropic Cognitive Unsoundness*.

Then again, Lovecraft did seem to have a malign obsession with Negroes and Jews, which would have been forbidden by Bailey's father's book. 'Either stow 'em out of sight,' he wrote to one friend, 'or kill 'em off.' This was tiresome reading, and yet Lovecraft was hardly alone. A great many of the Americans Bailey most admired were, or had been, preoccupied with the precarious future of the noble white race. Robert Millikan, the founder of CalTech. William Cowper Brann, the martyred editor of the freethinker magazine *The Iconocolast*. Edward Alsworth Ross, the sociologist who blamed the replacement of private cabs by public streetcars for the high rates of miscegenation in the urban United States. And Henry Ford, famously. Well, perhaps the other races really were inferior and dangerous. Perhaps they weren't. Bailey didn't know; it didn't interest him . . .

'Did you have a nice time at the party last night?' said Adele.

For a moment he thought she must be talking about the Athenaeum Club in '35. But of course she meant the party last night at the Muttons' house in Pacific Palisades. Loeser had pestered him for months to go to one, and he still wasn't sure why. But that first time, he'd been surprised to find quite a few German and Austrian scientists present who didn't yet have tenured jobs in this country, and some of them knew rumours about the latest incremental advances in particle physics that hadn't even quite reached CalTech. Also, the hosts seemed delighted by his presence in a way that was unfamiliar to him (once, Dolores Mutton had gone so far as to invite him to join her and a few other guests for a swim in the moonlight, but he'd had to decline because at forty-one he'd still never even learned to tread water). So he'd voluntarily gone back three or four times since. 'Oh, not too bad,' he said. It was nearly seven o'clock, and the ultramigration accumulator had finished a cycle. 'Why don't you go home, Adele? You must be tired after all those rehearsals.'

'Not really,' said his assistant.

'I insist. You won't miss anything. I won't be doing any more experiments today.'

This wasn't true. There were some experiments that, for various reasons, could not be performed in Adele's presence. Which was a pity, since Bailey liked to have her with him whenever he could. His instinct about her at that party four years ago had been more correct than he ever could have hoped. He didn't know why, but whenever it was Adele who operated the Teleportation Device, the prototype seemed to perform a great deal better. Perhaps in a field as mercurial as teleportation, a lack of formal scientific training was an advantage. And she worked so hard. Her only disagreeable quirk was that every so often he would notice her gazing at him for so long that he began to think he must have something in his teeth. Most likely she was just lost in thought. It had not escaped his notice that quite a lot of men on campus were erotically infatuated with the girl. Loeser, for instance, could hardly have been more blatant about it, and neither could Slate. Bailey himself had never taken any interest in sex, even as a young man. Most of what he knew about it came from Lucretius, who did not make it sound at all appealing. 'When the lovers embrace and taste the flower of their years, they closely press and cause pain to the body, and often fasten their teeth on the lips, and dash mouth against mouth in kissing; yet all for naught, since they cannot tear off aught thence, nor enter in and pass away, merging the whole body in the other's frame; for at times they seem to strive and struggle to do it. They yearn to find out what in truth they desire to attain, nor can they discover what device may conquer their disease; in such deep doubt they waste beneath their secret wound.' Why on earth would anyone want to put themselves through that?

Some time after Adele left, Bailey decided to go for a stroll. Fresh air kept him alert. But on his way out of the Obediah Laboratories he was dismayed to see Rupert Rackenham standing there in just the same place beside a cypress tree. The Englishman had a cigarette in his mouth and he'd flicked butts in every direction as if sowing a field.

'Professor Bailey—'

'Have you been here all this time?'

'Yes. I really am sorry to pester you like this but, between you and me, I've already spent the fee for this article so you'd be doing me an incomparable favour if you could spare so much as a minute and a half to discuss your work.'

'Mr Rackenham, if you weren't a friend of Adele's I would telephone the security guard at Throop Hall and report you for trespassing.'

'Don't treat the gentleman that way, Franklin. You always were a well-mannered child.'

Bailey turned, and there was Lucy. For a moment he thought she was another one of these alarmingly vivid recollections that had been invading him all day, except that his recollection of Lucy wouldn't have had a walking stick, and she wouldn't have had those spotty subsident jowls, and she wouldn't have been able to respond when Rackenham said, 'Are you a friend of Professor Bailey, madame?'

'Since he was born.'

'I don't know this woman,' Bailey said.

'Franklin!' said Lucy.

Rackenham raised his eyebrows. 'I don't mean to be impertinent, Professor Bailey, but she does seem to know your name.'

'Anyone could find out my name.' Last year the State Department had offered to help tighten security on campus to protect the highly classified endeavours of Bailey and Clarendon and their colleagues, but Millikan had refused, saying he didn't want the Institute to feel like a military base. At the time, Bailey had been relieved, but he realised now how absurd it was that nothing really stood between him and the rest of the world but Mrs Stiles at Throop Hall. Bailey had always done his best to keep his Teleportation Device a secret, but on his long pilgrimage with his father he'd come to realise that secrecy, like kinetic energy, was continuously dissipated – so that a secret kept for ever was not just improbable, like a teleportation device, but inconceivable, like a perpetual motion machine.

'Have you been here all evening, madame, like I have?' said Rackenham.

'Yes,' said Lucy. 'They said he won't see me. But I have to see him. So I waited. I was watching you waiting too.'

'You must be hungry. I certainly am. Perhaps you'd allow me to buy you a spot of supper somewhere near by? You needn't worry,' Rackenham added with a smile, 'I haven't any caddish intentions. But we could talk a bit about the disobliging Professor Bailey.'

'You have no right!' said Bailey.

'To do what?' said Rackenham.

The last thing Bailey wanted to do was invite Lucy into his laboratory, but he didn't have a choice if he was going to get her away from Rackenham. 'Lucy, come inside.'

'I thought you didn't know her,' said Rackenham.

'Come inside,' Bailey repeated. He took Lucy's arm and pulled her into the Obediah Laboratories almost faster than she could go with the stick. Then he locked the door behind them. Neither of them spoke until they were back in room 11, when Bailey said, 'How did you find me?'

'My granddaughter, she lives in Pasadena,' said Lucy, panting a little. 'I came out to live with her last year after I retired. One day I saw you in the street. I knew it was you. Don't know how I knew – thirty years gone by at least – but I knew it was you. My little Franklin. But I didn't want to stop you right away. Too nervous. So I got in a taxicab and I followed you. Found out you're at the Institute. Found out you're calling yourself Bailey now.'

'My name is Franklin Bailey and it always has been.'

'What did your daddy tell you about your mama, Franklin? I always used to wonder what he told you. You remember when she passed on it was right around when she'd had that ruckus with your grandma about your confirmation. Did he tell you your grandma and grandpa did something to her? Did he tell you he had to take you away in case they did something to you too?'

The lock on the door of the chapel. The carvings on the altar like gutters on an operating table. The chalice that was polished almost too clean. 'You are a senile old woman.'

'He did, didn't he? Franklin, don't you want to know what really happened to your mama?'

'Nobody knows what happened. She disappeared and she was never found.'

'She was found, child. She hadn't been found by the time your daddy took you away. He only waited a day. She was found after that. But you were already gone, so you never knew.'

'No more of this gibberish, please.' She was going to tell him that his father had murdered his mother. She was going to tell him that his father had run away because otherwise he knew he'd be caught. She was going to tell him that it was the police that he and his father had been fleeing, not the agents of the Phenscots and the Catholic Church. She was a liar. He knew she was a liar. He knew. He knew. He didn't know. He'd never known. He thought of Lucretius. 'These men, exiled from their country and banished far from the sight of men, stained with some foul crime, beset with every kind of care, live on all the same, and, in spite of all, to whatever place they come in their misery, they make sacrifice to the dead, and slaughter black cattle and despatch offerings to the gods of the dead.'

Lucy smiled sadly. 'Franklin, your mama fell down an elevator shaft.'

'What?'

'She was in a hotel and she didn't have her eyeglasses and the grille opened when it shouldn't have and she just stepped right into the elevator shaft. Broke her pretty neck. They didn't notice her down there for a day and a half. Your daddy just jumped to conclusions.'

'Do you still worship the gods of the dead, Lucy?' said Bailey.

'Are you listening to me, child?'

'Do you still worship the gods of the dead? The gods those priests taught your grandparents about on the island where your people come from?'

'I'm a good Catholic now, Franklin.'

'That's a pity,' said Bailey. 'Your grandparents were wrong – there are no gods of the dead – but they still understood more than you could possibly know.'

'Professor Bailey?'

He looked up. Clarendon stood at the doorway of room 11. When had the Obediah Laboratories turned into Union Station? And then for the first time he wondered whether all this had really happened in just one day – whether, in fact, it wasn't a week ago that he'd seen the Ford on the roof of Dabney Hall, and two weeks ago that he'd watched Adele in her rehearsal – whether he'd just let the transitions drop from his memory like a cutter down in Studio City. He found it hard to be certain. How was it possible for a person to be in one place, and then in another place, or to be in one time, and then in another time, without ever seeming to traverse the distances between them? 'Yes, Dr Clarendon?' he said.

'I thought we might have that talk now about the trouble I've been having with the phasmatometer. But, uh, I see you're busy,' said Clarendon, obviously puzzled by the presence of an elderly black woman in Bailey's laboratory.

'No, I'm not busy. This lady is just lost. Why don't you go back to your lab and I'll come by in a few minutes?'

'All right.' Clarendon nodded to Lucy and then left.

'Who is that man, Franklin?' said Lucy.

'A colleague.'

'There's something about him puts a frost on my bones.'

'He's not very genial, no.'

'I don't know if you should be on your own with him, child.'

Bailey wondered if Lucy had heard rumours about the deaths at CalTech. 'I've been on my own with him a hundred times. He's harmless. Now, it's time for you to leave. You'd better go out by the back entrance. I don't want you ever to come back here and I don't want you to say one word to that Englishman.'

'Franklin, please . . .'

'I don't know you. You didn't know my parents. You have probably come here to cheat some money out of me and you are trespassing just as much as Rackenham.' Then he turned his back on her and started fiddling with the controls of the ultramigration accumulator. He would stay like this for ever if he had to, but after a short while he heard her give a long sigh and then depart, cumbersome as black cattle.

When the ultramigration accumulator was at full power, Bailey put his toy steam engine into his pocket and went upstairs to Clarendon's laboratory, where the other physicist was in the process of disassembling his phasmatometer. 'As you can see, I've added this extra pair of valve coils,' he said when Bailey came in, as if they were already in the middle of conversation. 'I think that might be causing the trouble. What do you think?'

'Actually, Dr Clarendon, there's something I'd like to show you in Dabney Hall. I believe it has some bearing on your difficulty.'

'What is it?'

'I'll explain on the way. Then we can have a closer look at your valve coils when we get back.'

'If you really think so,' said Clarendon, and reluctantly put down his screwdriver. Together they left the Obediah Laboratories. This time, to Clarendon's relief, there was no sign of Rackenham, Lucy or any other pursuer.

'Do you know anything about Adriano Lavicini?' said Bailey as they walked.

'A little. I read that novel about him.'

'*The Sorceror of Venice*. Yes. Then you remember that Rackenham proposes that the destruction of the Théâtre des Encornets was the result of the sabotage of the Teleportation Device by a stagehand. That hypothesis is implausible, most obviously because it gives no explanation for the unusual phenomena reported by members of the audience. The fall in temperature. The disagreeable smell. The tentacles. I've done a lot of research into Lavicini, and I believe I know what caused the Teleportation Accident. The truth is, it wasn't an accident at all. The destruction of the Théâtre des Encornets was the express purpose of the Extraordinary Mechanism for the Almost Instantaneous Transport of Persons from Place to Place.' They were at the main entrance of Dabney Hall now, and Clarendon made as if to go inside, but Bailey shook his head and led him around the corner to the utility staircase.

'Why would Lavicini want all those people to die?' said Clarendon. 'And what has this got to do with the valve coils?'

'You remember, of course, that the basis of my teleportation research is to delete a particle's physical coordinates and replace them with new ones. Well, I once said to Adele, my assistant, "What's the one thing in the world that can uproot almost anything?" She's a very good assistant but she can be sentimental, and I could tell from the vapid expression on her face that the answer she had in mind was love, or something of that sort. That's what it would be in the motion pictures. But it's not love. Love does nothing. Love is only a type of anthropic cognitive unsoundness. What uproots things is violence. You must already understand that, Dr Clarendon. After all, a ghost could only be possible if a violent death caused some localised distortion to the physical laws of the universe. And it does. Unfortunately, not in the way you think. There is no such thing as a ghost. No one will ever build a working phasmatometer. All your research has been futile. If you were a better physicist perhaps you might not have wasted so many years.'

Clarendon looked taken aback. 'But, Professor Bailey, I always had the impression . . .'

'It was not the right time to break it to you. If you gave up your research, the State Department would have had no one at CalTech to bother but me, and that might have been inconvenient. Now, Lavicini knew no more of physics than Lucretius. But, like Lovecraft, he came to the truth by other means. This was Paris in the age of the Court of Miracles. And Lavicini's temperament was an empiricist's, not an artist's. He'd worked as an inventor at the Venetian Arsenal. Theatre was just a diversion. He wanted to build a real teleportation device, just as much as I do. And he succeeded. Did you know that in 1684, five years after Lavicini was supposed to have been killed in the Teleportation Accident, he was reported to have been seen back in Venice?' By now they were at the top of the utility staircase. Clarendon followed Bailey out on to the roof, where the Model T Ford was still parked at the edge. Beyond that, you could see the whole distribution of CalTech's buildings, like the parts of the phasmatometer laid carefully out across Clarendon's table.

'What are we doing up here?' said Clarendon.

Bailey opened the driver's side door of the car. 'Get inside,' he said.

'Why?'

'Get inside. You'll see why.'

Clarendon did as he was told. Bailey shut the door after him, then went around to the other side of the car and got into the passenger's seat.

'Hurry up and shut the door,' his father said.

The noise of the rain on the roof of the car was so loud that Bailey had to raise his voice to speak to his father. 'I didn't know they had storms like this in California.'

'They have tornadoes here sometimes, son. Hail. Mudslides. It's not all sunshine.'

The rain had started all at once, as if some part of the sky's masonry had suddenly collapsed, and they'd been caught outside with no shelter near by except a few inadequate trees. Then his father had spotted the Model T Ford parked a short way up the slope, and they'd dropped their bicycles and sprinted over, gambling that they would find its doors unlocked.

'What if the man who owns the car comes back?' said Bailey. There was a folded roadmap of southern California at his feet and he saw guiltily that the water dripping off him had already soaked it through. He could smell that a big dog sometimes travelled in this car.

'He won't come back. You can't drive in this rain.'

'Do you remember that Model T we saw on the roof in that town in South Carolina that time? What was it called?'

'Scarborough. I remember.'

He heard thunder, not far off. 'What are we going to do now, Dad?'

That morning, beneath one of those glassy March skies with a few grey stormclouds like the smears of soot on the inside of a blown light bulb, they had finally arrived at Tiny Lustre. Five years it had taken them to bicycle from Boston to California; five years of doubling back and turning aside and looping around and hiding out; five years as a mad doodle on a map of the continent, a housefly exploring a sunlit ballroom, a western vector so faint it might as well have been a statistical accident; five years avoiding the agents of the Phenscots and the Catholic Church, and the bustles in which those agents might lurk; five years of hotels and flat tyres and *De Rerum Natura*; five years to get to this freethinkers' colony not far from Temecula where they could hide in safety until the despotism of religion had been overthrown. Every few months his father had sent coded letters to Tiny Lustre to update its leaders on the progress of their *clinamen*, but of course he couldn't ever reveal their current location in case the letters were intercepted and the code was broken, so he had received no news in return.

The colony was approached by a dirt road winding up through the pines. As they came near they had got down off their bicycles as they always did, and Bailey had realised almost with disbelief that this might be the last time they would perform this little ritual. Tiny Lustre was intended to be self-sufficient, so among the log cabins there were goat pens and chicken coops and vegetable patches. But all that seemed to be in a state of some neglect, and they couldn't see a single human being. At the far end of the colony there was a big meeting hall with cracked clerestory windows, and they wondered if everyone might be assembled in there, but when they pushed open the door they saw only two tiny white rodents skittering away like backgammon dice between the benches. If he were a Pentecostal Christian, Bailey thought, he would probably assume that the Rapture had come. Except that the men and women of Tiny Lustre were all atheists. Could atheists have a sort of Rapture, too? Could the sheer heat of your scepticism be so great that you were converted instantaneously into gamma rays?

'Perhaps they're all swimming in the lake,' his father said. 'Hello?' he shouted after that. 'Is anyone here?'

They heard a noise behind them and they turned. An old man in dungarees stood there with a carrot in his hand as thin as a chisel. 'You looking for Yoakum and the others?' he said.

'Yes.'

'They're gone.' He bit the end off the carrot. 'Hope you haven't come far.'

'What happened?'

'No gossip behind other people's backs,' said the old man. 'That's a rule here.' He looked around. 'But I guess the rules don't mean much any more. Well, the long and the short of it is, Yoakum was having relations with other men's wives. Three of them at least. All came to light at once. No violence here, that's another rule, so we just sent him away with his things. Week later, police came up here from Temecula and said they'd had a report we'd been keeping women and girls chained to trees and suchlike. Must have been Yoakum. They didn't find anything – nothing to find – but they started clearing us all off. Said we didn't have a right to farm this land. They never liked us down in town.'

'We were coming to live here,' Bailey's father said.

'You the ones been writing to Yoakum? In the special code?'

'Yes.'

'He talked about you. He couldn't make head nor tail of that code most of the time, but he knew you were coming. Well, you can hang around here as long as you like. Can have your pick of the cabins. But the police ought to be back before long. They know I'm still here and they want me gone.'

'In that case, we won't stay. There's another community like this in Ohio. Not as big as this one, but we can go there. Thank you for your help.'

So Bailey and his father had got back on their bicycles and gone back down to the road at the foot of the wooded slope. Then the rain had started and they'd found shelter in the Ford. 'What are we going to do now?' Bailey asked again.

'We'll go to the colony in Ohio, as I told the man. We'll find our sanctuary there instead.'

'How long will it take us to get there?'

'I don't know. We'll have to take all the same precautions, of course. Remember that man we saw in San Jacinto: there's no reason to think They've relaxed Their vigilance. What fallacy would that be?'

For Bailey not to answer his father's question with the correct subheading from *The Complete Taxonomy of Anthropic Cognitive Unsoundness* was physically uncomfortable. But instead he said, 'That'll take years.'

'Perhaps.'

'I don't want to do that, Dad. I want a life. I want to go to college.'

'That's not possible just now.'

'I'm not going to Ohio with you.'

'What else do you suggest we do? Take the train back to Boston? I haven't protected you all this time so that They can do to you what They did to your mother.'

Thunder so loud that Bailey could almost see ripples in the air. 'What did They do to her?'

'You know it's best not to dwell on that, son.'

'You think she was a human sacrifice. You think They drained her blood in that chapel because she was going to leave Their religion.'

'It's best not to dwell on that.'

'You've never said it right out, but that's what you've always wanted me to think. But it might have been anything. It might have been an accident. Or she might have taken her own life.'

'There's no evidence for that,' said his father.

'Or you might have murdered her yourself.'

'I know you're disappointed about Tiny Lustre, son – I am too – but it isn't rational to let your anger get the better of you.'

'Is it rational to care more about your mother than about some woman in Mongolia? Is it rational to mourn your own mother's death when so many others just like her die every hour of the day?'

'As you know, I address this question at length in the third chapter of the *Taxonomy*, and it is my conclusion that—'

'What about your father?' said Bailey. 'Is it rational to mourn your own father's death? Or doesn't it mean anything at all if he's found dead in a car by the side of the road?'

'I don't understand what you're talking about, Professor Bailey,' said Clarendon. 'My father is still alive. I thought we were talking about the Teleportation Accident.'

'Yes. As I was saying. The Teleportation Accident was an act of human sacrifice. Just like the Aztecs used to practise. And Lucy's grandparents on Hispaniola. And the Court of Miracles in Paris. And the Esoteric Order of Dagon in Innsmouth. Except that Lavicini made it work. He understood what violence can do. And if he'd been born in this century, he would have understood, as Wittgenstein did in the *Tractatus,* that "gravitational force" and "electric charge" and "Planck's constant" and even "causation" are just the same as Dagon and Tezcatlipoca and Yahweh and Ryujin – patterns that men think they've seen, when the real pattern is far, far too complex for them to see, like a child with a crayon finding funny shapes in a logarithmic table. He was a brilliant man. And at the moment all those people

267

died, he gained the power to appear and disappear anywhere he liked, as the devil himself can, according to the Bible. He was able to shift his own spatial coordinates so that he wasn't crushed under the Théâtre des Encornets. My Teleportation Device will do the same with any object. You are giving far more help to the State Department now, Clarendon, and more to your country, than you ever could have with your phasmatometer. I had thought of using Lucy tonight but then you saw me with her and you might have caused difficulties when she was found.'

'You don't look very well, Professor Bailey. I think we should go back downstairs.'

'There is void in things,' Bailey said. He heard the squeak of a green wheelbarrow. 'Have you seen it? I've seen it. There is void in things. Lucretius says so and I've seen it.' He reached out.

'What the devil are you doing, son?'

'There is void in things!' he began to shout. 'There is void in things! There is void in things!' To do it sitting side by side like this was awkward, and the Ford's suspension wasn't built for any kind of tumult inside the vehicle, and his father was trying to peel his fingers away from his throat, and Clarendon was batting impotently at his face like a moth trapped between the sashes of a window, but Bailey kept up a steady asphyxiant pressure, feeling the hyoid bone break obediently under his left thumb – and after that it was only seven or eight more seconds until the other man went limp and the struggle was over. Bailey sat back and rested for a while, watching a last bead of sweat run most of the way down his father's ruddy forehead before it paused at the hummock of a swollen vein. Then he took his toy steam engine out of his pocket and drove it again and again into Clarendon's torso until at last it broke through the physicist's ribcage. He reached into the tunnel he had made, used a sort of brisk corkscrew motion to wrench Clarendon's heart out of its cavity, and bit deeply into it, leaning forward over the warm corpse so that blood didn't drip on to his trousers. To distract himself from the taste, he thought of Lucretius. 'For it is clear that nothing could be crushed in without void, or broken or cleft in twain by cutting, nor admit moisture nor likewise spreading cold or piercing flame, whereby all things are brought to their end. And the more each thing keeps void within it, the more it is assailed to the heart by these thing and begins to totter.'

When he had finished, he spat out a last oyster of gristle on to the dashboard and wiped his mouth and glasses with Clarendon's handkerchief. Then he got out of the car, descended the utility staircase, and went back to his laboratory to take some readings from the ultramigration accumulator. Tomorrow, he would ask Adele to run some more tests on the Teleportation Device. He already knew they would be successful. He'd seen it in his father's eyes.

7

LOS ANGELES, 1940

When the US military attacked Loeser's house with poison gas, it was a short while after dawn and he was still in bed. He awoke to find his nostrils being savaged by an odour about a billion times worse than anything he had ever smelled in his life – a cacodemoniac swirl of rubber and garlic and dysentery and murder, perhaps not unlike what the audience at the Théâtre des Encornets began to detect just before the Teleportation Accident of 1679. Remembering something he'd read once about British soldiers and chlorine shells early in the last war, he lunged for a discarded cotton undershirt, folded it over twice, pulled his penis out of his pyjama bottoms, and pissed until the undershirt was saturated with urine. Then he held it tightly over his mouth as he ran through the sitting room and out of the house, still in his bare feet. He looked around, but he couldn't see any bombers in the sky, and indeed on Palmetto Drive there was an old woman walking her cabbage-faced black pug as if nothing had happened. Cautiously he took the undershirt away from his face. The air out here was as glib as ever. So Loeser really had been the lone target. It was clear that President Roosevelt, as lazy as any other modern American, had decided to begin his vengeance on Germany with the citizen of that nation who happened to be most conveniently at hand.

When Woodkin answered the front door of Gorge's mansion, he looked like he'd already been up and dressed for so many hours that just meeting his eye was enough to give Loeser a mild feeling of circadian vertigo. 'Good morning, Mr Loeser.'

'Have you gone into the war?'

'The United States, you mean? Not yet, sir, although the Colonel believes it's only a matter of time. Would you like to come in? Perhaps I could take that for you?'

Loeser realised he was still clutching the urinous wad of undershirt, as if he'd wanted to bring Gorge a nice gift and had opted for a bold alternative to the usual bottle of wine or bunch of flowers. On the way here he'd been intending to ask if he could hide in Gorge's cellar, but instead he said, 'Can you come over to my house? Something's happened.'

'Certainly, Mr Loeser.'

Even just outside the threshold, they couldn't smell anything. Only once they were through the door did the horror make its presence known. 'I think it's poison gas,' said Loeser, no longer quite convinced. 'Methyl heptin carbonate or something.'

Woodkin wrinkled his nose. 'You've had some very bad luck, sir. It's a skunk.'

'A skunk? Don't be ridiculous. Skunks squirt about a teaspoon at a time. A skunk would have to be the size of an Indian elephant to make a stink like this.'

'Not in every case. When a skunk dies and begins to decompose, its glands will sometimes swell up with microbial gas and then explode. I've only encountered it once before, but one doesn't readily forget the smell.'

'I may be untidy but I think I would have noticed if a skunk had died in my wardrobe.'

'A house like this has more voids than you realise. It might have gotten under the floor. Or into the walls.'

Loeser thought of his ghost. 'Or into the roof?' he said.

'Yes, sir. I did once have a raccoon that established a pied-à-terre in my roof space.'

'What can I do about it?'

'I'll have someone sent over. We'll have to hope the body of the skunk is accessible. In many cases, there isn't any way to get to the animal without demolishing part of the house. Until then, I suggest you put out bowls of tomato juice and baking soda to absorb the smell. I'm afraid you may find that it has already worked its way into your belongings.'

Loeser had rather hoped that a prelate as senior as Woodkin in the religion of cleanliness might have the power to drive out odour by verbal incantation alone. 'So all my clothes are going to smell permanently of putrid skunk venom?'

'It could be worse, Mr Loeser. There exists a rare genetic disease called—'

'But I don't have time to deal with this now! The first performance is tonight!'

Conspicuous not far from where they now stood was the contusion on the wall from the day in September when Loeser had hurled a German–English dictionary across the room upon discovering from the *Los Angeles Herald* that Eric Goatloft, director of *Scars of Desire*, was planning to film an adaptation of Rupert Rackenham's *The Sorceror of Venice*, with Ruth Hussey as Princess Anne Elisabeth, Tyrone Power as Adriano Lavicini, Charles Coburn as Auguste de Gorge and Gene Lockhart as Louis XIV. At the time he left Berlin, Loeser had been determined that he would put on *The Teleportation Accident* as soon as he got back; even seven years later, and even after all the success of Rackenham's worthless novel, he still felt that Lavicini's story belonged to him, and there was no way he would allow himself to be pipped to its first dramatic rendering by Mr Don't Slip into the Dark. So he telephoned Millikan and demanded that the 1940 Christmas play at the Gorge Auditorium should not be *The Christmas Carol* as planned but instead the world première of his own magnum opus. Millikan told him that the students and faculty of the Institute would prefer to see something appropriate to the season. Loeser made an ultimatum, which they both knew was at best a penultimatum or an antepenultimatum. Negotiations bumped along, and at last it was agreed. This year, the California Institute of Technology Players would present a heart-warming historical fable by writer-director Egon Loeser entitled *The Christmas Teleportation Accident*.

Loeser was annoyed by that compromise, but he was hardly surprised. After all, in Pasadena, motorised sleighs were rolling along the streets like tanks, men in Santa Claus costumes were standing guard on corners like infantry, and carols were blaring from loudspeakers like patriotic anthems. As far as he could tell, Christmas here was equivalent to a sort of martial law. Perhaps he was lucky not to have any elves billeted in his home.

With the first performance of *The Christmas Teleportation Accident*, Loeser was – yes – painting the devil on the wall. In October, on the way to a party at the Muttons', he'd mentioned the play to Bailey, and it had turned out that Bailey was already acquainted with Lavicini's story from *The Sorceror of Venice*. In fact, the physicist had gone so far as to ask if he could help with the production – the Obediah Laboratories, he said, were full of devices that could very easily be adapted as novel theatrical effects. And although Loeser had decided not to attempt to replicate the mechanical Teleportation Device that had sexually upgraded Klugweil back in Berlin, it was true that in all the years he'd worked on *Lavicini* he had never had a clear idea of how he could convey the climactic destruction of the Théâtre des Encornets. So he had told Bailey he was welcome to help. And Bailey had now spent over a week up on ladders and gantries in the Gorge Auditorium, installing his experimental stagecraft prototype, but he still hadn't quite finished, and Loeser still didn't know what it actually did. Meanwhile, his cast this year were on the brink of mutiny.

So he shouldn't have had anything on his mind except how to make sure tonight's première wasn't a total catastrophe. After Woodkin left, though, all Loeser could think about was his ghost. If those noises over his head at night had been no more than a mustelid squatter, then half the reason to believe in her was gone. Perhaps the late Dr Clarendon had been right after all. But then Loeser had no explanation left for the girlish *objets trouvés* that had continued to appear in his house. That antique wooden chest was like a forensic evidence box maintained by some aberrant police detective to investigate a sex crime that might never take place. Where did all its contents come from? How could so much just materialise? It was almost as if . . .

He telephoned Adele.

'Egon, I haven't even had breakfast yet. If you're about to tell me you've rewritten the last scene again, then you will have to find an understudy.' He heard her light a cigarette. In *The Christmas Teleportation Accident*, Adele had the part of the doomed ballerina (who was not, on this account, Princess Anne Elisabeth in disguise).

'You want to fuck me.'

'What?'

'You want to fuck me,' Loeser repeated. 'You don't want to admit it to yourself, but I can prove it. You're still running your own experiments on the Teleportation Device, aren't you? Nocturnal experiments that Bailey doesn't know about? Well, I know what you've been putting in the chamber. Your little romantic tributes. Stockings and brassieres and lipsticks and handkerchiefs and so on.' Adele choked on smoke and Loeser knew he was right. 'You told me you can't control where the objects go, because you can't control your heart, and the teleportation device runs on love. But it doesn't run on love. It runs on desire. And, unconsciously, you want to fuck me, so you've been sending everything straight here. You might think you're in love with Bailey – chaste and unrequited – but that's classic Freudian displacement. My parents were psychiatrists, remember? I know about this stuff. "Love is the foolish overestimation of the minimal difference between one sexual object and another." You told me that once. There's more than a minimal difference between Bailey and me, but we're the same in some ways. Each of us is an isolated genius who wants to build a teleportation device. You've just got confused between us. He's your metonym for me. At first I wasn't even sure I believed that Bailey's Teleportation Device worked. But now I know I was right to follow you all the way to America!'

'That is irredeemable nonsense,' said Adele.

'Then how do you explain all these intimacies of yours I still have in my house? How else could I possibly know what you put in the chamber?'

'You've just made a good guess. Perhaps you've been taking some sort of evening class in feminine psychology.'

She was more correct than she knew, thought Loeser, but *Dames! And how to Lay them* had not been any help in this particular case. From a long way off he thought he heard laughter, but out on Palmetto Drive nothing stirred. Ziesel had once told him about the heat death of the universe, in trillions of years' time, when all thermodynamic free energy would have dissipated and so there would never again be motion or life: quite often west Pasadena felt like that. Millikan, apparently, had argued that cosmic rays were the 'birth cries' of new atoms being created all the time by God to delay this heat death, but Loeser found it hard to believe that God was forever slapping the face of the universe like a policeman trying to stop a drunk from falling asleep. 'Let's have dinner after the performance tonight,' he said.

'And I suppose if I don't sleep with you, you'll tell the Professor I've been defiling his Teleportation Device. You're as bad as Drabsfarben.'

Loeser frowned. 'What do you mean? What has any of this got to do with Jascha?'

'You understand perfectly well what I mean. I should have guessed you'd copy his methods before too long.'

'Drabsfarben is trying to seduce you?'

'Don't play ignorant. You know all about Drabsfarben and the Professor. What about those parties in the Palisades?'

'I just take Bailey to the Muttons' house sometimes because Dolores Mutton told me to,' said Loeser. 'On my parents' graves, if there's some intrigue afoot there, I'm not part of it. Come on, give me the rest. Is this why you've been so bad tempered in all the rehearsals this year?'

'You really don't already know?'

'Adele, I smoked cigarettes for five years before I learned to inhale properly. I am not always' – he reached for the American phrase – ' "quick in the uptake".'

'Drabsfarben's blackmailing the Professor,' said Adele.

'What?'

'He claims to know some secret about the Professor's past. He says if he tells everyone, the Professor will be ruined. But he's bluffing. The Professor's never lied about his past. Why would he? Honestly, Egon, I can't bear the thought that I tried to get Drabsfarben to go to bed with me once. Berlin seems like somebody else's life now.'

To Loeser it didn't feel as if any time had passed at all. 'Adele, as it happens, I'm getting blackmailed by Drabsfarben myself. That's what I meant about Dolores Mutton. He's obviously a very prolific extortionist; a Balzac of the form. Can I please emphasise that I'm not about to use the same tactics to get you into bed?'

'Let's see what happens later when you're drunk.'

'Why doesn't Bailey just go to the police about Drabsfarben?'

'I keep telling him to. But he refuses to involve them.'

'And what does Drabsfarben want from Bailey?'

'I don't know. The Professor won't tell me.'

'You don't have any idea?'

Adele hesitated. 'He did once mention something about Russia.'

'Russia?'

'Look, Egon, you specifically forbade me from going into the lab today because you said I had to be relaxed for the first night. This conversation has not been very relaxing. I'll see you backstage. I hope you forget about all this by then.' She hung up, and Loeser felt the last five years of his life begin to disrobe at last.

'Couldn't this have waited?' said Dolores Mutton a few hours later as she sat down opposite Loeser on a red velvet banquette in the bar of the Chateau Marmont. He'd telephoned to demand a meeting in private, and since her husband was at home she'd reluctantly agreed to drive out as far as Hollywood. 'Stent and I are coming to your play later. And what's that smell?'

'Death,' said Loeser. He took a sip of his beer. 'Is Drabsfarben a spy?'

Like a flock of blackbirds just before it knew which way to fly, the decision not yet made but already scribbled in its wings, Dolores Mutton's face, in the three or four seconds that followed, seemed to disclose the whole polyphasic transit of her deliberations; but Loeser knew that it was only when you were in love with a woman, or at least had once been in love with her, that you could look up and follow the transit, read the wings, join the flight. And although Loeser would have mortgaged his bone marrow to see Dolores Mutton naked just once, he wasn't in love with her, so he didn't anticipate that she was about to call over a waiter, ask for a double vodka, wait patiently for it to arrive, and drink most of it down before replying: 'Whenever I used to practise what I'd say when someone finally came out and asked me that, I used to assume it would be Stent. Or someone from the FBI. Or someone who mattered. I never guessed it would be somebody like you. I didn't rehearse for this. And I'm trying to remind myself now why I'm supposed to say what I'm supposed to say. But this morning I feel closely comparable to somebody who doesn't give a damn.' She grimaced as if she'd only just noticed the taste of the alcohol. 'You know, it's hard to imagine now, but there was a time when I really believed in it all. Years ago, back in New York, when they first got their hooks into me. I read *Capital* to the end – I don't even think Bill Foster read *Capital* to the end! And I was happy to help, although I was never their favourite because I wasn't one of those girls who'd put on lipstick and screw some diplomat for the good of the Party. Then I met Stent and we got married and we moved out here. I forgot all about it. Until one day in thirty-four Drabsfarben came to see me and said he'd been told I was a loyal friend of the Communist International.'

Loeser had always thought that was a song. He nodded.

'At first, he just wanted Stent to put his name on some petitions. Then there were the letters to the newspapers. Then we had to go on that trip to Moscow and Stent had to write those articles. And meanwhile the novels all had to be anti-capitalist, anti-bourgeois, anti-government. I didn't really mind any of that. It still felt like doing good, sometimes. But then Drabsfarben wanted us to help out more directly. He had people coming to California. Gugelhupf was the first. Do you think I ever wanted to live in that ridiculous glass box? Maybe in Berlin it's a political gesture to build a house like that. Here, it's no different from building a Gothic chateau or a Tiki hut or whatever the hell else. Except the house builders here don't know what to do with the sort of blueprint you get from Gugelhupf, so not a damn thing fits together and there are nails sticking out of everything. And half the time it's too hot to think! But Drabsfarben said we had to have Gugelhupf build us a house because it was the easiest way to get him set up in California. They needed him here. I still don't know why. And how did that asshole thank us? He rehashed an old design. Then Drabsfarben made me set up the Cultural Solidarity Committee as a cover. We started having the parties. I hate those parties. I always hated parties. I never threw a party in my life before Drabsfarben told me to. Do you know what I like doing at night? I like cooking dinner with my husband and then making love on the beach. But Drabsfarben makes me fill our house with strangers twice a week so he can catch them in his lobster trap. Every year, it gets worse. Every year, Drabsfarben wants more.'

Loeser remembered that conversation he'd misunderstood five years ago at the Muttons' party. One is always wrong, he thought now, always, always wrong about every single thing; if some young cousin was ever stupid enough to ask him for advice about life, that was all he would be able to tell them. The truth ran back and forth over your head at night but you never saw so much as the colour of its fur. 'And what does your husband think about all this?' he said.

'Stent? He's never had any idea! He just likes how I take an interest in his work. He likes how I always have suggestions and corrections. He says I'm the best editor a writer ever had.' She shook her head. 'I don't care what happens to me any more. I don't care if I get locked up for spying. I don't even care if Drabsfarben shoots me and dumps my body in the ocean. But Stent can't know. I love that man more than anything in the world. I love that man so much it makes me grind my teeth at night. If he found out I'd been fooling him for our entire marriage . . . That's why I can't stop. If I stop doing what Drabsfarben says, he'll make sure Stent finds out about everything I already did. You know, I met Sinclair Lewis's wife once. She was in the same hole as me. But in the end she went to the FBI. I guess I'm not that brave.'

'What does Jascha want with Bailey?'

'When the NKVD found out Bailey was working on teleportation, they told Drabsfarben they wanted Bailey to defect. That was supposed to be his top priority from then on. But Drabsfarben only really knew artists and writers and musicians and architects. Back then, he didn't have a connection to CalTech. He didn't even have a connection to a connection. Then we saw you going to dinner at Gorge's house. Gorge bought himself a lot of juice at CalTech with that million dollars for the theatre. Drabsfarben thought you might be useful one day.'

Ever since he noticed Dolores Mutton, the barman across the room had been polishing the same side of the same glass in ever smaller and more rapid circles. 'So that was why you called me afterwards and took back all your threats and offered me that job,' said Loeser.

'Yes. And in the long run, it worked out nicely. Drabsfarben's plans almost always do. We put on a little pressure and you brought Bailey right to us. The NKVD were thrilled. But after about another year, Drabsfarben decided Bailey wasn't going to defect voluntarily. So he tried blackmail.'

'Adele told me that. What's this secret about Bailey's past?'

'Maybe he's a bootlegger from North Dakota? I don't know. Drabsfarben hasn't told me. But that's not all Drabsfarben knows. He has something else on Bailey. Something much bigger. Something so big he says it's too dangerous even to bring into play right now. In any case, blackmail hasn't worked either. And Drabsfarben's getting worried. The NKVD have taken the Comintern apart, and they see Drabsfarben as a Comintern man all the way through. That means he has to watch his back. He goes out in public now less and less. Did you hear what happened to Willi Münzenberg?'

'Who is that?'

'Didn't you know him in Berlin? He came up in the Comintern at the same time as Drabsfarben. They worked together for years. They used to leave parcels for each other at some second-hand bookstore.'

'Luni's!'

'I don't know. But a couple of months ago Münzenberg was found hanging from a tree outside an internment camp near Lyons. Drabsfarben thinks the same thing could happen to him. He thinks the only way he can save himself now is to get Bailey to Moscow. I just hope he fails.'

'So do I! Bailey's supposed to be running my Teleportation Accident tonight.' Loeser finished his beer. 'Are you still going to pay me the thirty dollars every month?' he said.

'No. If the Cultural Solidarity Committee carries on, I want it to do some honest good for honest exiles.'

'Oh. All right, well, one last question: have you really seen Jascha kill someone?' For the first time Loeser wondered if Drabsfarben might have had something to do with the deaths at CalTech.

'Maybe I was just saying that to scare you. Either way, though, if you breathe a word about any of this to anyone, you'll have a hell of a lot more to worry about than those forged cheques.'

'You needn't worry, Mrs Mutton. I won't tell anyone. Whom would I tell?'

The answer, of course, was Blimk. He told Blimk. After Dolores Mutton left him alone in the bar of the Chateau Marmont, Loeser paid the bill, walked down to the shop where he still spent most of his afternoons, and repeated every sensational detail.

'I don't think I've ever seen a more persuasive demonstration of why you shouldn't get involved in politics,' Loeser concluded.

'I feel sorry for the lady,' said Blimk, who had not made any comment on Loeser's odour, perhaps because, by the standards of the shop's regular customers, it was not memorably unpleasant.

'I shouldn't still be scared of her, but I am.'

'So you want a number for my buddy in Washington?'

'Your Lovecraft man at the Department of State? Why?'

'Probably easier than calling the FBI out of the blue.'

'Why would I want to call the FBI?'

'Tell 'em what's going on in the Palisades.'

'I'm not telling anyone about this except you. If getting Bailey to Moscow is really Drabsfarben's last chance to save himself, then there's nothing more he can make me do for him now. I don't have to worry about it any more. I can just sit back and watch what happens.'

'But he's a commie spy. Probably wants to bring the whole country down.'

'I thought you weren't political.'

'I ain't, but a fella's got some responsibilities to the place he lives.'

'Not me,' said Loeser. 'I am what is sometimes termed a rootless cosmopolitan. I had no responsibilities to Berlin and I certainly have no responsibilities to Los Angeles. Anyway, so what if Drabsfarben does bring the country down? What would anyone mourn? Jell-O salads with mayonnaise?'

'You been here five years and you're still pretending you hate this place? Five years and you're still worried about what your buddies from back home would say if they heard you admit you kinda liked it?'

Blimk had never spoken so sharply to him before. 'Look, I read an article in *The Nation* last year by some English writer,' Loeser declared, 'where he said, "If I had to choose between betraying my country" – well, not that this is my country – but anyway, "If I had to choose between betraying my country and betraying my friend" – well, not that Drabsfarben is my friend – still, "If I had to choose between betraying my country and betraying my friend, I hope I should . . ." – well, I can't remember exactly how it ended, but the point was . . . until you've seen Dolores Mutton in a red dress you can't comprehend the position I'm in.'

'You think it won't make any difference to you if the commies get this teleportation fella? You ain't read about all these deals Hitler and Stalin keep making?'

'I try not to pay attention to any of that.'

Blimk put down his cup of coffee. 'Get out of my store.'

'What?'

'I might not love my country like I ought to, but I like it okay, and I think it's been nicer to you than you deserve.'

'Would you still like your country so much if it took your store away?'

'What's that supposed to mean?'

'Have any more of those men from the Traffic Commission come by recently?'

'So what if they have?'

Loeser was about to tell Blimk all about the elevated streetcar terminal, but he knew the information was too important to give up in haste. 'I just mean your opinion might change one day.'

'I said get out of my store. Out.'

Loeser decided he just did not have the inner faculties to resolve a quarrel with his best friend on the same day as the première of *The Christmas Teleportation Accident*; but he couldn't go straight to the Gorge Auditorium, because he'd always taken a sort of Berkeleian idealist approach to first nights, believing that problems didn't really start to multiply until the director was there to deal with them; and he didn't want to go home because of the skunk bomb. So instead he sat in a drugstore on the edge of Elysian Park long enough to arrive at CalTech with only about an hour to spare, no more than was sufficient to give Bailey's new theatrical effect the proper test run it had been awaiting for so long. Passing the Obediah Laboratories on his way to the Gorge Auditorium, however, Loeser was dismayed to see Bailey himself going inside. He pursued the physicist upstairs to room 11, too impatient to knock.

'Professor Bailey? I'm sorry to interrupt, but we really both ought to be at the theatre by now.'

'Just a minute, Mr Loeser.' Bailey was already bent over the controls of the ultramarine accomplishment or whatever it was called. Loeser sighed and looked around the room. On a desk nearby was Bailey's toy steam engine, and beneath it Loeser noticed a slim white book with a familiar yellow illustration of a row of shacks: *The Shadow Over Innsmouth* by H.P. Lovecraft.

'I had no idea you were a Lovecraft aficionado, Professor!' said Loeser.

'What?' Bailey looked up from his machine, and then an expression of displeasure passed across his face as he saw the novella in Loeser's hand. 'Would you mind putting that back, please?'

Thumbing through the book, Loeser discovered that Bailey had even annotated some of the pages in pencil. He'd never seen such tiny knotted handwriting. 'I should introduce you to . . .' He was about to say 'my friend Blimk', but stopped himself ruefully. 'You know the whole story of Lavicini, don't you?' he said instead. 'Not just what Rackenham put in his travesty?'

'Yes.'

'The tentacles and the smell and so on. Doesn't it seem to you sometimes as if Lovecraft could have written the story of the Teleportation Accident?'

'I can't say I've noticed any commonalities,' said Bailey. 'Now, Mr Loeser, I've just come from the theatre and of course I shall be rushing back directly, but if you'll excuse me I do need a short while longer to get this experiment running.'

Loeser put down the book. 'It's the first night! Why are you running an experiment now?'

'I promise it won't distract me from tonight's Teleportation Accident. But I think Adele and the others were very anxious to see you. They didn't seem to know what to do about Lavicini.'

'What do you mean?'

'Oh, I assumed you knew – there's been some sort of problem with your leading man. I didn't catch all the details.'

In Berlin, from the beginning of his career, Loeser had observed that even among the most pugnacious of the New Expressionists a degree of nervousness was to be expected before any first night, but the atmosphere he found backstage at the Gorge Auditorium suggested a cast and crew awaiting the audience like sinners an apocalyptic judgement. Then Adele rushed up to him. 'Egon, you idiot, where have you been? We've been calling your house for three hours! And what's that smell?'

'I wasn't at my house. Forget about the smell. Tell me what's happened.'

'Dick's in hospital.'

'What?'

'There was an accident. He was just walking along near that bakery on Lake Avenue and a car swerved to avoid a little girl running across the road—'

'God in heaven, Dick's been hit by a car?'

'No, the car hit the bakery and it knocked down that big papier-mâché cupcake and the cupcake rolled straight into Dick. He's got a concussion and they won't let him leave until tomorrow morning. Who's going to play Lavicini?' Loeser thought of the time Hecht had put on a 'performance' of *The Summoning of Everyman*, which had consisted of informing the audience half an hour after the play had been due to start that the lead actor had drowned in a well (false) and that their tickets would not be refunded (true). 'I thought maybe we could ask Rackenham,' added Adele.

'He wouldn't know any of the script.'

'But he's so charming it almost wouldn't matter.'

'Absolutely not.' Loeser straightened up to his full height. 'I'll have to play Lavicini.'

'Oh, Egon, no!'

'Well, who else? I don't think we're about to compromise on Ziesel. I'll just need a last look through the script. Tell everyone not to worry. By the way, I want to return something you lent me.' Loeser took from his pocket the pair of pearl-handled nail scissors that he'd brought with him from his house and held them out to Adele with a smug flourish.

'Those don't belong to me.'

'Yes, they do.'

285

'I've never seen them before.'

And as crucial as it was that Adele should be lying to him about this, it did look as if she were telling the truth. Discouraged, Loeser put down the nail scissors on the prop table and let her hurry away to put on her make-up. Half an hour later, he emerged from a dressing room in a costume that felt a bit dejected by the absence of Dick's big surfer's shoulders but was otherwise not too bad a fit. Hunched in a nearby corner, Mrs Jones, who played Montand in male drag, was repeating her three lines to herself over and over again with such heavy emphasis that she seemed to wish to exclude the possibility of any other grammatically valid sentence ever being formulated in English by anyone. Peering around the side of the front curtain at stage right, Loeser observed that the audience were already taking their seats. The Muttons had joined the Millikans for cocktails at the Athenaeum Club before the show, and now all four sat together in the front row – along with Jascha Drabsfarben. As if he stood before a favourite painting after consulting for the first time an essay on its symbolism, Loeser tried to find in the familiar features of Drabsfarben's face all that he had now learned about his old acquaintance. But the spy still looked, to Loeser, like a composer.

Further back, Gould, Hecht, and Wurtzel passed back and forth a bag of peanuts. And even Plumridge was here with his wife. Loeser couldn't see Rackenham or Gorge, but he did see Woodkin, who was saying something to a girl next to him who caught Loeser's attention immediately. She was around twenty-two or twenty-three, with shiny hair the reddish-brown of a rooster's hackles and dark, narrow eyes, and she wore an expression of such cold, fathomless, authoritative boredom that if you happened to catch sight of it at a public event like this one, you would not just feel stupid for enjoying what she was not enjoying, but also, somehow, ugly and culpable. Loeser couldn't look away, until he remembered that in only a short while he was actually going to have to go out on stage in front of her.

Loeser didn't feel nervous, though. He was Lavicini. He always had been. He could already see the lights of the Arsenal reflecting off the lagoon. Perhaps he wouldn't even let Dick reclaim the role for the remaining four performances. There was still a short while before the curtain went up, so he went looking for Bailey, and soon found him talking to Adele next to the prop table.

'Is everything ready for the Teleportation Accident, Professor?'

'Indeed it is,' said Bailey.

'You're sure? We haven't had a chance to test it.'

'You must trust the Professor, Egon,' said Adele.

'Can you describe it to me, at least?'

'Well, since there are only four people on stage at the time, but Lavicini kills twenty-five people and a cat, I thought the best way to represent—'

' "Kills"?'

'Pardon me?'

'You said Lavicini kills twenty-five people. Lavicini doesn't kill anyone. The Teleportation Device goes wrong and twenty-five people die as a result. That's why it's called the Teleportation Accident.'

'Oh, yes, of course,' said Bailey. 'I misspoke.'

'I don't mean to be pedantic but it's just that if Lavicini destroyed the Théâtre des Encornets deliberately' – Loeser coughed – 'it would be . . . it would be a very different play.'

That cough, rather like a death rattle, was the faint and involuntary laryngeal expression of a vast and imperative internal crisis, because it was just at that moment that Loeser made a deduction about Bailey – making this deduction as a sort of breech birth, upside down, so that somehow he had the conclusions in his forceps before he could count off the premises – realising, all at once, that Bailey really did think Lavicini had destroyed the Théâtre des Encornets deliberately; that Bailey planned to do much the same to the Gorge Auditorium; that Bailey must have killed Marsh and Clarendon and Pelton and all those others – and remembering only afterwards so many separate facts that he already knew but had never put together: that the State Department were working with Bailey on new weapons; that Cordell Hull, the Secretary of State, thought everything Lovecraft wrote was true; that *The Shadow Over Innsmouth* was about human sacrifice; that Bailey had always seemed to know a lot more details about Adriano Lavicini than Rackenham had bothered to put in *The Sorceror of Venice*; that no one knew for certain which mysterious force was supposed to power the Teleportation Device; that Drabsfarben cherished some secret about Bailey too big and dangerous, somehow, to exploit for blackmail; and even that there had been a certain piscine calm to Bailey's expression when Marsh's body had tumbled out of the storage cupboard in the basement of the Obediah Laboratories on that day in 1938.

'Excuse me for a moment, Professor,' said Loeser. Then he turned and walked as fast as he could to the costume rails, where Ziesel, who had been promoted this year from sound and lighting technician to stage manager, stood with a clipboard. Loeser didn't know if he could apprehend Bailey on his own, but Ziesel had bulk. 'Come with me,' he said.

'I think we might have lost one of the carnival masks,' said Ziesel.

'Come with me right away,' Loeser repeated. So Ziesel followed him back to the prop table – where Bailey and Adele were no longer waiting.

Loeser looked around. Dismissing an unhelpful recollection of the time Rackenham had taken Adele away from him at the corset factory, he was about to begin a search for the pair. But then he realised what must have happened.

Bailey knew that he knew.

Loeser's cough alone couldn't have been enough to betray him, but something in his eyes, or something in his voice, or just something in the psychic torsion of the space between them must have told Bailey that Loeser had finally worked it all out.

'Fire!' Loeser shouted. No one noticed. 'Fire!' he shouted again, and this time a couple of student stagehands turned to look at him. 'Fire! There's a fire! There's a huge, raging fire!'

'Egon, what in heaven's name are you doing?' said Ziesel.

Loeser ran past the flats to the curtain and pushed through it to the stage. There was some confused applause. 'Fire!' he shouted. No one moved. 'Fire! Fire! Fire! *Feuer!* Fire! Get out if you value your lives!' And Stent Mutton was the first one to rise.

Running back into the wings, he almost collided with Slate. 'Make sure everyone gets out,' he said to the janitor. 'Everyone!'

'Where's the the the the the the the the the the the the the the the the—'

'It doesn't matter. Just do as I say.'

Backstage, Loeser found Ziesel again. 'If your stage fright was really that bad, Egon, you could just have—' began Ziesel before Loeser grabbed his arm and pulled him towards an exit. At a creditable pace they sprinted together across the lawn to the Obediah Laboratories, and then up the stairs to room 11. Loeser pushed open the door.

'No further, please, Mr Loeser,' said Bailey. With one hand he covered his assistant's mouth to stop her screaming, and with the other he held the pearl-handled nail scissors to her carotid artery, the two blades hinged halfway open like a drafting compass ready to plot a small circle on the pale plane of her neck. Behind him, the heavy steel door of the teleportation chamber was wide open, and the ultrasonic accordionist was making a noise like a portable vacuum cleaner. Loeser thought he could feel a static itch in the hairs on his arms.

'We've evacuated the theatre,' said Loeser. 'I don't know what your "novel theatrical effect" really was, but it won't hurt anyone now.'

'Then Miss Hister will have to be the sole subject of this experiment,' said Bailey. 'There is void in things. Remember that, Mr Loeser, whatever happens. There is void in things. Cross this country in a wheelbarrow and you will see it.' Unsteadily, as if practising some awkward new dance step with a reluctant partner, he began to pull Adele backwards towards the teleportation chamber. Loeser's hands were both fists of panic but he didn't know what else to do except stand there next to Ziesel and watch. He'd known Adele for twelve years, longer than anyone on this continent, and she was going to be made a human sacrifice right in front of him.

Then Bailey, not seeing where he was going, knocked the back of his thigh on the edge of a desk. And he relaxed his grip on Adele for an instant, but it wasn't quite enough for her to get free – until she lunged sideways, grabbed the toy steam engine from the desk where Loeser had put it down earlier, and jammed it backwards into Bailey's left eye.

Bailey gave a surprisingly feminine scream and thrust the nail scissors into Adele's flank. 'Adele!' Loeser shouted. Which was when Ziesel bowed his head, charged forward like a rugby player, and propelled Bailey backwards into the teleportation chamber.

'Dieter, don't let him close the door,' cried Adele through tears of pain. 'There's a time lock! You'll be trapped in there with him!'

So Loeser, galvanised at last, made his own dash forward. But just as his fingertips brushed the handle, the door of the teleportation chamber swung shut with a terminal clunk. With one hand, Ziesel had been trying to wrench the nail scissors out of Bailey's grasp. With the other, he'd locked himself inside.

Loeser punched the door in frustration and then dropped to his knees to attend to Adele, who lay curled on her side. The twin wounds from the nail scissors, like bite marks from a vampire bat, didn't look especially deep, and Loeser was grateful that he'd designed Adele's ballerina costume in tough Neo-Expressionist stingray leather instead of the more traditional silk. Near by lay the toy steam engine, its tinplate pilot slick with optical gore.

'I'll be all right,' said Adele. 'But we have to save Dieter.'

Loeser pressed his ear to the steel door for a moment, but he could hear nothing from the other side. 'How can we get into the chamber?'

'I don't know. Run. Find someone.'

Loeser kissed her on the lips for the second time in his life and then did as he was told. Outside, a crowd was milling around by the doors of the Gorge Auditorium. Mrs Jones, still in costume, stood hugging a purposeless fire extinguisher. He rushed up to the Muttons.

'Egon, what in the world is going on?' said Stent Mutton.

'We need help. We don't know what to do.'

When Loeser returned to room 11 with the Muttons, Adele was sitting up against the wall with her hand pressed against her punctures. She explained to the Muttons about Ziesel and the time lock.

'Can't we just break the mechanism somehow?' said Stent Mutton.

'Even if we could, it's on the inside of the door,' said Adele.

'Disconnect it from Bailey's device?' said Loeser.

'The timer's already started – that won't do anything.'

'Then we need one of those oxya-such-and-such cutting torches,' said Mutton. 'Like my bank robbers used in *Silent Alarm*.'

'Dr Pelton used to have one of those for taking apart his old rocket prototypes,' said Adele.

'Where would it be now?'

'I don't know. They cleared out his lab after he . . . After the Professor . . .'

'We'll split up and search,' said Mutton.

So Loeser went down to the basement, but he tried every storage locker that wasn't locked, even Marsh's erstwhile tomb, without success. Upstairs, he found Mutton returning from a similarly fruitless search of the nearby laboratories.

'There must be some other way.'

'I know how to to to get in.'

Loeser turned: it was Slate.

Hobbling as fast as he could, the janitor led Loeser along the corridor, up a flight of stairs, and along another corridor, where there was a lavatory with a padlock on the door and a sign that said 'Out of Order'. Loeser realised that they must be directly above room 11. With a key from the loop on his belt, Slate got them into the lavatory, in which Loeser observed an extendable metal ladder leaning against the wall and a neat square gap in the floor about two feet on each side. Then Slate got down on his hands and knees, reached down into the hole, and hauled up what Loeser recognised from its grey rubberised panels as a section of the teleportation chamber's ceiling. Evidently not every inch of the chamber had really been lined with lead.

Frightened, Loeser peered down into the room below. Ziesel lay on his back next to the platform, his head in a halo of blood, his eyes wide open, nail scissors still protruding from his neck. The struggle had probably ended within a few seconds of the door shutting.

Bailey, however, was gone.

With no one to rescue and no one to apprehend, Loeser turned back to Slate. 'Did you set all this up yourself?' he said, gesturing at the hole and the ladder.

Slate nodded.

'Why? Why would you want to go down into there while the time lock is on?'

Slate didn't reply, but instead turned and went out of the lavatory. Loeser followed him back down two flights of stairs to the basement, where Slate unlocked a storage locker in a far corner with another key from the loop of his belt. Then, with an oddly showmanlike sweep of his hand, he stepped aside.

Here, Loeser saw, was a strange cousin of the antique wooden chest in his own house, except that it less resembled a police evidence box than the collection of holy relics in some decrepit Black Sea chapel. Slate had installed six little wooden shelves inside the storage locker, and arranged carefully on those shelves were the same varieties of private female oddments that Loeser himself had been puzzling over for four years: knickers, stockings, garter belts, brassieres, hairclips, lipsticks, eyebrow pencils, nail files, perfume bottles, handkerchiefs, sleep masks. No jewellery, though.

'Do these all belong to Adele?' he said.

Slate nodded.

'She puts them in the teleportation chamber, and then you climb down the ladder and steal them and bring them back here?'

Slate nodded.

'Are you in love with her?'

Slate looked at his feet.

'My sympathies,' said Loeser. Leaving the janitor to his *Wunderkammer*, he went back up to room 11, where Dolores Mutton was with Adele. 'Stent's gone to find a stretcher,' she said.

'Where's the Professor?' said Adele.

'Gone,' said Loeser. 'Ziesel's dead, but Bailey's gone.'

'How?' said Dolores Mutton. 'Was there another way out of that closet or whatever the hell it was?'

'Not from the inside. But maybe from the outside.' Part of Loeser was reluctant to say any more, but if Adele knew now that her beloved was a lunatic, it couldn't do her all that much more harm to find out that her experiments with his Teleportation Device had never actually worked. 'Slate – the janitor – he had a way.'

'So Jascha got him after all,' said Dolores Mutton.

'What do you mean?' said Loeser.

Dolores Mutton glanced at Adele, then beckoned Loeser out into the corridor where they couldn't be heard. 'Jascha was running out of time, remember?' she said in a low voice. 'Maybe tonight was his last chance. Maybe he knew that, whatever happened, he'd be gone by tomorrow. Either on his way back to Moscow with Bailey, or bundled into the trunk of a car by some NKVD agent and taken out to the desert for execution.'

'But he was in the theatre with you.'

'Yes. He was. But then you called your fire drill, and by the time we got outside, he'd vanished.'

'How could he have known about Slate's skylight?'

'He probably has something on this Slate guy. Like he has something on everyone.'

Drabsfarben could have picked the padlock on the lavatory, thought Loeser, or just used a duplicate key, and then lowered the ladder so that Bailey could escape. After that, he could have replaced everything as it was. There would just about have been time during the search for a cutting torch. Perhaps Slate had even made sure to delay telling Loeser about toilet cubicle until Drabsfarben had made his escape with Bailey. Up and down through the trapdoor was always how the devil made his entrances and exits. 'But if Drabsfarben's gone,' said Loeser, 'that doesn't prove he got anywhere near Bailey. Maybe the NKVD picked tonight to retire Drabsfarben. Maybe they had someone on campus. You told me he goes out in public less and less now. Maybe this was their best opportunity.'

'In any other circumstances, if Jascha had just disappeared like this with no warning, that's what I might have thought.

But Bailey's gone. You said he couldn't have got out from the inside. So it must have been Jascha. There's no other explanation. Jascha's saved himself. The son of a bitch.'

'I'm going to talk to Slate again.' Loeser went back down to the basement, where the janitor now sat smoking on a bench, his body hunched tensely around the cigarette as if he thought it was only half dead and might still escape from him.

'Are you you you you you going to tell Adele?' said Slate.

'I don't know yet. But listen to me, Slate, did Jascha Drabsfarben know about your shrine? Did he blackmail you with it? Did he ask you questions about Bailey? Did you ever tell him about your secret trapdoor?'

Slate just looked at his feet.

'Come on, Slate, answer me. Jascha Drabsfarben.'

'I don't know who who who who who that is.'

'Tell me the truth. You didn't have to show me your shrine. But I think you looked almost relieved afterwards. Was that because Drabsfarben can't hold it over you any more now that he's not the only one who knows?'

'I don't know who that is,' repeated Slate. And Loeser couldn't tell if this rare forbearance of his stammer was a sign that he was lying or a sign that he was telling the truth. He went back upstairs to room 11 and, as he entered, he heard a sound from the door of the teleportation chamber like a bolt slamming back.

'What was that?' said Dolores Mutton.

'The ultramigration accumulator should have finished a basic cycle by now,' said Adele, 'so the time lock's disengaged.'

Loeser pulled open the door of the teleportation chamber, and then took a step back as a gush of liquid ran out over the threshold. He hadn't noticed before when he was looking down from the room above, but the whole chamber was puddled, as if someone had emptied out most of a bath full of water in there. Curious, he squatted down, wet his finger on the floor, and then licked it.

'Egon, what are you doing?' said Adele.

'It tastes salty.'

'That's probably Dieter's blood. You're going to make me vomit.'

'No, it's more like . . . sea water.'

'We're twenty miles from the ocean. A pipe must have leaked or something.'

'Why would there be salt water in the pipes here?'

'Dr Carradine and his eels are upstairs, maybe it's something to do with that.' She glanced sideways at the open door of the teleportation chamber. 'I can't make myself believe it yet. About the Professor.'

'I believe it about the Professor, but I don't think I really believe it yet about Ziesel. When he shut that door he must have known he'd probably die in there.'

'He did it to save you and me from the Professor. After all those years you bullied him . . . You should say something nice to Lornadette.'

'Who?'

'His wife.'

'Oh. Yes.' Loeser knew he never would.

Adele glanced at Dolores Mutton, then beckoned for Loeser to kneel down next to her so she could whisper in his ear. 'Egon, do you really still want to fuck me?' she said.

'What?'

'I'd probably let you, when I stop hurting, and when you've washed. You saved my life just as much as Ziesel did. But when you kissed me, earlier, it didn't feel as if you really still wanted to fuck me. So do you?'

Did he? Loeser felt like a wrinkly and complacent Professor of Euclidian geometry who had consented to take a few questions after a lecture and had just been asked, for the first time in his entire career, how he could be absolutely sure that all right angles were equal to one another. He swayed at his lectern with a mixture of terror and joy. For nine years his desire for Adele had been the basic axiom from which all other truths could be inferred. If it were false, then everything might be false. He had to want to fuck her. He had to.

Which was, perhaps, exactly why he didn't.

Loeser realised that he could no more arouse himself with the thought of Adele's willing body than he could comfort himself with the thought of the equality of right angles. It had been so deep in him for so long that it almost didn't mean anything any more. There was no music in the sound of your own heartbeat, no savour in the taste of your own mouth. There was no lust in an axiom.

'I'm very confused,' he said. And then, as if in sympathy, the whole room shook. He looked up at Dolores Mutton. 'What the hell was that?'

'Sounded like a bomb going off.'

Loeser ran outside, and saw what Bailey had wrought. The Gorge Auditorium looked as if it had been dropped from the height of a weather balloon and had just now crashed down in the middle of the campus, so that the roof was gone, the east wall was gone, the other walls were still crumbling as he watched, and a thick grey ruff of dust was rushing after the audience of *The Christmas Teleportation Accident* as they scattered in panic from where they had stood near the theatre's doors. Beyond that he could just make out an orange glow, perhaps a fire beginning to spread through the velvet upholstery of the seats, an oven from which he'd stolen the meat. There were no tentacles. Loeser looked at his watch: it was half past eight. In the play, this was just about when the Théâtre des Encornets would have been destroyed. Bailey must have had his 'novel theatrical effect', like his Teleportation Device, on a timer. He went back into the laboratory. Adele, belatedly, had fainted.

After he'd accompanied her as far as the little hospital in Pasadena, he decided to walk straight home. Stent Mutton had told him that he ought to stay on campus to answer questions for the police, but he felt sure they had no chance of finding Bailey, so a delay would hardly matter, and after all that had happened he very much needed a solipsistic whisky. When he turned off Palmetto Drive on to his own street, however, he saw that the lights in his house were on. Was even Woodkin so efficient that he could already have engaged some sort of skunk mortician?

Loeser unlocked the front door. 'Hello?' he said.

'Oh, hello, Loeser,' said Rackenham, who stood naked in the middle of the sitting room. 'I didn't think you'd be back until later. Isn't it your play tonight?'

Loeser closed his eyes and told himself that it would be an overreaction to ajudge that this was the absolute worst thing to which he could possibly have come home. Lots of other things would have been worse. A ghost, for instance; or a skunk; or a giant ghost skunk; or the vengeful and newly cyclopean Professor Franklin Bailey digging his spurs into a giant ghost skunk like some grim mounted herald of the fish god Dagon; or even his ex-girlfriend Marlene.

No. There was nothing. There was not one thing worse than Rupert Rackenham standing there naked. 'What the fuck are you doing in my house?' said Loeser in German.

'I can promise it will be much better for your peace of mind if I don't tell you.'

'Just tell me.' He was trying not to look at Rackenham's penis but it seemed to occupy about two thirds of his field of vision.

'Fine, if you must know: I was with Gorge's wife. We didn't know what the smell was – I'd be fascinated to learn, by the way – and there wasn't time to find anywhere else to go before her appointment with her psychiatrist, so I insisted we make the best of it. At Winchester I slept in a dormitory with eight other boys every term for five years, so this strikes me as pretty mild. But we'd only just got the motor running, so to speak, when she began to feel queasy. So she got dressed

and left. I would have left too, but it occurred to me that if the stain on the air turned out to be indelible I might not have any occasion to come back here again, and I ought to find Delia Sprague's nail scissors at last, so I stayed. They're some sort of cherished family heirloom and she's been pestering me for weeks. Wealthy women learn to be forgetful because they know everything can pleasurably be replaced – except that once in a while it can't. To tell you the truth, when I looked in that box of yours, I couldn't quite believe the quantity and variety of the rejectamenta. I'm surprised you never wondered where it was all coming from.'

'Of course I fucking wondered! How many women have you brought here?'

'A good deal. When you're out. They can hardly receive me at home, can they? They're millionaires' wives. The servants would talk. And my house in Venice Beach is an hour's drive away. Los Angeles is so spread out. Why do you think I was so keen for you to take this place? And so helpful about bringing you the key after I got it from Woodkin? I hope you haven't forgotten that when I got you that first invitation to dinner at Gorge's house, you said you'd owe me a favour.'

There were quite a lot more questions Loeser wanted to ask, but in his bewilderment he could only manage: 'So why are you still nude?'

'It's a warm night for December. Now, old chap, I really must find these nail scissors – might you have any idea where they are?'

'I can promise it will be much better for Delia Sprague's peace of mind if I don't tell you. Just get your clothes.'

The skunk's colleague gathered his clothes, went into the bathroom to get dressed, and came back out. 'You know, as it happens, I could ransack a pot of tea: I don't suppose before I go I could just—'

'No,' said Loeser.

'By the way, have you heard about Brecht?'

'What about Brecht?'

'He's coming to Los Angeles. He's in Finland now, but he's going to apply for a visa.'

'Please just leave my house before you tell me anything else that makes me want to walk into the Pacific.'

Since the only regular visitor to Loeser's bungalow was the postman, the sound of Rackenham's departing footsteps was enough to remind him that he hadn't checked his mailbox that day. He went outside and found in it a letter with a Berlin postmark. When he looked at the address, he recognised the handwriting, and breathed out the vapours of an overwhelming relief.

Loeser had never replied to that letter about the incident on the tram that Blumstein had sent him in 1938. But his former mentor had persisted in his attempt to patch up their friendship, continuing to write every three or four weeks. Each time, Loeser got through about a paragraph, and then as soon as Blumstein made any reference to the conditions in Berlin, he would stop reading and throw the letter away. Loeser told himself that he hadn't come to live six thousand miles from the Allien Theatre just to endure rambling appeals for sympathy from his irrelevant former mentor. He began to resent them more and more. Each ivory envelope was like a ragged little emigrant from Blumstein's life that could not be turned back at the border because it had all the right stamps from all the right officials – like a pestering ghost condom, a dead French letter, stuck down with the warm fluid of all that Loeser had not done but probably should have – as unwelcome in his mailbox as any strange deposit from the domestic spirit in which he had once believed. And as the months went on, it became harder and harder to persuade himself that, when the sight of his own address in Blumstein's handwriting made him feel as if he had his head caught in a bear trap, it was just some banal combination of boredom and annoyance, rather

than, for instance, guilt: because to concede that he felt guilty about Blumstein's letters, or even to concede that there was any reason whatsoever why he might expect to feel guilty, would demand an internal readjustment of a magnitude not unlike his recent experience with Adele – except without a comparable sense of liberation. And no one could make him concede any of that, so he didn't.

Then the letters stopped.

When Blumstein was writing letters, Loeser wanted him to stop writing letters. But then when Blumstein stopped writing letters, Loeser wanted him to start writing letters again – and he wanted it ten times as much. When Blumstein was writing letters, Loeser had to force himself not to think about Blumstein. Then when Blumstein stopped writing letters, Loeser still had to force himself not to think about Blumstein – and he had to force himself ten times as hard. Quite often, he'd dreamed about getting more letters, but nothing had actually come until today.

Loeser closed the mailbox. He went back inside. He sat down and he tore open the envelope. He saw that there was nothing inside.

And for some reason the sight of the empty envelope made him think of Ziesel lying dead in that locked chamber, and he coughed twice on the skunk rot, and his eyes filled with tears, and at that moment he knew for sure that Blumstein was going to die before he ever wrote another letter.

This wasn't logical, of course. There were all sorts of reasons why an envelope might have arrived empty. Blumstein might have made an absent-minded error; or his wife Emma might have; or it might not have been an error at all, but rather a deliberate performative metaphor for the end of any chance of reconciliation; or some postal official might have steamed open the envelope for the purposes of censorship or espionage or theft and neglected to replace the contents afterwards. All those explanations made some sense, whereas there was no causal connection at all to be drawn between an empty envelope and Blumstein's doom.

Nonetheless, Loeser was certain. He would never see Blumstein again. Not without a phasmatometer.

The telephone rang and Loeser went to pick it up. Just like the very first time a missive from Blumstein had arrived at Loeser's house, it was Woodkin, mercifully interrupting his thoughts with a summons to the mansion.

He hadn't seen Gorge since the summer, and upon Loeser's arrival Woodkin stopped him in the hall. 'Before you go any further, Mr Loeser, I must warn you that my employer's condition has continued to deteriorate.'

'What now?'

'He can no longer read.'

'*Mein Gott*, he's that ill?'

'Please don't misunderstand me. Colonel Gorge is still perfectly capable of interpreting words on a page. That, you might say, is just the problem. When the Colonel reads the word "hurricane" in a newspaper, he now actually believes himself to be in the presence of a hurricane. It's a further extension of his ontological agnosia – the trouble he has distinguishing between representations and the objects of those representations.'

'You once told me reading wasn't one of Gorge's hobbies.'

'No, but the Colonel did used to pay close attention to Sky-Shine's ledgers. Now, however, when he reads "$898,854.02", for instance, he sees 898,854 actual dollars and two actual cents there in front of him, even though in reality all hard currency was banned from the residence after the third time the Colonel took up arms to rescue George Washington from kidnappers. And when he reads "-$898,854.02", he sees – well, in the event, after he recovered from his seizure, he was still not quite able to describe the experience – but from what I can understand, it is a kind of palpable and marauding embodiment of a nine-hundred-thousand-dollar deficit. Unpleasant for any businessman. Colonel Gorge, like your compatriot Mr Gödel, is now an adamant mathematical realist. As you would expect, he must conduct his affairs by telephone and get his news from the radio.'

'What about when he reads a word that signifies an abstract concept?' said Loeser. ' "Regret", say? What does he see then?'

'Fortunately, as the Colonel has often told me, abstract concepts mean nothing to him. That is one of the personal qualities to which he attributes his success.'

Despite all this, Gorge didn't seem at all subdued when Loeser found him in the billiards room. 'Macbeth, Krauto?'

'Sorry?'

'Said Macbeth when they shouldn't have?' joked Gorge. 'One of your actors?'

'Professor Bailey destroyed your theatre. Not a curse.'

'Yes. Bailey. Dynamite, he used. Pounds and pounds of it, police are saying. Enough to blow up this whole plaaa—' And then Gorge rolled like a commando over the side of his armchair and lay on the ground with his hands over his head.

Loeser was now so well trained in the psychopathology of ontological agnosia that it took him only a moment to work out that the tycoon had begun to make an expansive hand gesture signifying the hypothetical destruction of the mansion, caught sight of that hand gesture, mistaken it for the actual destruction of the mansion, and attempted to take cover. 'That wasn't an explosion, Colonel, that was just your own hands.' An expedient as crude as dynamite, thought Loeser, was a poor tribute to Lavicini on Bailey's part, although perhaps not incompatible with the New Expressionism.

Gorge returned to his seat. 'Hands! Right. Beg your pardon. Anyway, seems to run in the fucking family, theatres falling down. Not all bad. Still get the tax break. And none dead. Got you to thank for that, Woodkin says?'

'I take full credit, yes.'

'And vanished, Bailey, they tell me. Last we're going to hear about his Teleport Gizmo. So: verdict. Out with it. Real or not?'

'Bailey certainly hadn't perfected it. And now there's no one to continue his work.'

'Not the point. Told you before. Doesn't much matter, Bailey's Teleport Gizmo in particular. Works, though? Means anyone could make one. Means they will, give it a year or two. Means I don't have to bother about squashing Plumridge and his damned streetcars. Well?'

Loeser thought back to his argument with Blimk that afternoon. If he really did have responsibilities to the place he lived, then he ought to assure Gorge that teleportation was possible. That would mean Los Angeles might still get its streetcar network – might still become a tolerable place to live. But that would also mean Blimk might lose his shop. So what was he supposed to do? Betray his adopted country, or betray his friend? According to that English writer in *The Nation*, he ought to pick the former. But in this case, his friend had specifically instructed him to be patriotic, so he was betraying his friend either way.

And then he thought of the empty envelope from Blumstein, and he made up his mind. Blimk might be right, up to a point – a man did have responsibilities to the place he lived. But Loeser was beginning to think now that a man's ultimate responsibility was a lot simpler. Don't be a total prick to the people who try to be nice to you.

'Bailey's Teleportation Device was a fiction,' he said. 'His assistant was faking the results. I saw no evidence whatsoever that teleportation is possible.' The lie tasted briny on his tongue.

'Not what I hoped you'd say,' said Gorge. 'Still, can't be helped. Like rotten skunk, by the way. Stink on you. Not to be rude.'

Loeser realised this might be his last chance. He'd seen an old acquaintance killed today – he could manage one awkward enquiry. 'It is, indeed, rotten skunk. Now, Colonel Gorge, I spent more than two years at CalTech watching Bailey on your behalf. I don't expect to be paid, because you've been generous in so many other ways, but there is just one thing . . .'

'Stop there, Krauto. Know what you're going to say.'

'I don't think you do.'

'Book of mine that you want. French. Very rare.'

Loeser was astonished. 'How did you know?'

'Not hard to guess after you asked Woodkin about my books. Probably why you came to me in the first place.'

Loeser was even more astonished. 'Yes, it was.' Had Gorge smelled that on him too?

'Told myself I'd never part with it. No use to me now, though – books with words. And no son to pass it down to.'

Loeser was about to point out that the text in *Midnight at the Nursing Academy* amounted to no more than a few suggestive captions, but he stopped himself. He could hardly believe that after all this time he was now only a few ticks of the clock away from that holy hour.

'Woodkin?' Gorge shouted.

The personal secretary came into the billiards room. 'Yes, sir?'

'Take Krauto to the treasury. Then call Clowne and tell him he can have Mildred.'

'Yes, sir. If you'd follow me, please, Mr Loeser.' They took the stairs down to the mansion's wine cellar, which didn't, of course, contain any wine. 'This is a fortified room containing all the items that Colonel Gorge would most wish to protect in the event of a burglary or anarchist insurrection,' said Woodkin as he unlocked a heavy door, and Loeser was half reminded of the teleportation chamber and half reminded of Slate's storage locker. At the same time he realised that in this, as in everything, Gorge was showing good business sense. If the rule of law were ever shattered, perhaps after the big earthquake, then so many people would already have had the idea of stockpiling gold or shotgun shells or tinned peaches that those commodities would be badly devalued in the resultant barter economy. But hardly anyone would have thought to hold on to books. Not *Berlin Alexanderplatz* or *Ulysses* or *The Sorceror of Venice* or even *Assembly Line* – all those would be worthless when everyone forgot how to read. But there were certain types of printed matter that would never lose their intrinsic value. The wisest shop to loot, in those first days, would be Blimk's.

Except Loeser now saw that the treasury was not lined with bookshelves, as he'd expected. Instead, the room was dominated by two old sedans with broken windscreens and twisted fenders, parked there underground like escapees from a wrecking yard.

'Why are these here?' said Loeser.

'Colonel Gorge acquired them in 1925 after hearing of an accident that had taken place in Nevada. It was a warm Sunday afternoon, and by coincidence both drivers had spent the morning industriously polishing their cars with Sky-Shine. They were driving in opposite directions, and as they drew near, each was dazzled by the reflection of the sun on the mirrory hood of the other. There was a swerve and a crash. Both drivers survived uninjured, and Colonel Gorge intended to use the cars as part of an advertising exhibit. Later, however, he decided against it.'

'Why?'

'Three small girls and a terrier were killed in the accident.' Woodkin continued the tour. 'This is a signed photograph of the actress Marlene Dietrich. This is the coyote whose glands were transplanted into the Colonel by Dr Voronoff. This is the authentic skeleton of a Troodonian cantor. This is a flagitious puppet from the Colonel's great-great-great-great-grandfather's puppet show, discovered last year in an attic in New Orleans. This is a drawing made by the Colonel's daughter when she was five. And this is the book that the Colonel wishes you to have.'

It was French, and it was rare, but it wasn't *Midnight at the Nursing Academy*. It wasn't a photo album at all. It was a much older, smaller book, bound in dark red leather like that copy of Dante's *Inferno* that Loeser had bought in the Marais, entitled *Un rapport de la confession sur son lit de mort d'Adriano Lavicini comme elle a été dit à son ami Bernard Sauvage en l'an de grâce 1691* – a record of the deathbed confession of Adriano Lavicini as it was told to his friend Bernard Sauvage in the year of grace 1691.

'But the Teleportation Accident was in 1679,' said Loeser.

'Yes,' said Woodkin. 'Lavicini survived it, however. And when Auguste de Gorge, my employer's great-great-great-great-great-great-great grandfather, discovered this fact some years later, he became determined to have his revenge on the Venetian for destroying his theatre. But at that point his resources were meagre, and by the time he found out where Lavicini had been hiding, Lavicini was already dead, so de Gorge's sole consolation was a copy of this book. Bernard Sauvage had printed only a dozen, intended for his closest associates. It is one of the very few inherited possessions that has survived all the changing fortunes of the Gorge patrilineage. No other copies are now known to exist. All Lavicini's secrets are here.' Woodkin paused. 'Is something the matter, Mr Loeser?'

'Oh, no. Not at all.' Loeser knew that this was probably the most extraordinary gift he could ever hope to receive in his whole life. He did his best to conceal his disappointment. 'Did Lavicini really plan the Teleportation Accident? I think that's what Bailey thought.'

'Yes.'

'Why?'

'Because of a woman,' said Woodkin. 'He went to Paris because of a woman. He perpetrated the Teleportation

307

Accident because of a woman. He went back to Venice because of a woman. So the testament states.'

'He really killed all those people because of a woman?'

'That is not precisely the case, no. I hope you'll forgive me for suggesting that it would be best if you read the truth for yourself, Mr Loeser. Now, I imagine this has been a demanding evening, and it occurred to me that you might not have had time to attend to your own needs. I understand that Watatsumi is preparing a light supper for the Colonel's daughter. Perhaps you would like to join her. And perhaps before that you would like a bath and a change of clothes.'

Loeser had never met Mildred Gorge, but when he was shown into the dining room later that evening, he recognised her at once: here was the redhead who had been sitting in the audience at the Gorge Auditorium – forced to attend, he surmised, by her father, who could not go to his own theatre for obvious reasons. Woodkin introduced him. He sat down. She barely acknowledged his presence. And within half an hour, Loeser had decided he was in love.

As prolegomena to an explanation of this surprising turn of events, there now follows a partial list of subjects covered in Loeser's conversation with Mildred Gorge that night that failed to arouse even the smallest perceptible quantum of approval or interest from the heiress. The delicious seared tuna steak and artichoke salad prepared by Watatsumi; any of Watatsumi's cooking; any meal she'd ever had; food in general, and also drink; the weather in Los Angeles; the weather anywhere; sunshine in general, and also shade; the generous postgraduate scholarship she had been offered by Cambridge University to study moral sciences; learning in general; rationality in general, and also madness; Britain; Europe; the civilised world; travel in general, and also staying at home; the Gorge mansion; her family fortune; money in general, and also anything bought with it; hypothetical boyfriends; romance in general; human company in general, and also solitude; theatre; art in general; her lucky escape from an explosion that could have claimed her life and the lives of hundreds of others; her continuing survival in general, and also her death; sailing boats; tiger cubs; daffodils; cinnamon; laughter.

She really just didn't like anything. And although this might almost have sounded almost like an illness, the truth was that Mildred Gorge didn't seem to be depressed or morbid or arrested in adolescence: her opinions on the world didn't derive from a mood or a temperament or a pose, but rather from a rational evaluative position. There was nothing to rule out the possibility that at some point in the future, perhaps in only a few moments' time, she might be girlishly surprised and delighted by some notion, event, object, or human being, but it happened that, just now, everything still bored her. In other words, although one might have supposed that a conversation with Mildred Gorge would have been like auditory ketamine, to Loeser she was the opposite of tiresome. There was nothing more attractive than a girl who was difficult to impress. And he'd never met a girl more difficult to impress than Mildred Gorge. She was a perfect negation of the city in which she'd been born, a pearlescent kidney stone that California had grown in its own gut, one shake of her head enough to shame a million nodding, nodding, nodding oil derricks. He thought of that drawing he'd seen in the treasury: rain falling on a crippled old man alone in some sort of quarry. Five years old, living in Pasadena, and that's what she'd drawn.

Loeser had never wanted to marry anything so much in his life.

'It's strange we've never met before,' he said as a maid cleared the plates. Woodkin still stood in the room, presumably as a chaperone, but Loeser had known skirting boards that were more obtrusive.

'Not really,' said Mildred. 'Since I left Radcliffe I've been going to stay with my friend Goneril quite often.'

'I'm sorry, did you say Goneril?'

'Yes. Why? Do you know her?'

'No, but my parents are psychiatrists, and they once had an American patient who called one of his daughters Goneril, and she would have been about your age by now, and it's such an unusual name . . .'

'She has a sister named Regan.'

'Yes, that's the one.'

'And he named his yacht *Titanic* and his company Roman Empire Holdings.'

'To prove he was the master of his own fate. What happened to him?'

'The yacht sank, the company went bust, and his daughters had him certified insane.'

'Oh.'

'Luckily Goneril got some money from an uncle.'

In parallel with his realisation that he wanted Mildred Gorge to be his, another new knowledge was now surging within Loeser: that this city, to him, was his bungalow, the Gorge Theatre, his longing for Adele, his monthly cheque from the Cultural Solidarity Committee, parties at the Muttons' house, the definite absence of Bertolt Brecht . . . But now he couldn't rely on any of those things. California was a patient who had never left Dr Voronoff's operating table, who had accepted transplant after transplant after transplant until its limbs bubbled with moist grapevines of every imaginable foreign gland – but after five years of dribbling sour juices into his new host, a xenograft called Egon Loeser had finally been rejected. And he didn't know what to do next. Except that when Gorge shouted for Woodkin, and Woodkin left the room for the first time since Loeser had sat down, he knew he had to say something.

'Your father's going to make you marry Norman Clowne,' he blurted.

'Who's that?'

'The Secretary of the Los Angeles Traffic Commission.'

'Why is he going to make me marry the Secretary of the Los Angeles Traffic Commission?'

'Because I told him teleportation isn't real.'

'Oh,' said Adele, apparently satisfied by that explanation. 'I don't want to marry the Secretary of the Los Angeles Traffic Commission.'

'I don't want you to either,' said Loeser boldly.

'I guess I don't have a choice.'

'You could run away. You could get out of Los Angeles.'

'And go where? Cambridge?'

Loeser thought back to *Dames! And how to Lay them.* 'If you've got the fever hots for a velvety piece, but the egg timer's running out, you may need to put your balls in your mouth and just straight up swing for an elopement. You might think it's a one in a million shot, but sometimes the lady's so surprised her brain will flip upside down and she'll say yes and kiss you. That, see, is how God made her.' Could that actually work? Could the gland skip off and take with it the kidney stone, no anaesthetic required? Of course, if Mildred wasn't around to marry Clowne, then Clowne would have no reason to stub out Plumridge's streetcar scheme, and that would probably mean Blimk would lose his shop. But it was lot easier to stick to tiresome rules like 'Don't be a total prick to the people who try to be nice to you' when you hadn't just fallen (mostly) in love. And if Lavicini could kill twenty-five people over a woman, or whatever it said in the book he hadn't read yet, then this didn't seem so bad in comparison. He'd never tried anything like this in his life, but he knew now that he had to leave Los Angeles whatever happened. He had nothing to lose.

'New York,' he said. 'Come to New York with me.'

Mildred regarded him for a while and then shrugged. 'All right,' she said. 'It's not as if I have anything better to do.'

311

Part IV

Zeitgeisterbahnhöfe
(four endings)

8
VENICE, 1691

The gondolier wore the mask of a plague doctor, with a long white beak, and when he shook his head the gibbous moon flashed in the red glass of the mask's eyes. 'You don't want to go to Vignole.'

'Why not?' said Sauvage.

'It's nice enough on a warm afternoon, but there's nothing much there. I haven't been across for months. I'll take you to Murano instead. Much more pleasant. Much more to do at night.'

'I have business on the island.'

'Are you in negotiations with an old lunatic to buy a dead vegetable patch?'

'Perhaps I am.'

'You really don't want to go to Vignole. If I don't talk you out of it now, you'll just blame me afterwards. And rightly so. You're a Frenchman, aren't you? In Venice we look after our visitors.'

Sauvage, who wore an ordinary gilded *bauta* that left his mouth uncovered, took two gold *zecchini* out of the purse at his belt and pressed them into the gondolier's gloved hand. 'In that case, please indulge me.'

The gondolier was silent for a moment and then gestured for Sauvage to step down into the boat. As they pushed off into the lagoon, Sauvage looked up at the two guard towers that rose to the west above the ramparts of the Arsenal. Often since coming to Venice it had seemed to him that the city was not an island but a great loose raft, tied together only with bridges and washing lines and the complacency of pigeons, ready to cut loose and float off south if at any time it began to lose interest in the mainland.

'Why do you wear that particular mask?' he said.

'Plagues come into Venice by sea,' said the gondolier. 'Not for a while now, but they will again. We in the boats live in the kingdom of plague just as much as any doctor.' He rowed fast but there was no exertion in his voice. 'Also, my nephews love it.'

When they got to the other shore, a wolf sat there watching them like something crystallised in an alembic out of the reflection of the moonlight on the surface of the water. For a moment the beauty of it made Sauvage's spine ring like a xylophone, but then the gondolier banged his oar several times on the side of the boat and the wolf rose and trotted away, unhurried, on its surprisingly spindly legs.

'You'll wait for me here?' said Sauvage when they knocked against the little wooden jetty.

'I'd better come with you. For all you know there could be a whole pack near by.'

'I've never heard of the wolves in Venice attacking a human being.'

'Not over there,' said the gondolier, pointing his thumb back in the direction of the Arsenal. 'But out on Vignole they don't get so many scraps.'

So Sauvage waited while the gondolier tied up his boat, and then they set off along the shore towards a small church, with only the stump of a collapsed steeple, which stood next to a copse of trees.

'Do you know anything about that place?' said Sauvage. After a week in Venice, he was struck by the silence of Vignole at night.

'Not much. It's old, I think. Goes back to Barbarigo's time at least. But during the plague that killed my great-grand-mother, the priest there started taking in the sick. Before long it filled up, and then the priest himself died, and after the

316

plague went away there was no one who wanted to take it over.'

Instead of heading straight for the church, Sauvage made his way up the low hill on his right, and the gondolier followed. When they got to the top, Sauvage unfolded a sheet of paper that had been tucked inside his purse: a workmanlike pencil sketch of the view from the hill on which they stood, with the Arsenal on the left and the marshes stretching off to the right. 'I came here to check something I couldn't quite confirm from the other shore. This drawing was made fifteen years ago by a Siamese man who came to Venice to learn to paint. The church should be here in the foreground, next to the trees. But it isn't.'

'Maybe he just left it out. Orientals are godless, after all.'

'He's a Christian, actually, and he didn't leave anything out. I asked him.'

'You met him?'

'Yes. He's still in Venice. I bought this from him and he made me a gift to go with it.' Sauvage took a small cloth bag from his belt and showed the contents to the gondolier.

'What are those?'

'What do they look like?'

'Armoured raspberries.'

'They're called lychees. They come from Siam.'

'How do they get all the way to Venice?'

'I don't know.' Sauvage ate one, then peeled three more and dropped them on the grass. 'Maybe the wolves will find these and it will make up for some of the scraps they don't get.' It saddened him to think that in a hundred years there would be no wild animals left in cities.

They went back down the hill towards the church. Pink flowers burst from the bark of the Judas trees near by as if their trunks were stuffed beyond capacity. 'Why are you so interested in this church?' said the gondolier.

'You say it was – oops – abandoned sixty years ago,' said Sauvage, nearly tripping on a dead vine. 'And that's how it

317

looks. But fifteen years ago, it wasn't here. Don't you think that's interesting?'

As they came closer, they could see that not only had the steeple collapsed but also the front wall of the church, leaving the whole structure open like a cart shed. Inside, there was nothing but rotting pews leading up to an altar and a stained-glass window at the opposite end, which confided none of its colours in the moonlight. 'Have you ever seen anyone enter or leave this church?' said Sauvage.

'I told you, I don't often come to Vignole. But I can assure you no one uses this place.'

'How can you be certain?'

The gondolier pointed. 'Bats.' And indeed Sauvage could see the silhouettes of dozens of the little creatures hanging upside down from the rafters, a few of them stirring or swaying in the gloom. The stone under his feet was scurfy with dried guano. 'Rats don't mind people. Nor do cats or birds or spiders. But bats can't stand to be disturbed too often.'

'Let's see if you're right,' said Sauvage, moving further into the church. He spoke louder than usual, trying to weigh the echo.

'We shouldn't be here. A lot of people died where we stand.'

'I'm not afraid of ghosts.'

'We should go back to the boat.'

'If I'm wrong, we will.'

'Turn back.'

'Not yet.'

'I told you to turn back, Frenchman.'

'Or what?' said Sauvage. 'You'll peck me to death with your beak?'

And then Sauvage was flat on the ground with the gondolier kneeling on his back and a blade of some kind pressed against the side of his neck. 'De Gorge sent you, didn't he?' shouted the gondolier.

'No! De Gorge is my enemy!'

'How many others does he have in Venice? Tell me or I'll kill you.'

'My name is Bernard Sauvage, son of Nicolas Sauvage.'

'I think I'll just kill you either way.'

But at that moment the air itself seemed to shuffle, faster than Sauvage could follow, like a card-sharp setting up a crooked game of *bonneteau*, and at the same time there was a sound of cogs turning and pulleys running, and then there was a bright doorway in front of him where before there had only been darkness and empty space. If the option to inhale had at that moment been available to Sauvage, which it wasn't, he would definitely still have been rendered breathless.

'Let him go, Melchiorre.'

The order wasn't much more than a croak. But the gondolier did as he was told. Sauvage got to his feet, rubbing a bruised shoulder. Probably, he thought, it was only his cheap *bauta* that had saved him from a broken nose when he was knocked forward.

The room beyond the doorway was lit by oil lamps, and far bigger than it had any right to be. In the centre of the room was a bed, and in the bed lay a man in a mask. The wooden frame of the bed was hinged in the middle so that the man could sit up in it, and a draughtsman's table was suspended by a complicated skeletonic sort of crane at an angle in front of the man so that he could work without changing his position. At the edges of the room were workbenches cluttered with tools and brushes and paint and twine and cloth and metal.

'Come inside, boy, and sit down,' said the man in the bed, gesturing to a stool. As he entered the room, Sauvage reached instinctively to take off his *bauta* out of respect, but the man stopped him. 'No, keep your mask on,' he said. 'It's Carnival. I intend to die in mine.'

'The Théâtre des Encornets,' said Sauvage softly as he came closer.

'You recognise it?'

'Of course. I lived in Paris until the year it was destroyed.'

The man's mask was a gilded replica of the grand front of the opera house as it had stood until 1679. The density of detail was astonishing, a hundred times more exquisite than any doll's house or architective ornament Sauvage had ever seen, so that you could see every nipple on every nude on every marble frieze; and yet the mask was not quite mimetic, because the façade had been artfully distorted to imply the shape of a human face; and not just a general human face, but the face of a man who had visited Sauvage's childhood home in Paris several times before Sauvage's father's death.

'Was it difficult to find me?' said Lavicini.

'Very,' said Sauvage.

'So you know the lengths to which I've gone to hide myself. And yet you didn't care who you brought with you?'

Sauvage glanced at Melchiorre. 'He told me that he hadn't been to Vignole for months. But he hopped over that loose plank in the jetty without even looking down. I knew he was lying.'

'Yes, Melchiorre has been very loyal.'

'When did you build this place?'

'Eleven years ago. A few seasons after I left Paris.'

'Why build a false church? Why not just a false cottage? A false barn?'

'No one ever looks at a chapel and wonders what it's hiding.'

'And the bats?'

'Melchiorre, show him a bat,' said Lavicini. The gondolier duly retrieved an object from one of the workbenches and then came back to show it to Sauvage. The bat had an iron skeleton, black velvet wings, and no face or feet. 'They hang on a frame, and after Melchiorre winds the spring, they move in their sleep all night.'

'And that wolf?'

'The wolves are real.' Lavicini coughed as if his lungs were brimming with hot tallow, and Sauvage was glad of his mask because he couldn't help but wince. 'Is it common knowledge that I am alive?'

'De Gorge knows, of course, but not many others. It took me a long time to be sure.'

'Yes. No one should ever have been able to find out. But after everything went wrong, I started to be careless. I didn't bother to take all the precautions I'd planned.'

'What do you mean, "everything went wrong"?'

'You still haven't worked out what happened at the Théâtre des Encornets?'

'I know most of it, I think. I know you planned it all. But there's one thing I've never been able to understand.'

'What?'

Sauvage hesitated. 'You were a friend of my father's. He thought you were a good man. I can't believe you would have let two dozen men and women die like that. It doesn't make sense.'

'I did not let two dozen men and women die.'

'I watched them dig out the bodies the next morning.'

'You've seen my bats, and you still believe that?'

'So no one died that night?' said Sauvage.

The other man shook his head. 'That is not quite correct either.'

The circumflex of reflected candlelight in the drop of almond syrup that oozed slowly down the pale dough of the choux bun at the creamy summit of the chocolate *croquembouche* that was served one summer night in 1677 in the patisserie belonging to the only real Parisian pastry chef in Venice: that had been Lavicini as he sat opposite the ninth of de Gorge's deep-pocketed emissaries to visit him since he left his job at the Arsenal to become a designer for the opera. He, too, hung in that drop of syrup, quite ready, if it was licked up by this fat Frenchman, to be licked up with it.

Every previous offer from de Gorge he had rejected out of hand. He didn't want to work for a monster like that. But the day after Pentecost the only woman Lavicini had ever really loved had told him that God wanted her to go back to her husband. His friend Foscolo, the playwright, had drowned himself in the Lagoon last year after a courtesan broke his heart, but Lavicini wasn't seriously considering suicide. All the same, he couldn't bear to go on living in the same city as his Wormwood, his star who had made the waters bitter. He didn't care any more where he was, or what he had to do, as long as he would never again have to worry about catching sight of her by accident as he hurried across the Rialto Bridge. So he waited for the Frenchman facing him to take his first bite of the *croquembouche*, and then announced that this time he was ready to take de Gorge's job. The lackey guffawed in triumph, spraying flecks of cream across the table, and shouted for brandy. Two weeks later, without ever having quite sobered up, Lavicini arrived in Paris.

He'd been at the Théâtre des Encornets nearly a year before his Wormwood wrote to him. She said she'd been arguing with God night and day ever since he left. And God simply would not back down. He still wanted her to be faithful. But she didn't care so much what God wanted any more. God could hang. If Lavicini would come back to Venice, and forgive her for her indecision, then they could be together again.

He nearly jumped on a horse there and then. But he had another nine years left on his contract, and he knew de Gorge defended his contracts like other men defended their virgin daughters. He might get away for a few weeks, but eventually he would be hunted down, beaten, and brought back to Paris. The only way out of the contract was death.

And it was around this time that his friend Villayer disappeared. Lavicini guessed straight away that Louis had ordered the assassination, but it wasn't until a few weeks afterwards that he discovered it was his own employer who had actually paid the assassin. There was often business in Paris with which Louis didn't wish to dirty his soft hands even from the safe distance of Versailles, so de Gorge was sometimes called upon to make arrangements on his behalf, and in return Louis kept on attending the Théâtre des Encornets, ensuring that it would remain the most fashionable venue in the capital. Lavicini wanted to avenge his friend, but much more formidable men than he had gone against de Gorge and ended up dining on their own noses and ears. Also, he had no appetite for violence. Instead, he decided that he would have to find a way of staging his own death that would not just utterly dupe de Gorge, but also utterly destroy de Gorge's livelihood. And some months later, when Nicolas Sauvage died in the same circumstances as Villayer, it redoubled his determination.

On the night of the premiere of *The Lizard Prince*, twenty-five costumed automata sat fidgeting in private audience boxes. Lavicini had been obliged to buy them all tickets at full price under false names. Many years earlier, when Louis XIV was still a child, a toymaker called Camus had reportedly designed for him a little carriage complete with mechanical horses, mechanical coachman, mechanical page, and mechanical lady passenger, but Lavicini's own creations were so far advanced that he did not believe even such experienced eyes as the Sun King's would recognise them for what they really were. Hidden in the ceiling above the automata, packed into crates along with two tons of broken ice, were twenty-five corpses that Lavicini had purchased from a porter at a failing anatomy school, explaining that he was an upholsterer who had received a very elaborate and unusual request from an aristocratic English client. And in place all throughout the Théâtre des Encornets were the contrivances that would be required to give the appearance that it was the devil himself who had destroyed part of the Théâtre des Encornets when he came to claim the soul of

323

Adriano Lavicini, the Sorceror of Venice, while leaving no identifiable trace of the automata.

Towards the end of the second act, Lavicini poked his head hastily into every room backstage to make sure they were empty, and then slipped out of the theatre by a side door. Some superstitious instinct prevented him from turning back to watch as an apocalyptic rumble rose within the building behind him. Instead, he hurried on towards the convent of the Filles du Calvaire, opposite which there was a cold vacant room above a butcher's shop where he intended to spend his last night in Paris.

So it wasn't until the next morning, when he returned in disguise to the ruins of the Théâtre des Encornets, that he heard about the dead ballerina. He moved through the crowd of onlookers, listening to conversations, needing to be certain that the truth was not suspected. And indeed no one knew that Lavicini was still alive. But everyone knew that a dancer called Marguerite was dead. He had to wander a long time before he could complete the story: she had fainted at her first sight of the Extraordinary Mechanism, and had then been carried backstage and deposited on a couch, where she was still lying when the opera house collapsed. Lavicini remembered then that the couch faced away from the door to that dressing room. That was why he hadn't noticed her on his final backstage inspection. He'd never spoken to Marguerite, but he remembered her face, because Montand always seemed to pay special attention to her during the rehearsals.

Lavicini knew then that he could never see his Wormwood again. He'd planned to live with her in Venice under a false name until her husband died, and then they'd run away to some exotic place where no one had ever heard the name Lavicini. But now, if he returned to her, he would have to confess that a girl had died to help bring them back together, as if sacrificed to their love, a proxy for the suicide that Lavicini himself hadn't had the conviction to commit. Adultery was one thing, but the guilt of being party to a murder would drive his Wormwood out of her senses. She couldn't ever find out. But he couldn't keep back the truth if he was with her. He decided it was better if, like the rest of the world, she never found out that he'd survived the destruction of the Théâtre des Encornets.

Nevertheless, he went back to Venice. If he couldn't have his Wormwood, he would at least have his home. Out on Vignole, he could live out his penance in a sort of exile, while still in sight of the Arsenal, where he'd worked as a younger, happier man. And during the months of Carnival he could wander the city, like Hephaestus returned to Olympus, in the masks he built and painted like tiny stage sets the rest of the year. Even if he jostled past his Wormwood a dozen times in a day, it wouldn't matter, because he would never have to know it was her.

'All the way to Paris, and all the way back, because of a woman?' said Sauvage when Lavicini had finished his story.

'Because of two women, really.' Lavicini coughed again for a long time. 'Why have you come here?'

Sauvage gathered his resolve. 'I've written a play,' he said, 'and I want you to design the set. I had to find you because no one else can do it.'

'I have many talented successors in Paris.'

'No. The play is set two and a half centuries in the future. I don't believe there is another man alive who could make that seem real. It's about a young man whose friends are about to be murdered by a tyrant just like the Sun King. But instead of trying to save them, he runs away to a colony in the New World.'

'What happens to him?'

'He meets a man who has become very wealthy from the sale of currycombs, who sends him to find an inventor who is trying to build an Extraordinary Mechanism for the Almost Instantaneous Transport of Persons from Place to Place. But not a stage device like yours – a real one. A sort of reproducible miracle. The hero does find the inventor, but he also encounters an agent of the Ottoman Empire who wants to take the inventor back to Constantinople.'

'Does this agent succeed?'

'I haven't decided yet. The important thing is that the hero comes to realise his cowardice and he returns to the land of his birth to overthrow the tyrant. But he is too late to save his friends.'

'De Gorge always used to tell me that the hero of a successful play must be a man the audience would be happy to invite into their homes for supper. Otherwise no one will want to sit through the whole thing. Your "hero" who abandons his friends to their deaths – he doesn't sound like that sort of man.'

'De Gorge knows no more than a low pimp.'

'A very astute low pimp.'

'The point is that the hero has a change of heart. He redeems himself by his rebellion. Without that, the story is meaningless.'

'And I assume you hope to encourage the same sort of thinking in your audience?'

'Louis killed my father. I don't know how else to take my revenge. I'm no Cromwell. I'm a playwright.'

Lavicini shook his head. 'I'm sorry, Bernard, but I can't design your set. I'm much too ill. Before more than a few more moons have risen, I'm going to die here, inside the Théâtre des Encornets, just as I was supposed to in the first place. You were lucky to find me still warm. I'm grateful for your visit, but I'm afraid you'll leave empty-handed. Swap masks with Melchiorre before you go. If you were followed, that will cause some confusion.'

'I certainly will not leave empty-handed.'

'If you want to keep the clockwork bat you are welcome to it.'

'No,' said Sauvage. 'I'll leave with your story. You've told me a part, but I want the rest, the entirety, from the very beginning. I'll write it down and then after you're dead I'll publish it and it won't be lost. You know, my father wanted to write the story of his life. But he never had a chance before he died.'

'I won't pretend I have no pride left here in my languor, but are you quite certain?' said Lavicini, amused. 'There is a lot to tell.'

'Of course.'

'Very well. I hope you won't come to rue the idea as the hours drag on. Melchiorre, would you be kind enough to bring our guest some paper and ink and a quill, and myself a little water?' The gondolier did so. Lavicini drank and then sat back against his pillow. 'Ready, Bernard?'

'Yes.'

'So then: I was born in Paris in the year of grace 1648 . . .'

9

WASHINGTON, DC, 1947

THE CHAIRMAN: The Committee will come to order. The next witness will be Egon Loeser.

THE CHIEF INVESTIGATOR: When and in what country were you born, Mr Loeser?

MR LOESER: I was born in Berlin, Germany, in 1907.

THE CHIEF INVESTIGATOR: And you are appearing before the Committee in response to a subpoena served on you Tuesday, 23 September – is that correct?

MR LOESER: Yes.

THE CHIEF INVESTIGATOR: Are you a citizen of the United States?

MR LOESER: No, I'm not a citizen. I still have only my first papers.

THE CHIEF INVESTIGATOR: When did you acquire your first papers?

MR LOESER: In 1935, when I washed up on the shore of this country.

THE CHIEF INVESTIGATOR: Where do you live now?

MR LOESER: In New York City with my wife.

THE CHIEF INVESTIGATOR: At what address?

MR LOESER: At 36 West 73rd Street, near Central Park. Shall I expect a Christmas card?

THE CHIEF INVESTIGATOR: Mr Loeser, are you now, or have you ever been, a member of the Communist Party?

MR LOESER: No. But I have a short statement I'd like to make.

THE CHAIRMAN: Mr Loeser, you may read your statement after you testify.

MR LOESER: I'd like to read it now.

THE CHAIRMAN: Only after you are finished with the questions and the answers.

MR LOESER: I've already told you I'm not a communist. I have never had any political affiliation. What else is there to say?

THE CHIEF INVESTIGATOR: Mr Loeser, you have been called before the Committee as a witness because we are investigating the nature of the association in the years 1934 to 1940 between a certain Soviet agent operating in Los Angeles and the novelist and screenwriter Stentor Mutton, who will testify tomorrow. Is it correct to say that you have some special knowledge of that association?

MR LOESER: Most of the time I had no idea what was going on.

THE CHIEF INVESTIGATOR: But you were acquainted with both parties?

MR LOESER: Yes, I knew Drabsfarben and I knew Mutton. Well, I still know Mutton.

THE CHAIRMAN: Excuse me, Mr Loeser, but what are you doing?

MR LOESER: What does it look like I'm doing?

THE CHAIRMAN: It looks like you've taken off your tie and you're whirling it around your head like a gaucho's bolas.

MR LOESER: Yes. I wanted to see if it would show up in the transcript.

THE CHAIRMAN: What do you mean?

MR LOESER: The strange thing about a transcript like this is that it contains no stage directions. I could beat you to death with your own gavel and the stenographer wouldn't even be able to hint that it had happened unless somebody got up and said, 'Let the record show that Mr Loeser has beaten the Chairman to death with his own gavel.'

THE CHAIRMAN: Are you making a threat against the life of a congressional official, Mr Loeser?

Mr Loeser: I was only making a theoretical point.

The Chairman: Please put down your tie. May I remind you that you are standing before a Congressional Committee appointed by law?

Mr Loeser: But I don't think I'm standing before any such thing. I don't think I'm standing at all. I think I'm asleep in bed in the Shoreham Hotel about three miles away from the Capitol.

The Chairman: How can you possibly justify such an assertion, Mr Loeser?

Mr Loeser: Because I don't remember getting here. All I remember is making love to my wife a little while after the alarm clock woke us.

The Chief Investigator: In what position?

Mr Loeser: I was on top of her, with my right arm hooked under her left knee in order to hold her thigh up against her stomach.

The Chief Investigator: Why not both arms under both knees?

Mr Loeser: That's a lot of work. I'm forty years old. May I continue?

The Chief Investigator: Please.

Mr Loeser: I ejaculated, withdrew, rolled off on to my side, kissed her on the neck, and closed my eyes. Then before she went into the bathroom to take out her little rubber womb veil, she shook my shoulder and said, 'Egon, you'd better not doze off again, it's already nine and you have to be across town in an hour.' I grunted in full and sincere agreement. Then I dozed off again. I think I may still be dreaming.

The Chairman: Does this feel like a dream to you?

Mr Loeser: Not really. But that doesn't prove anything. Schopenhauer would say we all have a case of chronic ontological agnosia. 'Life and dreams are pages of one and the same book.' Our senses give us a few flickers and hums and tickles, and we mistake those representations for real objects and real experiences, even though every single bleary morning reminds us that we can't tell dreams apart from life until we wake up. None of us are really any saner than Colonel Gorge. I loathe Brecht—

THE CHAIRMAN: Mr Brecht is scheduled to appear before this Committee in a few weeks so please keep your language respectful.

MR LOESER: – but I can't help admiring the way he makes it impossible for the audience to forget that they're only watching actors on a stage. In the theatre we develop a special temporary type of ontological agnosia and Brecht injects us with the cure against our will. But who can give us the same injection at double the dose when we're out of the theatre and walking down Broadway? Nobody reads the philosophers any more.

THE CHIEF INVESTIGATOR: So what you're contending, Mr Loeser, is that history is a nightmare from which you are trying to awake?

MR LOESER: No. History is an alarm clock I want to throw through the window. Can I make my statement now?

THE CHIEF INVESTIGATOR: Not yet. Why did you come to the United States?

MR LOESER: For the good of my health. If I'd dropped dead before I left Berlin the doctors would have cut open my spleen and they would have held it up to be photographed and they would have said, 'Do you see these patches here and here, the colour and texture of rotten dog food? The patient was only just twenty-six, and yet we wouldn't normally expect to find such a toxic accumulation of bitterness and jealousy in a man younger than sixty years old.' That, and Adele's eyes.

THE CHIEF INVESTIGATOR: What will you say if you are asked that same question again later this morning?

MR LOESER: I have no idea. By the way, are we speaking in German or English? I can't tell, which really does suggest this might be a dream. You two already seem to be on the point of admitting it.

THE CHAIRMAN: No more of that sort of talk, please.

THE CHIEF INVESTIGATOR: What is your occupation?

MR LOESER: I have none. I was once a set designer.

THE CHIEF INVESTIGATOR: Why did you give that up?

MR LOESER: After I read the Lavicini book, there didn't seem to be any point any more. He'd already covered it all. The man was perhaps the second ever professional set designer, after Torelli, and yet he anticipated almost every advance in the history of set design. Today, we only remember his conjuring machines, but he wasn't just a technician. He was an avant-gardist.

THE CHIEF INVESTIGATOR: Have you really adopted as your 'role model' a man who abandoned the city of his birth, and of all his early success, because of a break-up? Not a death, not even a divorce, just a break-up? Is that rational?

MR LOESER: Thoroughly rational, yes. I am full of admiration for anyone with such strength of character. Sometimes when there's a dead skunk in your roof you just have to write off the whole house.

THE CHIEF INVESTIGATOR: If you're no longer a set designer, how do you support yourself and your wife?

MR LOESER: For most of the war we were almost penniless. Mildred's father cut off her inheritance when we eloped. But then a judge declared, with retroactive effect, that he was mentally unfit to make a will.

THE CHIEF INVESTIGATOR: Why was that?

MR LOESER: Gorge's ontological agnosia, which I mentioned before, has developed to its inevitable final stage. Now, he just has to hear a word spoken aloud and he will see before him whatever that word represents. It's as if his disease got so strange that it circled all the way round to boring again – you can hardly tell him apart from any other delirious old man. Even Woodkin can't talk to

332

him, except in pure abstractions, like bad transcendental poetry. Mildred goes back to Pasadena sometimes to see him.

THE CHIEF INVESTIGATOR: They reconciled?

MR LOESER: Yes. He says he only changed his will because he wanted her to come back, and he's forgiven her for going away. He still calls me Krauto, though. 'My son-in-law, Krauto.'

THE CHIEF INVESTIGATOR: Now, please relate the circumstances in which you received your subpoena.

MR LOESER: I was eating dinner with my wife and a man came to the door who described himself as a United States deputy marshal. He wanted to give me a document of some sort. I didn't tip him. My wife and I sat down and I handed her the document and asked her to read it to me.

THE CHIEF INVESTIGATOR: Couldn't you have read it yourself?

MR LOESER: I was enjoying my steak. But then she said something about Congress, something about un-American activities, and something about going to Washington to testify, so straight away I dropped my cutlery and snatched the document out of her hand.

THE CHIEF INVESTIGATOR: Why so alarmed?

MR LOESER: For some weeks I'd been in correspondence with a librarian at the Library of Congress about their copy of *Midnight at the Nursing Academy*. I was posing as a researcher from Columbia University, but my real intention was to travel to Washington, break daringly into the Library after dark, and steal the book. When the subpoena arrived, my first assumption was that my plot had been discovered – by some means I couldn't even imagine, since obviously I hadn't said a word to anyone – and I was being called to trial. I didn't know what to do. I just stared at the subpoena in silence. (I have never met anyone who is more comfortable than Mildred with long and unexplained silences.) At last my wife finished eating and lit a cigarette. 'We have to go to Washington,' I blurted with a pubescent glissando.

THE CHIEF INVESTIGATOR: What was her response?

MR LOESER: She simultaneously rolled her eyes and blew cigarette smoke out of the side of her mouth as if her whole face was being hoisted to the right. This occurs only once every few weeks due to the respective periodicities of the two actions and I find it supremely beautiful.

THE CHIEF INVESTIGATOR: More beautiful than her smile?

MR LOESER: Yes. Anyway, she very seldom smiles.

THE CHIEF INVESTIGATOR: More beautiful than her laugh?

MR LOESER: Yes. Anyway, she very, very seldom laughs. Except when she's reading *Krazy Kat*.

THE CHIEF INVESTIGATOR: What's *Krazy Kat*?

THE CHAIRMAN: I believe it's a newspaper comic strip.

MR LOESER: By George Herriman, yes. Last year, for Christmas, on the recommendation of the bookseller Wallace Blimk, I bought her a 192-page *Krazy Kat* anthology published in New York by Henry Holt and Company with an introduction by EE Cummings. I've never understood what's funny about it, but quite often I come home to find her slumped in an armchair with the book in her lap, snotty and straggly and red-faced like someone who's just been informed of the death of a close relative.

THE CHIEF INVESTIGATOR: Doesn't that make you jealous of Herriman?

MR LOESER: A bit, but he died in 1944. And has never, to my knowledge, given my wife an orgasm.

THE CHIEF INVESTIGATOR: To return to the matter at hand, for how long were you under your misapprehension about the nature of the subpoena?

MR LOESER: All the way to Washington. As a matter of fact, I was still squashed under it like a cockroach yesterday afternoon, when I left the hotel to buy some stockings for my wife, who had forgotten to bring a spare pair. I was walking down Calvert Street when I caught sight of someone it took me a moment to recognise. I hadn't seen him for nearly fifteen years. It was Hans Heijenhoort – Ziesel's sidekick from Berlin. We shook hands and went into a coffee shop to sit down.

'When did you leave Germany?' I asked him when my hot chocolate had arrived.

'At the end of the war,' Heijenhoort said. He has strong, almost heroic features, but his face is both much too long and, at the base, much too wide, so it's only when he bows his head and the trapezoid proportions are foreshortened by perspective that he's contingently quite handsome, like something from a parable about humility.

'And you live in Washington?' I said.

'No, I live in New Mexico. I'm here for some meetings. Are you still in touch with any of the old gang from university?'

We began to go through them one by one, as people do in these situations. 'Did you hear what happened to Ziesel?' I asked.

'Yes. Terrible.'

'I was right there in the room. What about Klugweil?'

'Yes, I heard about that too,' said Heijenhoort.

'I didn't! What happened to him?'

'Oh, quite an exciting story. He got conscripted into the Wehrmacht and ended up working for an army propaganda unit stationed in Paris. No one seems to know all the details, but somehow he got involved in the Resistance over there – something to do with a girl. And he became a very enthusiastic traitor. He used to pass along information, for instance, about where the next security sweeps were supposed to take place. Well, one day he realised that his commanding officer had begun to suspect him, and he fled. The Resistance hid him in a farmhouse just outside Paris, and the following morning they were going to try to smuggle him out of France. But that same night the SS came to the farmhouse – perhaps the Resistance had a traitor of their own. They beat him up, tied him to a chair, and then set the farmhouse on fire with paraffin. They told him he was going to burn alive.'

'And then?' This was not a dignified moment, I decided, to bring up the time Klugweil unacceptably started sleeping with my ex-girlfriend.

'After the farmhouse was reduced mostly to ashes, the SS men went back inside for a look around. They were expecting to find Klugweil's blackened skeleton. But there was nothing there. He'd escaped out of a window. Several months later, he turned up in Switzerland.'

'What happened?'

'The SS know how to tie a man up, of course. Even if you could dislocate your own arms, you wouldn't have been able to wriggle out of those ropes. But Klugweil managed it. I heard he was never willing to explain exactly how.'

'What about Achleitner?' I said.

'He died in the Battle of Berlin.'

'And Blumstein?'

'Dora.'

'Who's that?'

'A work camp.'

'Oh.' I was silent for a while. Then I said, 'What were you up to during the war?'

'Physics. Just the same as ever.'

'Still at university?'

'No.'

'Where, then?'

Heijenhoort picked up his cup of coffee and then put it down again without taking a sip. 'For a certain period I was attached to the Ordnance Department.'

'No! You were working for the Wehrmacht?'

'Just an accident of organisational structure. My work was almost all theoretical physics. I wasn't building rockets underground with slave labour like von Braun.'

I leaned back in my seat, suffused with gloating warmth. 'You know, Heijenhoort, I always thought it was unnatural how indiscriminately nice and helpful you always were to everyone, and now I know I was right! I bet you were just as indiscriminately nice and helpful to the Third Reich! Good nature is deviant, like I've always said. You should meet my wife, she could teach you a thing or two.'

Heijenhoort got up and started to put on his scarf. 'I had no choice, Loeser. You wouldn't understand. You weren't there.'

'Oh, Hans, come on, don't go! I haven't seen you in fifteen years!' I knew he wouldn't be so self-assured as to leave after I'd asked him to stay. And sure enough he sat down again. 'How did you get out of Germany?' I said.

'In that last April of the war, we were evacuated from the laboratory. We ended up hiding in the mountains. We weren't under guard any more, but we were terrified that the SS would shoot us all just so no one else could have us. The next worst thing would have been the Russians. They might have taken us straight back to Moscow for torture. The British or the French would have been all right. But it was the Americans. They made us some good scrambled eggs. After that they put us in a barracks for a few weeks, and then on a plane to Boston, and then a train to New Mexico.'

'And now you're working for the State Department?'

'Yes.'

I wondered how different I, too, might have found America if my first years there had been arranged for me in detail by some government office – and then as a sort of toy theodicy I tried to imagine the baffling aims that such an office would have to have had in order to arrange my first years there as they actually were. 'Is Cordell Hull making you read a lot of H.P. Lovecraft?' I said.

'Who's H.P. Lovecraft? Anyway, no, Hull's not there any more. He resigned a few years ago. Sarcoidosis.'

'So what are you doing for them?'

'I'm sorry, Loeser, but I'm sure you understand that I can't say anything about that.'

'Presumably the same sort of thing as you were doing for the Ordnance Department,' I said. 'That's why you're valuable. But what did the Ordnance Department care about theoretical physics? Was it anything to do with the atomic bomb?'

'No.'

'What, then? Are you going to make me guess? That's no use. I spent a few years at CalTech but I don't know anything about the state of the art. Apart from ghosts and robots and that fellow trying to build a machine for making eel congee out of electric eels that was itself powered by electric eels, all I ever heard about back then was . . .' I leaned forward. 'Oh my God. Teleportation. You were working on teleportation, weren't you? The Nazis were trying to develop teleportation as a weapon of war.'

This time Heijenhoort held my gaze. 'Yes, Loeser. That's right. And we didn't do so badly. Why do you think the Soviets pretended Hitler's remains were burned and buried?'

'God in heaven, you're telling me Hitler teleported himself out of the bunker?' I shrieked. 'So he's still alive?' There were puzzled looks from nearby booths.

'Yes, Loeser. That is the world-shaking secret I am telling you, here in this coffee shop.'

'Oh, are you being sarcastic?'

Heijenhoort got up again. 'I'm sorry, Loeser, but I must be going.'

'When did you become capable of sarcasm?'

'Things happen in war.'

'Hey, listen, they must have told you a lot of secrets in New Mexico?' I said.

'Not really. We're still Germans.'

'But do they know what happened to Bailey?'

Heijenhoort nodded as he put down a quarter-dollar for his coffee. 'They spent almost a year studying his device after they removed it from CalTech.'

'And?'

'Goodbye, Loeser. I'll see you around.'

'Come on, you have to tell me! Did Drabsfarben rescue him from the chamber, or did he accidentally teleport himself into the Pacific?'

'The answer is not what you think.'

'But I haven't told you what I think. Heijenhoort, stop! Come back!'

But he was gone. And I don't suppose I'll ever see him again. I hope the stenographer won't have too much trouble with the punctuation of dialogue. Can I read my statement now?

THE CHAIRMAN: Not yet.

THE CHIEF INVESTIGATOR: When did you discover the real nature of your summons to Washington?

MR LOESER: I didn't go straight up to the room when I got back to the Shoreham with a pair of stockings. Instead, I went to the bar and sat down on my own and ordered a whisky. All the way to Washington, I'd been praying for some sort of miraculous reprieve, but now there was only about seventeen hours left until I was due to testify here and I couldn't see where it could come from. I was going to have to tell Mildred that her husband had been caught planning to steal a book called *Midnight at the Nursing*

339

Academy from the national library of the United States; that he was going to be humiliated in front of the press and public; that he was probably going to be deported. I'd just finished my drink and was deciding whether to order another when Stent Mutton walked into the bar. I hadn't seen him since the summer of 1943. That July, there was the first really caustic smog in Los Angeles, thick enough to humiliate the sun, as if Wormwood the Skunk had died and rotted up in the roof of the world, and naturally everyone assumed, just as I had a few years earlier, that it was an attack from some unseen enemy. No. Just cars.

'Loeser!' He wore a white suit with coral buttons. 'Are you staying here too? I didn't think I'd see you until tomorrow.'

'Tomorrow?' I said.

'Yes. I'm testifying in the Caucus Room right after you. But you know that, of course.'

'For the defence or the prosecution?' I asked.

He smiled. 'Very funny.'

But I was quite serious. 'Do they think you were in on it somehow?'

' "In on" what?'

'*Midnight at the Nursing Academy*. The Library of Congress. The heist.'

I won't bore you with the untangling that followed, or the relief that I felt. But before long, Mutton was explaining that there would be no need for me to conceal any facts when I testified today about his relationship with Drabsfarben. My account of the truth would not incriminate him (or me) any further.

'But what about you?' I said as his drink arrived. 'What are you going to tell them?'

'That I never knew Drabsfarben was a spy and neither did my wife. They can't prove otherwise. Dolores and I

340

have had so many hours of practice at telling that particular falsehood that we could enter some sort of conservatoire. And the final proof: how on earth could we have lived in that house if we'd had anything at all to hide?'

'So when did you really find out?'

'Loeser, I knew Drabsfarben was working for the Russians from the first time he came over for dinner.'

'That's impossible. Just before I left Los Angeles, your wife told me you'd never even suspected she was working for the Comintern.'

'So I should hope. I never let her know that I knew.'

'But she was manipulating you. You had to go to Russia and write all those articles about how puppies love Stalin.'

'That wasn't so hard. You must understand, I had a choice. Either I was a little dumb and a little blind but I still thought my wife was a perfect goddess. Or I wasn't so dumb and I wasn't so blind and I found out my wife had been fooling me to keep Moscow contented. My marriage survived the former but it could never have survived the latter. I would have forgiven Dolores anything. But I don't think she would have let herself be forgiven. You're married yourself now, Loeser, you understand what it's like. You must have made some unspoken bargains of your own.'

Yes, perhaps I have. 'You were prepared to keep all that up for ever?' I said.

'No. But I could tell Drabsfarben wouldn't last that long in Los Angeles. He didn't cast the right sort of shadow. Did you know Dolores and I have a six-year-old son? My wife fell pregnant only a few months after Drabsfarben disappeared.'

'So until then you hadn't been . . .'

'Oh, quite the contrary, we'd been trying for years. But I think Dolores's womb refused to bring a child into a lie. An ethical organ.'

'Do you all still live in the glass box?'

'Yes. Although it wasn't easy during the war. Our neighbours – and when I say "neighbours", I mean interfering strangers who lived about a half-mile down the beach – got together a petition. They thought the Japanese pilots would use the lights of our house for navigation on their all-too-imminent night raids. In the end we papered over the whole place with birch bark. Not quite what Gugelhupf intended. But to perdition with Gugelhupf. Do you know what he did for most of the war? He got a job with the Chemical Warfare Corps, erecting replica Berlin tenements in the New Mexico desert, full of replica Bauhaus furniture. They burned them down again and again to improve the design of their incendiary bombs.'

So Germany City really had been built in America, only to be razed each week like a torment from Greek mythology. Did Gugelhupf, I wondered, imitate the streets and squares he missed the most, so that he could he could walk through them once more before they perished in trial by fire, or did he imitate the streets and squares he missed the least – we all have a few marked on the maps of our memory that we associate for ever with rejection or despair – so that their arson would be a secret revenge? And since then had Heijenhoort and his colleagues ever been rewarded for their hard work with a coach trip from their own laboratory across the orange desert to the site of this fitful dream of *Heimat*? Mutton and I had a few more drinks – he told me he's writing science fiction now – then I went up to fetch my wife, who was dressing after a bubble bath, and we all had dinner together at a Chinese restaurant not far from the hotel. Mutton's lawyer had forbidden him from eating in the Shoreham itself in case the waiters were eavesdropping on your behalf.

THE CHIEF INVESTIGATOR: We don't employ waiters.

THE CHAIRMAN: We do bug telephones, though.

THE CHIEF INVESTIGATOR: And Woodkin was working for us all along.

LOESER: Really?

THE CHAIRMAN: For the purposes of the present hearing, yes, he was.

THE CHIEF INVESTIGATOR: Mr Loeser, one last question. Why are you such a total prick all the time?

MR LOESER: Excuse me?

THE CHIEF INVESTIGATOR: Do you think it's something to do with your parents?

MR LOESER: 'Something to do with my parents.' With insights like that you should be a psychiatrist.

THE CHIEF INVESTIGATOR: You don't seem to think about them very much or talk about them very often.

MR LOESER: That's because they're dead.

THE CHIEF INVESTIGATOR: Yes. The Teleportation Accident.

MR LOESER: Not a Teleportation Accident. Just a traffic accident.

THE CHAIRMAN: Accidents, like women, allude. You remember, Mr Loeser, what Nietzsche said about the French Revolution? 'The text has finally disappeared under the interpretation.' So often the case.

THE CHIEF INVESTIGATOR: A lot of people had to die to get you to America. Your parents, and all those millions of Jews. Quite an advance on Lavicini's two dozen.

MR LOESER: You say that as if they were human sacrifices. But I didn't kill anyone and neither did Lavicini (except that one girl) and there was no causal connection at all.

THE CHIEF INVESTIGATOR: Perhaps not. But they died, and you don't seem to care any more than if they'd been clockwork automata.

MR LOESER: Oh, grow up. We're all clockwork automata.

THE CHAIRMAN: Mr Loeser, you ought to remember that you are a guest of this nation.

THE CHIEF INVESTIGATOR: Did you follow the Nuremberg Trials in the newspaper?

MR LOESER: Not if I could help it. Can I please read my statement now?

THE CHAIRMAN: Yes, Mr Loeser, you may now read your statement.

MR LOESER: Oh, I'm sorry, I . . .

THE CHAIRMAN: Is something wrong?

MR LOESER: I don't understand what's written here.

THE CHAIRMAN: You wrote it yourself, didn't you?

MR LOESER: Yes, I thought I did, but . . .

THE CHAIRMAN: What does it say?

MR LOESER: It says . . .

THE CHAIRMAN: Yes?

MR LOESER: It says, 'Wake up, Egon, you're going to be late. Put some clothes on while I call down for a cab. Wake up, Egon. Can you hear me? Wake up. Wake up.'

10
BERLIN, 1962

Fitzgerald Estate Says *'Sorrowful Noble Ones'* is Forgery

A lawyer for the estate of F. Scott Fitzgerald released a statement yesterday charging that *The Sorrowful Noble Ones*, a purported lost work by the late author, is a deliberate fabrication. The statement reports that there is no reference to *The Sorrowful Noble Ones* anywhere in Mr Fitzgerald's letters or notebooks, and that his daughter, Mrs Frances Scott Fitzgerald Lanahan, has no recollection of such a book ever being mentioned. This contradicts the claims of Herbert Wolf Scramsfield, a self-described former friend of Mr Fitzgerald who attracted international publicity last week when he announced that he had been guarding the manuscript since 1931.

Interviewed by telephone from his home in Paris, Mr Scramsfield strongly denied any allegations of fraud. 'The fact is, Scott trusted me to decide when the world was ready for this book,' Mr Scramsfield said. 'That's why it's been a secret all this time. Honestly, I'm flattered that anybody thinks I could write something as good as this. But that's preposterous. I never wrote a book in my life, let alone a masterpiece.'

However, an enquiry by this newspaper has found that earlier in his career Mr Scramsfield did in fact write a manual of seduction, *Dames! And how to Lay them*, published pseudonymously in 1930 by the Muscular Press of Los Angeles, California. Reached yesterday for comment, *Esquire* magazine editor Arnold Gingrich said that he has cancelled plans to publish excerpts from

'Rupert?'

Rackenham looked up from his newspaper. A woman of about his own age stood there in the posture of someone who has just dropped a fragile antique.

'Yes?' he said.

'Don't you recognise me?'

Rackenham smiled in apology.

'You promised you'd keep me in your heart until the end of time.'

'Oh. Did I really?'

The woman burst into tears. Rackenham searched his pockets for a clean handkerchief and his memory for a name or at least a context. He couldn't help but feel she was behaving with extraordinary rudeness. Thankfully, after a few minutes, she seemed to accept that he wasn't going to ask her to sit down with him, but before she'd leave him alone he still had to take down her address and promise to write her a long letter. Even her full name didn't so much as gesture at a bell, and so, in the usual manner of these things, it wasn't until she was on her way out of the café that Rackenham got any inkling. At the door, she looked back at his table, Orphean, and as she did so you could see in her face that she was already rebuking herself for her weakness, and then she turned away again and forced herself on, but too hastily, so that she bumped into a fat man on his way in and had to apologise in her bad German. The whole sad procedure took him straight back to 1932 or 1934 or whenever it was and he remembered her at last. One night she'd asked him to tie her naked to a clothes horse with shoelaces but it had collapsed and he'd had to pay his landlady for a replacement.

He was still a few minutes early for his appointment, but he decided that now his peace had been disturbed he might as well pay the bill. Outside, on Kurfürstendamm, the sky was a grey paving stone with a few dirty bootprints of darker cloud and the sparrows conducted their usual patrol among the tourists for unattended pretzels. Turning right at the Kino Astor, he went down a passage into a potentially pleasant courtyard that was rendered rather gloomy by a huge plane tree with the apparent ambition to expand like a gas to fill every cubic inch of available space. He found the doorway, buzzed for entry, and went upstairs.

'You never seem to age, Rackenham,' said Loeser when he invited the other man inside. 'And I don't mean that as a compliment. It's sinister.'

'Do you live on your own here?' Rackenham didn't really need to ask – in its resonant frequencies this flat was so much like his own in London that he could tell at once no woman shared it. The place was not untidy so much as rationalised in a precise and stable way to the habits of its occupant: a bottle of vodka on the floor by the armchair, an electric razor keeping a place in an etymological dictionary, a corduroy jacket on a hanger that was hooked over the door of the fusebox cupboard, and then by the window some chrysanthemums in a vase, alive but wilted, like a small delegation from a more feminine land who knew that their presence at these negotiations was a pointless diplomatic formality.

'Mildred and I divorced in fifty-four,' said Loeser. 'That's why I came back to Berlin. I have a "girlfriend", though,' he added, nodding at the flowers. 'The word sounds ridiculous, of course.'

Last year, Rackenham's cousin Etty had come to his flat in Paddington for tea, and she'd adopted such a tone of condolence as she looked around it that he was provoked to ask for an explanation. 'It's obvious you can't be happy here, Rupert,' she'd said. 'Living like this. All alone.' He'd assured her that, as reluctant as she might be to believe it, he was happy – much happier, in fact, than she was, with a husband and two children who were all visibly sick of the sound of her voice. But whether Loeser was happy here, he couldn't yet tell. How strange, he thought, that Loeser should ever have been married to the Gorge girl, so that with respect to sexual genealogy Rackenham was to the German a sort of father-in-law. Did mother and daughter fuck the same way? He remembered all those afternoons with Amelia Gorge on Loeser's sofa in Pasadena, cold dimes kissing his knuckles as he groped between the leather cushions for purchase, when he'd been obliged to accept that nothing he did to her body would ever match the ecstasy she milled from that nasty rumour he'd helped her to spread about the contents of her husband's wine cellar. 'Do you like being back here?' he said.

'I can't find the old neighbourhoods any more. I tried to steal Ryujin's daughter from his palace and when I came home without her it was all in ruins as if three hundred years had gone by. Puppenberg, Schlingesdorf, Strandow, Hochbegraben. What happened to them?'

'Bombed. Demolished. Walled off.'

'But they can't all have been. Not every single street. It doesn't make sense. I must say, though, yesterday I was in Kreuzberg and the wind made one of those hurricanes of blossom and it made me very happy to be here. I'd forgotten quite how fecund this city is.' He sat down and gestured for Rackenham to do the same. 'I spent quite a while trying to work out why you wanted to see me. But I can't guess.'

'I'm making a documentary film for American television,' said Rackenham. 'It's about what Berlin was like in the last few years before the war. Kristallnacht and the rallies and the Gestapo and all that. I came to see if you'd agree to be interviewed. The idea is to mix my own recollections with those of some other prominent acquaintances of mine.'

'But we both left in 1934. We missed the worst.'

'The network don't know that, nor is there any reason why they should find out.'

Loeser blew out a sceptical plosive. 'How would I even know what to say?'

'Oh, it's easy. "I went to a cabaret and I saw an SS officer with an evil face slap his mistress for spilling a glass of champagne and then I knew the good times were over for ever." You know the sort of thing.'

'No, Rackenham. Absolutely not.'

'There's no formal fee for an interview, but the budget for expenses is almost unlimited. We can make something up. Bill them for an essential unicorn.' Rackenham could see that this did interest Loeser, so he said, 'How do you make your living these days?'

'I'm writing a book.'

'You've got an advance?'

'No. I don't have a publisher yet. But I got a grant from the Norb Foundation.'

'What's it about?'

'The role of mass transit in the *Endlösung der Judenfrage*,' said Loeser.

'Are you joking?'

'No. The Third Reich moved eight million people on sixteen hundred trains with two hundred thousand railway employees. And this is while they were fighting a war on two fronts. It's an extraordinary feat. When people talk about the cattle wagons, it's always as if the Nazis used them chiefly as some sort of demeaning symbolic gesture. But those cattle wagons can tell us so much more if we understand them as a logistical necessity. A hundred and fifty people in every wagon, fifty-five wagons on every train, at least four days for every journey. They could only manage it because there was so much redundancy built into the Deutsche Reichsbahn from before the war, and because they had so much coal, and because the French and Dutch and Belgian state railways were so helpful.' Loeser was silent for a moment. 'You know, when I went to Washington in forty-seven, there was no metro, but now they're finally building one. And the truth is that anyone planning a public transport system now is trying to solve a lot of the same problems that the Nazis had to solve. Just for different ends. If you leave an Enlightenment running for long enough, eventually, one way or another, it will become preoccupied with the moving around of large numbers of people. Were you still in Los Angeles in forty-three? For the first big smog? I was back in Pasadena that week. Everyone said it was the Japanese. They didn't want to believe it was their own cars turning against them. That same year the Nazis started using transportation vans where the driver could flip a switch so that the exhaust from the engine would be pumped into the back and suffocate the passengers. All those people, killed in transit – killed by the weight of their own bodies, in a sense, because the heavier they were, the more fuel the engine would burn, so because they'd been starving for months they'd have a few more minutes to live – an equation about calories and masses, like all the rest of history . . .'

Rackenham decided not to let Loeser go too much further down that hole. 'They never built that streetcar network in Los Angeles,' he said.

'When I left, I thought they would. I took Mildred, so Gorge had nothing to give Clowne, so there was nothing to stop Plumridge.'

'What happened?'

'Plumridge got drafted. He established the Army Transportation Corps almost single-handedly in forty-two. And he liked the army so much he never went back to California. Without him there was no one to push for the streetcar network. So nothing I did could ever have made any difference. A few years ago they started dropping the old streetcars into the sea near Redondo Beach to make artificial reefs for fishing. Imagine them, all submerged like that. You know the only place in California that has real public transport? Disneyland. In Disneyland they have trams and steam trains and monorails and it all works perfectly.' He sighed.

'I've put all this in the book. I'm going to have to take it all out again.'

'I didn't expect to find you writing a book about genocide.' Rackenham wanted to change the subject, but he also wanted to know: 'When did you start to . . .'

'Care?' said Loeser.

'Yes.'

'I don't know. It happened gradually. Very gradually. Remember in that taxi when I bet Achleitner that Hitler would never make one bit of difference to my life? I was right. I was nearly right. All those years, all that history . . . Everyone was else was packed into a tram and I was riding along in my car with the air-conditioning on and the windows closed and the radio up. Still, I wasn't the only one. Brecht was always so "political" but he never understood what was happening any better than I did.'

'How would you know?'

'I've been reading him a bit since he died. The poetry's not so bad. "We know we're only temporary and after us will follow/Nothing worth talking about."'

'And that one on how LA is just like hell.'

'He didn't leave until forty seven,' said Loeser. 'Much later than me.'

'You got there earlier.'

'Yes. I never lived there, though. Not in a sincere way. Did you ever hear about that question Bailey used to ask? "What's the one thing in the world that can uproot almost anything?" And that's what he thought he wanted to invent. But what he should have invented was the opposite of that. The opposite of a teleportation device. That's what we all needed. Something that could actually root a man in his surroundings. Wipe off some of the lubricant.'

'A bit of *in-der-Welt-sein.*'

'No Heidegger in this apartment, please. I feel *zum Tode* quite enough of the time as it is.'

'I think a man with a teleportation device could do good business in a city with a wall through the middle.' Rackenham noticed a book on Loeser's desk next to a bottle of cologne. 'You're rereading that?'

'*Berlin Alexanderplatz*? Rereading? No. I've been reading it for thirty years. I only have eleven pages to go. I hope to finish by next autumn.'

Rackenham got up. 'Can I open the window?'

'If you want.'

So Rackenham opened the window, picked up *Berlin Alexanderplatz*, and tossed it out. The book slid down through the branches like an exhausted wood pigeon and then lodged itself between trunk and bough.

'What the hell did you do that for?'

'I just had a sudden conviction that if you ever finish that book you will immediately drop dead. Like something from Han Chinese medicine.' Rackenham shut the window and sat down. The truth was, in spite of everything, he liked Loeser. 'Will you do this film or not?'

But Loeser ignored the question. 'Just tell me something.'

'What?'

'How did you do it?'

'Do what?'

'How did you fuck all those women? Adele and Gorge's wife and a million others? What was the secret? I still want to know. It's too late to be of any use to me now but I still want to know.'

'Loeser, if there really existed some trick that I could put into words, I'd . . . well, I suppose I'd write a manual or some-thing. And get rich. Anyway, I never actually slept with Adele.'

'What do you mean?'

'After that party at the sewing machine factory or whatever it was. I left with her but she changed her mind.'

'You're serious?'

'Yes. She said I reminded her too much of her father.'

'*Gott im Himmel*, if I'd known that, I might never have become so pathologically obsessed! I might never have gone to Paris. Or Los Angeles. Everything might have been different.'

'Oh, don't be ridiculous. You left Berlin because you hated Berlin. You would have gone either way. What happened to her in the end?'

'Adele? She stayed in Los Angeles. Married Goatloft, that director. I hear she's very happy. Meanwhile Brogmann's just been appointed Minister of the Interior and Marlene's just been made film critic for *Die Zeit*. Seems like everyone from those days did all right for themselves. Everyone that survived. You know, last month I was on Kurfürstendamm and I was almost certain I saw Drabsfarben walking a dog. It can't have been, of course.'

Rackenham took out a packet of Sobranies and offered one to Loeser, who shook his head. 'I've got some coke,' he said as he lit a cigarette for himself.

'What?'

'I've got three grams of really good coke that I bought from my cameraman. If you'll be in my documentary, you can have as much as you want, on top of the "expenses". We can do some now if you like.'

'I haven't taken coke in thirty years,' said Loeser.

'Then it will be a wonderful, sentimental reunion. Come on, just repeat after me: "In 1938 I went to a cabaret and I saw an SS officer with an evil face slap his mistress for spilling a glass of champagne and then I knew the good times were over for ever." An hour of that tomorrow afternoon. That's all it will take.'

Loeser didn't answer straight away, and for a while the two men sat watching each other in silence. Outside, the breeze changed, and *Berlin Alexanderplatz* slipped from the tree.

11
LOS ANGELES, 19310

The gondolier wore manatee-bone goggles, with pornographic engravings on the snout bridge, and when he cocked his head to the right in the Troodonian gesture signifying negation, the afternoon sun flashed in the smoked glass of the goggles' lenses. 'You don't want to go to the temples.'

'Why not?' thought Mordechai.

'Electric eels,' thought the gondolier. 'The biggest electric eels you've ever seen. They can shock you to ashes. May my slit close up if I lie.' He chirruped the oath aloud for emphasis.

'I can barter. I have manna.'

'I don't care. I'm not taking you into those waters. I value the life God gave me.'

So Mordechai knocked the gondolier unconscious and stole his boat.

As he paddled, he watched the turquoise surface of the lagoon, knowing that electric eels had an amateurish obligation to come up every so often to breathe. He'd licked the face of death more times than he could count as a soldier in the East, so he wasn't afraid, but he didn't want to be caught unawares. Every so often, to cool down, he flicked his tail through the water to douse his snout, then fluttered his dewlap feathers so they wouldn't get too crusted with salt. In the distance, through their caul of heat shimmer, the viny white tops of the temples rose out of the water like a ribcage lying half submerged in a rock pool, and on his left were the rias of the mainland, their slopes fuzzy with groves of lychee trees. Many octaeterids ago, before Dagon-Ryujin's half-fish came, when the Troodonians had still had the leisure to enquire into their world, archaeologists and playwrights had lived in villages on this coast, diving every day among the drowned conurbations of the apes. But now they were all gone, which was how the electric eels had begun to proliferate so menacingly in the lagoon, untroubled by hunters or trappers.

Like every Troodonian, except for a few thousand sickening heretics who had gone over to Dagon-Ryujin, Mordechai understood that all time was one instant, all space one point – that only God had the privilege of extension, and his creation was only the very tip of a claw – that any appearance to the contrary was just a sort of stereoscopic illusion. And so, like every Troodonian, he struggled with the paradox of how it could be that in the time of the half-fish, God wanted them to fight, and yet in the time of the apes, God had wanted them to humble themselves as shrunken quadrupeds, when the two periods were of course not only equivalent but simultaneous. Nonetheless, he knew that God did now want them to fight, and God did now want them to win. And that was why he, Mordechai, had abandoned his comrades and trudged across a continent to this lagoon. Whatever their clerisy might say, the Troodonians were losing the war, and if they ever hoped to drive the half-fish back into the sea, they would need either a direct intercession from God or some unimaginable new weapon. Since he did not dare rely on the former, Mordechai had come to these temples to look for the latter. The apes hadn't understood much, but they'd understood fighting. There might be something here, forgotten in the ruins, an accidental legacy from an unmourned and intestate species. The chances were laughably slim. But he had to try, because no one else would. He was lost in these thoughts, and in the rhythm of his rowing, when his boat was flipped over like a dried peapod.

Smashed into the water, limbs flailing, bubbles streaming from his snout because he was too surprised to hold his breath, Mordechai stared for a moment into the eel's monstrous right eye. Most of its gigantic body was dark grey, but its belly was a mottled orange not unlike the colour of his own intertarsal scales. He began a prayer that he knew he wouldn't have time to finish.

Except that, somehow, he did finish. He opened his eyes and he wasn't dead.

And then he realised that perhaps to this beast he was neither a threat nor a meal. The eel wouldn't go to the trouble to fire its voltage organ just because it had bumped against something on its way up for air. Thank God he'd lost the oar when he went under, or he might have been stupid enough to try to use it as a weapon. He held as still as he could without sinking any further down, and just as the grinding of his empty lungs was becoming unendurable, the eel swam off into the cloudy water, its long anal fin rippling like shadow congealed into a dainty membrane. Mordechai's knitted skullcap twirled in its wake and then was also lost to sight. Not since the half-fish themselves had he come across a creature that so obviously owed allegiance to Dagon-Ryujin as this long gullet with a face.

He floated, panting and retching, at the surface until he'd regained enough strength to right the stolen boat. The hull had sprung a small leak, he had nothing to row with, and he'd badly grazed his elbow climbing up over the side. But there wasn't that much further to go until the temples. Cursing himself for coming here in such a puny craft, cursing the gondolier for being so correct, cursing the sun for being so plump, he began to paddle.

And that was when he saw it. The lone figure standing on the roof of the nearest temple on his right like a soliloquist on a raised stage. An animal that hadn't walked God's earth for more than eight times eight times eight generations.

An ape.

Mordechai began to paddle as fast as he could, his elbow stinging with every splash of brine. As he drew closer, he could make out the ape in more detail. It had a bald, pink, snoutless face, with sparse grey fur only on the top of its head, and like a Troodonian cantor it wore woven clothing that covered almost its entire body. The fabric of the clothing looked soaked through, but at low tide the lagoon here wasn't nearly up to the level of the roof, so the ape must have ascended from some lower section of the temple. And instead of a left eye the ape had a meaty tunnel – although Mordechai had no way to be sure if that was a wound or just a characteristic of its species – a collateral sense organ or supplementary orifice.

The ape was barking loudly, and of course the noise itself meant nothing to Mordechai. But by the time the prow of his boat bumped up against the cracked and barnacled wall of the temple, he was close enough to hear the relict mammal in his own head.

'I don't know where I am,' the ape was thinking. 'I don't know where I am. I don't know where I am. I don't know where I am. I don't know where I am. I don't know where I am.'

A NOTE ON THE AUTHOR

NED BEAUMAN was born in 1985 and studied philosophy at Cambridge. His writing has appeared in the *Guardian*, the *Financial Times*, *Dazed & Confused*, *AnOther*, the *Awl*, *Literary Review*, and elsewhere. His first novel, *Boxer, Beetle*, won a National Jewish Book Award and the Writers' Guild of Great Britain Award, and was shortlisted for the Desmond Elliott Prize and the Guardian First Book Award.